Canadian **Dani Collins** k... ... that she wanted to write ... Twenty-five years later, a... ... high school sweetheart, having two kids with him, working at several generic office jobs and submitting countless manuscripts, she got The Call. Her first Mills & Boon novel won the Reviewers' Choice Award for Best First in Series from *RT Book Reviews*. She now works in her own office, writing romance.

**Kelly Hunter** has always had a weakness for fairy tales, fantasy worlds and losing herself in a good book. She has two children, avoids cooking and cleaning and, despite the best efforts of her family, is no sports fan. Kelly is, however, a keen gardener and has a fondness for roses. Kelly was born in Australia and has travelled extensively. Although she enjoys living and working in different parts of the world, she still calls Australia home.

# HIS FORBIDDEN TOUCH

DANI COLLINS

KELLY HUNTER

MILLS & BOON

First published in Great Britain 2024
by Mills & Boon, an imprint of HarperCollins*Publishers* Ltd,
1 London Bridge Street, London, SE1 9GF

www.harpercollins.co.uk

HarperCollins*Publishers*, Macken House, 39/40 Mayor Street Upper, Dublin 1, D01 C9W8, Ireland

His Forbidden Touch © 2024 Harlequin Enterprises ULC.

Marrying the Enemy © 2024 Dani Collins

Stolen Princess's Secret © 2024 Kelly Hunter

ISBN: 978-0-263-32021-3

08/24

This book contains FSC™ certified paper and other controlled sources to ensure responsible forest management.

For more information visit www.harpercollins.co.uk/green.

Printed and Bound in the UK using 100% Renewable Electricity at CPI Group (UK) Ltd, Croydon, CR0 4YY

# MARRYING
# THE ENEMY

DANI COLLINS

MILLS & BOON

To my editor, Laurie,
who called this one her new favorite.

Thank you for being so wonderful to work with. <3

# CHAPTER ONE

*Five years ago...*

EVELINA VISCONTI PICKED up a text from her middle brother asking which club she and her friends were visiting tonight.

She texted back.

Tell Mom I'll call her tomorrow.

Their mother would have called him the second Eve refused to pick up her call, texting instead that she was out for the night.

Seconds later, her friend, Hailey, looked up from her own phone.

"Your brother wants to know which club we're at. He wants to drive down from Naples to join us. Should I tell him we're actually in Budapest?"

"No," Eve said with beleaguered annoyance. Why was her family *like* this?

Eve was twenty-one, celebrating the end of her university years and the beginning of life as an adult, not that any of her family saw her as such. It wasn't as though she had a history of getting into trouble, either. She'd been determined to prove herself academically so her partying had been confined to inviting friends onto her parents' yacht between semesters. Drinking a glass of wine during reading break was her version of bacchanalian excess.

When she had finished her latest exams, these friends from boarding school had urged her to come to the Amalfi Coast with them. Hours after arrival, Hailey had coaxed her uncle into flying them to Budapest for a pub crawl through the ruin bars.

Eve's mother had been chilly about her coming as far as the Amalfi Coast, having planned an introduction between Eve and her future husband. Or, a contender at least.

Allowing Eve to finish her degree before marrying her off had been an exercise in patience for Ginny Visconti, an American heiress herself. Ginny had been matched by her own mother in a very advantageous and comfortable arrangement when she was nineteen. If she or Eve's father had ever cheated, they'd hidden it well, but they weren't soulmates. They were partners in the business of securing and advancing Visconti Group, primarily a hotel and resort conglomerate with holdings and interests in related industries. Ginny had done her part by producing three sons, one every two years, before she closed up shop. A girl arrived unexpectedly, seven years later.

In many ways, Eve had been the overprotected, spoiled baby, always trying to catch up to her much older brothers. Her mother had discouraged her from horseplay and other tomboyish activities, constantly putting her in dresses and insisting she "act like a lady." The very second that Eve grew breasts, her mother had begun talking about her prospects and seeing her "settled."

Eve's entire purpose for existing seemed to revolve around the link she would forge between the Visconti dynasty and one of their cohort families. The fact her mother was going so far as to try sending her brother to chaperone her, to ensure her plan stayed on track, provoked a massive case of delayed adolescent rebellion in Eve.

She texted her brother.

Leave my friends alone. I'll fly back to New York Monday.

She turned off notifications and tucked her phone into the wallet that hung from a cross-body shoulder strap and let it drop against her hip.

"Isn't it time to go dancing?" she asked.

Everyone nodded. They'd started their evening in a quaint garden café for dinner, then made their way to a billiards bar to enjoy a cocktail. They had listened to a band for an hour in another outdoor bar and now headed into a stone factory built in the late eighteen hundreds. It was renowned for being converted into a labyrinth of bars, music venues and dance floors.

"If you decide to leave with someone, text the rest of us, yeah?" Hailey said, then tucked her chin to add playfully, "But assume that's what I've done. I'll see you sluts on the walk of shame tomorrow."

Everyone laughed, but Eve only smiled weakly. She didn't know *how* to hook up and had never really aspired to. She occasionally dated—mostly men her mother threw at her—and had kissed far too many toads, but she hadn't found anyone who tempted her into a long-term relationship, let alone his bed. Besides, her mother expected her to remain a virgin until she married, which Eve knew was grossly outdated, but she had been busy with her double major in marketing and hospitality management so that's exactly what she was.

Her lack of sexual experience made her feel like a terrific spinster against her friends. They were all sending speculative looks around the crowd as they entered the first bar, where a heartbeat of syncopated electronica seemed to pulse from the stone walls. Flashing lights rotated to spill color across the bouncing bodies on the floor.

Eve skipped ordering a drink. She loved good wine or a tangy, refreshing cocktail on a hot day, but she didn't enjoy feeling drugged or the cotton-headed nausea of a hangover so she always paced herself.

"Are you still playing dorm mother?" one of her friends teased.

Eve laughed off the remark and began to sway her hips as she moved onto the dance floor. She genuinely loved dancing and stayed there for several songs before breathlessly visiting the bar for a sparkling water.

A boisterous noise drew her attention as she moved to the end of the bar where she could watch the dancing.

A group of young men were coming in, a bachelor party, judging by the plastic shackle on one man's ankle. The chain was long enough to drape over his arm and the ball must have been full of alcohol because he brought it to his mouth and popped open a cap like a water bottle to pour something into his mouth, eliciting approval from his friends.

Their antics reminded her of her brothers except *that* one was different.

A visceral tugging sensation accosted the pit of her belly as she studied the one who wasn't laughing. He was older than the rest, close to thirty, and definitely came from money.

They all did, she noted with another brief glance at

tailored cargo shorts and T-shirts with discreet designer logos. The mystery man was also casually dressed, but in sophisticated linen trousers that were barely creased. His short-sleeved button-down exposed beautiful biceps and a watch that she suspected was a Cartier Tank.

His cheeks wore a well-groomed stubble, his dark hair was combed back off his forehead and his straight brows suggested he was a man who never compromised. His mouth was unsmiling. Unamused.

He looked bored. *So* bored.

Which made her chuckle around the straw she had tucked between her teeth.

At that second, his gaze seemed to laser through the flashing lights and burn into her.

A fresh punch of intrigue tightened her abdomen, but she actually glanced behind herself, thinking *Me? No.*

The man said something to his companions and began winding his way toward her.

The tempo of her heartbeat increased, matching the music so closely, she felt as though she *became* music.

At the last second, he veered into the bar and waved a credit card, leaning in to place his order.

Well. Wasn't she full of herself? Apparently, her friends had lied when they had said this hot-pink halter top and sequined silver miniskirt were sexy on her. She wasn't the curviest figure in the room, though. She tended to run miles when she was stressed and, having just finished exams, was lean as a greyhound. Her mother was always trying to push her into padded bras, "for a more attractive silhouette," but Eve preferred to go without a bra altogether. In that way, she was happy to be less Marilyn Monroe, more ironing board.

"Are you alone?"

Her nerves leapt then froze, as though a panther had snuck up on her and took a curious, abrasive lick of her arm.

Mr. Tall, Dark and Disinterested was suddenly right beside her, leaning close so he didn't have to yell. His voice was like dark chocolate, too deep and earthy to be sweet, but enticing all the same.

She choked slightly at how close he was and covered her mouth, shaking her head.

"With friends." Her voice was so strained he had to read her lips. The sting of his stare made them tingle. She pointed to the dance floor, but there was no way he could tell who she meant.

Was that his aftershave that closed around her like an embrace? It was a delicious mingle of nutmeg and carnation, cedar and citrus, bergamot and black pepper. His aura of power was even more overwhelming, enveloping her in an energy field that paralyzed her body, yet left her nerve endings humming.

She wanted to touch him. That's all she could think as she skimmed her gaze across his chest and fixated on what looked like an ancient gold coin in the hollow of his throat.

"How old are you?" He sounded American, like her.

Affronted that he suspected she was underage, she said pithily, "Almost twenty-two."

"So twenty-one." His mouth quirked, equally pithy as he withdrew slightly.

"How old are you?" she challenged, instantly wanting him back into her space, even though it was like standing in the blast of a furnace.

"Almost too old for twenty-one." He turned to gather up the full tray of shots he'd ordered and balanced it easily on one hand. He paused long enough to offer her one, taking one for himself. "I'm Dom."

She bet he was a Dom. She'd read enough erotic romance to easily picture him as the sort who liked to control everything, especially sex. A sensual shiver worked its way from her nape to her navel.

"Eve." She took a drink off the full tray.

They shot their shots, he nodded, then took the tray to his friends.

She breathed through the fiery burn in her chest, left her empty glass on the bar, then rejoined her friends to continue dancing.

She didn't look to see where Dom had gone, but she knew exactly where he was. Through the next hours, as their two parties moved through the various tunnels and bars and clubs, down to the cellar and up to the terrace, she was always aware of him. Not because his group was big and rowdy, which they were, but because she could feel him. She knew when he was at the bar, or left the room, or was approached by a woman to dance. It was as though an invisible signal pulsed inside her, connecting her to him.

At one point, when she was in the ladies' room, her friend said, "My sister used to date one of those guys in that bachelor party."

"Which one?" Eve asked with a sharp pinch of jealousy.

"The sloppy one. That's why they're no longer dating. You go ahead," she added to Eve as she slid a flirty look to the woman who came to the sink.

Far be it from Eve to block anyone's good time. They'd already lost Hailey to a German fellow wearing skinny jeans and a tongue pierce. All her friends seemed to be finding a romantic partner except her.

Literally everyone was, Eve thought with amusement, as she left the washroom and passed an alcove where a couple was doing their best to have sex against a wall.

She was about to enter the club again when a drunken man lurched toward her.

She dodged him, thinking he was merely staggering, but he caught her around the waist from behind and tried to pull her into him. He slurred something in a language she didn't catch.

Reacting purely on instinct, Eve shifted her hips to the side so she could give his crotch a hard slap. As he choked out a pained, "Oof!" and released her, she spun to clip him on the ear.

She left him slumping to the floor against the wall and practically walked into another man. She pulled back her arm, ready to deliver a solid punch.

Dom closed his hand over her fist and leaned in. "Nice work."

Her adrenaline spiked anew, flooding her with the thrill of his touch and the proximity of his lips to her jaw.

"I have brothers." Just because her mother had discouraged her from wrestling with them didn't mean they hadn't taught her to "go for the groin" and protect herself.

"Come dance with me." Dom brought her hand down and slid his fingers between hers, leading her onto the dance floor.

She had already surreptitiously watched him move, mesmerized by the way he rolled his hips and rocked his wide shoulders. He had the grace of an athlete, every move smooth and perfectly timed.

For a moment, she felt off-beat and self-conscious,

then his gaze slithered down her like a spell. Her body began to match him move for move, even though they weren't touching. He seemed completely focused on her, but she realized after a few moments that he was putting himself between her and other men, subtly turning her away from them or inserting himself, forcing them to keep their distance.

It was possessive and weirdly exciting, feeding the sizzle in her belly. She felt free to be as sexy as she wanted and looked him right in the eye as she set her foot between his and brushed up against him, then turned so her backside was nearly in his lap.

She barely touched him, but the hum inside her was a scream of anticipation. His wide palms held her hips as they began to grind together. His chest was against her back, his body caging hers.

This was how he would make love to her. Like an animal.

Arousal exploded through her at the thought. She saw, for the first time in her life, the raw appeal of sex. She wanted to be covered and held safe while he filled her and made her his. She wanted that so badly, she thrust her buttocks deeper into his fly, rubbing against the hardness there. Inviting more.

His touch firmed on her hips, pressing her to his erection before he released her and spun her to face him, then clasped her close. The sudden impact with his chest punched her breath from her lungs. His thighs were hard against hers, the ridge of his erection against her stomach, filling her mind with crude fantasies. She could feel those muscled legs pushing hers open. His weight would crush her pelvis while his mouth came down on hers—

He spun her away, catching her hand and twirling her.

She stood in flames, licked and lashed by the heat of his lust-filled gaze.

He brought her back against him, bending his knees so they were pelvis to pelvis. She had never been so aware of her own sex. Had never felt such an ache there, like a signal pulsing between her thighs, yearning for that thick shape that rubbed with such promise.

Connect. Join. *Mate.*

His teeth caught her earlobe, scraping lightly before he growled, "I have to keep my cousin's groom from drinking himself to death. Be good."

His mouth dipped into her neck and his arms tightened to hold her still while he marked her with a small hickey. He left her swaying in the crowd of strangers.

Be good? *Shut up.* She was tired of being good.

She was gone.

Domenico Blackwood took it like a chest punch when he could no longer see the midnight hair that picked up the purple hues of the flashing lights. The clock and his inner radar told him she was gone, likely with someone who would exploit the blatant sexuality she had pushed so tantalizingly into his lap.

He cursed, still aroused from the feel of her, and now he had a pool of tarlike anger in his belly.

She was too young for him, he reminded himself. She was a doe-eyed twenty-one to his jaded twenty-nine and he was a man with "a cold, empty heart." According to his ex-fiancée, at least. And popular opinion, no doubt.

At first glance, Eve and her squad had reminded him of the woman who'd broken off his engagement a few months ago. They might be party girls slumming with backpackers for a night of dancing, but their rich girl roots were as clear as the daddy-bought diamond studs in their ears.

Dom was more than ready for a rebound affair, but cold heart or not, he had promised his aunt on his mother's side that he'd ensure her soon-to-be son-in-law didn't do anything to ruin the extravagant wedding she'd spent a year planning.

The role of big brother to a bunch of drunks was painful, but at least Dom had had the eye candy of legs that went on for days. Eve's breasts were pretty teacups he craved to sip and her hair was long enough to wrap around his fist two or three times. The sparkle off her skirt as she'd swayed her hips gripped him like a hypnotist's pocket watch every time they crossed paths, moving in and out of the various bars and dance clubs.

When he'd glimpsed her heading to the ladies' room an hour ago, he had lingered to watch her come back, then grew concerned when he saw a swaggering club goer headed into the same tunnel.

By the time he got there to ensure she was all right, she was dusting her hands. Dom had been so turned on, he had wanted to press her to the wall and test the limits of public decency.

Asking her to dance was as much dereliction of duty as he allowed himself—and it was pure, erotic torture. She had natural rhythm and undeniable sensuality. When she had boldly looked into his eyes and rubbed up against him, he'd caught the fragrance of anise and lilac and the tang of her sweaty night. He wanted that smell all over him.

He had wanted her badly enough in those moments to recognize the danger she posed. He'd proposed to his fiancée specifically because she didn't get under his skin.

He'd had a front row seat to a man consumed by his own emotions—two, in fact. His memories of his grandfather were dim, but they were similar, chilly recollections of a man haunted by a desire to settle a score. His father had been driven by the same crusade of anger, his grudges wearing away any softness in his soul, leaving only the hard, gnarled center.

Growing up in that fugue of antipathy had taught Dom to tamp down, bottle up and otherwise ignore his own feelings, lest they twist him into a similar, embittered version of himself. He never allowed anyone to needle him past his own control so, when Eve's lissome figure and alluring gaze had tempted him to forget his responsibilities, he'd made himself walk away with only that tiny taste of her against his lips.

There was nothing satisfying in being so noble, especially when he finally poured his future cousin into his hotel bed and went to his own in the penthouse. Dom had every kind of shower, trying to douse the hunger gnawing at him, but still only tossed and turned.

When he couldn't stand it any longer, he rose and dressed for a grueling, early-morning workout, planning to punish this craving out of himself, if that's what it took.

The fitness room wouldn't be open yet, but he owned the hotel. He owned the whole chain, in fact, along with the corporation that oversaw dozens of similar resorts and developments around the world. His card was all access, all the time.

When the elevator stopped midway down, he expected a family with young children to join him. Or a businessperson hurrying out for an early flight.

It was her. Eve. She wore a pair of shorts and a bright yellow windbreaker and a look of exactly as much surprise as gripped him. His sister would call this kismet. He didn't believe in such things. For him, it was merely coincidence. A convenient opportunity.

The hunter inside him leapt on it.

# CHAPTER TWO

WHEN HER LAST friend had paired up with a woman wearing bright blue lipstick and an armful of bangles, Eve had caught a rideshare back to the hotel—which was the *real* crime she was committing here in Budapest. If her family knew she was staying in a WBE hotel, they would drag her out by the hair.

Eve hadn't realized where they were booked until they arrived. Hailey's uncle had paid for everything as a graduation gift to his niece. As their guest, Eve hadn't wanted to make a fuss so here she was, waking alone in a mini-suite that was as luxurious as any of the Visconti hotels.

She hadn't really slept. She blamed the alcohol and Hailey not coming back, but she knew what the real issue was. Dom had left her in a state of arousal that kept her fantasizing about a kiss she hadn't received. She had spent the restless hours imagining he had brought her back to this hotel and did more than kiss her.

At six thirty, when the sun came up and other early-morning joggers had started to emerge on the streets below, she dressed for a run.

She was skimming through her playlists as she waited for the elevator when the doors opened to reveal *him*. Dom.

A jolt of electricity gripped her, freezing her in place.

"Are you just getting home?" she asked, even though he wore gym shorts, sneakers and a plain blue T-shirt.

He shot out a hand to hold the door. "I can't sleep." His growled voice seemed to blame her for that, which sent a flutter of smug pleasure into her chest.

A wispy scent of risk stung her nostrils, though, even as anticipation teased her stomach. She had cursed herself for not speaking to him before she left, not that she knew how to invite a man to her room. The carefree come-hither woman she'd been a few hours ago was long gone, leaving a tongue-tied virgin who was blushing over the thoughts she'd been thinking all night.

"Do you have your own room?" he asked in that same gritty, intent tone.

Or he could just invite himself, she thought with mild hysteria. The churn of nervous excitement increased in her abdomen. Be good? Or...?

"My roommate isn't back yet." She tried to project a sophistication she didn't possess. "Would you like to see it?"

"I would." He stepped out, seeming bigger in daylight than he had at the club. More intimidating.

He'd showered off the sweat of the club, but hadn't shaved. The edges of his beard were scruffy, his eyes alert, but sunken into the dark circles of a sleepless night.

He nodded in a command for her to lead the way.

Her blood turned to champagne, bubbling and fizzing as she walked, making her feel lightheaded. She wished that she was wearing her club clothes, not this bust-flattening sports bra and baggy shorts with a windbreaker colored for visibility, not flattery.

Nervously, she let him into the sitting room. The pair of queen beds was visible through the open double doors to the bedroom. Hailey's bed was untouched, the other was tousled, revealing her fitful sleep.

She waved in a lame *Here it is* gesture. She had opened the drapes when she rose. The view of the river and the historic architecture on the far side was beautiful.

"It's great," he said, not taking his eyes off her. "Do you have condoms?"

Wow. She held his stare and swallowed the heart that had risen into her throat.

She could have demurred and told him he was moving too fast, but he wasn't. That was the weirdest thing. In any other case, such earthy bluntness would turn her off, but something more intuitive inside her was responding to his wavelength. She liked knowing he was feeling exactly as urgent as she did. It flooded her with erotic heat and more yearning than she could stand.

"Yes," she replied, because Hailey had made sure she knew there were some in the nightstand if she needed them.

"Do you want to show me where they are?" He sounded as though he was being deliberately careful and neutral, not sarcastic. Perhaps he realized how aggressive he was sounding and wanted to give her an opportunity for second thoughts.

All she had to say was "no." She could easily tell him she'd rather go on her run and would see him at breakfast. She could open the door and say nothing at all. Her hand was still on the latch.

But her fingers were twitching to explore his smooth arms and she wanted to nuzzle her nose into his throat. Her lips were still dying for the press of his and the rest of her... The rest of her really, really wanted to know how his naked body would feel against hers. How his erection would feel inside her.

Her knees felt wobbly as she walked into the bedroom and opened the nightstand to take out the box. She set it beside the base of the lamp then kept her back to him, struck by bashfulness.

His weighty steps were silent on the thick carpet, but she felt his energy like a force as he arrived behind her. The heat of his body pressed like a physical touch against her back.

"What are you wearing under that?" His voice was a velvety caress in and of itself.

She turned and started to lift her hands to the zip, intending to show him, but realized she was still holding her phone. She tossed it onto her unmade bed and took hold of her collar with one hand, then slowly, slowly, drew her zip down.

He watched the descent of the tab the way a cat gave its single-minded attention to an unsuspecting prey, but his chin dipped in the smallest nod of approval as she let the jacket fall open to reveal her mauve bra.

"Sexy, right?" she said of its flattening fit.

"Very," he said in a low rumble.

He stepped closer and touched her chin. She thought he was going to kiss her, but his gaze slid to her throat. A faint smile eased the line of his stern mouth. He trailed his fingertip down to where he'd left the barely-there shadow of a love bite.

"I want to cover you with those." His voice was raspy from his late night and something else. Want?

"Maybe I'll do the same to you," she suggested boldly.

"Be my guest." He took hold of the open edges of her jacket and drew her into him.

She instinctively brought her hands up, but they only landed on the satin smoothness of his bare upper arms.

"You drove me crazy all night, Evie." He released her jacket and his wide hands slid inside to splay against her bare waist.

She gasped at his hot, possessive touch. Her skin tightened and tingled while her brain short-circuited over the way he had turned her name into an endearment.

"All I could think about was having your long legs around my waist. Around my neck."

Oh, that was dirty. Why did she find it so titillating? A helpless sob thrummed in her throat.

"My roommate might come back," she warned, voice as abraded as his.

"Does that turn you on?" He traced tickling patterns in her lower back that made her squirm in reaction and press closer to him in an attempt to escape it. "That we might get caught?"

"No." Yes. A little. Her senses were being bombarded by a lot right now. The heat and hardness and scent of him. The touch that was both light and merciless at the same time. A sense of anticipation and wonder and nervousness of the unknown.

"Do you want to lock the bedroom door?" he asked.

She should, but his hands were sliding into her shorts at the back, pushing them off her butt cheeks along with her underwear, leaving her backside bare to the cool room and the exploring massage of his hot palms.

It was incredibly disconcerting. She felt vulnerable and wicked and turned on. His roaming, claiming touch incited her to the point she could hardly speak, let alone move to do something so practical as…

"I want you to kiss me," she confessed in an aching whisper.

His reaction was a noise of approval and a firming of his hands on her ass. He dipped his head to capture her lips with his own.

This man knew how to kiss. Maybe there would have been a gentler preamble if they hadn't spent last night priming themselves for this moment, but he slicked his tongue between her lips, creating a damp seal that allowed him to consume her then he *did*.

Helplessly, she swept her arms up to cling around his neck, arching into him so she could find and feel his erection again. His hands on her backside pressed her mons firmly into that implacable ridge while he hungrily rocked his mouth against her own.

This was what she had wanted last night. What she had always wanted. Passionate oblivion. He was strong and sure and she instinctually knew he would keep her safe while absolutely ravishing her. She rubbed blatantly against him, stoking the heat that was gathering in her loins, seeking pressure against the knot of nerves that was swollen with every libidinous thought she'd had of him and a thousand new ones.

"I want that, too," he said, holding her hips tight to his as he lifted his head.

She was panting, so disoriented she wondered if she'd spoken her thoughts aloud, but she couldn't have. Her mouth had been occupied.

He kept her hips braced in his wide hands and ground his erection against her, making her eyelids flutter.

This was a perilous moment, she realized with muted alarm. Not because he seemed to be violent or cruel, but the way he drew her so effortlessly into acting without inhibition was sobering. She liked to believe she was a strong, confident, independent woman, but this stranger was using her own sensuality to undermine her sense and willpower.

He proved it by casually skimming her shorts down her legs, taking her underwear with them.

She gasped in surprise, but her only struggle was the fight to get her shod feet free. She should have unlaced and removed her shoes, but he was peeling his shirt over his head and catching her close again.

A small cry escaped her. The heat of him! He was tensile muscle and silky hair and slow, wicked hands as he guided her to rub her near-naked chest against his. She moaned, reveling in the brush of skin on skin, not realizing he was easing her onto the bed because it happened so effortlessly. She was too enthralled with mapping his back with her fingertips and using her inner thigh to caress his leg. His arm was a hard band around her, his other hand feathered touches behind her thigh and into the heat between.

His knee went onto the mattress as the cool bottom sheet arrived against her back. He stretched out alongside her, bracing on an elbow as he pushed her bra up to reveal her breasts.

"I want to tangle you up in this thing and have my way with you. Would you like that?" He caught the arm that was between them and tucked it under her lower back. The position arched her breasts up to him while lightly trapping her. He bent to lick at her pouted nipple, making it contract into a taut, sensitized peak.

"You're a little bit kinky, aren't you?" she accused breathlessly, turned on but also overwhelmed by his casual control. She was half-naked, still wearing her shoes, excited, but also wary. "Do we need a safe word?"

"'No' works. Do you want me to stop?" His golden-brown eyes glittered with amusement as they met hers.

"You're evil," she accused, since she couldn't answer his question without risking that he would, in fact, stop. "Keep going."

"Tell me what you like." He watched his hand as he trailed his touch down her quivering abdomen to the damp line of her folds. He lightly traced the seam, his touch stirring the fine hairs there until she thought she would die of need.

She bit her lip, breath catching.

"You have to tell me you want this, Evie. Open your legs if you don't want to say it."

She did. And she closed her eyes because it felt so flagrant to offer herself this way, but he made it worth it. A rumbled noise of approval resounded in his chest as he found her damp with readiness. He opened his mouth over her nipple and sucked while he explored her intimately, stoking the fire that was threatening to consume her. He circled where she pulsed and delved into the ache with one long finger, sliding and caressing while he pulled at her nipple until she thought she would die.

It was too good. She twisted in agonized pleasure, moaning with torture, tense with the struggle of fighting off a climax that had been building since she'd danced with him.

She had never orgasmed with anyone else in the room. Definitely not from someone else delivering it. It made her feel incredibly exposed to let him play with her this way, but the pleasure was so acute, so relentless, she was losing the fight.

He released her nipple. "Do you want my mouth here?" He slowly pressed a second finger into her then eased his touch up to press the swollen, needy, shivering bundle of nerves.

It was the final straw. The coiled tension within her released. She groaned long and loud, catching at his hand to hold it against her mound as she abandoned anything like dignity and bucked, consumed by ecstasy.

His mouth smothered hers, capturing her moans while he caressed her through the crisis and into the shuddering aftermath.

Then he chuckled and freed her arm from beneath her. He shifted over her. His arms caged her beneath him as he settled his still clothed hips against the damp, overly sensitive flesh of her bare pelvis. His hand took hold of her hair in a fist that was just tight enough to keep her head still while he kissed her again, deep and hungry, dragging at her lips and searching out her tongue with his own.

"I'm going to be buried in you to the root when you do that again," he promised when he let her up to breathe.

She couldn't wait. She roamed her hands over his back and into his shorts at his hip, shyly moving her touch forward, but stalling when she heard the muffled xylophone keys of an incoming call on her phone.

"My mother," she muttered in apology. She pulled her hand free of his shorts and searched beneath the bunched blanket where the phone had slid. "I'll turn it off."

As she drew it from the sheets, however, Dom grabbed her wrist. He stared at the screen.

"How the hell do you know that man?" His voice had gone ice-cold.

Jealous? Because it wasn't Ginny Visconti.

"That's Nico. My brother," she said dismissively.

Dom pushed off the bed. Her lover of seconds ago had left the room, the building and the country. *This* was a man who was dangerous.

"You're Evelina Visconti?" His lip curled with repulsion.

"Yes?" She ought to sound more certain. She knew who she was. Kind of. She had never behaved like this with anyone so she was a bit of a stranger to herself in this moment. She was definitely someone else to him, though. Someone he didn't like.

She reached for the edge of the sheet.

"Get the hell out of my hotel."

"Your—What?" She sat up, trying to drag her bra back into place while tucking the blankets across her naked lower half, but he'd already seen everything and was looking at her as though he found her to be the lowest form of filth. "You're not..." He couldn't be. But his name was suddenly drumming in her ears. Dom, Dom, Dom. "You're not Domenico *Blackwood*."

As in Winslow-Blackwood Enterprises? WBE. *No.*

"Don't pretend that's a shock. What the hell is this? Do you have cameras in here or something?" He looked around while pulling his shirt over his head.

"What? No! That's disgusting."

"It is disgusting that you would do something like this. I can't believe how low your family stoops."

"You came onto me," she cried. "You asked to see my room! And my condoms." Along with her breasts and her body and, apparently, her humiliation. She had thought the rivalry between the Blackwoods and Viscontis was ancient history, but it was real and here and she suddenly felt very sick. "Did *you* plan this?"

*"No."* He looked as outraged at the accusation as she had been. "I would have had you removed if I'd known you were staying here. I'm going to have you removed now."

"Get out of here and I'll remove myself." She hated that crack in her voice. And the scald in her throat that was climbing to press behind her eyes.

"You don't tell me where I go in my own hotel." He punctuated that with a derisive point. Contempt flashed in his bronze gaze as his gaze flickered to the sheet across her waist. "Don't try to use this against me. I'll bury you."

"Same to you," she said in such a puerile response, it only earned her a snort and a final, dismissive curl of his lip.

"Security will be here in twenty minutes. You had better not be." He walked out.

# CHAPTER THREE

*Six months later...*

DOM WALKED INTO his father's empty office and left the lights off, allowing the wet, New York day to cast everything in shades of pewter and ash. It suited his mood.

Not because he was depressed and grieving. His responsibilities were heavy and his thoughts grim, but there was relief in his father's passing. Thomas Blackwood had been a bitter, combative man and, when his heart began to fail, had been even more quick to punish those around him who still possessed optimism for the future.

The funeral had been a somber affair, but there had been a collective exhale from everyone in attendance, Dom's mother especially. Dom's stepmother, Ingrid, had been the only one still projecting tension and discord. She didn't like that she'd lost the ear of the patriarch. She would live out her life in comfort with a suitable allowance, but like everyone else, she was now reliant and beholden to Dom. The heir.

Dom glanced at the open bottle of Scotch in the refreshment nook, but as much as he would like to disappear into oblivion, he had too much to do—starting with fending off the Viscontis.

In the ten days between his father dying in his sleep and his body going into the ground, Romeo Visconti and his three sons had swept across the globe like an invading army.

Granted, WBE wouldn't have been in such a vulnerable position if Thomas Blackwood hadn't insisted on staying at this desk while he had breath in his body. Dom's father had made some terrible decisions in the last years, determined to see the Visconti Group destroyed before he died. Dom had regarded that vendetta as a waste of time, energy, money and resources, but there had been nothing he could do except argue and watch.

Privately, he had hoped the feud between the Blackwoods and Viscontis would end with his father. *He* had been prepared to let it fall away into history since that's all it was.

Dom's great-grandfather had bootlegged and smuggled alcohol with Christopher Winslow during the Great Depression. When Prohibition ended, they turned their stills into breweries and their speakeasies into nightclubs. They invested their ill-gotten gains into hotels and casinos then, to ensure their combined fortunes stayed in the family, they arranged for Maria Winslow to marry Michael Blackwood.

Maria hadn't turned up at the church. She eloped with Aldo Visconti instead.

Humiliated, the Blackwoods did their best to ruin the Winslows, taking ownership of their shared properties and cutting them off from income streams. The Winslows hung onto a few assets, barely, then reconciled with the daughter they had shunned and used Visconti money to rally.

Through the ensuing years, there'd been some territorial disputes between the Blackwoods and the Viscontis, but the fight should have stayed between Michael and Aldo. Dom's grandfather had pushed it into the next generation, though. When his twin sons, Thomas and Peter, had discovered that Romeo Visconti was at Harvard with them, Michael goaded his sons into an academic rivalry with the Visconti heir. That enmity carried into their business dealings when they all began working at their family companies.

A war of empires ensued through the eighties and nineties. Visconti Group and Winslow-Blackwood Enterprises became synonymous with five-star accommodation, luxury entertainments and a battle as competitive as those between the top cola brands. At one point, Romeo had launched a trademark suit, coming at Winslow-Blackwood for continuing to use the Winslow name—which he had no right to, either. The suit itself was frivolous, but he won over public sentiment, forcing the rebranding of Winslow-Blackwood Hotels and Resorts to the less elegant WBE.

Dom had vague memories of his father from those days. Thomas had never been gregarious or fun, but he hadn't been mean. He and his siblings had been the product of a fraught marriage so they were all taciturn people who showed little emotion except anger. Uncle Pete had never married, hadn't had children, but he'd worked side by side with Thomas at WBE. They'd been focused and intent. Workaholics to some extent, because their father constantly whipped them to work harder, be more. *Win*.

After Michael Blackwood died, there'd been another chance to take the personal out of the battle. Elbowing for

market share was to be expected, but there was no reason
for Dom's father to hold onto a grudge against Romeo.

Perhaps he would have let it go if Romeo hadn't been
implicated in Peter's death. Romeo was cleared of wrong-
doing, but losing his brother changed Thomas. From then
on, he had one goal: to annihilate the Viscontis. His thirst
for vengeance cost him his marriage to Dom's mother,
but Thomas simply found a wife who agreed with him
and kept on his one-track quest to punish.

Dom was sorry for his father's loss. He felt cheated of
what might have been a better relationship with him if
things had been different. His childhood had been iso-
lating at best and too often punctuated with his father's
harsh moods, bullying and unreasonable demands. Dom
had shouldered responsibilities well beyond his years,
purely because his father was trying to turn him into a
foot soldier in his personal war. Dom had been caught in
the impossible position of wanting to inherit something
he knew inside out, something he believed he could do
great things with, but he had to appease the old man to
do it.

He had never blamed the Viscontis for any of that.
Never hated them or wished them ill.

Until now.

Now those opportunistic carrion-eaters were taking
advantage of his father's death to raid and pillage. In a
matter of days, they had scooped up majority shares in
half a dozen WBE properties that were mid-development.
They were buying WBE debts so they could call them.
They were attacking Dom on all fronts and *he knew why*.

Evelina.

He dropped into his father's chair, but refused to close
his eyes because, whenever he did, all he saw was her. He

saw long black hair and long tanned legs. He saw small, high breasts as she twisted in erotic anguish under his touch. He saw white lips shaping his name while her dark brown eyes widened in horror.

For the millionth time, he looked back on every second of his time in Budapest, from his last-minute agreement to oversee the party to how Eve could have made that elevator open at that specific moment. There was no way she could have orchestrated any of it. He was only trying to convince himself that she was a criminal mastermind so he could absolve himself of blame for having touched her.

She hadn't waved him to approach her from across a crowded club. His own feet had carried him there. She hadn't danced with him until he'd asked. She hadn't tried to come home with him.

She hadn't known who he was.

And even though he had relived their interactions a thousand times, punishing himself for not recognizing her, he simply hadn't. Why not? He knew all three of her brothers by sight and reputation, if not personally. He should have seen the resemblance.

Not that she looked much like her older siblings. They had wide jaws and broad shoulders and were full of machismo. Evelina was the happy surprise who was several years younger. Aside from her height, she took after her Italian grandfather's family. That's where she got her black hair and dark brown eyes and that touch of gold embedded in her skin.

She had attended an all-girls boarding school in Switzerland and she'd been too young to be in any of Dom's social circles, not that Visconti and Blackwood worlds were allowed to overlap. After the loss of his brother,

Dom's father hadn't allowed a Visconti name to be spoken in his earshot, let alone suffer the presence of one in a room with him. They were "that family" or, if he was referencing Romeo, "the mongrel."

Thus, Dom hadn't had a clue he was lusting after Romeo's daughter that night.

All he'd known when the elevator opened was that he couldn't let her go again. Compelled by what could only be called a primitive imperative, Dom had made all the advances, barely capable of his usual restraint. He always made sure a woman wanted his sexual attention, but he'd been more assertive than usual. More driven.

Eve had seemed surprised by his directness, but when it came down to it, she'd matched his level of carnality. That's what still made him hard in a heartbeat, that she'd trembled and moaned and climaxed when he'd barely touched her.

He'd wanted inside her more than he'd wanted his next breath.

At that point, the gods had had their biggest laugh at his expense. They'd delivered the message he'd so far failed to grasp. Her phone rang and there was Nico Visconti's smug face turning Dom's lust to disgust. To ire at being thwarted. And rage at feeling tricked.

Eve had seemed equally aghast. Maybe it really had been a series of outlandish coincidences, but their innocent mistake didn't make any of their actions less criminal. Not in his mind. Certainly not in the mind of his father if he ever found out.

For weeks, Dom had debated coming clean about the incident, wanting to get ahead of his father's tantrum. No matter how or when Thomas learned of the betrayal, it could literally stop his heart.

Ultimately, Dom had stayed silent not out of shame or concern for his father, but from a misguided sense of decency. He had sisters. He knew that pinning a Scarlet A on a woman, humiliating her for having a sexual appetite, was as sexist and hypocritical as it got. His father would do it anyway. If it would hurt Romeo to have his daughter disgraced, Thomas would revel in making her suffer.

Dom's heart was not quite as charred as his father's. He kept his mouth shut and waited to see if she would move first. If *she* would reveal the intimate things they'd done.

There'd been nothing but silence.

Until his father died.

Now Eve's father and brothers were jumping on WBE like hyenas on a wounded gazelle. There was a small chance they were acting independently, Dom supposed. As far as he could tell, Eve had recently been given a midlevel position with their head office so she didn't have the frontline ability to lead these sorts of attacks, but she easily could have spun some story to her father that would fuel this action.

Either way, Dom's father was dead. That meant the Viscontis were coming for *him*.

Dom understood his father's perspective now, even his grandfather's. The Viscontis were leaving him with no choice but to fight. He was angry enough at their tactics that he wouldn't rest until he had his teeth in their proverbial throats.

A memory flashed of the mark he'd left on Eve's neck. Heat pooled behind his fly.

Damn it, he wanted her out of his head! He wanted her and her family relegated to the fringes of his perception, where he would never think about any of them ever again.

It might take years. It might take playing the wounded

antelope to lead them down a path toward an ambush, but he was a smart, patient man. He could do it.

One way or another, he would end this feud once and for all.

# CHAPTER FOUR

*Four years later...*

HE WAS HERE. God help her, Dom Blackwood was attending this freaking wedding.

Which wouldn't be such a nightmare if it had been a typical afternoon-evening affair, but no. This was a weeklong extravaganza in the Whitsunday Islands of Australia.

How many times had she considered calling off her agreement to come? Every day since she'd been asked. Eve didn't even know the couple getting married. She was the plus-one for a man she'd only been seeing for two months.

Her date, Logan Offerman, was a handsome lawyer with political aspirations who came from a big family with old money. He liked dogs and hiking and supported right-to-vote legislation. He had gone to school with her middle brother, Jackson. His parents were friends of her own from the country club.

Eve's mother, who had always told Eve to guard her virginity like it was the Hope diamond, wanted this marriage. Everyone did. Her father kept saying, "It's a good match." Her eldest brother, Nico, was starting to sound like a used car salesman, he was selling it so hard. Her

youngest brother, Christopher, was indifferent, but happy
that she was taking the heat of family attention so he
could live his bohemian life in Hawaii unbothered.

Ginny had essentially poked a sword in Eve's back to
get her onto the plane.

"Spend some time with him. You'll soon see how right
this is for both of you." Eve suspected her mother believed that if Eve finally slept with a man, she might actually marry him.

Eve had been finding fault with her mother's suggested
suitors for four years. Even she was tired of it. She really,
really wanted to fall for Logan, if only to finally have
some peace from this constant pressure to marry. Nevertheless, all she could think was that Logan reminded
her of sunscreen. He offered important protection, but
made her feel sticky and suffocated.

Logan was a groomsman in the wedding party so
they'd been given a beautiful two-bedroom suite at the
eco-resort where the guests without yachts were being
housed. Eve knew that Logan was hoping they would
start sleeping together while they were away. He didn't
take it for granted, though. He set her suitcase in the second bedroom without asking, only sending her a brief,
hopeful look that resembled a puppy tapping its tail.

"I think I'll nap before the welcome reception," Eve
said, closing herself into her room.

She was actually going to scream into her pillow because what else could she do?

While they'd been ferried across from the mainland
with some of the other wedding guests, she'd overheard
someone ask a very beautiful woman, "Isn't Dom with
you?"

"WBE just bought a hotel in Airlie Beach," the woman

had replied. "He's staying there for meetings. I want time with my family and I'm a bridesmaid so…"

Eve had drifted away, ostensibly to enjoy the view, but mostly because she had feared she would lose her breakfast over the rail.

She had managed to avoid Domenico Blackwood for four years—mostly. She had compulsively learned far too much about him online from how many women he dated to the fact he was named for his mother's favorite uncle. He lived in New York, but he had properties around the world and was very hands-on so he was rarely home.

Even when he was there, the chance of running into him was low. Her parents were very good about vetting guest lists. There had only been a handful of times that Eve had glimpsed Dom from across a restaurant. The one time she had walked into a Fourth of July party and noticed him, she had claimed a migraine and left immediately.

Each tiny encounter had left her unable to sleep for days, though, always wondering if he'd seen her and whether he would finally turn on her, exposing her behavior to her family and anyone else who would listen. Over the years, she had only grown more mortified by the way she had behaved with him in Budapest. The fact he'd been a stranger was embarrassing enough, but her father had genuinely hated Dom's.

Romeo's hostility toward Thomas Blackwood was understandable. The man had accused him of murder, but it had all been cleared up. Nevertheless, when Thomas had died, her father had rallied her brothers to attack WBE.

Eve had questioned her father on that. It seemed like a dirty move when Dom had been grieving and finding his feet as the head of the company.

"Michael Blackwood didn't let up on me when *my* father died," her father groused.

At that point, Eve had distanced herself, still unable to think of how uninhibited she'd been without cringing. Dom had both ignited and derailed her passion, making it impossible for her to feel anything with anyone else.

Eventually, her father had determined WBE was on its last legs. He had retired and handed the reins to Nico.

Eve should have seen an upward trajectory in her own career at that point, but Dom and WBE had quickly begun to rally, apparently not so beaten as they'd seemed. Nico spent all his time countering offensives while she was left to languish in the marketing division. In fact, the resort that Dom had just purchased here in Queensland had been targeted as the next Visconti property. Nico was furious that he had not only lost to Dom *again*, but had lost the significant time and money he'd put into his attempt to acquire it.

Eve couldn't help wondering if Dom's relentless attack was fueled by what had happened between them. She hadn't told a soul about meeting him in Budapest and never would, but dreaded that Dom might. He could be waiting for exactly the right moment to slay her with a pithy revelation that would destroy her reputation, turn her family into a mockery and lower her family's view of her.

She hated that he held that over her!

Her stomach churned as she dressed for the welcome reception two hours later. The schedule of mix-and-mingle activities through the week included day trips and shopping, sailing and diving and hiking, all culminating in the ceremony and reception five days from now. It was organized like an all-inclusive trade conference, which was the real reason she had accepted this invitation. Her middle brother, Jackson, had reminded her that there would be a lot of quality connections to be made.

"Bring value to the table," he had advised her, well aware of how frustrated she was with their older brother's reluctance to advance her in the company. "That's the kind of thing Nico notices and appreciates."

Nico did nothing but stonewall her. No matter how hard she worked, he treated her as though she was five, not twenty-five, but Eve was willing to try anything to get him to take her seriously.

Even face Dom again.

Or maybe not. Ugh. She was regretting everything about being here as she and Logan arrived at the outdoor dining room—including the fact that she'd left her hair down because there was just enough breeze and humidity to make tiny strands stick to her face and neck.

Running back to her suite for a scarf wasn't an option. It would look like another retreat, not that Dom even noticed her, but *she* would know that she was being a coward.

After her first sweeping glance—and the painful awareness that sliced through her when she spotted him—she looked anywhere but where he stood with the tall brunette she'd overheard earlier. Was that woman his wife? His fiancée? He'd been engaged ages ago, before they'd met, but nothing of the sort had been reported lately.

*Not that she cared.*

Eve barely noticed what the other woman looked like. Dom's image dominated her vision. She forced herself to smile as they began moving through the receiving line, but all she saw was Dom's athletic frame in bone-colored

trousers and a pale blue Henley in fine cotton. His jaw
was shaved clean which made him look even tougher
than when he'd worn stubble. Maybe it was the aviator
glasses reflecting the sinking sun against the water that
gave him such an air of remote arrogance. Maybe it was
a stronger air of command that had developed in response
to his takeover at WBE.

Maybe it was the same belly-deep loathing for an ad-
versary that sat in her own stomach.

*But who is your loathing really for?* a sneering voice
mocked deep inside her.

It was for herself. She had been so *eager* that morning in Budapest. So *easy*. It was the great irony of her
life that she'd resorted to telling men she was waiting for
marriage as an excuse for not sleeping with them. The
truth was, the only man she'd ever wanted to have sex
with was that man, the one she hated most on earth. The
very last man she would ever touch.

Logan introduced her to the bride and groom and their
parents.

Eve forced her bright smile to stay in place as the
mother of the bride drew her aside. "I'm so sorry, dear.
I was just informed of the bad blood between you and
one of our guests."

"What?" A wet sack of cement landed in her gut.

"The professional rivalry between the Viscontis and
the Blackwoods. Dom is here as a guest of my niece."
The woman glanced over, but Eve refused to give in to
the temptation to do the same. "I wouldn't want anyone
to be uncomfortable…" The woman meant her niece and
her daughter, the bride.

"Are you referring to the court case between our fathers?" Eve asked with manufactured confusion. "Oh,

that trademark dispute was settled ages ago. It's old news." She dismissed it with a wave of her hand. "Besides, I understand there are more than seventy islands to explore here. I doubt we'll even speak." She leaned in to add with forced levity, "Maybe don't seat us together, just to be sure."

The woman chuckled with relief and went back to the receiving line.

Eve took a subtle, shaken breath, hoping her request would be taken seriously. She absolutely did not want to talk to Dom.

"Everything all right?" Logan appeared beside her to offer a glass of white wine.

"Mmm. She…um…warned me that Dom Blackwood is here. I've never met him." She used the excuse to glance around, deliberately looking the wrong direction.

"Over my left shoulder. Your brother won't be happy," Logan said ruefully.

Eve did her best to appear disinterested, sipping and glancing past Logan.

Dom's attention seemed angled her way, but with his mirrored sunglasses it was impossible to tell if he was looking at her. Her heart rattled in her chest anyway. Hot coals of yearning glowed brighter in her midsection. It was shameful to react this way. It took all of her control to hide her response behind a blank expression.

*You mean nothing to me,* she transmitted, before looking to Logan with a sweet smile.

"What do you want to do tomorrow?"

She really did hate Dom, she decided, as Logan's voice turned into a drone that was as pesky as a mosquito's whine while the rest of her senses were amplified with proprioception.

Dom had broken her with their early-morning dalliance in Budapest. No one had ever made her feel so much want. For the first time, she had let herself go with what she was feeling. She had let him see her at her most vulnerable, in the throes of passion. She had been in a state of shock, half-naked, the rest of her clothing askew, when he had ordered her to leave.

She had felt rejected and dirty and mortified as she hurried to pack. She hadn't wanted to stay another second. She had texted Hailey on her way to the airport that something had come up and she'd waited with trepidation for Dom to say something to the press or leak something on a grapevine. She had been sure he would use her behavior against her.

He hadn't. Which was no consolation. She only felt beneath his notice, which was somehow worse. He seemed to have wiped her from his mind and she ought to be able to do the same. It was her deepest shame that she still fantasized about him.

Did he touch that woman's arm? A barb of envy pierced her chest. Now her ears strained for his voice, hearing him order a drink with, "Extra ice."

"What do you think?" Logan asked.

She bit back a bewildered, *What?* He'd been saying something about snorkeling off the groom's yacht, but she hadn't been paying attention.

"That sounds fun." She kept her smile on her face even though Dom moved closer, to speak to a couple nearby.

Her back felt his presence like a tropical sun was radiating a third-degree burn into her skin.

Logan, bless him, said, "Darling, come meet my friend Dave and his wife."

The whole evening was like that, drifting into striking

distance of a deadly viper, trying not to draw Dom's attention while gripped by tension, waiting for him to say something to her or about her or force her to speak to him.

Most disgraceful of all, when she and Logan were on their way to her room, all she could wonder was whether that cousin of the bride would be screaming Dom's name later.

"He's staying at his property on the mainland," Logan said as the door to their suite closed behind them.

"Pardon?" Good God. She hadn't spoken her thoughts aloud, had she?

"Blackwood. I checked. And I texted your brother, letting him know I'll make sure he doesn't bother you, so you can relax."

Eve blinked, wondering if she was supposed to be flattered that Logan was acting so proprietary, as though she couldn't make her own decisions or look after herself.

"I would have thought all of that rivalry had died with his father," Logan continued as he casually kicked off his shoes and left them in the middle of the floor. "Your brother sounded pretty agitated, though, asking whether WBE was expanding elsewhere in Australia, beyond that resort he just bought. I said I'd ask around."

"Boys will be boys," Eve said blithely. "I don't pay much attention."

That was another huge lie. She wished she could ignore Dom and what her brother did to antagonize him, but she couldn't. She should probably be grateful she was still being held at arm's length from the top-level decisions or she might betray her excess interest, but she was mostly indignant at being relegated to branding and décor, never included in big decisions or given real responsibilities.

A light hand slid along her arm. She tensed in something that felt a lot like repulsion.

"Darling? I respect that you want to wait until your wedding night, but… We could do other things," Logan persuaded. "Perhaps get in the hot tub and see what happens?" He nodded toward the terrace.

"I have a headache." Not a lie. "Can we talk about that tomorrow?"

"Of course. But if you're going to bed, I'll change and pop down for a nightcap." At least he didn't pout about it. Maybe marriage to him would be okay.

"Sleep well." He kissed her cheek, leaving her cold.

*"Of all the gin joints in all the towns…"*

Dom had thought those grim words more times than Bogart himself had said them. Why that night, in that bar, in that rabbit warren of a playground in Budapest? Why *her*? A Visconti?

And why was he still fascinated by her four years after he had resolved to erase her from his mind?

Because he still carried a sense of something unfinished. It was no mystery why. He hadn't slept with anyone since. No matter how sexually frustrated he got, no matter how beautiful and receptive his date might be, they all left him unmoved.

Yet all Eve Visconti had to do was lift her hair off the back of her neck and he was hard as a rock, barely able to restrain himself.

Aside from one haughty glance past her lover's ear, she had avoided looking at him during the welcome reception last night. Yes, he had noticed, even though he'd done his best to ignore her, too. It was a skill he'd perfected the handful of times he'd seen her in New York. It didn't matter if he looked at her or not, though. His inner radar always tracked her when she was in the vicinity. He knew where she was and which man she spoke to and how she sounded when she climaxed.

When she'd left the party last night, Dom's blood had turned to acid as he wondered whether that stick puppet of an attorney was making her shatter. He hadn't slept and blamed her for that, too.

Now he'd arrived for a buffet brunch and beach activities. He was pretending not to notice Eve as she came out of the pool. Her wide-brimmed hat and retro sunglasses hid most of her face, but her lithe figure was on full display in a red one-piece with waist cutouts. Her nipples hardened despite the full sun of midmorning. Water beaded against her golden skin. Her legs were still a mile and a half each way, accentuated by the high cut of her suit and the heeled sandals she stepped into. She accepted a towel from that toothpaste ad of a boyfriend.

"—need a special permit because they limit access. If we want to see it, we have to go tomorrow."

Dom dragged his gaze off the pert cheeks of Evie's ass where the V of her suit left a portion of the pale globes bare and looked to the pretty face tilted up to his.

"They're expecting a storm, though," Cat continued. "We have to be off the island by two. My brother will take us on his sailboat."

"Okay." Dom wished he'd brought his own yacht or at least rented one. He had a speedboat operator at his beck and call, but anything larger had seemed superfluous when he had the penthouse in his new, five-star hotel on the mainland—the one he'd scooped away from Eve's brother.

Dom's battle with Nico for key properties was coming

out in his favor almost exclusively these days. When he'd taken over WBE, it had been struggling, but he'd shored up its cash position and had a sizable cushion these days, one that allowed him to enter bidding wars that forced Visconti Group to either back off or pay through the nose for what they wanted.

Dom had a strong feeling that financial pressure was the reason Eve was here with Logan Offerman, second son of a multimedia tycoon.

"The kids will be aboard," Cat added with an appealing expression.

Dom made himself pay attention to what she was saying. Spending time with Cat and her family was the point of his being here. His middle sister had set him up with Cat, urging him to be her date to this wedding since he was planning a trip to Australia anyway.

Dom was trying, genuinely trying, to like her. Cat was everything he ought to look for in a life partner—well-mannered, well-connected and well-off. Children liked her. So did his sister and, seemingly, everyone else.

"Oh!"

The startled pitch in Eve's voice snapped Dom's head around while his muscles bunched in readiness to attack.

She wasn't being assaulted, though. Her hat had blown off. It rolled toward him and fetched up against his feet.

She chased it with long strides of those forever legs and halted when he straightened to offer it to her.

They both wore sunglasses, but he knew they looked straight into each other's eyes. He felt the clash all the way into his chest. Lower.

She had shrugged on a cover-up of eyelet lace. Belting it had probably been the reason she'd failed to catch her hat.

"Thank you." She swallowed as she took it, then pressed something that looked like a natural smile onto her face as she said to Cat, "I apologize for interrupting."

"No problem. I'm Catherine. Cat." She offered her hand. "Have you met Dom?"

"I haven't. Eve. Nice to meet you both." She briefly shook Cat's hand, aimed a polite smile vaguely but not quite in his direction and said, "I won't keep you. Excuse me."

Dom bit back a hoot of laughter. They hadn't met? *Wow.*

Eve set her hat on her head and walked away with long, unhurried strides that made his blood itch.

"The animosity is real," Cat said in an undertone of amusement. "She didn't even shake your hand."

He had noticed. His palm felt scorched yet empty.

"Shall we get out on the Jet Skis before they're gone?" Dom suggested. He was too much of a workaholic to get much pleasure from such a pointless activity, but the greater goal was to get to know Cat. He was testing the waters, so to speak, considering whether to pursue a more formal arrangement.

He followed Cat toward the rental shack on the wharf, fighting the urge to look back at Eve.

He lost.

# CHAPTER FIVE

EVE HAD TO hand it to Logan. He'd taught her to carry a sensible assortment of items when leaving for a day hike—most of which turned out to be unnecessary today. They arrived with the rest of the guests at one of the uninhabited islands to find the groom's family had installed a pop-up store and takeaway shack on the beach.

The shack was on pontoons so it could be floated back to whence it had come, once the day was over. Its large wooden awning was levered up with poles to shade the order window. Racks of sarongs, beach towels, flip-flops and sunhats stood nearby.

"This was arranged last year, before they knew there'd be a storm," Eve overheard someone say while she was flicking through the sarongs. "They thought everyone would be swimming and snorkeling all day then dancing on the beach until sunrise. The band will perform at the resort tonight instead."

At least there was a portable loo. Eve used it before heading out with Logan across the island.

Logan was hungover after the stag party on the mainland last night. There'd been a hen party for the bride at the resort, but Eve had been happy to stay alone in the suite, catching up on reading after she composed a blistering email to her brother asking him to read her most recent proposal and give her the promotion she deserved.

She was taking out her frustration with Dom's imposing presence on her brother, sure, but she wasn't wrong.

Whether Dom had joined the stag party, she didn't know. He had looked fresh as a daisy when he had waded in from one of the other boats. He wore loose swim shorts in shades of blue with a white surf shirt that hugged his torso so lovingly, she could count the muscles in his six-pack.

Disgusted with herself for noticing, Eve set a grumpy pace along the trail to the far side of the island. The track climbed up through the rainforest then across the top of a hill that opened into grassland. When they arrived at a lookout, they paused to photograph the stunning views of empty islands surrounded by swirls of white sand and turquoise waters.

The track then descended toward a bottle tree and a sign that marked a split in the track. One read Spit, the other Turtle Bay.

They chose turtles and descended to a private beach of powder-white sand with a sea turtle sunning itself in the lapping surf.

"This is beautiful." Eve stayed well back from the creature, but used the zoom feature on her phone to snap a photo of it.

"I think I'm going to be sick." Logan braced his hands on his knees. His face glowed with perspiration. "This isn't normal behavior for me," he assured her as he looked to the scrub at the edge of the beach. "Just old friends behaving like we're still in college. Oh, I meant to ask you…" Logan straightened to take out his electrolyte drink and sip it. "I picked up a text from your brother before we left. He asked me if Dom is upsetting you. Is he?"

"What? No. Why would he?" She lowered her phone, growing prickly. *From the heat.*

"I don't know." Logan shrugged. "Nico said you sent him an email that sounded bitchy. His word." He held up a staying hand as she snapped her spine straight.

"That doesn't make it okay to repeat! And wouldn't you be bitchy if you were being held back every second of every day?"

"He's not holding you back." He took another pull off his drink. "He's being realistic."

"In what way?" Why was he taking her brother's side?

"I'm not trying to insult you, Eve." His tone said, *calm down.*

"Yet you're managing to." She strained to sound ultra-reasonable instead of incredibly irritated, which she was. "I think it's very realistic that, after four years of dedicated service, my brother give me more responsibility in the family company. When Jackson was twenty-five, he was given all of Europe to oversee. Christo has the Pacific Rim. I'm not even *head* of marketing yet."

"Because Nico knows that you *claim* you want a top position in the business, but that will change once you're married and have children."

"I'm not *claiming* to want it. I know what I want." And she was affronted that Logan seemed to doubt that. "A husband and children could be years away. I don't know how I'll feel when that happens so how could Nico?"

"Years?" Logan's brows crinkled with a patronizing aren't-you-cute? expression. "Darling, we have to marry within the year so I can hit the ground running with the next campaign cycle. If you want to put off children for a short time after that, I suppose I can agree, but voters prefer family men, not power wives who put their career ahead of their husband's. I think you'll find that between raising our children and keeping up with the duties of a congressman's wife, you won't have time to spare for Visconti Group. Which is what I told your brother when you and I started dating—"

"Oh, my God," she cut in, putting up a staying hand. "Was that your marriage proposal to me just now? I respectfully decline."

"Eve." His mouth tightened with dismay. "Don't be like that."

"I'm not saying that with hard feelings, Logan. Honestly. I'm glad we've established that we want different things." In fact, she was profoundly relieved. "I'll go back to the landing beach where I will catch a lift with the first boat willing to take me to the hotel. Then I'll pack and leave you to enjoy the wedding and the rest of your life with whoever wants to dedicate her life to being your wife and only your wife, because that woman isn't me."

"Wait, stop. Come on. You can't leave. What would I tell people?" He put out a pleading hand.

"Say I had a family emergency." She paused in starting toward the track. "My brother will definitely need surgery to remove the job I'm about to shove up his—"

Logan cursed and clutched his stomach, then staggered toward the weeds.

*What a catch.*

"Bye, Logan." She spun to push herself up the winding incline with such force, her thigh muscles burned. She was impelled by anger at Logan and his assumptions, and her brother and his sexist dismissal of her, and her whole family for only seeing she had value as a wife, not as an employee. Not as a person.

She was panting and sweating as she arrived at the bottle tree in time to hear Dom and Cat on the lookout above her, taking photos.

*Ugh.* He was the *last* person she wanted to see when she was ready to burn down the patriarchy with the sheer force of her glare.

She veered down the track labeled Spit. It had taken less than an hour to hike across the island and the boats weren't leaving until two. She would easily get back in time.

Or so she believed.


Dom was not a quitter, but nor was he a liar.

This wasn't working with Cat. She leaned into him, eyes limpid, mouth soft and inviting and all he could think was, *Don't.*

He couldn't reject her days before she was supposed to be a bridesmaid in her cousin's wedding, though.

At least they weren't sleeping together. She might accuse him of leading her on when they had The Talk, but he'd barely kissed her cheek since a certain someone had arrived under his nose to torture him all over again.

"Dom?" Cat murmured, drawing a circle around the small logo above his heart. "Are we o—? Oh!" With a self-conscious smile, she stepped away, glancing beyond him. "Hi."

Dom turned to see Logan coming up from the trail down to the far side of the island. He was sweaty and red-faced with exertion. He paused to give them a curt nod of greeting.

Dom braced himself for the sight of Eve, but she didn't appear behind him.

"Where's Eve?" Cat asked, looking past him.

"She had to leave," Logan said with a sullen pout. "Family emergency."

When? Dom had seen her leaving on her walk with Logan and they would have passed her on the trail if she'd already gone back. Or Dom would have felt her walk behind him while they were taking photos. He didn't *want* a sixth sense where she was concerned, but he had one.

"Is it worth hiking down to see the turtles?" Cat asked Logan.

"There was only one and it went back into the water. I'll see you at the thing later." Logan's gaze refused to meet his, striking Dom as shifty before Logan headed back to the cove where the boats were mustered.

Dom didn't think the other man had done anything nefarious to Eve, but a sense of wrongness abraded his insides as the other man left. Dom's ears felt pricked for her voice, his nose twitching to catch her scent.

"Trouble in paradise?" Cat elevated her brows in amused speculation.

Dom shrugged, irritated by the question. "Do you want to see the turtles?"

"He said there weren't any. If it's just a beach, let's go back to the one we can swim at."

The weather was turning cloudy and the water was too choppy for comfortable snorkeling. That's why they had decided to walk instead of swim. Dom was reluctant to leave the trail, though. It was a gut-level response that he relied on when he made big decisions at WBE, the kind that wasn't always backed up by logic and facts, but never steered him wrong.

Leaving the trail went against his instinct, but he took

Cat back to the cove, compelled to see if Eve was, in fact, there.

She was officially an unhealthy obsession, he decided, when they arrived and he couldn't see her. He scanned the crowd and counted the boats, noting that one yacht had left. It was feasible she'd been taken back to the resort. She wasn't his responsibility anyway. She was his *enemy*, for God's sake. Her whole family was a pile of thorns in his side.

He told Cat to swim without him and pondered whether to radio a boat he couldn't identify while he watched Logan pour margaritas down his throat as though he was being paid to do it. Guilty conscience? *Was* there trouble in paradise?

"She had to leave," he overheard Logan say to someone. "Family emergency."

Dom knew he was behaving like a Victorian spinster, worrying about someone he had no business caring about, but he couldn't shake a sense that Eve was still here. Just not *here*.

As the wind picked up and the first raindrops fell, boats began pulling in gear and families started gathering children and toys from the beach. Two boats left and the one that had been missing came back from circumnavigating the island. Eve wasn't on it.

"Go with your brother. I'll find someone going to the mainland," Dom said to Cat, glancing at his watch. "I'll catch up to you at dinner."

Cat was surprised, but her sister-in-law asked for her help getting the children to the sailboat so she moved down the beach.

Dom glanced at the takeaway shack, thinking to tell

the man running it not to leave until he'd checked back in with him, but Cat's uncle was at the window.

Dom veered from admitting aloud that he was concerned about Eve. He barely wanted to admit it to himself. She was likely fine and had done exactly as Logan had said. She'd made her way back to the eco-resort and was on her way to the airport.

He glanced at his watch again, deciding to be sure. He worked out constantly, both cardio and strength. He could easily sprint across the island and be back before this regatta of disorganized boaters had launched itself.

He slipped into the trees and ran up the track, seizing the challenge, grateful for the sting of rain as he traversed the plateau, keeping him from overheating.

The goat track down to Turtle Beach tested his agility and the area was reassuringly empty. Logan hadn't murdered her.

Dom decided to seek counselling when he got back to New York. This fixation he had developed wasn't healthy.

He started climbing back up and almost ignored the sign labeled Spit, but his feet took him that direction before he'd consciously recollected Logan's assertion that Eve had gone ahead.

A strange tingle hit him as he began jogging that direction. It was the same subconscious polarity that oriented him in an unfamiliar city back to his hotel or car. The same tingle that said, *She's here.*

Just as he began to think he'd been bitten by a hallucinogenic spider, he heard a feminine voice swear a blistering and imaginative blue streak.

Relief crashed over him like a surge of surf, followed by a disorienting anger. Could she not tell time? Now they would arrive back at the resort together and have to make stupid explanations—

He came around a bend in the path and saw she was hurt. She was using a stick of driftwood as a cane. Her foot was out of her shoe with only her toes tucked into it as she limped-slid it forward. She was watching where she put her feet against the various roots protruding across the path, continuing to spill robust curses.

Her ankle was the size of a grapefruit and grossly discolored.

His heart stopped.

"Did something bite you?" That was bad. In this country, that could be very, very bad.

She snapped her head up. Her expression blanked before she cried indignantly to the sky, "Really? *This* is the help you send me?"

"Eve," he said through his teeth. "Did something sting or bite you?"

"*No*. I turned my ankle. It's sprained."

He looked again and realized the bulge was actually an ice pack secured with—

"Is that a *condom*?"

"News flash, they can be used for other things. I took an ibuprofen, but I can't walk on this foot. Can you go tell the boats to wait?"

"I'm sure they'll do a head count." He was not sure of that at all, or of its accuracy, given how people had been jumping on and off each other's boats. "The kid in the takeaway shack won't leave until everyone else does." He hoped.

Dom moved to her side and slipped his arm around her. They both jolted at the electrical charge that zapped like an entire winter's worth of static between them.

She glared at him. He glared back.

She shrugged him off and tried to continue walking without holding onto him.

"Don't be stupid, Eve. You can't do this without—"

"Don't call me stupid." She squared to face him, chin set at a belligerent angle.

*Screw it.* They could stand here and fight, missing the last boat, or he could duck, which he did, and throw her over his shoulder, which he also did.

"Don't you dare!" she screamed as he straightened from grabbing her shoe. The day pack she wore slumped to knock into the top of his ass.

"Give me that." He reached back to tug it free of her flailing arms and looped it over his free shoulder so the sack was against his chest.

"Put me down you freaking *animal.*" She kicked her feet and braced a hand against his spine, trying to straighten.

"Watch your head," he commanded as he started back the way he'd come.

"Put me *down.*" She slapped his ass hard enough to sting.

"Bad news, Evie. I *like* that." He did. Not because he had a kinky streak—although he did have a small one—but more because finally, finally, he was discharging some of his pent-up sexual energy. He wanted a tussle and a pillow fight and *sex*. Raw, dirty, endless sex.

He would settle for a slap on his ass and her weight on his shoulder while he puffed his way up the hill, muscles seared with strain. Her filthy mouth calling him filthy names while her hands clutched into his shirt and her breasts brushed his back was a dream come true.

She tried grabbing the sign as they passed the bottle tree.

"Settle down." He gave her butt a warning tap, very tempted to let his hand linger there. "No one knows I came looking for you. We have to hurry or we'll be stuck here."

"I would rather fall down a crevasse and be eaten by goannas than be held by you."

"You think I woke up today hoping I could run a marathon with radioactive waste on my shoulder?" They arrived at where the lookout gave a view of the back side of the island. He turned a slow circle. "See any boats?"

"No," she said on a whimper.

"Hold onto my waist so you don't bounce. I have to hurry."

With another infuriated noise, she sagged down and hugged her arms around his chest. The temperature was dropping. Clouds were thickening on the horizon and fat, spattering rain was starting to soak their clothes.

"Why are you even here?" she mumbled into his back.

"Why are you?"

She didn't answer, but after a few minutes of his half jog across the grassland stretch, she said, "This hurts my stomach."

"I just want to get to…" He swore as he arrived at the spot where they could see the stretch of water toward the main island. He let her slide down and braced her while she balanced on one foot.

She lifted her hand to shield her eyes from the rain and followed his gaze to the loose armada of boats already well into the distance.

"That little silver one at the back is the kid from the shack." At least he wasn't towing the shed, probably because the water was too rough.

A desolate noise broke from her throat. "They'll do a head count when they get back, though, won't they?"

"Some of them are going to the mainland. Cat thinks I caught one of those. I won't be missed until dinner." He looked to the desperation on her face. "Logan said you had a family emergency?"

"Don't get excited. Everyone's fine," she said crossly. "I told him to say that to cover the fact I was leaving early." She chewed her lip. "Hopefully, he'll notice my things are still in my room and wonder where I am."

"*Your* room? You two aren't sleeping together?" Satisfaction shouldn't have glowed so ember-hot in the pit of his gut at that news. "Is that why you were fighting?"

She scowled resentfully. "What makes you think we were fighting?"

"You're making up reasons to leave early. He was doing his best to get drunk once he got back to the beach. He won't notice you're missing." He shook his head.

"Men are the bane of my existence," she muttered, fists in knots beside her hips.

"So you don't need a lift the rest of the way to the beach?" he asked with false pleasantness.

"Why are you even helping me?" Her voice strained with aggravated emotion.

"Because I don't have your father's stark absence of conscience when it comes to leaving people to die."

# CHAPTER SIX

"THAT WAS A cheap shot." Eve was both hot and cold. Her blood was simmering with a mix of anxiety and sexual frustration. Rain was beginning in earnest, soaking her clothes enough to chill her skin as the wind cut across the top of the island. Her ankle hurt. A lot.

She resented the hell out of this man whom she had tried to avoid by taking that stupid trail and wound up injured and stranded and alone. Now she was stuck with him and he thought he could throw old lies in her face?

"I will make my own way down thanks." She would crawl if she had to.

He swore under his breath and ducked again, moving so fast he had her over his shoulder before she could finish her cry of protest.

She didn't bother struggling, though. She passionately hated relying on him, but this was a more efficient way of traveling, especially down the knotty, zigzag path through the rainforest.

Plus, there was a part of her that thrived on the feel of his strong body shifting and flexing under hers. She reveled in the excuse to pin her arms around his chest, hugging herself into his strength while pressing her face into the smell of his skin beneath his shirt.

They didn't speak until they were on the beach. Which was empty. Very, very empty.

She pulled open the Velcro pocket of her shorts and took out her phone. There was no signal here, either. The entire island was out of range.

With a huff of despair, she limped her way into the loo, thankful for *that* small mercy.

When she came out waving her hands, drying the disinfecting lotion, Dom was at the door of the shack, scowling at the locked knob.

"Got a hairpin? I can't kick it in. It opens out."

"What about the window?" The wooden awning was secured with two dead bolts on either side, neither of which was locked.

She slipped each free and Dom lifted the awning, propping it with the dangling sticks. The sliding order window was small, but it slid open when she reached up to touch it.

"Look at us with our teamwork," she said with a sunny smile of triumph.

It faded as she glimpsed his humorless expression.

He linked his hands and bent to offer a stirrup. "Knee," he said. "See if you can unlock the door from the inside."

Oh, this was going to be even more graceful than being slung over his shoulder.

She took hold of the window ledge and set the knee of her injured foot into his hands.

In another show of his supreme strength, he boosted her high enough she dove headfirst through the opening where she knocked a few caddies of condiments and utensils to the floor.

She caught at the counter on the far side as she dragged

her feet in, then under, herself. There wasn't much room to step, though.

"Good news. We can get roaring drunk," she told him through the window as she picked her way over crates of alcohol and around the racks of sarongs and towels to reach out and flick the lock.

He opened the door from the outside and peered in. "Radio?"

She looked around. "No."

Another curse, one with more resignation than heat.

"He has to come back for it at some point," she said.

Dom made a noise of agreement and took the well-used plastic milk crate from inside the door. He set it as a step, then reached for the nearest box of bottles. "I'll throw some of this underneath so we can both fit in there."

There was only a small strip of floor between the counters and the cupboards that lined the walls. The back of the shack held a sink, a stove and a deep fryer that was covered and thankfully empty, despite the lingering funk of grease. The front counter serviced the window. Beneath it was a small refrigerator stocked with bottled water and a few unopened jars of pickles, but little else. The cupboards over the window held canned and dry goods. The ones at the back were full of cooking implements.

Eve stowed what she could of the things she'd knocked over and stacked the sarongs and beach towels onto the shelf by the window, since they would only blow away or fill with sand if they were left outside.

When the last rack and box of alcohol was removed, she hitched to sit on the counter beside the sink, instantly feeling claustrophobic when Dom stepped inside.

He set a six-pack of premade Bloody Mary cocktails on the ledge by the window.

"It looked like the only thing with nutritional value." His shirt and hair were soaked. His nipples were sharp points beneath his shirt.

*Not that she noticed.*

She handed him a towel. He ran it over his face and hair, then his bare arms.

He'd secured the door open, but it rattled in the growing wind as did the awning. She made herself look at those things, then above where the rain had become a steady drum on the roof.

"Power?" he asked, flicking a switch by the door.

Nothing happened.

"He must have taken the generator with him." He released another tired curse and gave his damp face a final swipe before tossing the towel onto the pile of clean ones. "Why the hell didn't you come straight back to the beach when you left Logan?"

"Really?" Just like that, her temper was back at explosive. "You want to make this *my* fault? I didn't want to see you," she spelled out belligerently. "Okay? You were standing at the lookout with your girlfriend and I was sick of men, given what Logan had done—"

"What did Logan do?" he asked in a tone that was so lethal, her scalp prickled.

"He said something to my brother that I didn't like," she grumbled. "Why didn't you tell someone you thought I was missing and ask them to find me?"

He muttered something about this being an unproductive conversation and closed both window and door, leaving the awning open to provide light and a view of the heavy surf as it crashed onto shore.

"Is there anything to eat?" He started to open a cupboard.

"Potato chips and candy bars, crackers and caviar, pickles and olives, canned pineapple and beets. When that runs out, each other."

She regretted her sarcasm as soon as she said it. She heard his thick voice asking, *"Do you want my mouth here?"* She remembered his tone perfectly because she'd been replaying it for four years. Her body flushed with heat and her cheeks stung.

He stared right at her, smug as he reached for a Bloody Mary, opened it with a pop, then drained half of it in a few healthy swallows, never taking his eyes off her.

God, she hated him.

But when he offered her a can of her own, she took it and opened it, taking a big gulp of the tangy, vodka-laced drink to wet her dry throat.

"You really didn't know who I was in Budapest?" he asked in a voice thick with suspicion. He leaned his hips beside her against the back counter so he stared at the water, but she felt his attention on her as though she was under an interrogation light.

"No," she choked. "I would never—Did you know who *I* was?"

"Hell, no." His profile was carved from granite. "Did you tell anyone? Your brothers?"

"Gawd, no. I'm dreading having to explain this." She started to sip, then had to ask, "Did you? Tell anyone?"

"No," he scoffed, sounding as though he'd rather have a bullet dug from his chest with a rusty knife and no anesthetic.

His repulsion was as insulting now as it had been then,

making her reach for hostility to hide the fact she was so deeply stung.

"And by the way, my father did not leave your uncle to *die*. Your father and his brother were horrible to Dad while they were all at Harvard. Dad didn't have any love for either of them and didn't even want to be at that party with your uncle. Which is why he was leaving when your uncle asked for a lift. Dad thought he was drunk so he said his car was full. Yes, it was spiteful, but he didn't know your uncle was diabetic and needed his medication. It eats at him to this day that he brushed him off instead of taking him to where he might have got help. But there were dozens of other people there who also could have helped him. It wasn't Dad's fault."

"Yet he had no qualms about keeping up the pressure on my father after that, pushing him into an early grave. Then he came after me while I was burying him."

"Look." She put up a hand. "I was sorry to hear about your father. That must have been a difficult time for you."

"You think?" He snapped his head around to pin her with his hard stare, making her heart stutter and thrum in her chest. "Did you set them on me? Your brothers?"

"*No*. I was trying to forget we'd ever met!"

"I'm sure," he said facetiously. He took a pull off his can and returned his attention to the surf and the falling rain.

"I don't have a say in the business one way or another," she said with a surge of resentment. "My brother is being a sexist jerk about it, if you want the truth. But think about it. Your father accused mine of *murder*. Dad has had to deal with that for decades. So yes, it was tasteless of him to go after WBE when your father died, but he felt justified. He said your grandfather did the same to him when Nonno Aldo died."

Dom drained his can and set the empty can in the sink, making her stiffen as the air stirred beside her hip before he resumed his stance against the counter, ankles crossed and arms folded, glaring at the foam washing up the beach.

"How has this feud persisted this long anyway?" she muttered. "My grandmother didn't want to marry your grandfather. Maybe Michael Blackwood should have got over that instead of dedicating his life to making my family suffer?"

"He was insulted that she preferred a *war criminal*."

"Oh, please. Nonno Aldo could be accused of being a profiteer. Maybe. But people do what they have to when times are tough. Your great-grandparents were bootleggers trying to survive the Depression, same as mine. Don't throw stones at Nonno because he sold olive oil and cheese on the black market during the war."

He snorted, unmoved.

"And so what if my grandmother preferred someone else? She fell in *love*. Your family didn't have to steal— yes, I said 'steal,'" she stressed as he shot her a warning side-eye. "They pulled some questionable stunts, cutting the Winslows out of all their shared assets. *That* was profiteering from a war they instigated. Maybe, once they stole everything, they could have let up? There was no reason our fathers should have been involved, let alone our generation." She pointed between them.

For a few moments, there was only the buffeting wind and the rattle of the awning and the heavy patter of rain on the roof. The light was fading, making the shack seem colder than it really was.

"My father and his brother were twins," Dom said flatly. "Dad never got over losing him. He needed someone to blame. To hate." He picked up another can to shake it, but didn't open it, only set it aside with a grimace of discontent.

Something in the dourness clouding his face made her wonder what sort of father that had made Thomas Blackwood.

"Let's look at your ankle," Dom said abruptly.

"Why?"

"I want to play doctor," he claimed with a fake smile.

She knew he was taunting her, but she couldn't help her reaction of both tension and, deep in her belly, anticipation.

The ice pack, which was the instant, disposable kind that she'd snapped to activate when she'd realized her ankle was sprained, had long lost its cooling properties. Now it was purely for decoration so she tried to bring her ankle into her lap.

Dom turned toward her and caught her leg behind the knee, burning her bare skin with his hot palm.

She reflexively tried to jerk away.

"Would you stop?" He scowled at her.

"I can do it myself."

"I've removed one of these before," he assured her and started rolling down the rim of the condom.

"Can you *not*?" She brushed at his hand.

"What?" he asked with tested patience. "I'm trying to help."

"You're getting your kicks by taunting me. I don't like it."

"Just let me see what we're dealing with."

She tsked as she let him work the condom down and

off. He let it fall with the ice pack then gently cradled her calf and heel while he carefully tested her range of movement. His thumb lightly explored the faint blue swelling.

"Hurt?"

Only in her chest where an ache of yearning pulsed.

"Not too much," she said huskily, wishing she could cure herself of this intense reaction to his clinical touch.

"Keep it elevated." He propped her foot on the edge of the front counter. "Is there a first aid kit? We should wrap it."

"I didn't see one. Stop!" she ordered as he started to remove his shirt. "Use a sarong."

"These sleeves are stretchy. I was going to cut one off." He shrugged and shook out a pink-and-blue sarong before tearing it in half lengthwise.

Eve silently promised to pay for whatever they used while they were here, then succumbed in silence while Dom took up her leg again. He began winding the strip of cotton from the base of her toes toward her ankle. Perhaps he *had* played doctor a time or two. He seemed to know what he was doing, keeping the fabric taut and neat despite the tricky bend around her heel.

He was being very matter-of-fact about it, too, which made the tendrils of arousal that wound through her all the more agonizing. When he tucked the tail in and set her foot back on the counter, she was both relieved and swimming in renewed awareness.

"I'm trying to defuse the sexual tension when I say those things." His golden eyes seemed to visibly spark as he met her gaze. The air between them crackled. "It doesn't work."

He felt it, too? That actually made hers worse. She swallowed a protest that would have been a lie while a wicked swirling sensation in her stomach pooled and slid like quicksilver. She stared stubbornly past him, out the window.

He picked up another can, put it down.

"Are you trying to ration our food? How long do you think we'll be here?" she asked with alarm.

"I'm trying not to get drunk enough to make a pass at you," he said through his teeth.

She clenched her hands around the edge of the counter, aware of how her outstretched leg left her thighs open.

"You don't even like me."

"Yes, I know that, Evie. But *this*—" he waved at his crotch "—isn't listening."

# CHAPTER SEVEN

SHE AVERTED HER GAZE, MUTTERING, "Quit calling me that."

"Evie? Why?"

"Because it implies we're more familiar with each other than we are."

His hoot of laughter cracked the air like a gunshot.

"Would you *stop*," she implored. "You're behaving like a child."

"No, you are. Budapest happened, Evie. Walk out of every restaurant in Manhattan just because I'm there. Tell people you don't know me and look right through me. I don't care. It doesn't change the fact that we turn each other on. Or that I hate it as much as you do." The bitterness in his voice was an insult.

But she knew exactly why he was being so acrimonious. She resented him for still enthralling her after all this time. She despised him for making her feel more during the dispassionate wrap of her ankle than any other man had ever made her feel with French kisses or romantic gestures.

And she was so *tired* of feeling stuck and frozen. Rebuffed. Denied. She was stunted by her experience with him because he had been the first and only man she had wanted to have sex with. He had taken her to a height she hadn't known existed then plunged her abruptly back to earth before abandoning her altogether.

She'd never recovered. It wasn't even a matter of courage when it came to other men. She simply didn't want them. She only wanted *this* man. She feared that would never change and that filled her with despair.

"Well, I'm not going to have sex with a man who is involved with another woman so…" She said it as much to forestall any ideas that might crop up in her own mind as his.

"Cat and I aren't involved," he muttered.

"Oh, please. You're her date for a wedding."

"Because the timing worked with my takeover of the resort in Airlie Beach." He was staring dourly toward the water. "My sister has been trying to set us up for a while. I had dinner with her twice before this. We're not sleeping together. Either," he added with quiet significance, alluding to her arrangement with Logan.

That shouldn't make a difference, but it did. There was no obstacle of other people that would have kept her from sleeping with him. Now there was only a potent silence that thickened with sexual tension.

"So what?" she blurted. "We have sex just to get it over with?"

"Possibly the sexiest invitation a man has ever received."

"Oh, go to hell, Dom! You just said you hate that you feel this way. You think that was the romantic sentiment I've been waiting for?"

She immediately wanted to bite back her words, thinking they were too revealing. She braced herself for some arrogant, sarcastic remark, but he only expelled a grim curse.

"We're like cats in a cage, aren't we? We're going to keep swiping at each other until it happens." He didn't even turn his head to look at her, but he seemed to cast out a net that snared her.

She felt his proximity. She refused to look at him, either. She was fearful he'd see the tears of frustration standing in her eyes.

Outside, the clouds had turned sooty and thick. The wind was gusting hard enough to pick up the awning and make the shack rock on its pontoons.

"Do you have more condoms?" Dom asked gruffly. "If you don't, that will end this. I *cannot* get you pregnant."

A pang hit deep in the bottom of her heart while a fearful excitement filled her lungs.

*Lie*, she told herself. *Just say no.*

"Two. They're in my bag."

"You couldn't lie?" he asked with exasperation, twisting his head around to glare at her.

"You could simply not use them," she suggested with a bat of her lashes.

A wild flash of lust glinted in his eyes, one that seemed very excited by the idea of naked sex.

"I always use them," he said in a voice that dropped several octaves so it abraded her skin as he spoke. "And *you* could say 'no,' Evie. Say it," he commanded.

She stubbornly sealed her lips and lifted her chin in challenge.

"You're such a pain in my ass." He reached for her bag where it was lying on the floor and passed it to her, holding onto it when she started to take it. "It would only be sex, Eve. Once. We get it out of our system, then we never tell anyone. We don't talk about it. We never see each other again. This isn't the start of something."

"You're saying that as if I want it to be." She noted that he called her Eve when he wanted to impress the gravity of his words upon her.

She took the bag and brought it into her lap, realizing he was doing it again, making her offer him the condoms as a tacit demonstration that this was her choice.

She dug around, brought out a protein bar. "Still hungry?"

"Not for that." The grit in his voice was making her skin feel too tight to contain her. She remembered that voice all too well.

*"You have to tell me you want this, Evie."*

She found the condoms, two squares stuck together, and offered them.

He didn't take them. He clasped her wrist and said, "You're shaking. Is that fear?"

"No." She wished the helpless pang in her voice didn't make it so obvious this was desire. *Yearning.*

He lifted the bag off her lap to set it out of the way, then edged into the space between her outstretched leg and dangling calf, pushing her thighs farther apart.

"If you want me to stay on my side of the shack, say so." He waited a millisecond before he clasped her hips and dragged her to the edge of the counter so the placket of her shorts was flush to the hard ridge inside his.

A squeak left her.

He might have breathed, "Last chance," then his hand was clasping her ponytail to drag her head back while his mouth came down on hers.

Lightning struck again, strong and sharp enough to hurt. Eve moaned and his arms wrapped around her, almost reassuring before they crushed her. She wormed her arms out of the space between them and up around his neck, then opened her mouth wider beneath his.

No soft seduction here. They picked up where they'd left off in Budapest, kissing as though the other held the last drop of water available on earth. He cupped her head and kept her where he wanted her as he angled his mouth across hers and delved for all the secrets of the universe. He stole and plundered and gave. He poured heat and passion into her. Want. Feral, angry, desperate want.

She absorbed it all with a groan of delight and dragged his shirt up, trying to find his skin. He wrenched it up and off, then pulled her T-shirt over her head. Her bikini top was a tug of two strings, then it also fell to the floor.

His wide hands shaped from her waist up her rib cage, covering her breasts in heat. His mouth dragged from her lips to her neck, heading down.

"I want to give you a collar of hickies," he said against her throat.

"You can't," she moaned.

He lifted his head long enough for her to see the bitterness in his gaze, then his thumbs dragged across her nipples and he was kissing her again.

She wrapped her good foot behind him and levered herself almost off the counter, balancing on her tailbone as she rubbed and rocked, inciting them both.

Or so she thought until he drew back, expression remote and harsh.

She dropped her hands to the counter and inched herself more firmly onto it.

"Don't lose your nerve now, Evie. We're getting to the good part." He released the button of her fly and lowered the zip, then clasped the waistband of her shorts with two hands. "Lift."

Heart slamming with a sense that she was doing something very bad, she did as he ordered, letting him drag away shorts and bikini bottoms in one go.

She'd been here before, naked while he was still half-dressed and fully in control. She licked her lips and looked for the condom, but he dropped to his knees.

"Like it was built for this," he said with guttural satisfaction. "Like you were. No, keep your leg up like that. I want you right on the edge. Hold on, Evie. Hold on."

He draped her good leg over his shoulder so the contact with his skin burned the back of her thigh. He blew softly across the fine hairs protecting her mound. She twitched and wriggled, but he wrapped his arm behind her hips, not letting her retreat as soft kisses made her thighs twitch, trying to close.

"If you want me to stop, say so."

She couldn't tell if he was mocking her reaction or being sincere. She could only bite her lip and close her eyes as he nuzzled closer. Her flesh was so sensitized and swollen with anticipation, she couldn't speak.

*Please*, she thought. *Please.*

Without any hurry at all, he painted a slow wet stripe against her inner lips, then again, with more pressure. Deeper.

She groaned. And shook.

He rumbled a noise of satisfaction that she barely heard over the sheets of rain and the crash of surf and the rattle of the awning in the keening wind. As the storm closed in and the day turned to dusk, her world shrank to this, the clever play of his tongue on her most intimate flesh. He brought his hand into the game, delicately parting her, fondling and adding to the sensations so she was nearly arched right off the counter. She pressed her head to the wall behind her, vaguely appalled at how uninhibited she was being, but she had yearned for this for four years. She needed it more than she needed air.

Why was it him that did this to her? Why? Why was he so perfectly skilled at swirling sensations through her like a tornado, teasing her and drawing her up and up into a greater storm of pleasure. Climax beckoned, glowing, expanding.

He gave her inner thigh a juicy, openmouthed kiss then stood.

"Don't stop," she panted, hearing herself beg and hating herself for it.

"I told you I wanted you right on the edge," he said with a cruel grin.

Her stomach clenched and, for one second, she thought he was doing this to her again. That he'd wanted to bring her to this point of flagrantly offering herself so he could reject her.

But he picked up a condom and tore it open with his teeth. He pulled the drawstring on his shorts at the same time, dropping them. He wasn't wearing underwear and his thick erection sprang out, ready and hot as it brushed her thigh.

"It's time." He efficiently rolled the condom down his length.

It was past time. It was the only time.

"Help me. Show me you want this," he urged, guiding his tip against her aching flesh.

She did, bumping her trembling fingers against his, touching the steely shape of him, exploring briefly then catching at his shoulder as he notched the wide dome of his head so he could penetrate her.

The pressure increased. She tensed, nervous.

"Hurt?" He flashed a frown up at her.

"No." It didn't. Not really, but it was more profound than she had expected. She wanted to cry, she had waited so long for this. And she had always thought that love-making would fill her with a flood of love, but she hated him. Didn't she?

Not right now. Not when he said in a voice that was almost gentle, "It's okay. I won't let you fall." He took a firm grip of her thigh. "Tilt your hips."

She did and the thick shape of him slowly filled her, stretching and forging his way in until he was, as he'd promised in Budapest, buried to the root.

She couldn't breathe. She could only hold onto his shoulders and press her open mouth against the side of his neck. She swore she could feel his heartbeat inside her. Her abdomen began to shake. A symphony of con-tractions worked through her pelvis and loins and she simply *lost*.

She felt his jolt of surprise, then his arm locked low behind her tailbone, securing her exactly where she was. His other hand cupped her neck while he covered her mouth with his own, drinking every cry and moan from her lips as he pulsed his hips, holding himself deep in-side her while subtly riding her through the shudders of her climax.

Was it supposed to happen like this? He wasn't even thrusting. All he'd done was arrive inside her and she fell apart. She could have wept, she felt so overwhelmed and helpless. So completely at his mercy.

"I'm starting to think they're going to find us like this," he said in a rasp, scraping his teeth along the edge of her jaw. "Because if that's what I can expect while I'm here, I'm never leaving."

She was still shivering in the aftermath, leaning weakly against him, trying not to sob over how powerful that had been. He kissed her once. Twice. Bordering on tender as his mouth traveled into her neck and across her shoulder while his caressing fingertips teased along her spine and rib cage, then grazed the underswell of her breast.

"Lean back."

She did, not wanting to lose the warmth of his chest against hers, but she braced her hands behind her.

He trailed his touch across her belly and down to where their flesh was locked. His caress was sure and intimate, but light and frustrating as he avoided the spot that would provide the sharpest sensations. Then he brushed the knot of nerves that was still so sensitive she gasped in a mixture of pleasure and discomfort.

"Mmm." She jerked and he did it again. The thickness of him filling her amplified everything, bringing an immediate flood of heat.

"Mmm," he mocked. "You like that." He circled his thumb, avoiding, avoiding, then skimming across in a tease.

She gasped again, accusing, "You're mean."

He dragged his gaze up from watching the play of his thumb. "When it's necessary. Tell me if I'm too rough."

Her heart lurched, but he was rubbing her own moisture against the swelling bundle of nerves at the top of her sex. She bit her lip and arched in reaction, starting to need more of that. Starting to think she needed that for the rest of her life.

Her movement shifted him inside her, promising the friction she hadn't known she desired. His free hand braced her hip as he withdrew in a sensual drag before returning in a slow, deliberate penetration that sent delicious shivers through her nerve-endings.

A small cry of joy escaped her.

This was what it was about, she realized as she splayed her hands behind her, holding herself still for his steady thrusts. This was why there were eight billion people on the planet. This was what everyone was chasing, this sense of being made from gold dust. Of being made for this. For him.

She gloried in the pace he set, layering sensation upon sensation into her. They were folding time so it was compressed and stalled and they could be right here, like this, forever. Like ancient life trapped in amber.

"Evie."

She dragged her eyes open to see his eyes were glittering through the fading light, his cheeks dark, his teeth bared.

"It's me." He lightly pinched her nipple. "I'm the one doing this to you."

"I know." Did he think she was fantasizing about someone else? He was her entire world.

"Good." He set his hand on her lower back and brought her all the way off the counter before he began to thrust with more power.

She grunted in surprise and clasped onto him.

She was bathed in fire, open and defenseless, but safe. Even as tension wound through her, even as she wanted to claw his back for the release he was promising, and even though she knew he resented this as much as she did, she knew they were in this together. That made it better than okay. It was wrong and messy, but perfect.

The rain had cooled the shack, but they were both

sweating. They were sticky and clinging and making noises as though working hard.

"Don't stop," she cried as climax danced tantalizingly close, yet remained out of reach, like a star at her fingertips. "Don't stop."

Now he did get rough, shifting to hold her tighter as he thrust with wild, barely couched power. She loved it. She had needed to know she could wreck him as thoroughly as he wrecked her and she could feel how he was shaking and about to shatter.

"Come, damn you," he ordered.

She opened her mouth against the crook of his neck and bit him. Not hard, just hard enough for him to feel her teeth.

They detonated. She didn't know whether it was him or her that hit the culmination first, but they were thrown into the abyss together, screaming and shouting with pleasure. He kept thrusting and the edge of the counter cut into her backside and her ankle bumped something sending a zing of pain through her, but none of that mattered.

Only *this* mattered. The feel of him buried deep inside her, pulsing against her internal clenches. His arms were locked around her and the slam of his heart was against her breast and pleasure radiated through her whole body.

It was a glorious disaster.

# CHAPTER EIGHT

DOM THOUGHT HIS orgasm would never end. The hammer-like throbs rang through him, taking forever to slow and fade before becoming latent pangs and twitches.

His arms and legs were trembling with exertion, but he waited until he felt himself slipping out of her before he clumsily made sure she was balanced on her foot. He secured the condom and withdrew, wrapped it in a napkin and tossed it into the bin under the sink.

Then he walked out into the lashing rain, still shaking and soft in the knees.

It was rude, he knew, to exit in silence like that, but he didn't have a word in him. He was too stunned.

Had it been worth the four-year wait? Quite the opposite. He resented that lost time, which was a ridiculous reaction. That was like saying he wished he'd tried heroin four years ago. He shouldn't have tried it *today*.

He walked naked into the crashing surf, then dove into the bracing water, only realizing as he came out that that was also stupid. He could have been stung by jellyfish or carried away on a rip current into the dark ocean. The beach had been deemed safe earlier in the day, but there had also been a hundred people here looking out for each other.

Where the hell were all those good people when he

was taking an even bigger risk with his life? If this affair ever got out, both of their families would come after him. Evelina Visconti was absolutely off-limits, taboo and forbidden.

Which had to be the reason that had been the most incredible sex of his life. By a long shot. That, and breaking such a long dry spell.

He knew, though. Deep down he knew it had been like that before he'd known who she was. That's why he'd obsessed over her for the last four years. That's why he hadn't had sex with anyone else. It had to be her.

That's why, like a rube fresh off the turnip truck, he'd fallen for the "We'll do it once to get it out of our system" rationalization.

When the heavy rain grew too unpleasant to bear, he made his way back to the shack and used the last light of dusk to find a bottle of wine from one of the crates he'd stored between the pontoons. He'd rather have the Scotch he'd mentally earmarked, but he really would do something stupid if he split a bottle of that with her.

He stepped inside to find her dressed in her shorts and shirt. Her complexion was ghostly in the upturned flashlight of her cell phone. Her ponytail was tidy once again, her profile unreadable as she prepared plates of food.

"Your clothes are there with a towel." Her elbow pointed in a vague direction toward him. "The tap works. I don't know whether the water is potable or how much there is so I only used it for washing. I'm drinking bottled."

"Are you sure the food is edible? Something smells off." Astringent. He set the wine on the counter and stepped into his shorts, ignoring the beach towel and T-shirt. One look at her and he was already too hot inside his own skin. Better to stay clammy and uncomfortable.

"I used some disinfectant."

"On yourself or…?"

Her hand faltered, then, "It's under the sink if you need it."

What a pair of comedians.

"Glasses?" He took up the bottle and realized it wasn't a twist-off. "And a corkscrew?"

She handed over both, then took a gulp of what looked like a freshly opened can of Bloody Mary.

"Are you all right?" He was disturbed by the way she was avoiding his eyes.

"Of course."

"Evie—"

"We said we wouldn't talk about it." She met his gaze for one flat second, mouth stretched into a meaningless smile.

Maybe she was having as much trouble processing their lovemaking as he was.

"But you'll tell me if I was too rough," he said gravely.

"I'm fine." She gulped again. "My ankle was hurting so I had another ibuprofen."

"Sit and put it up. I can finish that."

"I'm done. I was just fussing." She shifted a caddy of condiments out of the way and sat on the front counter, setting her back next to the window this time, using the pile of towels and sarongs as a backrest. When she propped her ankle, her outstretched leg was more of a closed gate than an open one.

It was also a more convenient position for her to reach the food, but he felt deliberately shut out by her body language and was irritated with himself for taking umbrage over it.

He poured out the glasses and handed one across, giving the small banquet a proper review as he did.

She'd used the remaining half of the torn sarong as a tablecloth. The pickles and crackers and canned fruit were arranged as beautifully as any thousand-dollar plate he'd ever seen. She'd even found some pistachio nuts and some kind of dip.

"The hummus is from a packet. I used bottled water to make it."

"It looks good." He could have eaten all of this himself. It had been hours since breakfast and he'd carried roughly a hundred and thirty pounds across the island before working up an appetite with her.

She was hungry, too. They attacked the food, not speaking again until there were only a few olives and a lick of hummus left.

"Oh. Dessert." She leaned to dig into her bag. "My protein bar is chocolate-coated."

He snorted. "I thought you were going to offer me the other condom."

The look she sent him made him want to bite his tongue. Or hers, now that the air took on an erotic vibration.

"Yes, I want to use it," she spat with resentment. "Damn you to hell."

"Oh, I'm quite sure that's where we're headed." He snapped out a beach towel, wafting it onto the floor. Then he stepped across to gather her up and take her down onto it.

"Dom!" Eve snapped awake in the secure spoon of his body. His solid chest warmed her back. His hot thighs were bent behind hers and his heavy arm weighed against her waist. There hadn't been any other way to sleep in this narrow space down the middle of the shack. As night had fallen, he'd closed the awning, she'd set down fresh towels and sarongs as bedding, and they had crashed harder than the surf.

Now the floor was shifting beneath them.

She urgently tapped his thigh, trying to sit up and find her phone on the counter above her, but his arm tensed, locking tighter than the safety bar on a roller coaster as he drew a long breath, pulling himself into wakefulness. She blinked her eyes wide, but couldn't see a thing in the pitch dark of this unknown hour. She didn't think they'd slept very long, though.

"What's wrong?" he murmured.

"I think we're floating."

"We are. It's okay." He roamed his hand down her front, ironing her more firmly into the hollow of his sheltering body. "It's high tide. There was only a short beach when we arrived. Remember? That's how he gets this thing onto the beach. It's anchored to concrete blocks underneath. I saw them when I put the booze down there."

"Oh. Okay." She relaxed. Mostly. Because now his hand was petting her thigh, fingertips tracing the seam where her legs were pressed together. He was hardening against her butt cheek.

"That means he'll likely be back in twelve hours to retrieve it," he added.

"We don't have a condom," she reminded, voice growing unsteady with arousal.

"I know," he grumbled and brought his hand back to her stomach.

"We could do other things." She rolled to face him.

"Hell, yeah, we could." He pressed her beneath him and kissed her with urgent, dark passion, invading the recesses of her mouth in a reclaiming of territory he'd conquered only a short time ago.

She met the electric dance of his tongue with her own, greedily taking all that he was willing to give because they had less than twelve hours.

"Stand up," she urged when he started to part her legs.

He did and she used the darkness to hide her inexperience while she learned how to take him in her mouth and pleasure him in every way she'd ever read a man enjoyed.

He seemed to enjoy it very much. He swore and hissed in shaken breaths and his thighs were like iron beneath her hands as she stroked them. When he hit his release, his jagged cries were both triumphant and vanquished.

Then, while she was still glowing with inordinate pride at delivering him so much pleasure, he lay on his back and arranged her in a most unseemly position to return the favor. It was the most sinfully erotic experience of her life on top of a night of generous caresses and life-altering orgasms.

That really should have exhausted their libidos, but the chuckle of a kookaburra woke her to predawn light and the quiet of a blown-out storm.

Dom was already awake. His erection pressed insistently against her backside. As she drew in a waking breath, her breast shifted in the hand that cupped it.

"Your nipple is hard. It's been driving me crazy, wanting to play with it while I waited for you to wake up." He skimmed his hand down and discovered she was already wet.

She moaned with something like relief, shifting her

leg so it rested on his, parting her thighs so he had more room to caress into her tender folds.

He groaned with appreciation and opened his mouth against her nape. "Once more? I'll pull out."

They shouldn't. It wasn't just the risk of pregnancy. It was who they were. This was supposed to be an inoculation against wanting each other, but she feared it was only going to make this incessant pull between them stronger.

"Unless there's something more to worry about?" He shifted his hand to her stomach. "I get checked regularly."

She couldn't bring herself to admit that she had never been tested because she'd never been with anyone before last night. She hadn't told him that and doubted she ever would. She wouldn't have the opportunity. They were never going to see each other again. Not if they could help it.

She turned her face into the crooked arm that was her pillow.

"It's okay," she whispered. "I don't have anything to worry about. I can take a pill once we're back in civilization, to be safe."

"Sure?" he asked in a gratified growl even as he drew his hips back and guided himself between her thighs, seeking.

"Yes," she breathed, arching to accept the press and penetration that sealed them together one final time.

He swore and clutched his arm hard around her a moment, sounding breathless as he said, "You feel incredible."

The lack of latex made it more intense. It wasn't just the heightened sensations, though. It was the intimacy. The naked danger. The morning light that took away the fever dream aspect and made it real.

How would she bear never feeling like this again? She would suffer an emptiness for the rest of her life, yearning for him.

She had him now, though. In this moment, she felt divine.

He moved lazily, fingertip stroking through her folds again. She braced a hand on the cupboard in front of her, holding herself still for his easy thrusts.

She was glad he was behind her. This was so good, tears were pressing against her closed eyelids, wetting her lashes. Her longing for this to last forever rose along with her arousal until both were acute. Before she realized it was happening, she broke with a cry.

"Greedy little Evie," he said against her ear, teeth catching at her earlobe while he pumped. "You just can't get enough, can you?"

Her sheath was still fluttering around his intrusion. Her nipples felt bruised under his caress. Her whole body ached from the nonstop lovemaking and the abbreviated sleep on a cold, hard floor. Her ankle throbbed like a migraine and she was tender where he penetrated her.

But he wasn't wrong. None of that mattered. All she wanted was for him to skim his touch down again and reawaken her desire. She pushed back, inviting deeper, harder thrusts, behaving lewdly because she couldn't help herself.

"Me, either," he said, pulling out long enough to bring her onto her hands and knees before him. "This really is the last time." He returned and she pushed back with a groan of welcome.

The surf was at their doorstep when Eve rose and put on her bathing suit and went for a cool, cleansing swim. Dom joined her, also wearing his shorts, as though there were any eyes here to see them beyond each other's.

As though they hadn't seen and touched and tasted every inch of the other's naked body last night.

They barely spoke, barely looked at each other as the glare of midmorning light forced an end to the madness. A reckoning.

A *wreck*oning, Eve thought with irony, as she lowered to sit on the overturned milk crate that had been washed up to the sand a small distance from the shack.

She drank in the paradise of powdered sand and sunlight glinting off turquoise waters and rip curls of foam edging ever closer to her feet, as inexorable as reality. She was stranded with the last man on earth she should want and she half hoped they wouldn't be rescued. She would rather live out their life as castaways.

Dom waded around to join her. He carried two bags of potato chips, her protein bar, and offered her a cup of—

"Coffee?" She sniffed, then sipped. It was terrible. He'd made it with cold, bottled water and it was black, but it was better than none. "Thank you."

"You cooked last night," he said drily.

It was such a domestic thing to say, as though they were a couple who took turns cooking for each other, it brought a hot scald of wistfulness to the back of her throat.

*What are we going to do?* she wanted to ask, but she already knew. Nothing.

His profile was rugged and remote, his jaw shadowed by stubble and his eyes hidden behind his mirrored lenses. It was not the face of someone who thought their upcoming separation was a problem.

"There he is," he said.

She shot her gaze to the water and saw the flash of a tin boat reflecting the sun. The last thing she felt was relief.

"I realized I had forgotten my sunglasses at the lookout," Dom said cryptically.

"You're wearing them."

"Because I went back for them. That's when I found you limping up the path."

He was feeding her their talking points.

"I went to the spit on impulse," she added. "After leaving Logan barfing on the beach."

"Really?" His mouth curled with amused contempt.

"I caught my foot on a root and twisted my ankle." It was true.

"Our slow progress back here meant we missed the last boat. We spent a sleepless night in the shack, but otherwise we're fine."

*Sleepless.* She caught back a ragged chuckle. "It's always best to stick as close to the truth as possible."

His mouth stayed in its cynical curl.

"Can I really trust you not to tell anyone?" The raw, searing sensation in her chest wouldn't subside.

"Can I trust *you*?" He was still looking out to sea, not giving her the merest smidge of comfort with that harsh profile.

"Yes." It was untenable that she had trusted this man with her body, with her life even, given how their families regarded each other, when she didn't know how to trust him otherwise. Yet here she was. Alive. Unharmed. So sexually satisfied, she was kind of stupid with it.

But changed, too. Not by sex. By *him*. By the fact they continued to have something between them and always would. Now they had two memories. They were a part of each other's history that couldn't be erased.

"I don't want anyone to ever know I let you…" Her voice dried up as he finally looked down at her. His glare seemed to pierce the mirror of the lenses so she felt it like a pin that poked through her and held her in place.

"You didn't let me do anything," he said in a grim tone. "We did that together."

She turned her hot gaze to the boat bearing down on their cove. The sound of its engine was growing louder.

"I know," she admitted in a small voice. "I just wish it had been anyone but you."

Dom snorted, muttering, "Same," before he waded into the lapping waves, meeting the boat as it cut its engine, but continued to drift closer.

The voice of the astonished operator carried across the water.

"Mate. You two been here all night?" He stammered that he'd been told everyone was off the island.

"No harm done," Dom assured him. "We helped ourselves to what we needed. Bill me for the alcohol that was ruined by the tide."

"I can cover the costs," Eve said when they came ashore. "It was my fault."

Dom shook his head once, abruptly, as though she had offended him.

That was pretty much the last thing they said to each other. While he helped the young man collect everything and secure the shack for towing, Eve combed the beach for any litter that their party had missed yesterday.

When the tide was high enough that the shack was floating, Dom boosted her into the boat. She watched the empty beach grow smaller as they motored away. Their tryst was over.

# CHAPTER NINE

IT WAS LUNCHTIME when Eve was dropped at the eco-resort.

She was dying for a long, hot bath and a long, undisturbed sleep, but she had promised Dom she would see first aid. She got her foot rewrapped and they gave her a pair of crutches. She then gave the manager of the resort the story they'd agreed on. The resort hadn't organized the day trip so they weren't liable, but the manager was horrified all the same. He said he would review procedures to ensure nothing like it ever happened again.

Eve made her way to her suite, dreading bumping into wedding guests and having to explain her injury. That would only lead to even more awkward explanations. Hopefully, Logan wouldn't even be here—

He was here. She heard his voice on the terrace. Ugh.

Expecting he was on the phone, Eve peeked out the door to say, "Hey, Logan—"

He was in the hot tub with Cat on his lap. They jerked apart and Cat leapt to the stairs, emerging naked as she hissed at him, "You said she *left*. That it was over."

"I am leaving. Oh, gawd." Eve hurried into her room and clumsily got her suitcase opened onto the bed, then started throwing things into it.

Logan came in a half minute later, belting a hotel robe

around his dripping body. "What are you doing here? I thought you left yesterday."

"I was stuck on the island overnight." Thankfully, the first aid attendant had also given her fresh painkillers which were starting to kick in. Not that she was hurt by Logan moving on within hours. She thought it was sit-com-level hilarious, especially given what she'd done last night and with whom.

Their being here gave her no chance to shower and catch her breath, though. She packed willy-nilly while Logan stood in the doorway and Cat hovered behind him.

"I thought Dom ghosted me," Cat said. "I called his hotel. They said he wasn't there."

"Is he even still alive?" Logan joked lamely.

"It was an uncomfortable night, but we're fine," Eve said mildly. "Would you call the bellman to carry my luggage? I have a flight booked."

She didn't, but ninety minutes later, she was on a chartered flight to Brisbane where she checked into one of the Visconti properties. She spent the rest of the week ambling from her king-sized bed to a pool lounger to pampering treatments in the spa.

She didn't turn on her phone, not wanting to see whether Dom had reached out, which he hadn't, she learned, when she was on her way to New York. She very nearly shut the thing off again when she saw the number of texts from her family, all outraged that she'd thrown over Logan and spent a night alone with Dom.

She sent one quick text to Nico, fueled by her anger over the way he had deliberately held her back because he had consulted *Logan* about her future, not her. It would be a long time before she got over that and forgave him.

As for her parents, she put off responding to their outrage until she was home, only realizing as she arrived at the building on Madison Avenue how embarrassing it was that she still lived with them. They spent most of their time on Martha's Vineyard now that her father was retired so remaining in her childhood bedroom—which had been redecorated three times since she'd been an actual child—in the penthouse apartment had always seemed practical, not immature. She worked in Manhattan so it was convenient, but it probably contributed to the way her entire family still saw her as a child.

Boy, did they ever, she thought dourly, when she came off the elevator to find her parents waiting for her, tapping feet and already wagging fingers. Nico, was here, too, wearing his most smoldering expression.

"I'm moving out," she informed them, hoping to take them by surprise, which she did.

"What? When? Why? Where are you going?" her mother responded in breathy panic.

"I don't know yet. Thank you." She smiled at the doorman who'd brought up her luggage for her. He sent her a "good luck" look and exited.

"What the hell is going on with you, Eve?" Nico asked.

"Did you get my text?" Six words from an old song had been all she'd needed for her resignation letter. "That's all I plan to say to you for a while."

"You're such a child," he muttered. He was twelve years older and unbearably arrogant.

"I'm not *your* child, though. Even if I was, how *dare* you ask a man I barely know whether I'm going to be too pregnant to work for you? Go to hell, Nico. Go all the way to hell, then go a little bit past it so you're completely out of my sight."

"Evelina," her father said in a dangerous rumble.

"No, Papà. He disrespected me first. This is about my working for him for *four* years and him not once giving me the challenge or opportunities that Jackson and Christo have had at my age. The only reason he's doing it is because I'm a woman. That is sexist and *wrong*."

"The Offermans are an important connection. You threw his proposal in his face then spent a night with *that* man?" her father railed. "Nico has a right to be angry. This is a bad look for the entire family."

"Logan didn't propose," she scoffed. "It was a job offer for domestic service. But you're right, Papà. I'm so very sorry, Nico, that you had to go through the terrifying ordeal of hearing that your sister rejected a man you shook hands with once. She was stranded on a remote trail on an uninhabited island in the Pacific and could have been stuck there for days before someone found her, might even have died, but *that's* not important. Refusing to give up her life and uterus because *you* think she should is the real anguish she's causing you."

"This is why I don't give you more responsibility. You have the temperament of a toddler," Nico bit out.

"Calm down," her mother insisted. "Eve, you're tired. Does your foot hurt? Come sit down."

Eve didn't move. She glared at her brother, then her father's stony expression, then her mother's pinched mouth.

"You all think I'm being hysterical, don't you?"

"Selfish," Nico provided. "We all act for the good of the family. Except you. Because you think you're special. Like Nonna."

Eve realized she was shaking. Her heart was pinched in a vise and all she could think was that she might have been able to comply with an arranged marriage eventually, if she hadn't slept with Dom. Now she knew what she'd be missing and it would make any other man's touch repulsive to her.

She picked up her purse and opened the door.

"Evelina! Where are you going?" her mother cried with alarm.

"I'll let you know when I get there."

Dom wanted to hate her, but he couldn't. He wanted to *forget* her. But he couldn't.

Not when he and Nico were once again playing a game of chicken over a property in Miami.

Eve had nothing to do with it. The timing of Nico's bid made that impossible, but Dom still wanted to believe she had something to do with it.

Why? Because it would prove she was thinking of him? That he was as far under her skin as she was under his?

Even if he was, Eve wouldn't resort to asking her brother to deliver a message in such a cryptic way. She wasn't afraid to confront someone directly. He'd seen it more than once. He'd felt the smack on his ass, even.

Plus, asking her brother to exact revenge would necessitate revealing why. She wouldn't do that. They'd agreed on a statement labeling their night a misadventure, nothing else. It had been released into a heavy news cycle, burying it. Like the first time they'd trysted, this was their little own secret and, for some reason, Dom liked that most of all.

What was he, nine? He didn't convey messages by decoder rings and peer at diary entries and share secrets under the covers. He didn't share anything with anyone. Ever. He didn't need special connections. He barely tolerated the required relationships of work and basic social fabric. He'd spent his whole life learning to live at a distance from the rest of the world. He liked it that way. It was comfortable.

But he knew so many secrets about Evie now. Intimate ones, like how soft her mouth felt around him when he stood like a lighthouse in the dark, feet braced and hands clenched on either side of the narrow aisle of the shack while she rocked his world.

Then there were the intriguing tidbits Cat had shared with him when she'd come to his hotel. Dom had planned to use the light scandal of his night with Eve as a clumsy excuse to cool things off, but Cat had sheepishly confessed where she had spent the night and with whom.

She must have had a guilty conscience about it because she'd spilled a few of Logan's confidences. As much as Dom had appreciated the information, he'd also realized Cat was a gossip. They definitely hadn't had a future so that was off his conscience, at least.

"Sir?"

There were eight people at the boardroom table behind him, waiting for him to decide whether to increase his bid against Visconti Group while he, yet again, had spiraled into making love with Evie.

"The clock is ticking on our ability to counter," someone else said. "It's already been three weeks. Visconti Group has it locked in unless—"

"I know." Nico had put funds into escrow to secure it.

Which wasn't why Dom was stalling on matching and exceeding his bid. He was suffering a pinch of conscience.

Cat had revealed that Visconti Group was overextended. If Dom wanted to topple the first domino on what could spell the beginning of the end of Visconti

Group, he would let Nico have the Miami property. According to Cat, they couldn't afford it.

Dom had been working toward a moment like this for four years. It was the culmination of three generations of bloodthirst. He could hear his father's voice shouting at him to, "Pull the trigger."

Because all his father had ever wanted was revenge. Suffering. He'd thought causing someone else to hurt would somehow make his own pain stop.

No. Despite the attacks he'd suffered through the years at the hands of the Viscontis, Dom knew that crushing his father's enemy wouldn't do a damned thing to fill up the empty spaces inside himself.

He needed to do something else.

"I want to speak with Eve." He turned to confront a sea of confused expressions.

Someone leaned to the person next to them and murmured, "The one in accounting?"

"Evelina Visconti," Dom clarified with exasperation.

"Really?" They all sat taller and looked warily at each other.

"Um, sir?" A hesitant hand went up. "I'm not sure if this is relevant, but when I was doing my research, I noticed she's no longer on their org chart."

"Why?" Because of him?

A startled shrug.

"Find out where she is," he ordered. "I want to speak with her."


Four days later, Dom was vacillating between livid and sticky nausea when he walked into the Miami hotel that Nico Visconti wanted so badly.

It was showing its age, definitely not worth the price

Nico had driven it to, but location, location, location. The view from the penthouse was exceptional.

Nico Visconti turned from the windows when Dom entered. He stiffened.

"What the hell are you doing here? I was expecting Perez," he said of the current owner of the hotel.

"I asked him to set this up. Where's Eve?" Dom's staff had delivered the disturbing news that she was quietly missing. Her family didn't seem concerned, but she hadn't been spotted by paparazzi or photographed since Australia.

"Why?" Nico narrowed his eyes.

"She's no longer with Visconti Group. Why?"

"Why do you want to know?"

Good God, they were never going to get anywhere.

"Did it have anything to do with our being stranded that night?"

"You have an exaggerated sense of your own importance." Nico looked at his watch, likely to appear patronizing and dismissive. "Why?" he asked again, gaze sly as it came up to meet his. "Is there a reason I should have fired her? Did you sleep with her?"

Dom had prepared himself for that question.

"Would you excommunicate her for that? How medieval of you. Especially when the grapevine has it that she's saving herself for marriage." Thank you, Cat, for that nugget. "Do you really think she'd break her vow for *me*?" Dom offered his best poker face. "Or that I'd tell anyone if she had? I hear the last man who claimed he had slept with her walked away with a broken nose."

"Because he was lying. My brother knew it. That was years ago," Nico muttered.

"So where is she?" Dom pressed.

"Why?"

Dom's temper started to slip, but he had a flash of memory of her saying, *My brother is being a sexist jerk.*

"You don't know, do you?" He couldn't help a smirk of dark amusement. He knew exactly how irritating it was to be ignored by Eve. "Who can tell me where to find her? Your mother?"

"Do *not* talk to my mother. No one in my family wants to talk to you," Nico said impatiently. "I'm already tired of it." He started past Dom toward the door.

"Wait." Dom pushed his hands into his pockets and rocked on his heels. This was it. Once he took this step, he couldn't un-take it, but he'd been going around and around in his mind, trying to find another way. There wasn't one.

"I want to propose marriage."

Nico froze beside him.

Dom braced for anything, a sarcastic, *Me?* A thrown punch…

He got a scoffing choke. "Are you on drugs? I'd rather throw you off this building and spend the rest of my life in prison than call you my brother-in-law."

"Why?" Dom asked with genuine curiosity. "Do you ever talk about the feud? With your father? With any of your family? We never did." Dom shook his head, not waiting for an answer. "Talking to Eve was the first time I even imagined there was another side to the story my father had told me about my uncle. All I knew growing up was that I was supposed to hate your family. Making the Viscontis miserable is simply what we do, like celebrating Thanksgiving and running hotels. Aren't you tired of it?"

"What's the matter, Blackwood. Are you feeling the

pressure? You can't afford this place so you came here to cut a deal that might soften the sting?"

"Oh, I can afford it, Nico. Can you? Does your father know how overextended Visconti Group is?"

Nico's poker face was good, but not impervious. There was the tiniest hint of a flinch in his right eye.

"Eve was supposed to marry Logan to get you out of trouble, wasn't she?" Dom was repeating what Logan had told Cat. "Offerman was a lousy bet on your part. Eve had zero interest in him and he spilled your money troubles to *my* date while they were wrecking his bed."

Nico swore and pinched the bridge of his nose.

"Where's Eve?" Dom asked again.

"You're right. I don't know." He dropped his hand. "She blocked me over how things went with Logan."

"Who does know?"

"Let it go, Blackwood. None of us are going to condone your marrying her. How could we ever trust you?"

"If I wanted to hurt her, I had ample opportunity in Australia," Dom pointed out flatly.

Nico's belligerent stare turned troubled. His mouth tightened and his nostrils flared.

"How bad was it?" Nico asked with gritty reluctance. "That night on the island. Was she scared?"

"It could have been very bad if she'd been there alone. At least I got her to the shack, otherwise she'd have been in the open all night during a storm." Dom refused to pull that punch. "While we were getting drunk, waiting for rescue, she said, 'My grandmother refused to marry your grandfather. Maybe he should have got over it.' She's right. It's time we all got over it. If we don't, who will? Do you really want to consign our children to playing this silly game?"

"We could just put down our swords," Nico said. "Eve doesn't need to be involved."

"True." But that wouldn't bring Evie into his bed, would it? "But you're not wrong about how little trust there is on both sides. We'll both keep expecting a betrayal unless we have an old-fashioned arranged marriage that binds both families into one. The way it was supposed to happen in the first place."

"Is that what this is?" Nico challenged. "Are you setting her up to be left at the altar, trying to settle that old score?"

"God, no. I'm tired, Nico. You've driven up the price on this property to the point it's not practical for either of us to purchase it. But if I don't counter your offer, you're going to be in a very tricky position. Aren't you?"

"So I can have this place or my sister? Is that what you're threatening."

Dom released a beleaguered sigh to the ceiling.

"Why do you even want to marry her?" It wasn't the same cantankerous question. Nico's eyes narrowed as he finally weighed Dom's proposal more seriously. "What exactly happened between the two of you that this is even something you would consider?"

"She's not exactly hard on the eyes." Understatement. "Financially, an alliance between our companies would put us so far ahead, no one will ever catch us. And, believe it or not, I don't relish destroying you. But I *can*." Dom paused to let that sink in. "Now tell me where she is. If she agrees to marry me, I'll buy this place for her as a wedding gift."

Nico's lip twitched into a sneer, but he only asked, "And if she doesn't?"

"Then we'll see."

After a long, unbroken stare, Nico muttered something foul under his breath. Finally, he took out his phone, tapped and brought it to his ear.

"Where's Eve?" Nico asked without any other greeting.

"Call her and ask." The bored male voice was loud enough for Dom to hear it.

"It's important, Christo," Nico said with impatience. "Tell me."

"Where do you think she is?"

"I'm not playing twenty questions."

"Nonna's. *Obviously.*"

"Oh. Of course." Nico ended the call. "Our grandmother's villa on Lake Como."

"Give me the address."

Nico did, then said with heavy sarcasm, "Good luck."

"Don't need it. But you do," Dom said and walked out.

# CHAPTER TEN

EVE WAS TRYING to go back to resenting Dom. In some ways she did, because she was even more obsessed with him than before their time on the island. It took all her control not to stalk him online or find the number to his head office and try to reach out.

For what, though? They had no future. Putting their family history aside, he was the last sort of man she'd want as a partner. He was too much. Too gruff and dynamic and good-looking and powerful in the ways that he affected her. Her ankle was mostly better, but anytime it gave a twinge, she thought of him throwing her over his shoulder like a caveman, or smirking about removing the condom, or wrapping her ankle so tenderly.

The truth was, she wished she only thought of him when her ankle twinged. It was more a case of thinking about him and feeling a pang through her whole body.

Why? Why *him*?

She feared she would live out her life as a spinster because she seemed to possess whatever instinct or imprinting gene made wolves and geese mate for life. It wasn't love. It was the sort of pair bond that formed as a survival tactic. There was no logic to it. It simply was.

At least, that's what she told herself this infernal reaction was. If she allowed herself to believe this weird bond went any deeper, into liking his dry humor or feeling touched that he'd brought her breakfast, she only felt raw inside because she knew it wasn't the same for him. He'd made it clear their affair was a one-night thing and purely physical. Their parting had been circumspect without even a kiss, the silence since then profound.

Piqued by that and Nico's high-handed behavior and her realization that she was entirely too reliant on her family, she'd come to Italy—where she owned a home. Kind of.

This was the house where Nonno Aldo had brought his bride, Maria, after he had stolen her from her wedding in America. They'd had two years and their first child, Romeo, here before returning to America to bail out the Winslows. They'd held onto this villa and, after losing her husband, this was where Nonna Maria had lived out her golden years.

After she passed, Eve's father had wanted to sell the house because it was small and impractical, not to mention turning into a money pit with age. Eve had a lot of fond memories of visiting Nonna here. She had begged him to hold onto it until she was able to access her trust, at which point she'd got a mortgage and began making it her own.

It *was* impractical, made up of three floors built into a hillside. It was tall and skinny, with small rooms and narrow windows. But it was very cute with its red clay tile roof and its shutters in robin's-egg blue. There was an outdoor kitchen, a small pool, and terraced grounds holding fruit trees and ornamental shrubs that wore autumn colors of scarlet and copper and sunny gold. The view of the deep blue lake was outstanding.

Eve was currently supervising much-needed repairs to a retaining wall while waiting for a headhunter to get back to her when her housekeeper, Odetta, tugged her attention from the work she was surveying below her.

"Signorina?"

Eve turned to see Dom on the terrace above her.

Surprise nearly knocked her over the edge and onto the workmen.

Dom was still gorgeous, the bastard. He wore a light-weight suit in sage-gray. His jaw was shadowed with stubble, his eyes hidden by sunglasses. His hands were in his pockets, his attention seemingly on the view, but she felt his gaze follow her as she crossed the lawn to the bottom of the stone steps cut into the hill.

She took her time climbing them. Questions were tumbling through her mind and conflicted emotions bounced like pinballs in her chest. She couldn't help leaping to worrying that something catastrophic had happened. An exposé of some kind? She'd been staying off socials and off grid, trying to reset her life, but clickbait websites never took a break.

The closer she got, the tighter her skin felt. She subtly cleared her throat, fearing her voice would come out thin and high.

"If you're looking for your next development property, this one is not for sale," she said.

He took his sunglasses off and looked directly into her soul. "It's beautiful."

Her throat contracted around a squeak that she barely managed to suppress. Why did he have to be so damned edible? That mouth. She wanted to press her lips to his and nuzzle the scent in his throat and lean against the column of his body. She wanted to touch him. Feel him.

She wanted to take his hand and lead him straight up to her room without another word except maybe "yes," and "more," and "harder."

She turned so she was facing the water, trying to hide her libidinous reaction.

"My grandmother would have spent her whole life here if she hadn't had to go back to America and bail out the Winslows. Will you make coffee, please, Odetta?"

Her housekeeper melted away and Eve waved at the table and chairs farther along the paved stones of the terrace.

Dom didn't move. He tucked his sunglasses into his jacket pocket and gauged the distance to the workmen before asking in an undertone, "Are you pregnant?"

*"No."* He'd taken precautions, if he didn't remember. Even during that risky third time, he had pulled out as promised. Plus, the timing had been wrong. *And* she'd taken the pill, exactly as she had promised.

Despite how impossible it had been that she could be pregnant, she had still shed a couple of tears when her cycle had arrived as faithfully as tulips in spring. It was yet one more foolish reaction in a list of foolish overreactions this man provoked in her.

"I had to ask. I've been wondering."

"Is that why you're here?" A humorless laugh scraped the back of her throat. "You could have called."

"I don't have your number." He moved to hold a chair for her before taking one for himself. "Why did you leave Visconti Group?"

"Reasons." She shrugged that off.

"Me?"

"No. Family stuff." She frowned pensively at the water.

"I didn't tell anyone, if that's what you're asking. We agreed," she reminded him with a sidelong look.

"They might have made assumptions."

"They might have. I didn't stick around to find out. Did your family? Make assumptions?"

"Probably." His mouth curled slightly. "My situation is different. My sisters are from my father's second marriage. We're not as close as you seem to be with your brothers."

"I'm not that close to them. They're a lot older than me. Well," she allowed with a tilt of her head. "I'm close with my middle brother, Jackson. He's here in Italy. I used to stay with him on long weekends when I was at boarding school, only flying home for the longer breaks. He's the one I feel most similar to. Nico is driven and ambitious. Bossy," she summed up with a grimace. "Christo is very laid-back and fun to be around, but kind of impossible because he does what he wants. Jax and I are middle of the road. Sensible. Mostly," she added ironically.

Dom hadn't asked for her to tell him all that, but he seemed to listen intently, then said, "My sisters are all younger. Five of them." He splayed his fingers. "I didn't spend much time with them growing up so I don't really know them."

"Is your mother still alive?" She realized she didn't know.

"She is." He nodded absently. "She's in New York and lives with her partner, but never remarried. It would have affected her support payments. My relationship with her is distant for a lot of reasons."

"Such as?"

"I never fought to see any more of her than my father

allowed, which was only a few weekends a year. We don't really know each other."

"Do you wish she'd fought for you?"

"No," he dismissed easily. "We both knew to pick our battles with him. And sometimes I wonder if she saw too much of him in me to make it worth it for her."

"The fact you're here tells me you're not that much like him," she said with an ironic tilt of her mouth. "In what ways are you like him?"

"I'm practical. Determined. I can be ruthless. Like the way I left you in Australia, not looking back. Not even thinking until later that there might be someone else to worry about."

"There isn't," she murmured, stomach doing somersaults above her empty womb. "This is probably the longest personal conversation we've ever had. Did you come all this way for *that*?"

"No."

"What then?" Her voice became a ghost of itself.

The indent at the corner of his lips deepened with humor.

"Oh, *don't*." Her breath shortened. All of her nerve pathways contracted with anticipation.

"I don't know what *you're* thinking," he mocked. "But I came to propose we marry."

If the entire mountainside had fallen down upon her, she couldn't have been more caught off guard.

"We can't. Why would you even want to?" Did he have feelings for her after all? That thought sent her own thoughts scattering. Her heart tripped and thumped, trying to take flight. Adrenaline zinged through her system, urging her to flee because she didn't want to have this conversation. She didn't want to examine how *she* felt about *him*.

"The feud doesn't serve anyone. It has to end," he said simply.

All her ballooning thoughts condensed into a wet sack and fell back to earth. This had nothing to do with her, then. Nothing to do with emotion or attraction or even sex.

A sting of scorn rose beneath her skin. She fought to keep her reaction off her face, but felt as though she wore a stiff mask.

"What makes you think our marrying would end it?" she asked.

"I've spoken to your brother. He saw the advantages."

"You've spoken to Nico." That was a kick in the stomach she hadn't expected. "And he agreed? What do you need me for?"

"This is how warring kingdoms reconcile, Evie. It's one of the few tactics that has worked in every culture for millennia."

Trading women as chattel? She bit back those ripe words.

"Can I show you something?" she asked, working at keeping an innocent expression on her face.

He blinked, puzzled, then curious. He shrugged. "Sure."

She led him through the house and out the front door to the paved pathway that led from the porch to the road above. A pretty wrought-iron rail lined the path. It was covered in grapevines and bunches of green grapes not yet ripe. On the other side of the porch was a small garden filled with Nonna's roses. A few late blooms perfumed the air with lemon and raspberry and vanilla. A silver car was parked on the road above. His, she presumed.

Dom stood beside her, head swiveling. "What am I looking at?"

"My answer." She walked back into the house and slammed the door.

As she turned the lock, she heard his crack of laughter.

She waited, but there was no knock, no demand she let him in. Moments later, there was only the roar of his car's engine.

She left her forehead pressed to the door, bereft that he had given up so easily.

Worry pierced her, too. Had this been a real chance to end hostilities? And she'd allowed pride to take over and throw it away? Maybe she had just poured fuel on a feud that she agreed did need to end.

In a state of turmoil, she made herself go back out to the terrace and drink the coffee Odetta had made while she brooded over yet another proposal that had fallen short of her romantic dreams.

*Maybe I want too much,* she fretted.

Then, not even an hour later, a florist delivered a unique blown glass vase filled with a stunning arrangement of fragrant lilies and sunny daisies and romantic pink roses. The card read:

*I'll pick you up for dinner at seven.*

*Be ready or I will not do wicked things to you later.*

"Oh, you wish!" she cried.

And meant it. Mostly.

Actually, she very much wanted him to do all the wicked, sinful, carnal things they'd done in the Whitsundays. But she wanted that lovemaking to be something *they* wanted. She didn't want it to be something he used to manipulate her, but she was very worried he could.

When she found herself in her closet staring blankly at her wardrobe, she realized she would have to do something she'd been avoiding. She called Nico.

"Eve," he answered abruptly. "Where are you?"

"You know where I am because you sent Dom Blackwood here to propose a marriage *you* arranged. How do I get it through your thick skull—"

"Stop," he commanded. "Listen. You need to know two things."

After a beat of surprise, she lowered onto the tufted bench at the foot of her bed. "Such as?" she asked loftily.

"Dad's health isn't great."

"What?" Her heart lurched. She put out a hand to steady herself while her reflexive ire at being the youngest and always left behind skyrocketed. "Why didn't anyone *tell* me?"

"Mom is the only other one who knows," he said gruffly. "It's his prostate."

"Cancer?" Her heart stopped.

"No. But he's embarrassed to talk about it. They're still figuring out how to treat it, but you need that information as you think about Dom's proposal."

"Because Dad's not immortal? Marrying a Blackwood could kill him, Nico."

"If you decide to marry Dom, I'll talk to Dad," Nico said heavily. "Make him see why it's a good idea."

"It's not a good idea," she cried, letting her pent-up emotions get the better of her. "You and Dom are grown men. Quit fighting. You don't need me in the middle of it."

"We do," he said grimly. "*I* do." He drew a breath, signaling reluctance to continue. "I said there are two things you need to know." This one sounded like a biggie.

"Tell me," she insisted as the silence drew out.

"You know we took a bath when the economy tanked. I made some decisions—for which I take full responsibility," he stressed. "But they were based on the assumption that you and Logan were locked and loaded."

"Oh, my God." She closed her eyes and covered them with her free hand, glad she was still sitting down.

"Mom made it sound like you two were going to happen. *Logan* did," Nico insisted.

"But you didn't ask *me*."

"No. I didn't. I'm asking you now, though."

"Asking me what, exactly?" She dropped her hand and popped her eyes open, but she could only see a blur of blue beyond the window. A cold shiver entered her chest.

"To consider Dom. Seriously."

"Nico."

"He knows he has my back to a wall. This isn't Mom wanting you to marry her bridge partner's son. This ends the attacks and gives us new resources. This is something we need, Li-li."

He hadn't called her that in years. It was the pet name the family had used when she was very small.

*Bring your dolls into my room, Li-li. I won't let the boys bother you.*

"Are you still there?" Nico asked.

"Yes," she said in a small voice.

"I know I was holding you back at work. I thought I was protecting you from seeing how bad things were. That's how Dad always did things. He carried the worries so no one else had to. Being on the inside comes with a lot of responsibility. Hard choices and heavy burdens. It's not as great as you thought it would be, is it?"

"It's not fair to put them on me now! Like this," she said crossly.

"No, it's not. And I know you like to see yourself as Nonna Maria, living life on your own terms, willing to run away and elope for love, but she left her family high and dry when she did that, Eve. Are you going to do the same?"

She swallowed a sob of helplessness.

# CHAPTER ELEVEN

WHEN DOM ARRIVED back at Eve's, he was unsure that she would come to dinner or even open the door. Had that been a tantrum earlier? Or her real answer?

He took the umbrella his driver offered him and moved down the path illuminated by hidden bulbs beneath the shrubs. As he hit the damp fragrance of the rose garden, the front door opened.

Eve's snug satin trousers shimmered above laced ankle boots. Below the mock turtle collar of her cashmere top a wide cutout revealed her collarbone and upper chest. Her long raincoat flared open like a cape as she strode toward him on those endless legs of hers.

She punched his breath clean out of him. He wanted to take a fistful of her black hair and press her to the ground and not come up for air until they were covered in grass stains and smelled of crushed rose petals.

And each other.

She stopped under the umbrella and looked up from the clutch she had just closed.

"You came," he said, because he literally couldn't think of anything else to say.

"I always do. Don't I?" Her pretty mouth, painted scarlet, curled with self-contempt. She looked to the dark water where lights dotted the far shore.

A cold hand reached into his chest and gave his heart a quarter turn.

"You've spoken to your brother," he surmised.

"I have."

That's why she was here, not because of him or them. Because she knew her family finances were in jeopardy. Why that disappointed him, he couldn't say, since it was a lever he'd pulled to get her address and propose this marriage.

"Where are we going?" she asked.

"Ladies' choice." He kept the umbrella over her as they walked to the car. "I have a table booked at Il Gatto Nero, but it could stir speculation if we're seen dining together." The paparazzi knew that restaurant was popular with celebrities so cameras were always trained on the entrance. "If you'd rather dine privately at my hotel, we can do that."

"Please don't pander to me with the illusion of choice, Dom. We both know I don't have one. The public option is fine."

He waited until they were in the back of his car and his driver had them underway to ask, "What exactly did Nico say to you?" He was dying to reach for her, but he was pretty sure she'd snap in half if he did.

"It's not what he said. It's what he made me realize." She pulled her attention from her side window. "I was very close to my grandmother. She was also the only girl in a family of headstrong boys. Her two eldest brothers had been drafted into World War II and didn't come home. She knew what it meant to be treated as an asset, not a person."

Dom's grandparents had lost brothers to that war, too. It was the reason their great-grandparents had tried to shore up their partnership with the marriage between Michael and Maria, to solidify what they'd managed to hang onto through so many difficult times.

"Nonna didn't want to be treated like a stock, traded and invested by her parents into an arranged marriage, so she defied them and eloped with the man she loved. That always seemed heroic to me. Aspirational. Even though the consequences continue to ripple into my life. I didn't want to see that our family is still paying interest on a debt she incurred. I wanted to believe that her taking a stand meant I could and would be valued for my intelligence and ethics and dedication. That I was a person, not a vessel whose only purpose was to conceive and carry a strategic alliance. These aren't childbearing hips, Dom." She looked right at him as she said that. "Do factor that into your negotiations with my brother when you're attaching a value to this marriage."

Her tone was dripping with bitterness, but all he could think was, Children? He hadn't considered what the reality of a family with her would look like. Some dark-eyed hellion planting her feet and closing her fists and saying a defiant, *No, Daddy*, most likely.

He smirked, entertained by that notion for absolutely no good reason at all.

He waited until they'd wound their way through a sea of glances and murmurs at the restaurant and were seated at a table by the window, wine in hand, before he spoke again.

"Was I your first?"

"What do you mean?" She played dumb, but her eyes flared in alarm.

"You know what I'm asking." He had his answer in the mortified blush that stained her cheekbones and the way her mouth flattened to a pugnacious line while she turned her gaze to the candlelight reflected on the window.

Virginity was not something he prized or even considered much of a thing. By the time he'd hit his first home run, he'd rounded all the other bases dozens of times.

Being her first wasn't gratifying in a possessive, ego-driven way. Well, maybe there was a little of that. He was growing more possessive of her by the minute, but he was doing his best not to be a barbarian about it. No, it was more about what being her only lover told him about her and them.

"You could have knocked me over with a feather when I heard that," he said.

"From *whom*?"

"I put it together from bits of gossip." He shrugged. "The first time I heard that you were saving yourself was in Budapest. To be completely frank, before that, I had never given you a thought. Your whole family was beneath my notice. The late arriving baby sister was never going to be a threat to me so your name was all I knew."

*Beneath my notice.*

"This is turning into a great first date." She took a hefty gulp of her wine and looked to the window again.

"After I left your room that morning, I caught up with the bachelor party, emerging from their hangover. I asked if anyone had recognized you as a Visconti. They hadn't, but one said he'd heard you were saving yourself for marriage. He knew of a man who'd had his nose broken when your brother defended your honor."

"Jax was demonstrating how it's done," she said with a flutter of her lashes. "So I could learn."

"I dismissed it as urban legend. I had been with you that morning and knew that if I hadn't stopped when I did, we would have had sex. There was no way you were saving yourself."

She sobered and swallowed and frowned at the window. "Can we not do this here?"

"You chose the location," he reminded her.

She threw an aggrieved look at him. "I thought you were only mean when it was necessary."

"This is," he insisted. "You need to hear it. The few times I saw you before Australia, we were in public, but you were always with someone. At the wedding, you were sharing a suite with Logan. Of course, I assumed you were sleeping with him. When you told me you had your own room, I wondered for about half a second if those old rumors were true, but you're twenty-five, Evie. And when *I* touch you—"

"Would you stop?" she hissed, glaring at him. "This is *not* necessary."

"It is. There's a septic little boil between us that needs to be lanced."

"Your love poems need work."

"I want you to understand, Evie."

"Understand what?" Her mouth trembled and her eyes sheened with persecuted tears. "That you have the upper hand? That you can make me do things that are out of character and self-destructive? I *know*. That's why I hate you."

And that was it. "That's why I hate you, too."

She flinched.

He took no satisfaction in it. In fact, concern hit him at her words. It was a worry that had been rubbing like sandpaper in him even before he'd fully grasped that their night together had been her first time having sex with anyone.

"I didn't really believe I was your first until right now," he said gravely. "I wish you would have told me, Evie. If you felt like you couldn't stop me—"

"I couldn't stop myself. Okay? Is that what you need to hear?"

"I need to hear that I didn't hurt you," he said through his teeth, leaning in because they were talking so quietly. "I need to hear that, in future, you will tell me if I do."

The gloss on her eyes thickened. "You're hurting me now. This is *awful*," she told him in a strained, angry voice. "You're putting me on the spot for your own entertainment. How much humiliation do you need, Dom? Tell me the exact degree so I can get there and get it over with."

God, he wanted to grab her and… Not talk. Not have to find words and admit to things that turned him inside out in the same way they were torturing her.

So he just said it.

"There was no one else for me, either. Not after we met in Budapest. No one interests me, not the way you do. And that made me very grumpy, Evie. *Very*."

Eve's heart swerved in her chest. Her stomach was already wobbling from his, *"I need to hear that in future…"*

After talking to her brother, her emotions had been all over the place and she'd gathered them all into blame and resentment toward this man because, well, who else would a Visconti target when life was not going right?

"You're lying." She realized they were both angled into the center of the table so they could spike their hot words across the candle at each other. She pressed back in her chair, body trembling as though coming off a wild ride at an amusement park.

"We do a lot of things to each other, Evie, but we don't lie." His mouth was a bitter line that he pressed to the rim of his glass, draining half the contents before he sat back and stared at her, seeming to say *Your move.*

The waiter seized his moment. He rushed in to drop their amuse-bouche before them. With a mumbled handful of words in Italian, he topped up their glasses and hurried away.

Eve took a shaken breath, wondering if the entire restaurant was watching the forks of lightning they were throwing at each other, counting as they waited for the roll of thunder.

"Our marriage will be an alliance that will benefit both our families," Dom said grimly. "I will exploit it in every way I can. I'm not stupid. But that's not why we're marrying, Evie."

She had come here believing she had no choice in this matter and her stomach dipped afresh at the resolve in his statement. At the way he talked about it like it was a done deal.

"We're going to marry because we don't want anyone else." His pinning gaze was impossible to break. "Do we?"

It seemed laughable that he was asking her to speak for both of them, but there was too much acrimony in him for her to believe he was being anything but truthful.

"No," she admitted with defeat. It didn't make any sense, but, "We don't."

He signaled to their server and ordered, "Champagne, *per favore.*"

As the man hurried away, Dom reached into his pocket and brought out a velvet box. He opened it to reveal a stunning oval-cut diamond with a halo of smaller diamonds around it. He set it between them then held out his hand.

Dimly aware of gasps and attention turning their way, Eve set her hand in his palm. The spark between them was almost visible as skin touched skin. She began to tremble all over.

Dom slid the ring onto her finger, sending a sensation like a lasso up her arm to loop around her heart and drag it into his palm so he kept it as he released her.

The ring fit perfectly. She admired it as he rose and came around the table to draw her to her feet. His heavy hand cupped the back of her head and his arm banded possessively across her back. He dragged his mouth across hers in a slow, devastating kiss that rocketed her into a black hole from which she'd never return. The pull was too strong.

Applause broke out as the bucket of champagne arrived.

# CHAPTER TWELVE

"WE'LL FLY TO New York tonight," Dom stated when Eve returned from fixing her makeup. "You're a resident there, yes? So am I. We can marry in twenty-four hours."

"Dom." Her knees were so weak, she needed the chair he held for her. They hadn't taken a single bite yet. This was their first date. They might know each other in a biblical sense, but, "We're strangers to each other. We can't marry that quickly."

"I'm not spending the next year listening to threats from our families that they're boycotting our wedding. I'm not giving *you* a chance to change your mind." His eyes gleamed hard as polished bronze. "This won't be an easy sell to either side so we're not going to try. It will be done and their only choice will be to live with it. In harmony," he added with the arid sarcasm she was learning was his trademark.

Eve was trying to rearrange her brain cells to take in all of this. Her brother's call had made it clear that her marrying Dom would solve a lot of problems for her family. Nico hadn't ordered or pressured her to accept Dom's proposal. He had outlined the stakes and *asked*.

He was right about the weight of responsibility, too. It was smothering her.

"What if it doesn't work out? We divorce? That won't be good for either companies or our families."

"No, it won't. We have to make it work, Eve."

He always sounded so grave when he called her that. It was disconcerting.

"What if I can't have children?" She tossed that out as a defense mechanism, since she was running out of arguments.

"Children are not a deal-breaker for me. Your delicate hips are safe if you'd rather not put pressure on them." The corners of his mouth deepened with facetious amusement. "I have a nephew who has the temperament to be my successor at WBE if necessary, but we'll cross that bridge when we have to. I'd like children if you're up for it. I don't see my nieces and nephews often, and they're absolute monsters when I do, but for some reason I enjoy them."

Oh, God. She didn't want to *like* him, but how could she not when he said something like that?

"Do you want children?" he pressed.

"I always thought I'd have two or three," she admitted. "So I could bring them here for the summer and yell at them not to track sand into the house, the way Nonna did with us."

"Sounds idyllic. Any deal-breakers?"

"Love. At least, it used to be." She dropped her gaze to hide how much disappointment lurked within her, then lifted her lashes to meet his cool, flinty expression. "I imagine that sounds immature to you?"

He took a moment to consider his words.

"I hated those four years of abstinence." His voice was hard, but reflective, not assigning blame. "Since the island, I keep thinking it was good that we didn't get together in Budapest. The first time I saw you, I knew you were too young. Not just for me, but for the sort of affair we would have had. I'm glad you have some life experience behind you."

Did she, though? She wished she'd had a dozen throwaway affairs and at least one broken heart instead of carrying fractures in her heart that he had put there. Either way, she didn't think anything could have prepared her for this. Him.

"Don't you want to marry someone you love?" she asked hesitantly.

"I won't say I don't believe in it, but love seems... It comes with high costs. It's as much a weapon as anything else."

"That's not true." Did he really believe that? Why? "Love is a cushion. A home base. A place of safety. Love protects you."

"From what? Meteors? Life is going to impact you, whether you love someone or not. I'll grant you that love can skew how you react to those impacts. In my father's case, his love for his brother set him on a mission of vengeance."

Was that the reason for his cynicism? She was still troubled by the things he'd said about his father in Australia.

"He sounds like a difficult man," she murmured.

"He was." His face closed up, becoming shuttered and remote. "My mother had the sense to leave him, but my stepmother was forever trying to pull redeeming qualities out of him. Because she loved him. It was painful to watch."

"Painful to be his son?" she surmised.

"Yes," he said with a blink that was a small, unconscious flinch. "He taught me that living without love is easier, especially if it was never there in the first place."

A vast plane seemed to open before her, empty and desolate. She had the sense he was out there somewhere and had the fleeting thought, *I'll never reach him.* An ache arrived in her throat.

"You grew up believing your grandmother running away with your grandfather was a demonstration of love, but for who? Herself?"

"What's wrong with that?"

"Nothing. Just be honest about it. Where's the cushion for her family in that?"

"She was nineteen. She couldn't have *known* your grandfather would react so harshly."

He ran his tongue across his teeth behind his lip, studying her as though weighing whether to say something.

"What?" she prompted.

"I believe my grandfather felt something for her. That's why he was so devastated by her eloping with someone else. I think my father never got over my mother leaving him, which added another layer to his bastardish behavior. Love is not the great, wonderful entity you want it to be, Evie. It's destructive."

She turned her face to the window, trying to hide how much it hurt that he was reducing her yearning for that emotion into a girlish notion.

"Have you never felt anything like it?" she asked. "A crush? What about the woman you were engaged to? Are you this jaded about it because of her?"

"No," he said without hesitation. "Our marriage would have been advantageous in many ways and she blew it up because I didn't carve out my heart and offer it to her. I have no hard feelings because I had no soft ones." His lip curled. "No, I've only felt anything remotely like a crush once."

*Who?* A scald of envy, of threat, engulfed her.

"That sexual crush has been torturing me for four years," he continued, voice pitched low with intensity. "I'm determined to turn it into something productive. Otherwise, I'll burn down the world around me. Or *your* world, anyway, like my father and his father before that."

It hurt to hear that she was only a sexual crush to him, and that he felt it was destructive, but his words also sent the unsteadiness of anxious anticipation infiltrating her belly, sending out fingers of tension and ready heat.

"You?" he asked with gentle mockery. "How many crushes have you had?" His eyes narrowed to golden, laser-sharp slits.

"I wish other men interested me," she admitted with a pang of despair. "Women. Anyone. I hate how helpless you make me feel. But I can't devote my life to being your...sex doll. If that's all we have between us, I'll need to find personal fulfilment elsewhere."

"Meaning?" The way his voice dropped to subzero raised goose bumps on her skin.

"Work. I just told you no one else interests me," she reminded him.

Dom blinked, then shrugged with something like impatience, as though this was a topic completely lacking in importance. "If you want to work, work."

"At a real job," she stressed. "Not some lame portfolio picking out wallpaper and cutting cake. Not something that's handed to me like a toy to keep me quiet."

"I'm insulted." He sat back to frown at her. "Do you see me as sexist? One of my sisters is a human rights lawyer. She has joined an organization that sends her to countries where men don't think women should speak, let alone have the level of education she brings to the table. I hate it. I think constantly about how I need to be available to fly at a moment's notice to bail her out of trumped-up charges, but I'm so proud of her, I can't stand it. If you want to work, I won't hold you back. I'm perfectly capable of finding my own dinner if you're not there, barefoot and pregnant, to cook it for me."

"Well, I don't have her level of ambition. If that's the bar she sets, you're going to be disappointed in whatever goals I pursue."

"I'll be happy with whatever makes you happy. I don't want to come home to a miserable wife, Evie. She won't want to have sex with me."

She rolled her eyes and buried her reluctant grin against the rim of her champagne flute. Damn him for being arrogant, truthful, and self-deprecating. For being charming in his crude way.

"We've covered children and work. Do you have a preferred religion? I have none."

"Judging by the way we behave, I don't think either of us do."

That earned her a snort of appreciation.

She shook her head in answer. "Nonna was Catholic, but I haven't gone since her funeral. What about a prenup? We need time for that."

"We'll sign something that ensures our properties remain our own until such time as we've worked out more formal contracts post-nup. You're right. Those negotiations could take months, but if we're already married, that should take a lot of the contention out of it."

"Because Nico needs your money? Dom—"

"No. I know what you're going to say and no, I don't

want to wait. We can put off sex until our wedding night, if that's important to you, but I want that night to arrive very soon."

"Are you laughing at me?" Because she hadn't been waiting for her wedding night. She'd been waiting for him.

"I'm laughing at both of us." He reached across the table to still the hand that was nervously playing with the stem on her wineglass. "We've wasted enough time, Evie."

Heaven help her, she felt the same. Even these weeks since Australia felt like time they'd thrown away out of stubbornness and stupidity when she could have had that hand all over her. The mere touch of it was making her tremble with desire.

"All right," she murmured. "Let's fly back to New York tonight."

This was likely to be a disaster, but she was marrying Domenico Blackwood.

By the time Dom's private jet landed in New York, rumors of their engagement had leaked from the restaurant onto the global airwaves. It was midmorning and, since Eve also had her identification on her, he had his driver take them straight to the courthouse to apply for a marriage license.

The law required they wait twenty-four hours so he booked them an officiant for precisely twenty-four hours later. At her request, he dropped Eve at a boutique while he made the rest of the arrangements for their wedding.

It was just a business deal with a side of sex, but an unfamiliar restlessness stalked him until they met again at his penthouse. Then he finally relaxed, which unsettled him in a different way.

Evie was crashing from jet lag so he put her in a guest room—reluctantly—and found his own bed a few hours later.

The following day, he invited his mother and Nico to his penthouse. He didn't tell either of them what was happening so his mother arrived without her partner, perhaps expecting an update on the stock portfolio he managed for her.

"Oh," Kathleen Blackwood said with a self-conscious touch of the pearls when he introduced Eve and explained what was happening. "I would have worn something nicer if I'd known." She was as elegantly turned out as always in a sweater set over a slimline skirt, hair coiffed and makeup flawless. "It was kind of you to invite me," she said as she pressed her cheek to each of Eve's.

"Dom said you were the one person on his side who might actually support this marriage," Eve said with a hopeful quirk of her brows. "And since my own mother isn't here, I wonder if you'd be willing to come zip me into my gown?" She was still in the yoga pants and loose T-shirt she'd put on when she rose.

"I'd be honored."

Kathleen came back to the lounge a few minutes later wearing a smile he'd never seen before. It was somewhere between serene and optimistic. Maybe even, as she found him across the room, pride?

An unsteady sensation hit the middle of his chest, one that made him look impatiently for Evie so he wouldn't have to examine whatever this inner wobble was.

"She'll be out in a moment," his mother said as she squeezed his arm. "You know, given how your father always talked about them, I don't think I could have imagined a Visconti being so charming. She's lovely, Dom.

I'm really touched that you chose to include me. I hope this means that... Well, that things can start to heal. For everyone."

The way she searched his eyes caused the wobble inside him to grow worse.

*It's practical*, he wanted to argue. *Just business. Just sex.*

It wasn't supposed to be an emotional tonic. That was too much pressure to put on either of them.

The elevator dinged, saving him from the sense of walls closing in.

"That'll be Evie's brother." He started to brush past her, but he hesitated and gave her arm a light squeeze. "Thank you for being here. I hope we can all move forward, too."

Nico entered and grew both confused and suspicious when Dom introduced him to his mother.

Evie came out from the bedroom in a gown the color of whipped cream. Its one-shoulder crepe fabric clung smoothly and seamlessly to her torso and hips, flaring midthigh just wide enough for her to walk. Her hair was in a simple knot held with a silver clasp.

Such a jolt of pleasure hit him at the sight of her, Dom could hardly breathe. He'd had a fresh haircut yesterday and shaved this morning. He was dressed in his best suit, but he suddenly wished he'd had time to have a new one made. As much as he wanted this union formalized and finalized—and consummated—he could see the care Eve had taken despite this not being the wedding of her dreams.

It struck him that his sisters had approached their own wedding days with giddy excitement. Eve was very subdued, especially as she came up against her brother's thunderous reaction.

"What the *hell*, Lina?"

Dom held out his hand in a silent command that she come to his side, which she did, but not because she needed his protection.

"What," she said in a mild voice. "You asked me to do this."

"I asked you to *consider* it." He glared at Dom. "Why the rush?" He snapped a look of fresh shock at Evie. "Are you pregnant? Did you two sleep together in Australia?"

"When have I ever asked you about your sex life?" Evie snapped right back at him. "I really need you to check this sexism of yours, Nico. It's 2015."

"No, it's—" His mouth tightened and her brows went up. "*Are* you pregnant?" he demanded.

"Still none of your business," she said coldly. "But, no. I'm not. Although, people will probably presume that, won't they?" She wrinkled her nose as she looked up at Dom.

"Dad already does," Nico warned. "He called me yesterday when the engagement rumors started."

"What did you tell him?" Her hand tightened in Dom's.

"That you were on your way back to New York and that you and I would come see them today to explain."

"You'll have to manage that on your own," Dom interjected. "We're leaving right after the ceremony for our honeymoon. We can only stay away a week since Evie has a job interview next Wednesday that she can't miss."

"Where?" Nico frowned at her.

"I don't know. Did I miss a call?" She looked up at him in confusion.

"WBE has three executive positions coming available this year. One starts in a couple of weeks, but they could all benefit from your skill set. I'd like you to meet with our hiring team and consider whether any appeal. It's not nepotism." He turned that onto Nico. "Or a continuation of our rivalry, although I think we both operate best with a healthy sense of competition. No, I genuinely think you have slept on her potential. I refuse to make the same mistake. Ah. Here's the officiant," he noted as the elevator pinged once more.

His housekeeper hurried from the kitchen with the bouquet and a broad smile.

"Evelina," Nico said, quiet and urgent. "Are you sure about this?"

She searched Dom's expression. Her dark brows were lowered to a tense, conflicted line as though searching for something in him that he very much feared he didn't have.

When she nodded jerkily, he relaxed.

Moments later, they were repeating the words their officiant provided. The vows were taken straight from city hall, short and sweet.

"Domenico, do you solemnly promise to love, honor and respect Evelina for as long as you both shall live?"

"I do."

"Evelina, do you solemnly promise to love, honor and respect Domenico for as long as you both shall live?"

"I do." Her voice was quiet, but steady. Her hand was soft and warm when he threaded her wedding band onto it.

Dom had never imagined wearing a ring could feel any more profound than wearing a tie pin or a wristwatch. This whole day should have felt as though he was only collecting one more person onto his list of dependents, but he somehow knew that no matter whether that gold band sat against his skin or in a safety deposit box, he was changed by it. Not branded or bound, but linked to Eve in a way that defied logic or description.

"By the power vested in me, I pronounce you married. You may kiss!"

As Dom took her in his arms, she tensed slightly and flashed an apprehensive look up at him. Anxious tears threatened to dampen her lashes.

*Don't let my brother see what I'm like with you.*

He heard her voice in his head as clearly as though she'd spoken the words aloud.

Dom angled so his shoulder blocked Nico's view of her. He cupped her cheek and pressed a kiss across her trembling mouth, holding there in soft reassurance. Her passion was for him and him alone, not something to be put on display for anyone else to witness.

But even in that brief kiss, need and desire danced toward urgency. Her lips pulled at his with invitation, tempting him to linger and feed the fire.

*Soon*, he promised, keeping his arm around her as they broke apart and smiled for his mother's snapshot. Moments later, the paperwork was finished. Dom texted his assistant to release the statement they'd agreed upon and carried their luggage into the elevator while Evie changed into travel clothes.

Nico rode down with them, muttering that he hoped to reach their parents before they saw the headlines.

Thirty minutes later, he and Eve were in the air, flying south. They each held a glass of champagne, but she was worrying her bottom lip with her teeth.

"What's wrong?" he asked her.

"My parents. I should have gone with Nico." She worried the edge of her phone with her thumb.

A surge of possessiveness had him wanting to dismiss whatever guilt or obligation she might be experiencing, but he made himself say, "Are you feeling strongly enough that I should ask the pilot to turn this plane around?"

"No," she said on a sigh. "Dad will need some time to cool off. Mom, too. She's been planning my wedding since she heard the words, 'It's a girl.'"

He let out a subtle breath.

"I'll foot the bill on the reception. Tell her to go whole hog."

"Ironically, it's always been a family joke to warn me not to elope like Nonna Maria. A joke, but not really," she clarified with a crooked smile. "Now I have, but instead of running from a Blackwood, I'm with one."

"Are you regretting that?"

"No," she said promptly, then grimaced slightly at how quickly she'd said it.

Which was cute. Endearing.

"No," he repeated as he picked up the hand wearing both his rings. He set his teeth against her bent knuckle. Her gaze hazed exactly the way he liked to see it.

"What are you thinking about, my pretty little Evie?"

"Um…" Her lashes quivered as she watched the play of his lips against her twitching fingers. "That…um…"

It was like a switch, this thing between them. It took absolutely nothing to flip it and once it was on, it was *on*. But he made her say it. He wanted her to acknowledge it. He needed her to. The small beast inside him needed to know she was exactly as helpless to it as he was.

"I've…um…" Her cheeks flushed with shy color. She glanced to the flight attendant in the galley before leaning closer to whisper, "I've always wondered how one joins the mile-high club?"

"Oh." He was absolutely addicted to her when she was both carnal and curious. It turned him on like nothing else. "It's a very exclusive club. You need a personal invite."

"By someone who's already a member?" Her tone grew piqued.

Uh-oh. "Not at all," he said smoothly. "You could definitely ask me to become a member with you."

"Well, then. Consider yourself invited." She unclipped her belt and rose.

# CHAPTER THIRTEEN

EVE'S THOUGHTS AND emotions were all over the place.
Part of her did want to turn this plane around and run
home to where she was safe. She had *married* Dom
Blackwood, essentially still a stranger to her. How had
she thought this was a good idea?

Oh, right. He only needed to skim away her light
jacket, fingertips grazing her bare shoulders and upper
arms and she was suffused in heavenly vibrations. He
slid the zip on her simple sheath down her spine and she
shimmied to help him drop the navy crepe over her hips
to drop it to the floor.

Turning to face him, she began working on the buttons of his shirt. He'd removed his tie and jacket when
they had boarded and pulled the tails of his shirt free of
his trousers.

"Evie." He caught her urgently working fingers into a
single, firm grip, halting her. His other hand found the
side of her neck. "I've just realized." He waited for her
gaze to meet the glow in his. "You're mine."

Her stomach pitched at the magnitude of that statement.

"Are you mine?" she asked shakily.

"This ring says so, doesn't it?" He tilted the hand that
was gently crushing her tangled fingers, making his gold

band wink. "We're going to spend the rest of our lives doing this. Why don't I show you I'm capable of seducing my virgin bride?"

After everything they'd done on the island?

"That look." A rusty chuckle rattled from his chest, then his expression sobered. He cupped her face in two hands as though she was precious and worth gazing upon. "Every time we've come together, I've leapt on you like you were my last meal. I would have been so much more careful if I'd known."

"It's okay." Her voice rasped from the bottom of her throat, cheeks stinging as she laid bare the truth. "I liked it."

"I know you did," he said throatily, making her want to pinch him. "I like that you match my appetite so closely, but let me have this." He dropped a soft, soft kiss on her lips. A quest and a promise, one that made all the small defenses she managed to keep up against him shift and waver on their foundations.

*I don't know you*, she wanted to say, but she was learning that he was capable of gentleness. He was almost tender in the way he reverently framed her face and brushed his lips across hers again and again, coaxing her to open for him. To cling and encourage and invite. To deepen the kiss by degrees until his kiss was all that she knew. All that she needed—to be held by him. Connected and suffused in these lovely, shimmering waves.

Her hands began to roam beneath his open shirt, exploring the warm planes and rough-smooth textures of his chest, his taut skin and the fine hairs and his pebbled nipples.

He sucked in a breath, abdomen contracting. He deepened their kiss, releasing her face to drag her into a more sensual embrace. The brush of his hot chest and crisp, open shirt against her mostly naked torso made her shiver.

Helplessness was stealing over her like the shadow of night. She would lose herself to him, she realized. When it came to enemies, he was the most insidious kind. He turned her against herself, weakening her from within.

She tried to take some measure of control by drifting her hands down to his belt.

He caught them and had them manacled behind her back before she'd realized how easily he could do it.

"I said slowly, Evie."

A catch of alarm went through her, then her breasts felt the heat of his gaze. They swelled in her bra, hardening from only a look. Her nipples stung.

He watched his own finger slide under the navy blue strap, drawing it to fall off her shoulder.

Her breaths were uneven, her nervous system vibrating with excitement and anxiety as she tested the strength of his grip. Her movement shifted her against the ridge of his erection.

His gaze was molten gold as he flashed her a look.

She held his stare and pressed her hips harder into his.

"You're the one who always breaks first," he taunted as he ran his hand over her ribs and around to her spine, casual in his claiming of her exposed skin. Proprietary in the way he pushed his hand into the back of her cheekies and palmed a soft round globe.

"You like controlling me," she accused.

"I like touching you," he corrected and slid his hand around to the front of the midnight-blue lace that covered her mound. "I like seeing what my touch does to you. I like feeling it."

She bit her lip, trying to keep her sob trapped in her

throat, and closed her eyes as though she could hide from the fact that her folds were damp and swollen with yearning for the fingertip that delved and explored.

"Look at me," he commanded quietly.

Her eyelids felt too heavy to lift, the exposure too raw. It hurt to let him see how much pleasure she derived from something so small as the light play of his touch against her most intimate flesh.

"Tell me when you're close." His voice had dropped into a low, hypnotic tone that centered her world on the glitter in his gaze and the lazy caress that drew her closer and closer to a dangerous precipice.

"Kiss me," she begged in a whisper.

"Not yet. Keep looking at me."

This was so flagrant! At least on the island, she'd had the dim light of the shadowy shack to hide behind. He was forcing her to let him see exactly how thoroughly he dismantled her with hardly any effort whatsoever. It was a show of dominance that was both disconcerting and a ferocious turn-on, making her squirm under the struggle.

Her heart was thundering, her skin burning. Her body grew taut with ever deepening arousal as he dipped and withdrew, caressed and circled and dipped again. She was caught in a slipstream of pleasure, arching ever tighter, breaths reduced to aching gasps of urgency.

"Please." She licked her dry, panting lips, so close she wanted to scream. "Please, Dom." She closed her eyes in bliss as the white-hot pleasure rose like the tide, about to consume her.

He withdrew his hand.

She snapped her eyes open to see the amused, gratified look on his face.

"You're being cruel!" She struggled against his grip

and he released her, only catching at her arms to steady her when she staggered drunkenly.

"It's a *game*, Evie."

"It's our *marriage*." She was shaking, wildly aroused and furious and reacting to the enormity of being tied to him when he was so arrogant and imperious. "If I can't trust you here—" She waved at the bed.

She suddenly wanted to cry, which felt like the greatest humiliation of all. She pushed the heels of her hands into her eye sockets, devastated in a way she couldn't articulate.

His clothing rustled. It sounded as though his belt hit the floor.

She dropped her hands to see him sprawl onto his elbow on the bed. He wore nothing but his wedding band. He was ridiculously beautiful, all lean muscle and tanned skin except for that pale strip across his hips, accentuating that he was unabashedly aroused.

A fresh wave of weakness attacked her along with a fresh flood of heat. She hugged herself, sliding her bra strap back onto her shoulder as she did.

"I said I'm yours, didn't I?" He was wearing his most remote expression, but for some reason it caused a pang of empathy in her chest. "Take what you want. Or walk out if you're that mad."

She bit her lips together, fearful they were quivering like a child's. "I don't know how to handle this." She threw that at him in a ragged accusation, as though it was his fault that she reacted like this. "The way you make me feel is too much, Dom."

"I keep telling you, we do this to *each other*. We have to stop hating each other for that." He held out his hand. "Come here."

She hesitated, but if she walked out now, the nascent threads of trust between them really would break. She had made this bed and longed to lie in it. With him.

She skimmed away the last of her clothes and joined him on the bed. He was still rock-hard and it only took the brush of his hands on her to reignite her own passion, but she curled into him on instinct, seeking more than sex. Comfort. Shelter.

He closed his arms around her and pressed his lips to her hair. "You're safe here, Evie. Always. I promise you that."

Physically, yes. She believed him. Emotionally? Not yet. Maybe never, but that wasn't his fault, either. He might play erotic games, but he didn't play mind games. He wasn't making empty promises to lead her on.

That was the part that really scared her, though. She didn't know how to cope with the way he made her *feel*. She was afraid that she could fall in love with him. Maybe already was and she wasn't even sure why. Because of the way he made her feel when he set adoring kisses on the side of her face? He was still a Blackwood. A stranger.

Yet he shattered her defenses with the warm crush of his mouth and the scintillating pleasure of his touch innocuously tracing the rim of her ear.

She abandoned her misgivings and turned her face into his throat, rubbing her cheeks against his skin like a cat sharing scent, marking him in her own way. She stretched out so she was long and lithe against his tensile strength and danced her fingertips down his spine then traced the line between his tight buttocks.

This time when he drew a sharp breath and caught her hand and pressed it to the mattress above her head,

"My purser informed me that my sister is in Jamaica, visiting her husband's family," Dom explained.

"You spoke to the purser like that?" She flicked her gaze to the naked, muscled thigh poking out from beneath the draped sheet.

"He used the intercom, so, yes. I did."

She was falling in love with that laconic humor of his. Wait. No, she wasn't. She scrambled to catch her slipping heart. Evie, *don't*.

Dom brought his phone to his ear. "I got your message. We're in the Caymans, but we can fly over for the afternoon. Is Ingrid with you?"

The woman's response was muted and puzzled. "No. Why would she be?"

"It was just a question. We'll see you later."

He ended the call, then looked to Eve with an unreadable expression. With a single fingertip, he guided her hair off her cheek and tucked it behind her ear. "And so it starts."

She bunched the pillow under her chest, hugging it. "Who's Ingrid?"

"My stepmother."

"Why were you asking if she'd be there? Are you worried she's going to hate me?"

"She already does."

"Ouch." She scowled at him.

He shrugged off his blunt words. "My father was extremely good at spreading his poison. She always sided with him, feeding into it. It was the only way she could be close to him. That led her to believe she had some influence or control over the family and WBE, but it was an illusion even before Dad died. My marriage forces

she only gave a moue of contrition and kissed the point of his chin.

"I'll be good," she promised.

"You're always good." He kissed her, once, twice, then shifted down to collar her neck with kisses. His lips trailed down, covering her breasts reverently, pausing to catch each of her distended nipples and rolling them with his tongue. He kissed her all over, down to her lurching abdomen and across her hips. He rubbed his lips against the inside of her thigh, breathing hotly, "So soft."

The pinprick joy of his kisses moved to her center where he easily brought her back to the fever pitch of a moment ago. When her muscles were strung wire-tight, she clutched her fist in his hair and moaned, "Dom."

He lifted his head.

"I'm not on the pill," she told him.

"What does that mean?" He opened his mouth on her inner thigh and sucked. Hard. "Should I wear a condom?"

"Only if you want to. And why do you *do* that?" She jerked away from the suction of his mouth against the top of her thigh. It hadn't really hurt, only threatened to, but she would have a small shadow of a love bite there tomorrow.

"If I get you pregnant, that's it, Evie." He rose to loom over her, hard knees pushing her legs apart so he could settle the hot thickness of his erection against her aching loins. "We're in this forever. Do you understand that?"

She nodded, even though she didn't think there was any way to fully comprehend the scope and magnitude of tying her life to this man.

In a single flex and surge of his body, the silken, aggressive shape of him forged into her. He was returned to her. Claiming her anew. The bleak emptiness she hadn't wanted to acknowledge was doused. Eclipsed. She was bathed in a halo of fire.

He muttered something and spared a moment to catch some of her hair and wind it around his fist.

"Evie," he said in a rasp of anguish right before he claimed her mouth with unrestrained hunger. As he began to thrust, she grasped at his shoulders and brought her knees up to cling her legs around him.

With each powerful thrust, he stole a little more of her. Possessed her a little more deeply.

This was what she had been afraid of, but in the throes of this pleasure, there was no fear, only glorious indulgence. He was driving her toward a wall. Driving them. The barrier might break when they hit it or they might be the ones to shatter. Either way, she was desperate to get there and urged him on with agonized gasps and the cut of her nails and the eager tilt of her hips.

"Evie," he said again. This time it was almost a curse. His heartbeat pounded against her breast and his ragged breaths stirred the hair near her ear.

They weren't going to survive it, but here they were. The world was fracturing and cracking and exploding. Perhaps they flew into the sun. Either way, she was nothing but white light. She and Dom were no longer physical or separate. They were made of the same, singular, eternal energy.

Then ecstasy crashed over her, ripping her breath from her body in a cry of sheer joy. His shout joined hers and the shock waves of his own culmination slammed up against hers.

They clung to each other, sweaty and groaning and lost to the maelstrom.

Eve only had one thought—that this would ha[ppen] again and again for the rest of their lives.

Eve woke with a start, naked in the wide bed in the stat[e] room of Dom's yacht. Sunshine and mahogany hit he[r] eyes. A tropical breeze came through the open windows, dancing across her skin where it wasn't covered by the sheet.

She was on her stomach and lifted her head to look for Dom.

He sat slouched against the headboard, also wearing only the corner of the sheet as he thumbed the screen of his phone.

*This is my life now,* she thought with sweet excitement.

She would fall asleep sated and wake to the sexy vision of his bare chest and sensual mouth, his stubbled jaw and the lazy, possessive gleam in his eye as he slid a look toward her.

"I thought we made vows," she said with mock indignance.

Both of their phones had been blowing up by the time they'd landed in Miami. Eve had spoken briefly with he[r] mother, who was concerned on many fronts.

"Your father is very upset with Nico," her mother [had] said. "He didn't want you to know about his doctor vis[it]

"Can I talk to him?" Eve had asked with trepida[tion]

"He's still in with Nico. Let him calm down fir[st]

She'd then exchanged a few texts with her othe[r broth]ers, both of them asking if she "had" to marry [Dom,] implying they presumed she was pregnant.

After that, she and Dom had turned off no[tifications,] promising not to check them until they were [home] again.

her to accept that. She won't take it out on you, though. I won't allow it."

Eve studied his dispassionate expression, thinking of his mother who had been near tears when she had zipped Eve's gown.

"This gives me so much hope, Eve," Kathleen had said with a misty smile. "He's always been so opaque to me. He learned to keep to himself out of self-defense. I did the same, not realizing I was losing him until he was already gone. But this… I mean it when I say I want the absolute best for both of you."

"What was your childhood like?" Eve asked him. "Did you spend most of your time with your mother or your father?"

A subtle stiffness came over him, one that made her think he was going to deflect without answering the question.

"Neither." His offhand tone sounded forced. "Dad married Ingrid very quickly after his divorce from Mom. Ingrid didn't like me underfoot, but she felt my father's influence was threatened if I spent too much time with Mom so I mostly lived at boarding school."

"Really? How old were you?" She frowned.

"School age." He shrugged. "Seven?"

"That's young to be away from home. Was the school in New York or…?"

"New York at first, then Eton so I can 'talk like this.'" He put on a somber British accent. He leaned to set his phone aside and plumped the pillow behind him. "I didn't mind. Being away was less drama and I made social connections that serve me to this day. I came back to America for high school, Andover, and spent summers abroad. Dad would send me to whichever property would teach me a new language and something about the business. Paris, Madrid, Athens, Tokyo."

It sounded very alienating and lonely. Her brothers might have called her a pest, but she hadn't been *unwanted*. She'd always known she was loved.

"You must have spent time in Sydney?" she joked lightly. "I heard you say, 'Crikey, mate' the day we were rescued. I was so grateful you could make our plight understood to the locals."

His mouth twitched. "You've missed a career in stand-up."

"There's still time." She rolled away, then pushed her pillows to the headboard. As she sat up beside him, she pulled the sheet across her naked breasts. "Tell me more about your relationship with Ingrid. Why didn't she want you around?"

"Because I wasn't hers," he said as though it was obvious. "That's why I have five sisters. She was trying to produce a contender for the throne."

"Are any of them not?"

He snapped his head around to give her a frosty look.

"You were the one who gets offended at being called a sexist."

"None want it," he clarified. "Freda is a lawyer. I told you about her. Astrid and our middle sister married young, likely to get out from Dad and Ingrid's thumbs, though they'll deny that. They're dedicated homemakers. The youngest is an artist. Glassblowing, mostly. She's very talented. My second youngest is brilliant in some ways and struggles in others. She works directly for me, remotely from her apartment. She analyzes data and does other nerdy things that no one else will touch, but she thrives on it."

kind, either." She was still sore about those things he'd said about that. "She did one thing for herself and here I am still paying for it."

"I'm the one who will be paying, Eve." He turned to face her, armor up, battle-ready. "Your brother's situation isn't all due to the feud. Quit playing martyr to history and thank me for bailing him out."

She curled her fist into the sheet, chest pierced by the lance he'd just plunged through her. She really had been traded for a bride price. Her eyes were hot, but she willed the tears not to well and pressed her quivering lips together, refusing to say anything at all.

After a long, charged moment, he muttered, "I need to arrange our flight," and walked out.

"And the nephew who could be your successor?"

"Zeke. Freda's son. He's twelve, very focused a
bright. A natural leader. To be honest, Ingrid had h
heart set on his ascension, believing she put in enoug
years with my father that she has as much right to WB
as anyone else."

"That tells me exactly how she'll react to me and any
children we might produce."

Ingrid would channel her late husband's antipathy
against a Visconti, but she would also see a threat to the
tentacles she had already wrapped around the Blackwood fortune.

Judging from the radio silence from Eve's father,
Romeo didn't seem to be coming around, either.

"What have we done, Dom? Did we burn down our
lives for the sake of a few orgasms?"

"They're very good orgasms, Evie." He floated a caress down her arm and tingles followed like stardust.

"I'm being serious. How is this marriage supposed to
build bridges? Did you marry me just to throw me in your
stepmother's face?" she asked with a twinge of suspicion.

"You know why I married you." He dropped his hand
away.

"Sex." She didn't mean to spit the word out with such
contempt, but it seemed such a paltry return for the challenge ahead of them. "At least Nonna married for love."

"Don't be naïve. She married for sex. She didn't wa
to sleep with my grandfather so she ran away with your
Dom left the bed and pulled on a pair of board sh
which was the extent of clothing he'd worn since t
cast off from Miami four days ago.

A chill settled over her chest.

"It was love, Dom," she insisted. "Not the de

# CHAPTER FOURTEEN

DOM WAS FEELING prickly and keyed up as he and Eve were driven from the private airfield to his sister's villa.

He wasn't one to navel-gaze and fret about conflict. It was the state he'd grown up in. His father had had a hair-trigger temper, always ready to become combative. Dom had learned to navigate those rough waters the way an experienced kayaker went through the rapids in a chasm. Sometimes you got bumped or bruised, but you always survived it.

So his argument with Eve this morning shouldn't have grated on him, filling him with a sense of *this is bad*. The argument shouldn't have happened at all. He shouldn't have risen to the bait of her dismissing their relationship as "just sex" and snapped at her over it.

What did they have other than sex, though? What did he want from her? He'd been raised to expect very little from those who were close to him. At least, he'd found that was the best way to avoid being disappointed so he typically clung to that strategy, but with her—

"Dom?"

Her small voice dragged his attention to her crinkled brow and the wiggle of her fingers in his too-tight grip.

He didn't remember picking up her hand. He released her.

"Are you worried about my meeting your sister?" she asked.

"No," he said with a dismissive scoff. Astrid was a people-pleaser by nature. He suspected the only reason she'd invited them was because it was the polite thing to do. Either that or Ingrid had asked her to.

The car turned through a pair of open gates and the villa came into view. Dom had never been here so he leaned to admire its architecture of glass and stucco arranged like building blocks that were stacked and fanned out to take advantage of the views offered by its private beach.

Dom came around to help Eve from the car and kept her hand as they walked past a water feature to the double doors.

"Astrid's husband, Jevaun, is a music producer. His father is a development banker, but the rest of his family are in the music industry. His mother is a famous folk singer here."

Jevaun opened the door to them himself. He was dressed casually in a T-shirt and board shorts, feet bare, brown head shaved bald and black beard shaved down to a narrow chinstrap. He held their youngest, Adio, who was slumped against his shoulder.

"Dom." Jevaun thrust out his hand. "Good to see you. Congratulations."

Dom liked Jevaun. He was ambitious, but not in a showy way. His clients were A-list superstars, but Dom only knew that from perusing the awards Jevaun had won. He was far more likely to brag about his kid's new tooth than any of the songs he'd launched to the top of the charts.

"This is Eve—I almost said 'Visconti.' Eve Blackwood. My wife." Damn, that was satisfying.

"Nice to meet you." Eve shook Jevaun's hand.

"Adio." Jevaun nodded at the boy whose head of short, tight curls was heavy on his shoulder. "I need to put him down. Astrid and the kids are outside."

Dom usually only saw his sisters on occasions like weddings or, perhaps, a birthday where he might make a point of taking one out to dinner. He'd seen them more often when his father had been alive, crossing paths with them in the six-story limestone mansion that Ingrid still occupied on the Upper East Side of New York.

He rarely visited their homes so this great room littered with children's toys and small clothes in bright colors was also new to him.

Dom's father never would have allowed so much disarray. Children were to be seen and not heard. If they were seen, they were clean, neatly dressed and stayed in one spot. They didn't run at you wearing paint and glitter, shouting, "Uncle Dom!"

Jayden's wide grin revealed front teeth that were too big for his six-year-old face. The top of his hair was in an intricate pattern of cornrows, the sides shaved up in a fade. His sister, Maya, was four. Her hair was in long braids with neon-colored beads swinging off the ends.

"Mama said we could go in the pool when you got here," Maya said, all big dark pleading eyes. "Will you come in with us? *Please?*"

"And throw me like you did before?" Jayden asked. "Please, please, please?"

"You remember that?" Dom hadn't been in a pool with these kids in well over a year.

"Jay. Maya. Can we please say hello properly first? This is your new Auntie Eve." Astrid came up behind the children, blond hair in a ponytail, freckled face clean of makeup. She wore a loose sundress that billowed over her baby bump. "Hi, I'm Astrid." She shook hands with Eve, eyeing her with open curiosity. "This was unexpected news. Congratulations, Dom."

She *hugged* him.

Dom honestly couldn't remember that ever happening and stiffened in surprise.

Astrid's smile faltered as she stepped back before he'd even thought to return her embrace. He caught the flicker of something across Eve's expression, but Astrid spoke again.

"I said we would see about swimming," she reminded the children while setting a quieting hand on her bouncing son's shoulder. "Jevaun's parents said they'd take them if we want adult time. Jevaun can drive them over."

"I don't mind. We brought our suits." Dom glanced at Eve.

She nodded.

"Wash up first," Astrid told the excited children, pointing them to the outdoor shower. "Uncle Dom doesn't want to come out of our pool looking like a unicorn. Jevaun will come in with you, but can I persuade you to visit with me in the shade, Eve?" Astrid waved at a pair of comfortable loungers placed in the shadow of the gazebo. "I'm dying to put my feet up. We have a housekeeper come in for a few hours every morning while we're here, but mostly we try to simply be a family. It's relaxed and messy and makes me appreciate the nanny, let me tell you," she added in a rueful aside. "Let's get some drinks for everyone, first."

Eve started to follow Astrid inside, but flicked a glance at Dom that was vaguely amused, as though she was conveying that she expected an interrogation and was willing to be a sport about it.

Dom watched her go, protective hackles raised, but also something more possessive. A voice in his head protested, *Evie is mine*. He didn't know where it came from. A lifetime of being on the periphery, he supposed.

Which was where he liked to be, he reminded himself, but that exclusion didn't sit as well this time. It was so disconcerting, he made himself move into the pool house to get changed.

"This invitation probably feels like a setup," Astrid said once she and Eve were settled on the loungers watching the men play with the children in the pool. "It is a little. When my sister called to tell me Dom was married, and to who, and that you were honeymooning here, she said, 'You have to invite them over and get the scoop.'"

Eve couldn't help her wistful smile. "I always wanted sisters. I love my brothers, but they're so much older, they've never really felt like confidantes."

"I used to think brothers were just harder to be close to, then I met Jevaun's family. You don't realize how dysfunctional your own family is until you meet one that works. They're so tightly knit, it makes me wish…"

Her troubled gaze fixed on Dom. He was helping Jayden balance on his shoulders before he stood up, launching the boy into deeper water.

Eve waited, but Astrid only reached for the glass of lemonade on the table between them.

"So what is the scoop?" Astrid asked. "Obviously, you two met in Australia. We've all read about that."

"I'm not pregnant. I'll quash that rumor before it starts," Eve said drily.

"Oh, that's too bad." Astrid smoothed her sundress over her bump. "I was hoping for more cousins in our mob."

"It really doesn't bother you, that I'm a Visconti?"

"Oh, I had to place an emergency call to my therapist, believe me." She grinned cheekily. "But it was more about me and my relationship with our father. How is your father taking it?"

"I'll let you know when he starts talking to me again." She grimaced, wishing she was joking.

Astrid made a face of sympathy. "Mom is pretty upset, too. But—Did Dom tell you how Dad reacted when Freda came home pregnant at sixteen?"

"She's the one who is a lawyer? He only told me she has a son."

"Yeah, he's great. I love that little man to bits, but it was a whole thing. Dad threw her out and wouldn't let any of us talk to her, but Dom found her a place to live— a nice place—and bought her groceries and paid her doctor bills and yelled at Dad until he came around. But that took years. I was kind of shoved into the eldest sister role and there were so many expectations on me." Her brow furrowed with anguish. "I was genuinely terrified Dad would rather ruin Jevaun than let me marry him so I introduced him to Dom and Dom told Dad that he could keep driving his daughters out of the house or he could smarten up. That's his version. I have no idea how it actually went. All I know is that we had a beautiful wedding and Freda was there. So I absolutely support Dom marrying whoever he wants, but I also know that if Dad were still alive, things would be really hard right now."

"I know," Eve said pensively. "And I won't pretend my family are a bunch of innocent victims. My dad and brothers have fueled the fire at different times, but Dom said your father never really got over losing his brother. That it made him bitter and looking for someone to blame."

"That's such an understatement." A sheen came into Astrid eyes as she looked to the pool again. "Dad was so proud of the fact that he had never hit us. That was his bar of good parenting because his father used to give them the belt. But the way he talked to us and things that he did, they were still abusive. Mom was totally codependent, feeding his moods and opinions so he wouldn't turn on her. I've had eight years of Jevaun and counselling and I was still a nervous wreck that Dom was coming over."

"Really? Why?"

"Because he looks and sounds so much like Dad," Astrid admitted in a pained whisper. "But look at him. My kids think he's the cat's pajamas. They hardly ever see him, but they were so excited he was coming."

Dom was on the diving board, holding Maya's feet so she could do a handstand before toppling backward into the water. He waited while Jevaun boosted her out of the way before he did a flip, making her scream with laughter as his splash swamped her as she clung to the ledge.

"If you're not pregnant, why did you marry him?" Astrid asked. "Is it really just to end the feud? Or something more? Love at first sight? I'm a romantic. Don't hate me."

"I couldn't hate you," Eve said truthfully. Astrid was far too earnest and nice.

But she couldn't look at her, either. All she could see was Dom, four years ago, walking into a club and looking straight at her.

He glanced over now as he came up against the edge of the pool. She felt the same hot arrow pierce her chest.

*Yes*, she thought. *I think that's what it was.* For her, at least.

"Okay?" Dom skimmed closer, maybe reading the conflicted joy that was closing around her like a fist.

Eve nodded and worked up a brave smile. "I'm just explaining to Astrid that being trapped on that island forced us to talk about how the feud was only causing pain on both sides. I suppose we could have tried matching one of your sisters to one of my brothers..." She was joking to deflect from deeper, trickier explanations around why she had agreed to marry him.

*Because I love him.*

Astrid seemed to find the idea of her sisters with a Visconti highly amusing. Her laughter pealed out and the conversation moved to other things.

"That was a fun day," Eve said sincerely as the tender motored them through the dark from Grand Cayman back to the yacht.

"It was," Dom agreed, sounding introspective.

"I was going to arrange a lunch with your mom and mine, to talk about the reception. Astrid suggested I do something similar with Ingrid, so she feels included in the arrangements. She thought that might help smooth the way with her. I wish Dad would get back to me."

Her father's silence, screaming of his sense of betrayal, was eating holes into her gut, especially now that Eve was realizing she'd been in love with Dom for years.

It sounded ridiculous even in her own head. She hadn't known anything about him when they'd met, not even his name. Maybe chemistry *was* what some called love at first sight, but her intense emotional feelings toward Dom were the reason he'd been able to hurt her so deeply by walking away that morning in Budapest. She'd felt *loss*. It had been amplified by the belief they would never have a chance. Ever.

However nascent and illogical that initial infatuation had been, she was learning it had underpinnings of deeper regard. As she came to know him better, she was learning *why* she loved him: because he was patient with children and stood up for his sisters and had overcome what sounded like a really difficult childhood.

She wanted to ask him about that, but a wave of compassion rose in her, one that wanted to hug the boy he'd been—shunted aside and living with the anger of a man his sister was still afraid of. Eve closed her hot eyes, looping her arm across his chest as she savored the weight of his arm across her shoulders. He tightened his hold, snugging her safe and warm against his side while her heart expanded too big for her chest. It hurt to swallow, her emotions were so sharp inside her.

"I shouldn't have said what I did this morning," he said in a low voice. "It's been bothering me all day. It's something my father would have done, trying to put someone in their place by saying something ugly. I don't want that feud between us, Eve. I want it *gone*."

"Me, too," she assured him. "I want us to be like Astrid and Jevaun."

"In what way?" His arm loosened and he looked down at her, expression shuttering.

*In love*. That's what she wanted to say, but she didn't want to set herself up for a stiff dose of reality so she described the love she'd seen between them.

"They're affectionate and trust each other to have their back. They're a team, especially where the kids are concerned. They make each other laugh."

She heard the rumble of acknowledgment in his chest. A frown of consideration settled on his face.

Was she watching him take a prescription for what she wanted out of their marriage and weigh whether he could deliver it?

She didn't know how she felt about that. It fell somewhere between pandering and endearing and made her wonder if he even knew what love *was*?

"Astrid said—" She glanced at the driver of their boat, who seemed far enough away not to hear them over the engine. "She said something about how dysfunctional she thought your family was." Eve didn't know if Dom knew that his sister saw a therapist so she skipped mentioning it. "Is that something you believe, too?"

"Yes." No hesitation.

"Have you ever talked to anyone about it?"

"Like who? Astrid?"

"Or a professional?"

"There's no point. You can't change history."

"But you can reframe how you think and feel about it."

"I don't want to talk about my feelings. I don't want to feel them." He didn't sound disparaging or even self-deprecating, only resolved. "This is what I'm doing about the past." He gave her another squeeze. "That history is over. We're moving forward from here."

*In what way exactly?* she wanted to ask, but they arrived at the yacht. And, because it had been several hours since they'd done so, they went directly to their stateroom to make love.

# CHAPTER FIFTEEN

DOM HAD NICO come to his head office for their first
meeting on the post-nuptial contracts. It wasn't meant
to be a power move. Eve was down the hall, finishing
up her meeting with his hiring team so she would join
them momentarily.

While he had her brother alone, however, he said,
"Your father is ghosting Eve. It's starting to upset her."

"He's angry with me, not her. And they're away, sailing
in the Galapagos with friends. It was planned ages ago,
before this and—" Nico let out a hacked-off sigh. "Dad's
had some specialist appointments lately that haven't gone
as well as he'd hoped. That's confidential," Nico added
with a warning look. "But it's adding stress to this situation that wouldn't have been here otherwise."

"Understood. But is that why your mother hasn't nailed
down a date for the reception?" They'd suggested a date
in November before the holiday parties started, but Ginny
had demurred, something else that was distressing Eve.

"Yes. Dad has a procedure scheduled as soon as he
gets back so they want to see how that goes."

Dom nodded at the assistant who glanced through the
window. She came in with a cart of fresh coffee and trays
of fruit and pastries.

"How long do you think this will take?" Nico eyed the

food. "I thought we'd agree on the high-level points and let our lawyers work out the nitty-gritty."

"Eve's been tied up all morning. She doesn't really eat breakfast."

"She's been like that since she was a kid," Nico said with a shake of his head. "And she runs when she's stressed so she gets too skinny at times. If that's what she's been doing lately then, yeah." He nodded with approval at the cream-filled eclairs and bagels with cream cheese. He waited until the assistant had left to ask, "She's definitely not pregnant?"

"My assistant?" Dom deadpanned. "I haven't asked. I'm not allowed."

"Eve. Obviously."

"Can I give you a word of advice?" Dom was enjoying this. "Don't ask about my sex life with your sister unless you really want to hear about it."

"This is why I'd rather keep hating you," Nico said without heat and helped himself to a cup of coffee.

Dom wasn't just protecting Eve's modesty. She'd been quite desolate to learn on the last day of their honeymoon that she wasn't pregnant. Dom had been surprisingly disappointed himself, not that he'd shared that with her. He hadn't wanted to make her feel worse, as though she'd let him down or anything. He wasn't even sure why he found the idea of having children so appealing. They'd been fresh back from watching the circus that was Astrid and Jevaun's life, which really was a lot of work, but he kept thinking about Eve saying she wanted what they had. The affection and tag team of parenting. The trust.

And there was something very simplistic about spending time with children. They were so unreserved, wrapping their wiry little arms around his neck, secure in the belief he would keep their head above water. He'd enjoyed watching Eve play a game with the toddler when he woke, holding him in her lap while she used the tail of her braid to tickle his arm and hand and cheek, both of them grinning and giggling.

He wanted to give her that. He wanted to give her everything she asked for if it would make her smile like that.

A sensation of the floor shifting beneath him struck, as though he stood on the tip of a diving board, toes curled on the edge, muscles gathering to jump and flip.

"Here she is," Nico said as Eve came through the door in a whirl of energy that pushed him into the deep end without any grace at all. Just a big, unexpected plunge with an accompanying rush in his ears and a loss of his breath.

"Hi." She hugged her brother very briefly, gaze on the table. "Oh, my God. Thank you. I'm starving." She came around the table to Dom. She clasped his arm and rose on her toes to kiss the corner of his mouth. "Seriously. You're my absolute hero for this."

She took the chair he held for her and began filling a plate from the tray, oblivious to the fact he felt punched in the face for no reason whatsoever. He didn't even know what had happened to him a moment ago. Low blood sugar, maybe?

"How did the meeting go?" Dom asked her as he and Nico also sat.

"Good. I'm leaning toward the London project, but we can talk later about how that would fit with your schedule. Why isn't Dad calling me back?" she asked Nico abruptly.

"They're sailing—"

"Oh. The Galapagos. Right. Mom was looking forward

to that. Tsk. Okay, we can cover family stuff later, too." She waved. "You two talk business while I eat."

They did, discovering quickly that they were mostly on the same page, even sharing the same concerns over how much they should integrate the two companies.

"You should put together a task force," Eve interjected. "Jackson would be a good lead, which might not be your first choice, if you're worried about bias," she acknowledged in Dom's direction. "But you want someone with attention to detail, who will keep you out of trouble with the FTC, but could find where the alignments would reduce costs versus where the individual branding is an advantage."

Dom looked to Nico.

Nico knew exactly what he was thinking and said, "I don't hate the idea."

"Of Jackson?" Eve looked up from her plate of fruit.

"Of you." Dom sent a patronizing glance at Nico. "This is what happens when you hold someone back. They lose sight of how much value they bring to a given situation."

"*Me?* I'm biased on both sides," Eve argued.

"Exactly," Dom said. "You'd want what's right for the whole, not one or the other. We'd need committees on both boards to provide arm's length oversight."

"Agreed. In fact, we can allocate a budget and let her run it as a consultant so she's not on either payroll. She could hire her own team to evaluate and make recommendations." Nico nodded. "But no more digs about how I can't see her potential."

"Sorry, Dom." Eve's hand came to rest on his. "Needling my brother over his colossal shortsightedness falls under my purview."

"I defer to your expert knowledge on that front." He

shared an amused smirk with her and pinched her fingers into his palm.

"Are you two having fun?" Nico asked with heavy sarcasm. "*Would* you be interested in running a team like that?"

"You know..." Eve nodded. "I think I would."

Eve was settling into something that felt a lot like marital bliss.

She hadn't started working yet. She had hired an agency to work out the structure of her consultation proposal and they were being absolute sharks about it. That was earning her good-natured complaining from both Dom and Nico about the cost, but there was rueful approval in those remarks, too.

The negotiations on the post-nuptial agreement were going smoothly, but the reception date was still in the air while she waited for her parents to return from their trip.

In the meanwhile, Eve had lunch with Ingrid and two more of Dom's sisters. Dom had wanted to come with her, acting so protective she couldn't help loving him a little bit more, but she'd finally reminded him, "I can stand up to you, can't I? Are you really worried I can't handle her?"

With a grumble, he acknowledged Eve was a "pretty tough cookie" and let her go alone.

Thanks to Astrid paving the way, it hadn't been too painful. His sisters were stilted, but Eve had the sense Ingrid's presence kept them from being as welcoming as they might have been if she hadn't been there.

Ingrid came across as cold and self-centered, but she also struck Eve as someone who lived in fear. Fear of being irrelevant, fear of losing what she had, fear of being judged. Eve left feeling sorry for her and the children who had to bear the weight of all that insecurity.

At least Ingrid had promised to put together a guest list which told her she was willing to attend. It was small progress, but progress all the same.

Finally, Eve's parents returned home. They stayed in the Martha's Vineyard house for a couple of nights to recover, then came into the city the day before her father's procedure was scheduled.

Eve invited them to the penthouse for an early dinner. She kept the menu light, conscious of the fact her father would have to fast before his surgery tomorrow.

"You're nervous," Dom noted, stilling her hand as she tremblingly shifted a butter knife two millimeters—as though its position would affect the outcome of this meeting.

"This is a lot bigger than Daddy's Little Girl marrying the town bad boy. I know you're ready to let bygones be bygones, but I'm not sure he is and that puts me in the middle."

"I would never ask you to choose between us, Evie." He rubbed her arm through the soft wool sweater she wore over tailored blue trousers. "You asked me once how our marriage would bridge the divide. You're it. You're the bridge."

"I hope that doesn't mean I get walked all over," she said wryly.

"No." He cradled the side of her face in a warm hand. "You're one of those feats of engineering that everyone marvels at because they thought it was impossible."

"Your poetic turn of phrase is a marvel," she teased, starting to lean into him, lifting her smiling mouth to invite a kiss.

The elevator sounded and she abruptly pulled back, then ran her suddenly clammy hands down her hips. They moved to greet her parents as they came out.

"Mom. Dad." Eve hugged each of them, feeling their stiffness as she did. "Have you two ever actually met Dom?"

"No." Her father stared coldly at her husband while he ignored the hand that Dom started to offer. "Nico said this was your choice. Is that true?" her father asked her bluntly.

"Romeo," her mother murmured.

"Yes," Eve answered firmly. "Come in. Let's talk." She waved toward the lounge.

Her father didn't move. He flicked his gaze around and shook his head. "This isn't right."

"Dad. Dom isn't his father. I know you had—"

"You *don't* know," he near shouted, making her jump.

"Let's keep this civil." Dom touched Eve's elbow and stepped forward so she was shielded half a step behind him.

"We're still out of sorts from travel," Ginny excused, earning a glare from Romeo.

"My mother would tan my hide for this." Her father's eyes dampened. "She refused to marry a Blackwood and I cannot believe Nico made you do it instead. We have options, Lina. I don't blame Nico for the mistakes he made. No one has a crystal ball, but he never should have pressured you to fix the problems he created. We'll restructure. You don't have to do this."

"Dad." She felt Dom's hand tighten on her arm. "It's done. We're married. Happily." Mostly.

"Don't lie to me."

"I'm not. I—" She looked up at her husband, not having expected to tell him like this, but she let the words spill past her lips. "I love Dom. I have since the first time we met."

His expression only stiffened further, which put a coil of tension into her belly. His cheek ticked.

Oh, no. He didn't welcome her feelings. A chill entered her chest, one that warned her she'd made a horrible mistake.

"And you?" Romeo challenged Dom. "Do you love my daughter? Is that why you married her?"

Dom took his time answering, jaw working as though he was looking for the right words.

"If you're asking me if I married her as an act of revenge, the answer is no. The feud no longer exists. Not in this house. If you're still carrying it, you should take it elsewhere."

She gasped, as did her mother, but Dom wasn't finished.

"Eve can come to you anytime she likes," he continued. "I told her I wouldn't ask her to choose between us and I meant it, but I won't fight you for her. I won't fight you. Not anymore."

"That doesn't answer my question," her father pressed.

"Romeo." Ginny touched his arm.

"You're really going to stay here?" her father demanded of Eve, eyes wet with outrage and disappointment. "Married to a man who doesn't love you?"

*You don't love Mom,* she bit back saying.

She was trying to keep this from devolving into something that none of them could come back from. Trying to keep from dissolving into tears when she was being forced to face that her husband didn't return her love.

She was hurt enough that she easily could have gone home with her parents and crawled into her old bed and cried for a week, but that's what an immature version of herself would do. She was a woman who had made a decision for herself that had far-reaching consequences, but she was willing to live with them.

"It's a good match, Dad." That felt like such a weak thing to say in the face of what he wanted for her. She was both shaken and touched that he did want more for her, but, "This is good for both families. You know it is. I can't walk away from it now."

"That's what I keep telling him," her mother murmured. "It's done and we need to accept it."

"You don't deserve her," her father said in quiet thunder at Dom before he turned to press the button for the elevator. It was still there so the doors opened immediately.

"Dad." Eve's heart lurched as he stepped into the car.

"I'll talk to him," her mother promised as she stepped into the elevator with him.

"I'll come to the hospital tomorrow and sit with you," Eve promised her mother while her father looked through her as though she was dead to him.

The doors closed and they were gone.

"Eve—" Dom tried to turn her to face him, but his touch burned past her skin, into the marrow of her bones.

"I want to go for a run. Please?" She pressed against his chest, refusing his touch.

He nodded curtly and released her.

# CHAPTER SIXTEEN

WHEN AN HOUR had passed and Eve was still pounding the treadmill as though she was carrying a message from the battlefield, Dom made her stop.

"Shower, then come eat," he urged her. He didn't have much appetite himself so he wasn't surprised when she only picked at the beautiful meal she'd arranged for her parents.

"Eve," he tried again as he topped up her wineglass.

"I don't want to talk." Her hollow-eyed gaze met his. "I'm going to pull a Dom and ignore my emotions, okay?"

He prided himself on keeping his emotions on the surface, rarely feeling anything at a deep level, but that rang through him with the agony of a broken bone.

He kept hearing her say, *I love Dom. I have since the first time we met.*

That seemed impossible. It made him angry because... He didn't know why it tripped his wires. Guilt? Because it made him feel as though he fell short? Or because he didn't believe her?

Evie didn't lie to him.

But she couldn't love him. Why would she? His heart was as empty as his father's and his father's father. If he was lovable, his life would have been different.

Wouldn't it?

When Eve went to bed, he came into the bedroom with her.

"Not tonight, okay?" Eve flashed him a glance as she hurried to put on silk pajamas. "I—"

"I just want to hold you, Evie." It was the rawest, most needy thing he'd ever said.

After a charged moment, she nodded jerkily.

A few minutes later, they were in the dark, under the covers. She curled into his chest as he drew her into him. He felt all her hurt radiate out of her and soak into him. It was hellish, especially when he realized the small shudders rolling through her were sobs.

Every breath he took burned his lungs. He had never felt so helpless in his life, but he cuddled and coddled her, so damned grateful that she let him pet her and kiss her hair, and said, "Shh. We'll get through this. I promise."

He didn't know how, though. That kept him wide awake most of the night, long after she finally relaxed into sleep.

He lurched awake when he realized she was up and dressed in skinny jeans and a cable-knit pullover. She was brushing her hair and fastening it into a low ponytail.

"Where are you going?" He came up on an elbow.

"To sit with Mom at the hospital," she reminded him.

"Eve—I know you don't want to talk. I don't know what to say," he admitted, sitting up. "I hope you know that I care about you. I don't want to disappoint you. I want you to be happy in this marriage."

"I know. It's okay, Dom. It really is." She sat on the bench at the foot of the bed with her back to him as she zipped knee-high boots over her jeans. "I just find it hypocritical of Dad to worry about whether you love me when he and Mom didn't marry for love. They care about each other a lot, I know they do. It's the same way you care about my well-being so Dad knows that's not a bad reason to marry. It has served them really well and gave us a stable, privileged upbringing. I don't have anything to complain about. I'm lucky to have what they have. I know that."

Was she trying to convince herself? Because he felt sick at how bland that sounded. It sounded as though he was forcing her to settle when one of the things that made Evie the amazing woman she was, was her belief in herself and her own worth.

"You said yourself that I want to believe love is magic and can cure anything. You're right. I do. And I know that's unrealistic. I don't expect you to love me, Dom. I don't expect anything more from you than what we already have." She rose.

"I'll come have breakfast with you." He started to throw off the covers.

"I'll get something later. And you have that meeting with the London team. I'll text you once I have news."

By the time he was dressed and down the stairs, she was already gone.

*Damn it.*

He was pacing restlessly, wondering if he should go to the hospital, when his doorman rang to say that Astrid was downstairs.

"Is everything all right?" he asked as she came off the elevator with Adio in her arms. They both wore speckles of rain and big smiles.

Astrid's cheerfulness quickly faded. "Is this a bad time? I was going to text from the pediatrician's, to make sure Eve still wanted to have coffee, but—"

"She probably forgot." Dom took the baby because he

was kicking off his boots. He set the boy on his socked feet and took his wet jacket, following him as he took off into the lounge. "Eve's parents are back from their trip and her father had a procedure at the hospital today. She's gone to sit with her mother, to wait for news."

"Why aren't you with her?" Astrid asked, pausing in hanging up her own coat.

"She's angry with me. I didn't think she'd want me there."

"Dom." She clunked the hanger onto the rung. "You go anyway. That's how she knows it doesn't matter if she's angry, you'll always be there for her. What happened?"

"I—"

*Don't want to talk about it.*

He didn't. But he kind of did.

Adio had found the piano and was walking his hands across the keys, releasing discordant notes.

"Evie said you said our childhood was dysfunctional."

"Am I wrong?" she asked.

"Honestly, Astrid? How the hell would I know?" he asked with latent frustration. Maybe some unrecognized pain. "I wasn't there." He moved a vase of flowers off the coffee table and set it where Adio couldn't reach it. "My childhood didn't look that different from the rest of the boys at school. Plenty of them had parents who were divorced so…"

"My parents were married," she said gently. "It was still a train wreck."

"I know." He scratched his eyebrow. "Have you ever talked to anyone about it? Like, a professional?"

"Weekly, for the last eight years." Her tone was blunt as a hammer. "Do you want her number?"

"Maybe." He wanted to be more for Evie. Not just that

weak sauce version of a marriage where he gave her stability and a few babies. He wanted—"Eve wants us to be like you and Jevaun."

He half expected her to laugh at him, but her brow crinkled in concern. "Do you love her?"

That sense of being on a diving board hit him again, only this time he was on the edge of a towering cliff, waves crashing into razor-sharp rocks below.

He drew a breath that felt like fire. "I don't even know what love is."

"Yes, you do," she said with a throb of despondency in her voice. "It's that thing we wanted from Dad and never got. That sense that it's okay to be vulnerable. I know it's scary to feel that way, Dom. But how do you think she feels if you don't love her? She's carrying around that same sense of not measuring up."

The pain that hit his chest was so visceral and sharp, Dom tried to rub it away with the heel of his hand. He couldn't stand for Eve to feel that cold and hollow. He would do anything to spare her. *Anything*.

"Pool?" Adio said, stretching to try to reach the latch.

Dom absently picked him up and said, "It's too cold for swimming." He opened the door so the wind gusted into their faces.

Adio cuddled into his shoulder. "Brr."

"Brr," Dom repeated. "That's right." He closed the door and rubbed the boy's narrow back. "Come visit when it's summer. Then we'll swim. Right now, I have to go see Auntie Evie."

"Abby Ebie."

"Exactly. Go put your boots on." He set the boy on his feet and Adio toddled to his boots.

"Thanks, Astrid." He could hardly look at her, finding that expression on her face too knowing, as though she saw all the way through him.

"Oh, you." She hurried across and hugged him.

He wrapped his arms around her shoulders and squeezed, compressing the abraded sensations in his chest, but when he released her, they weren't as bad as they'd been.

"It's like hugging a balloon animal," he said to cover how thin-skinned he felt.

"I dare you to say that to Eve once she's pregnant."

A stab of wistfulness pierced his chest. Would she still want that? Now that he understood how badly he'd hurt her, he didn't know how he'd make it up to her.

"I really like her, you know," Astrid said as she helped Adio with his jacket. "I can't help thinking you two were supposed to happen. Like it was fate or something."

"You know you sound like a hippie when you talk like that?" He held her coat for her. "But I think that's one of your most lovable qualities," he added, squeezing her shoulders.

"Nice save." She turned to face him. "Let me know how it goes, okay?"

"I will." Then he did the unthinkable and took the initiative to hug her again.

"What are you doing here?" Eve's heart lurched as Dom walked into the private waiting lounge at the hospital. "I thought you had a video chat with the team in London this morning?"

"I rescheduled. And brought brunch." He began unpacking the two cloth bags onto the small dining table, setting out pastries, yogurt parfaits and egg sandwiches.

"That was thoughtful of you." Ginny took a parfait and a spoon. "Thank you."

"I'll have one in a little while, thanks," Eve said, shaking her head when he offered one. She didn't mention there were ample meals available at the press of a button. This hospital catered to very wealthy patients. They ensured the comfort of families and caregivers during times of duress. "You don't have to stay," she added as he took off his overcoat. "It will be at least another hour, maybe two."

"I'd like to." He left his coat on a hook by the door. "Unless you'd rather I didn't?" His expression shuttered.

"No, you can if you want to. It's just that…" She hadn't expected this of him. She was incredibly touched and searched his eyes, wondering what had prompted this. Basic decency? Or something more?

The longer she looked into his whiskey-colored eyes, the more her heart felt pinched.

"Oh. Right." She remembered as Jackson walked in and came up short at the sight of Dom. "My brothers are coming."

"Traffic was terrible," Nico said as he came in behind Jackson and stepped around him. He nodded at them, then asked their mother, "Any news?"

"Not yet. Where's Christo?" Ginny set aside her parfait and stood.

"Chatting up a nurse, where do you think?" Nico kissed her cheek then came to peruse the food.

Jackson hadn't moved or spoken. In looks, he was a clone of Nico with more polish and style. Where Nico stuck to never-fail basics like a well-tailored, three-piece suit, Jackson wore things like striped trousers and chunky cardigans over a blue pullover and a winter scarf. They all would have teased him endlessly over his love of fashion if he didn't always look so effortlessly sophisticated.

He was still holding Dom's stare. Dom hadn't moved, either. Not one blink.

"Jackson." Ginny approached him. "It's good to see you."

"You too, Mom." He had to break the stare first to kiss her cheek, then lifted his head to say to Dom, "Let's go outside and talk."

"Oh, grow up," Eve muttered. "I married Dom to end the feud, not start a fresh one."

Christo came in wearing a fawn-colored coat over a black turtleneck and jeans. He frowned at Dom. "What are you doing here?"

"He's being a supportive husband." Eve was embarrassed by how rude they were.

"Is that what you're calling him? I thought this was a strategic alliance." Jackson curled his lip at Nico, apparently not confining his disgust to Dom and Eve.

"Maybe that is all I am to him," Eve said starkly, stepping forward to get in Jackson's face. "That's better than being his enemy. And maybe one of you could have 'made a strategic alliance' by now, instead of clinging to bachelorhood like you're Peter Pan and don't have any responsibilities to this family yourself."

They all had the grace to look away while Ginny said, "Eve, please. Can we have some peace while we're here?"

"Eve is more than a strategic alliance to me." Dom set the weight of his hands on her shoulders. His steady presence became a bolstering wall at her back. "If you want to hate me for marrying her, go ahead, but don't take it out on her. Not when Eve is creating peace for all of us. For me."

He squeezed her shoulders and she looked up, moved by the depth of emotion she found in his eyes. His expression was so tender, her heart swooped.

"When I'm with you, the battle stops. Everything inside me settles. That's worth everything to me."

Because he felt safe? Loved? The pinch in her heart clenched harder, but it felt oddly good, too. It wasn't being compressed. It was breaking past a thin shell, opening like a flower.

She covered one of the hands on her shoulder.

"You're acting like I'm asking you to surrender." Dom lifted his gaze to her brothers. "This marriage is a truce. Accept it."

"I have," Nico said gravely. "And I appreciate what you've done, Lina. Really. We *all* appreciate it," he said with a significant glower at her brothers.

Christo rolled his eyes and Jackson gave a discontented shrug as they both offered their hands.

"Congratulations on your marriage," Christo said.

"Look after her," Jackson added.

"I intend to," Dom vowed with such sincerity, hot tears of hope pressed behind her eyes.

"Dad was upset he didn't get to walk me down the aisle," Eve told Dom when they arrived back at the penthouse. "At least, that's what he said. He was pretty loopy from the anesthetic, but I think it was true."

She hoped it was also true that he loved her and only wanted her to be happy. She'd shed tears of relief all the way home because she thought he must be speaking from the heart, without his normal filter, and it gave her so much hope.

Dom took her coat, not saying anything.

Her glow of optimism dimmed. With her father's procedure successful and out of the way, their conflict from last night returned to sit between them like a coiled rattlesnake.

"Eve—"

"No, Dom, look. I'm fine. Honestly. I was upset last night because of the way Dad reacted. You've never lied to me about how you feel and—"

"You said you loved me from the first time we met," he interjected. "Why didn't you tell me sooner? Why did you tell your father instead of me?"

"Because—Because I didn't want to push you into saying something you don't feel. And because you make me feel raw and naked and like I'm waiting for you to notice me and want me and like me. Thank you for saying what you did at the hospital. It goes a long way, it really does, but can you at least show me a little pity? It's *hard* to love you."

He drew a sharp breath, head jerking back.

"Not because you're hard to love," she rushed to clarify. "You're so easy to love, Dom. You deserve to be loved. That's something I knew in here before I knew up here." She tapped her chest, then her temple. "I was so caught up in the feud, I didn't know I was falling for you. I only knew I shouldn't feel anything toward you except hatred. I knew that's all you felt toward me and that hurt, Dom. You don't know what it's like to love someone who resents you and—"

"Do I not?" he shot back. His voice wasn't loud, but it was so powerful, she felt it like thunder in her chest.

"W-what?"

"I didn't know what it was, either. How could I? I've never felt it. Yes, there was some weak version of it from my mother and my sisters, but it was drowned out by my father's nastiness and Ingrid's spite. All I knew was that I'd met a woman who was some kind of supercharged metal and I was a magnet that couldn't stay away. God, Evie." He ran his hand down his face. "It was hell to be apart from you. When I left you in Australia, I thought I was going to be sick. I tried to hate you, I did, but I couldn't even work up hatred for your family anymore. I just wanted you, damn it. I *need* you. I know that doesn't make sense, but..."

"It makes sense. I feel that way, too. So what is the 'but'?" She came close enough to pick up his hands. She held them close in the nook of her neck while she searched the tortured amber of his eyes. "I'm not trying to hurt you by making you say anything you don't feel, Dom. But I want to show you that it's okay. That I'm right here and it's safe. We have each other's back. We don't lie to each other. If you say it, I'm going to believe you and we are going to be stronger than we ever thought possible."

Her lips were quivering so hard, it was hard to talk. This was a huge chance on her part to say that. She was reaching for the thing she had always wanted and clenched her hands tighter on his, feeling as though she might shatter if this didn't go the way she hoped. But she needed all of him. Not the muffled, opaque shell, but the man inside. His heart.

"How is it so terrifying to say when it doesn't even express what I feel? I do love you, Evie." He flinched as though bracing for a blow, but a sudden brightness entered his gaze. His expression turned tender and a slow smile began to pull at his lips. "I didn't know it would feel like that. I love you so hard I'm afraid I'll break you with it."

"Impossible." She released his hands and stepped

into his arms, lifting her lips. "Our love is the healing kind. The kind that ends wars and builds kingdoms and changes history."

"You're changing *me*," he said as his mouth found hers. "I feel good. Hopeful."

"Loved?"

"Yes." His damp gaze met hers very briefly before he closed his eyes.

She cradled his face, allowing that small shield because this was new and delicate and deserved to be treated gently. She pressed her mouth to his, whispering, "It's okay. We don't have to talk right now. We can show each other how we feel."

He groaned and pulled her into a strong embrace. His kiss deepened, but stayed reverent and so imbued with emotion, she felt tears dampen her lashes.

They shed their clothes between kisses on the way to their bedroom, sliding between the sheets while gray skies hung low and fall rains gusted against the windows. They sheltered each other and warmed skin with hot kisses and kindled passion with the brush of thigh to thigh, belly to belly, chest to chest. They kissed soft and sweet and long and deep and then the flames caught for real, the way they always did, engulfing them in a bonfire that would burn them to ashes so they could arise anew.

When his body joined with hers, they both groaned in relief and stared in wonder at the other. She caressed his cheek and he brushed her hair off her brow and set a tender kiss there.

"Do you think we were destined to meet?" she asked him.

"Maybe it was just a very lucky coincidence. More than one."

"Despite the odds."

"Exactly." He withdrew and returned, making them both shake.

"It's so good."

"I know. Always." He did it again and her eyelids fluttered in pleasure.

He made a gratified noise. "Are you going to shatter for me, Evie? And let me watch you and feel it and know I give you this?"

A latent pang of exposure struck, but it faded as quickly as it arrived. She had no need to feel threatened by him. By this. Of all the places in the world, she was safest when she was in his arms.

"Yes," she said on a languid groan, nibbling his chin. "I have no secrets from you. No defenses left."

Emotions flickered across his face—satisfaction and tenderness and acknowledgment of the daunting power he held over her.

He slid his fingertip along her bottom lip and said, "Then you'll do the same to me, because you're my perfect match in every way, aren't you?"

"I am and I will," she promised as she ran her hand into his hair and brought his mouth down to his, urging him with the tilt of her hips to take her to paradise.

He did.

# EPILOGUE

*Two years later...*

EVE HAD A lot of sympathy for Nonna Maria these days. Astrid and her four children had left yesterday and she was still sweeping sand out of the kitchen.

"He needs a top-up before he goes to bed," Dom said, coming in with Oliver.

Their three-month-old son was pushing one little arm against Dom's shoulder. The other fist was in his mouth. He was gumming it vigorously, but he squawked when he caught sight of her.

"He had a really big diaper and a really big burp, then he turned into a lamprey when he found the skin on my arm. I'll finish that." He took the broom as she took the baby.

"Are you having a growth spurt?" she asked her son as she rubbed her nose to his. She was drowning in so much love for him, and the husband who watched her with such an indulgent look on his face, it was silly.

The September evening was mild and the sky was painted every shade from gold to rose to indigo. She stepped outside to sit on the swing and kick it into motion while she nursed. Oliver got down to business straightaway, but he was ready for bed so his eyelids began to droop very quickly.

She breathed the fresh air, soaking up this perfect moment because they were heading back to New York in a few days and even though she was technically on maternity leave, she was still very involved with all the structural changes Dom and Nico were implementing.

"It's our anniversary tomorrow," she said when Dom sat down and stretched his arm behind her.

"You keep saying you have baby brain, but you do know it's not April, don't you? There were tulips in the park when we had our photos done, remember?"

How could she forget? Their wedding reception had turned into five hundred guests witnessing them renew their vows. She'd worn an extravagant gown as Romeo had walked her down the aisle. Her mother had shed happy tears in the front row and Maya had been in seventh heaven as the flower girl. Even Ingrid had said a few kind words when all the toasts were made, right before they cut into the five-tiered cake.

The feud was over and everyone had turned out to celebrate that fact.

"Not our third anniversary," she chided him. "Our second. Our first was Budapest…"

"Oh. Now I'm embarrassed." He showed her an empty hand. "I didn't get you anything to mark the occasion."

"You can make it up to me once he's down for the night."

"Oh?" A slow smile crept across his lip and his voice dipped into that sexy one that made her tingle all over. "How do you suggest I do that?"

"I was thinking we could play 'stranded on a tropical island.'"

"Evie Blackwood," he said in a mock outrage. "You are a woman after my own heart, aren't you?"

"I thought it was already mine?"

"It absolutely is," he assured her warmly as he nuzzled his lips into her neck.

\* \* \* \* \*

*If you couldn't put down* Marrying The Enemy
*then why not dive into these dramatic other stories
by Dani Collins?*

A Baby To Make Her His Bride
Awakened On Her Royal Wedding Night
The Baby His Secretary Carries
The Secret Of Their Billion-Dollar Baby
Her Billion-Dollar Bump

*Available now!*

# STOLEN PRINCESS'S SECRET

KELLY HUNTER

MILLS & BOON

# PROLOGUE

'I'M GOING TO be a falconer when I grow up,' said Claudia, as she watched Tomas offered a sliver of meat to the fierce-eyed peregrine falcon perched on a stand in front of them. 'Just like you.'

'No, you're not,' he corrected, as he curled a soft leather strap around one of the falcon's narrow legs—its metatarsus, his father called it. The falcon, Lolo, was Tomas's first imprint, hand raised by him, and he tended her with every care. His father—the King's Falconer—made sure of it. Tomas gave his second bit of meat to Claudia—positioning it in her little leather-gloved hand *just so* and making sure she held her arm out properly so that Lolo could take it from her with ease. 'You're not allowed.'

'Because I'm a girl?'

'Because you're a princess. Princesses don't get to be falconers.' His eleven-year-old soul was sure of it.

'They do too!'

If he turned, he would see eyes as fierce as any falcon's glaring at him, golden for the most part with a wide rim of dark green around the edges. Those eyes would be accusing, so he kept his attention on Lolo. First, he fastened the anklets and then the jesses—crafted from a soft brown leather that he'd chosen from the pile and cut into shape beneath his father's watchful gaze. The points were as perfect as he could make them, the greased leather as soft as could possibly be. 'Maybe some of the time you can do falconry,' he allowed. 'In between the princessing.'

'Will *you* be my falconer?' she asked.

'That's the plan.' Both his father and grandfather had been falconers to the royal family of Byzenmaach. 'If I'm good enough.'

'You will be.'

She had a lot of confidence for a little kid. Maybe that was why the birds liked her. She wasn't afraid of their sharp beaks or claws or the fact that above all they were hunters. But she was still careful in their presence—doing exactly what she was told or shown to do, no matter if it was Tomas doing the telling or his father. She looked to him for guidance, and that made him feel big and strong and smart.

Maybe that was why he liked it so much when the little princess gave her tutors the slip and came to visit the falcons.

'There. All done,' he told Lolo. 'Look at you with your new jesses.' She was strong and swift and bred for racing. 'Maybe one day I'll take you to Saudi Arabia to compete in the time trials and you'll win a fine fortune.'

'Can I come too?' Claudia asked. 'What will you do with a fine fortune?'

'Nothing, because it won't be mine.'

'You are correct,' said the gravelly voice of his father from behind them. 'As much as any bird can be owned, these ones belong to the Crown, along with any prize money they may win.' His gaze fell to Claudia. 'Your governess is looking for you. Again.'

'I guess that means she's awake,' Claudia muttered, her golden eyes downcast. She didn't see the fleeting amusement that crossed his father's face, but Tomas did. His father was a stern man, no point thinking otherwise. But he was fair and never cruel, and there was none better when it came to gaining the trust of wounded animals. He had the touch.

Tomas badly wanted to have the touch too.

'I will escort you into her care,' his father rumbled. 'Tomas, prep enclosure three for incoming when you've finished here.'

Enclosure three was one of their bigger aviaries. 'What are we getting?'

'A mated pair of Steppe eagles.'

'Oh, wow! They're really rare.'

'Indeed.' His father favoured them with one of his rare smiles. 'So put Lolo away and get to work.'

'Yes, Father. Bye, Cl—' His father's quick frown stopped him mid-name. He'd had that lecture about knowing his place and not taking liberties with the young princess's friendship way too many times to want to hear it again. 'Bye, Princess.'

'Are the Steppe eagles coming today?' she asked. 'Do they have names? What do they look like?'

'You will see them tomorrow if your father wills it.' His father spared a meaningful glance for Tomas. 'King Leonidas and his hunting party arrive this evening. I've let the stable master know.'

Tomas nodded and secured Lolo to her stand. King Leonidas was a cruel man with a vicious temper and a swift arm—especially when he held a riding crop in hand. There were a dozen brood mares grazing the lower valley that would need to go into hiding in the mountains, because what the King did not see he could not ruin. The mares would stay hidden until the King departed, and then Tomas and his father would fly falcons with trailing green ribbon tied to their right legs to signal the all-clear for the stable hands staying with the mares to bring them back down.

Tomas hoped the King and his hunting party didn't stay long.

The light in the little princess's eyes had dimmed at the mention of her father. She too would be kept out of sight during his visit. 'Bye, Tomas, bye, Lolo.' The little girl gave a stiff wave, no bravery left in her, just fear.

His father always told him to make sure an animal felt safe, not scared. It was the biggest rule of all, so how come it never seemed to apply to *this* little girl?

He stepped forward, avoiding his father's gaze as he leaned to whisper in her ear, 'Remember that secret place I showed you?' The secret room in the fortress wall that he'd made his own with candles and hay bales and borrowed blankets and his collection of pretty feathers in an old clay vase. 'Go there if you need to and I'll find you. I'll never rat you out.'

Her lips tightened even as her eyes grew shiny with tears, and then she nodded, once, and flung her arms around his middle and hugged him hard before turning away.

Tomas met his father's hard gaze and squared his shoulders as Claudia set out for the castle. 'She's scared.'

'She has a brother. And a mother. And they are much better placed to withstand a king's wrath than you.' His father's hand on his shoulder was firm. 'You can't encourage her to come to you for comfort, do you understand?'

'Because she's a princess?'

'That, and because if you fall foul of the King, no one will be able to protect you from his wrath. Not even me.'

He shrugged away from his father's hand in a rare display of defiance. It wasn't right for Claudia to be so scared of her father. It wasn't right for her mother to lie in bed day after day and let her children bear an evil king's *wrath*. He didn't even know what the word wrath meant, but he knew what *he* meant whenever he thought of King Leonidas. Vicious, like some of the wild eagles in their care. Vicious and angry and impossible to understand.

'Why can't we ask if Princess Claudia can come here more often and help us with the birds? It would keep her out of sight, just like with the mares. She could imprint one of the peregrine fledglings as part of her lessons, and then she can be here with us more without having to sneak away. What's wrong with that? Can we at least ask for that?'

'You've far too much of your mother in you. Soft-hearted.'

Tomas's mother had died years ago from a blood cancer that had taken her within weeks of finding out she was sick. Tomas *liked* the thought of being a lot like her. She'd given great hugs and laughed when his hair refused to stay flat. She'd made his father smile and laugh the way no one else ever had. It wasn't wrong to be soft-hearted like her, surely.

'It's just not right that no one keeps a little kid *safe*. Please, Father. Can you ask if she can imprint one of the eyas? It's not a *bad* idea.'

His father bent down until he was at eye level. Hope filled Tomas's body, his soft heart and probably his puppy eyes, as his father nodded slowly. 'I'll try. But you have to promise to leave this to me, understand? You say nothing about wanting to protect her and this being a way to do so. You stay out of trouble and out of sight if her father comes hovering.'

'I promise.' Tomas nodded as hard and as fast as he could.

Days later, his father won permission for Claudia to take falconry lessons, and for a while Tomas's plan worked a treat.

But good intentions didn't always win against evil deeds.

In the end, none of Tomas's fine plans had been enough to keep the little princess safe.

# CHAPTER ONE

THERE WAS NOTHING unusual about the cool summer day with the bluest of skies and a fickle wind that ruffled feathers and whipped at his canvas coat. It was just another day in the life of Tomas Sokolov as he stood on the highest battlement of an ancient mountain fortress, with a hawk on his arm. He was the King's Falconer, and he'd been born to this blessed life and he wouldn't have it any other way.

Not for him the life of a nobleman with all its responsibilities and fancy trappings. He didn't particularly like people—apart from one or two who had slipped beneath his skin as a child, and he wasn't drawn to power. Or maybe it was more that when he stepped up to train his eagles and falcons and anything else that came his way, his will was absolute and he liked that a little bit too much. Tomas the tyrant, the dictator, the autocrat. Maybe he *was* drawn to power after all.

Byzenmaach, his homeland, had already seen far too much of that.

But old King Leonidas had passed, and the rule of King Casimir was upon them, and Tomas had no beef with Cas. Better a pragmatic statesman at the helm than a petty madman. Alliances were being built. Prosperity beckoned like a promise. All good, very good, and none of it his responsibility. He had no cause for complaint.

So why, on this fine and perfectly normal afternoon, was he up here looking to the north where the narrow mountain pass brought visitors down onto the plain? Why did restless anticipation ride him so hard?

The hawk knew what was coming her way—the freedom of flight and the hunting of prey. He untethered her, enjoying the look of fierce anticipation in her eyes as she sat perched on his gauntlet.

'Are you ready?' he murmured. 'Maybe you can tell me what's out there.'

Wolves or wolverine, brown bear.

Something.

'What are you doing?'

He didn't need to look over the parapet to know who he would find down there, but he did it anyway. 'You're back.'

At seven years old, young Sophia, newfound daughter of King Casimir, was almost a replica of her late aunt Claudia. She'd been conceived during a brief fling and had spent the first-six years of her life growing up as a normal kid with no knowledge of her father at all. The way Cas told it, he'd certainly had no knowledge of his daughter. Only after Cas had come for her and become engaged to her mother had young Sophia begun to live a life of royalty. Tomas often wondered whether she even liked her new life or whether she missed her old one. Did she enjoy her gilded cage?

She had Claudia's eyes—those remarkable golden eyes ringed with greeny-grey—along with a child's endless curiosity and tendency to roam the winter fortress with a pair of wolfhounds at her side. She was a sweet child and a bright one, and it wasn't her fault that Tomas could barely look at her without being swamped by unwanted memories of her aunt.

No matter how hard he tried to avoid her, ignore her, and—to his shame—be downright curt with her, she would seek him out. He'd vowed to be kinder and there was no time like the present. Steeling himself, he attempted to assemble his face into something resembling a smile. 'I'm about to fly a hawk. Where are your guards?'

Fortunately, the King was as rabidly protective of his daughter as Tomas could ever hope for. Round-the-clock security had become the norm for those living in and around the winter fortress. Tomas swiftly picked out two heavily armed guards with eyes on the child—one over by the stable door, the other stalking the battlements of the outer wall. There would be a third guard nearby, even if Tomas had yet to sight him.

A heavily armed man stepped out of the shadow of the wall and sketched a brief salute. He was new, and Tomas didn't trust new faces. He was young too. Fresh-faced warriors packed with youthful overconfidence were the worst. 'Master Falconer, may we join you?' he asked.

'If you must.' He sighed as Sophia and her guard made a race towards the outer stairs. It wasn't Sophia's fault Claudia had been snatched away as a child and held for ransom. Claudia's northern captors had wanted a seat at the table when discussing water rights. The King had refused to negotiate and Claudia had died.

Twenty years later, Cas was inviting the northerners to finally join the discussion on water rights and, as far as Tomas could tell, Claudia's death had been for nothing.

Sophia had arrived at his side and was trying to hoist herself up on the grey stone wall for a better view, and,

'No,' he growled. Hell, no, she would not sit up there and wriggle and move and give him a heart attack. He moved a few metres to the left, the hawk still perched on his arm as he pointed with his other arm towards a fat stone wedged against the wall. 'You stand on that, and not one part of you is to overreach the wall. You don't lean against it, you don't rest your elbows on the ledge, you don't stick your head over to see how high up you are. Are we clear?'

'Yes, Master Falconer!' Sophia beamed at him.

Why? Why did she have to beam with delight when he was being so stern?

She looked longingly at the hawk but was smart enough not to try and touch her. 'What's her name?'

He'd never known a child so fixated on names. Okay, that wasn't true. He'd known one other who'd been much the same. 'Carys. She's five years old.'

'Will she come back to us if you let her fly free?'

'She's bonded to me so she should return, but there's also a chance she won't.'

'What happens then?'

'We say goodbye and let her go.' He crouched and rummaged through the pack at his feet for a pair of binoculars. 'Do you know how to use these?'

'Yes!'

He handed them to her just as a high-pitched whistle sounded on the outer battlements. Two more short sharp whistles had guards converging and pointing to the north. Sophia, too, had the binoculars to her eyes and trained towards the north. It probably wouldn't be right to snatch those binoculars back, but only iron-clad control stopped him from doing so regardless.

'There's a lady on a horse,' said Sophia. 'Dressed in,

like, furs. And a man on another horse and two wolf-hounds.'

'Which way are they riding?'

'This way.'

He had the oddest feeling. A thundering in his heart that he couldn't explain.

'Give the master falconer his binoculars back, young-ling,' said the guard. 'And crouch down.'

Tomas had never been more grateful. 'There's a purple silk ribbon in my pack. Find it for me.' Keeping Sophia occupied was only part of that directive. Compulsion rode him now, as he focused on the riders. It was as she said. Two riders, two wolfhounds, two horses. And there was something about the dark-haired woman that turned his blood to ice.

*No.*

*But what if?*

*She's dead*, he argued to himself.

*They never got her body back.*

*She's been confirmed dead for twenty years.*

He'd been there the day she'd been taken by a guard who was supposed to protect her. He'd seen them in the garden. He'd thought nothing of it, and for years he'd blamed himself for not noticing that something was wrong. If only he'd been more observant. If only he'd waved to Claudia and called her over rather than hurrying after his father because he wasn't supposed to be friends with her when other people were looking… If only he'd done something *different*.

No one had ever seen her again.

He crouched down beside Sophia as she pulled the strip of royal purple silk from the bag. 'You know what this is?'

She shook her head, no.

'It's an old method of communication that falconers sometimes use when they fly their birds.' He wasn't even sure why he'd brought the silk with him in the first place, other than he'd been battling a memory of him and Claudia lying in front of his father's fire with a fragile book spread out in front of him that listed all the colours a royal raptor could fly and what they meant. He'd been the one reading, as usual. Claudia had been listening like a little sponge. 'When I attach it to Carys's right leg, like this, it means royalty is in residence and it offers incoming visitors royal protection.'

'Er, Master Falconer, sir, are you at liberty to be offering that?'

'Too late.' He lifted his arm and Carys shot into the sky. 'There are only half a dozen people alive who even know what that ribbon means.' So why was he flying that ribbon at all? Instinct?

*Instinct and false, fierce hope, and a thundering heart.*

Word went around the fortress that they had incoming visitors and curiosity grew. Visitors heading in from the high mountain pass, on horseback, was unusual. Carys had spotted the riders and was heading towards them. Nothing strange about that. He'd trained her to mark the presence of large animals.

And then the woman dismounted, pulled a gauntlet from her saddlebag and called that bird straight out of the sky.

*His* bird.

Using his signals.

It *couldn't* be.

*But what if it was?*

He could feel the blood draining from his face, leaving him clammy and shaken. Had there not been an audience, he would have sunk to his heels and leaned against the wall and taken strength from the only home he'd ever known. As it was, he had to put his hand to the wall to steady himself.

'Sophia, go get Housemaster Silas and tell him to get up here.' Silas and his wife Lor had managed the running of the fortress for decades. Out of anyone, he might, *might*, hear Tomas out.

Ten long minutes later he met the gaze of an out of breath Silas, and avoided looking at Sophia's mother—the soon-to-be Queen Consort Ana—and tried to project calm confidence as he explained the calling of his bird from the sky situation.

'So she's a falconer too,' said Ana.

'He thinks it's Claudia,' said Silas, his weary old eyes fixed on Tomas with unwavering intensity.

'I didn't *say* that,' Tomas protested.

'But you think it,' Silas replied.

'Just to be clear, you're talking Claudia, as in Casimir's dead sister?' Ana looked from one man to the other. 'You're serious.'

'We never got her body back,' Tomas said stubbornly.

'We got some of it back,' countered Silas.

'Okay,' said Ana hurriedly. 'Small girl on the battlements. Listening.'

Tomas felt himself flush. Silas shut his eyes and shook his head.

'Is there any way we can get a look at the woman's face?' Ana said next.

'She's wearing traditional headdress. Only part of her face is showing. It could be anyone.'

'But you think it's her.'

'I don't *know*.' Tomas swore and turned away before his control deserted him. Swearing in front of women and children, what next? '*She* knew about the coloured cloth instead of jesses and what they meant. It's in one of the royal falconry journals and I read that section aloud to her when she was helping me nurse a hawk with a broken wing. She was good with the birds. They trusted her. She knew all our call signals.'

'Why would she stay away all these years, only to return now?' asked Silas.

'Who knows?' Tomas snapped but he could take a wild guess. 'Because her father who left her to rot is dead, her brother is whole and happy, Byzenmaach is moving forward and she wants to come home? How should I know?'

'But you think it's her,' said Ana. 'Again, just to be clear.'

He stared at her and then Silas and finally young Sophia, with those eyes so wide and round. He didn't know. He couldn't be sure. But here he was staking his reputation and likely his livelihood on the return of a woman from the dead.

'Yes.'

'Then we have to tell Cas.'

The winter fortress stood exactly as she remembered it, starkly grey against a brilliant blue sky. Built into the side of a cliff face, there would be no attacking it from the south, just endless views over a secluded valley several thousand feet below. To the far north, and behind her now, rose a vast mountain range, inaccessible to all but the hardiest of mountain clans. Between mountain and fortress lay flat unwooded plains—a battleground of old with no place to hide. They would be seen. They *had* been seen—the hawk currently perched on her arm confirmed it.

A hawk carrying a strip of purple cloth.

*Welcome*, that strip of cloth said, if she remembered correctly. *We see you and you may approach. We offer our protection.*

She'd given no notice regarding her arrival. Who would believe her identity without seeing her in the flesh? And even then, she had her doubts as to whether anyone would know her on sight. So many years had passed. Her features had changed so much.

All she could hope for was an audience with someone who'd once known her.

Her brother, ideally, if he was in residence.

Silas and Lor, the older couple who had once managed the fortress, if they still served.

Tomas.

The bird on her arm spoke of his presence.

Or maybe she was just being hopeful.

'First smile I've seen from you in a week,' murmured her companion. Having Ildris by her side on this journey was a comfort, because he was a big brother to her in all ways that mattered, and twelve years older than she was. It gave him an aura of strength and maturity, those two words describing him perfectly.

'Coming home's a scary business,' she replied, pulling two ribbons from her saddlebag. White for peace. Purple for royalty. What a beautiful hawk to sit so patiently on her gauntlet and let her attach coloured ribbons to the left anklet. The ribbons hinted at who she was and what her intentions were. The King's Falconer would surely know what they meant. It was his job.

'It could have been less fraught for all concerned had

you allowed me to inform them of your return,' Ildris offered dryly.

'Who would believe you?'

'I think you just like creating drama.'

He wasn't exactly *wrong*.

'Then let's just say I've waited so long for this day, and it serves many purposes to claim the element of surprise. In that first moment of recognition, we'll be able to tell allies from enemies. And there will be enemies. Hopefully, my brother won't be one of them.' Her blood brother, Casimir, had grown to manhood beneath their father's cruel yoke. Who knew what kind of man he'd become?

Ildris sat comfortably in the saddle as she finished tying the ribbons and launched the hawk into the sky. 'What do you remember of him?'

'I have so many memories based on fear of my father and my mother's neglect, but Cas…he tried so hard to protect me. He took the lash for me, over and over again.' She shook her head to clear her mind of those bitter memories. 'One of my greatest regrets is not being able to tell him I was alive and happy. I don't know how that's going to go.'

'Tell him that no matter our initial intent, once your father refused to negotiate your return, you were safe with us. Tell him we nurtured you and love you. We are not forcing your return—you could have stayed with us for ever. This time, we could and *would* have negotiated without involving you.'

'I know.' And she loved him and the council of the northern clans all the more for making that clear. 'But I *want* to help him and his new wife and their little girl who looks just like me when I was her age. I want Byzenmaach to move forward. I truly want to serve my country and I'm uniquely positioned to do so. You always thought I'd return one day. You took me in and built me for exactly this moment.'

'Do you really think that?' he grumbled. 'My parents took you in because they were never on board with taking a child hostage. We gave you political survival skills so that no one would take advantage of you. Does it also not stand to reason that I'm wary of returning you to those who once considered you expendable?'

'I don't think my brother ever thought me expendable.'

'I hope you're right. Otherwise, we're in a bit of trouble. Yet another reason for telling people about you from a safe distance. The *trust* involved in expecting them to greet you with joy rather than suspicion. I shudder.'

'You're loving this.' She remounted and they continued on their way. 'You live for excitement.'

'*Live* being the operative word.'

'It's going to be fine. Cas has already reached out to the northern clans in peace. What better measure of good faith negotiation than the return of one of Byzenmaach's beloved jewels? And by that I mean me.'

For good or for ill, she was coming home and fully prepared to wield any scrap of power her identity afforded her.

'I'm ready, Ildris. For whatever comes next.' She watched the hawk soar, ribbons trailing, and hoped that if the owner of the hawk was Tomas, that he had not forgotten her. That he, of all people, would keep an open heart and mind. She had such sweet memories of him.

His boyish face in the firelight. His youthful voice as he'd stumbled over unfamiliar words as he read from books way too advanced for him. His hidey-holes and his smiles when he was absolutely certain no one else was looking.

It would take more than a lifetime before she ever forgot the fine mind and tender heart of her very first friend.

It took the riders what seemed like half a lifetime but in reality was measured by hours before they reached the outer walls of the fortress. There they had dismounted to shed layers of clothing and weapons. Rifles and scimitars, daggers and even the woman's hairpins. A dark plait had fallen to her waist in the absence of those lethal fasteners. She'd turned slowly in a circle, her arms out wide and her movements graceful. She and her companion were stating with vivid clarity that they were entering unarmed.

The stately, ceremonial nature of their approach had set people on edge. Cas had arrived by helicopter. Sophia had been safely stashed away inside the fortress and security was on full alert. The mysterious travellers were making their final approach, on foot, towards the stable doors.

'Let them come,' Casimir had commanded. 'No one is to ride out to meet them.'

The tension behind Tomas's eyes was excruciating. What were they even *doing*, adhering so closely to the old ways when they had all sorts of technology that could help to identify them without actually letting them in? It was as if time had slowed and hope had risen and reason had unequivocally left the building.

The stables were as they'd ever been. Twenty stalls capable of holding three or four horses apiece ran either side of a large central square. The square was covered in sawdust and the stable hands kept it immaculate. Huge wooden doors stood sentry on opposite sides of the square. Doors strong enough to hold invaders out rather than horses in.

Tomas stood in the centre of the sawdust square alongside Ana, with Cas on her other side. The stable master, stable hands and a company of guards took up other positions as Cas finally ordered the opening of the outer doors to let the visitors in.

The male rider entered first, leading his horse. He picked Casimir out of the crowd and steadily approached.

'Your Majesty,' he said with the click of his heels and a swift bow. 'It's been a long time.'

'Welcome, Lord Ildris of the North.' Cas clearly knew the man by sight, even if Tomas didn't. 'Who's your companion?'

The northerner waited a beat, as if taking a deep breath. 'She's the negotiator you requested and speaks for the people of the north and for herself. A future for a future, Your Majesty. Delivered to you in good faith.'

The woman entered the stables, swift and sure, and the horses and dogs followed, and Tomas knew who she was even before she lifted her eyes and made it a foregone conclusion. Her eyes were the same shape and colour as Casimir's. Same as Sophia's. The eyes of the royal family of Byzenmaach.

'Hello, Cas,' she offered quietly and then her gaze flickered sideways, passing over Ana to rest squarely on him. 'And Tomas. You're the falconer here now?'

He had no words. He could barely remember to breathe, so it was fortunate that Ana answered for him. 'Yes, he is.'

'I thought so.' She smiled as if they'd just shared a joke, but he could find no smile for her in return. He was too busy fighting a horde of emotions that threatened to overwhelm him. Astonishment. Disbelief. Anger. Relief. Where had she *been* these past twenty years or more?

And then Ana said something to Cas in Russian and then Cas was striding across the floor and pulling his sister into an embrace that left no one in any doubt of the depth of his supposed loss, or his joy at finding her alive.

'You were right, Tomas,' Ana murmured, and maybe he should have stuck around but he'd had enough of this day and all the drama, and if he was going to break down, he wanted to do it in private.

He turned on his heel and left without a word. Back to the house he'd been born and raised in, shedding his clothes as he headed for the shower and the tap that brought the icy underground river water into the homes of those living here, to be heated by a furnace and pushed through pipes so it could beat down on a man's head, hot and strong or icy cold and anything in between. A pleasure or a punishment, and today he chose the latter, standing beneath the stinging, icy spray far longer than was wise in an effort to wash away his confusion.

Claudia of Byzenmaach was *dead*. He'd *mourned* her. They all had. Her absence had coloured their lives.

Did the impossibly beautiful woman who stood there, so regal and composed, have *any* idea of the sorrow she'd left behind? Where had she been all those years? What atrocities had she endured? And to single him out. To remember his name and greet him like an old friend. She'd stood, magnificent and defiant, so impossibly alive and begging him with her eyes to acknowledge her existence...

Emotion after emotion broke over him. Confusion. Resentment. Rage. Where was it all coming from?

He didn't *want* to be drowning in emotions. *Get a grip.*

He was a man of firm control, not seething, unruly compulsions. A simple man, a falconer. Nothing more and nothing less. There would be no befriending the returned princess of Byzenmaach. No trying to protect her, no welcoming her home. *Definitely* no regarding her as an impossibly desirable woman capable of setting his body alight at a glance. He wanted nothing to do with her. Nothing!

He was *not* getting caught up in Princess Claudia of Byzenmaach's blast radius ever again.

# CHAPTER TWO

CLAUDIA COULDN'T SLEEP, and it had nothing to do with the warm and heartfelt reception she'd received from her brother and his family. Maybe it had something to do with the adrenaline-filled day and the capture of her senses as she'd built new memories over old ones and tracked all the changes that had occurred to people and possessions. Mostly, her wakefulness had to do with a certain falconer with an impossibly beautiful masculine face, eyes of darkest brown and stern lips that spoke of sensuality under rigid control.

Tomas had been standing there with Ana and Cas as she'd entered the stables and he'd known who she was in an instant. She'd seen it in his eyes—a kaleidoscope of feelings she hadn't possibly been able to decipher in such a short time before her attention had been forced elsewhere.

'The one who left the stables first is not your friend,' Ildris had told her just before bed, right before he'd withdrawn to his guestroom, and maybe that assessment was keeping her awake too.

Because Claudia absolutely disagreed with Ildris on that point. She stood at the bedroom window, staring out at the faint light in the building on the edge of the for-

tress that had once housed fledgling falcons and probably still did.

In all her reckonings of how this day would unfold,
Tomas welcoming her home had always been part of it.
A constant amidst ever changing variables. He would
know who she was at a glance and would be overjoyed
to see her alive and well and...

Well...

Apart from knowing who she was at a glance, reality
really hadn't delivered.

And that light in his window was beckoning and it
wasn't as if she was sleepy.

Donning her travelling cloak and nodding to the pair of
guards stationed just outside the bedroom door, Claudia
made her way through the corridors of the fortress to the
kitchen and from there to the herb garden and the deep
shadows of battlement walls. She was being watched, no
doubt, but she couldn't be caring about that. There was
only so much space in her mind to begin with and at the
moment it was full of Tomas the boy overlaid with an
image of Tomas the man, and her overwhelming desire
to make things right between them. Their friendship had
existed in the shadows all those years ago, and in the
shadows she hoped to find it again.

She knocked on the wooden door to the falconer's
workspace with every good intention and a dozen explanations on her lips, but when the door opened to allow
her entry and Tomas turned without a word and stalked
away from her down the narrow entry hall, speech deserted her. He was a presence. An unknown force, bat-
tering away at her senses. Too big to make sense of, his
shoulders too broad. Too stern. Ever so silent.

She followed him anyway.

He led her to what had once been the falcon nursery. These days it seemed to be an office with a couple of perches but no falcons currently present.

He took a seat behind the desk and motioned to the chair on the other side, all without saying a word. She had a feeling he could sit here all night, eyes stony and lips tight.

'Hi,' she murmured.

Icebreaker it was not.

She tried again. 'I'm guessing you have questions.'

'No.'

Oh. 'Because anything you want to know, I'll answer you. I mean, if you really want the deep dive into what happened we'll be here for days, but I could cover the basics quickly enough.'

Curiosity flared briefly in those assessing dark eyes. Curiosity and an internal conversation he seemed to be having with himself before he finally allowed himself a single slight nod. 'Then cover the basics.'

'Right.' It wasn't much of an invitation but it was enough. 'I got kidnapped from the palace by northerners hoping to force water concessions from my father. That didn't work. They wanted to return me. That didn't work either.'

His eyes narrowed. 'Why not? Why couldn't they have just given you back?'

'Because I was in the room when my father told them he didn't want me back. As far as he was concerned, I was damaged goods and better martyred than returned. He said that if they let me go, he'd kill me himself and blame it on them anyway. Is that a good enough reason to stay away until now, do you think?'

He had the most magnificent scowl.

'This presented a problem for my captors who, apart from the whole kidnapping thing, had treated me well enough up until that point. What were they going to do with me?'

'Tell me.'

She did like *this* Tomas's voice commands. He'd grown into his authority quite magnificently.

'A wealthy clan who'd voted against the abduction petitioned the council to think of me as an abandoned child and put me up for adoption. The council agreed, so the family took me in and gave me every opportunity to grow up strong and whole. I wasn't abused by them or anyone else.' She'd had to reassure Cas of this several times over and figured Tomas might appreciate similar emphasis. 'My father died, Cas wants to negotiate water rights with the northerners, finally giving them a seat at the table, and here I am. I know it won't be easy, fitting back in, but I can honestly say that so far it feels good to be home.'

'Your brother must be overjoyed.'

'I hope so. Are you glad to see me too? Because I really can't tell. Ildris thinks you're no friend of mine. I say you are.'

'Is this *Ildris* an abductor of children? Or is he of the clan of opportunists who took you in? Either way, I have no time at all for what he thinks.'

'Remind me never to seat you two beside one another at the dinner table.'

Savage little smirk from him at her words. 'Never going to happen.'

Civilised behaviour seemed to sit only lightly on this man. Boy Tomas had been softer.

Maybe if she stopped mapping every curve and plane of his face for traces of the child he'd once been, she could concentrate more on breaking the ice with him, although, to be fair, he was studying her just as closely.

'And you? I heard about your father's death in the papers and that you'd taken over here and were doing good things. You've been well? Life is treating you well?'

*I never forgot you*, she wanted to say. *I thought of you so many times. I never factored in that meeting you again would involve me wanting to fling myself into your arms, but here we are.*

Probably best not to mention any of that right now.

'I knew you'd grow up to be a falconer, of course.' Small talk was her friend. 'I did think you'd talk more and scowl less, but maybe you're just shy.'

'I'm not shy.'

'Standoffish, then, but that's okay too. I haven't forgotten any of your kindnesses. I'd like us to be friends again.' Start small. Build from there.

'I see.' He nodded as if they'd reached an accord. 'No, that's not going to happen.'

She reached out instinctively, her hand over his, and felt the sting of attraction rip through her skin and into her veins. He swiftly withdrew his hand from beneath hers and his eyes flashed fierce warning before he shielded them with long black lashes.

'What was that?' She knew exactly what it was, but did he?

'Nothing.'

'Then you won't mind if we try it again.' She held out her hand for him to shake, put it right in his line of sight. 'Hi, I'm Claudia.'

'No.'

'No to a simple handshake?'

'It's not a handshake. It's not simple. I'm not the boy you used to know.'

Maybe she needed a different approach.

'You should know that I don't give up on people easily. I'm *so* used to not being wanted at first glance. At second glance too. Even at tenth glance. I'm very persistent.'

'That's okay,' he murmured, echoing some of her earlier words with a smile that made ice look warm. 'You may be persistent but I'm as stubborn as they come. If you need someone to drive a team of oxen up a mountain, I'm your man. If I can be of service to you in any official or professional capacity, I will be. But I don't weather surprises well and I hate messy emotions and right now you're blasting both at me. I'm glad you're back, don't get me wrong. Surprised as hell, but glad you're alive and relieved your captivity wasn't terrible. God knows I never wanted you dead. But I don't have the time or the inclination to renew old friendships or go tripping down memory lane with you. I hope you can understand my position.'

'I don't understand your position.'

'What a shame. Maybe understanding will come to you in time. Now, if you don't mind, Princess, it's almost three a.m. and I have a sick falcon to see to. He stood and she looked up, up into pitiless eyes. 'You know the way out.'

Well, damn. Ildris had been right.

The King's Falconer was proving elusive.

Again.

In the three months she'd been back she'd caught up with the falconer only a handful of times, and every time he'd remained perfectly, excruciatingly polite and completely closed off to her overtures of friendship. This didn't stop her returning to the winter fortress whenever Cas could spare her, though. She loved it here on the edge of a cliff face, with her beloved mountain in the distance and a chill in the air even on the sunniest days. And this time she'd come armed with a missive from the King, all signed, sealed and soon to be delivered.

To Tomas.

Lor said he was in residence.

Her interest in the royal racing falcons and breeding and rehabilitation programmes was real, no need to pretend. She might not have the experience Tomas's apprentices were getting, but she had enough knowledge to ask sensible questions and be of use when it came to handling the raptors currently in royal care. Not that anyone ever let her help. They were under strict instructions not to let anyone near their charges without the King's Falconer's approval.

She'd tried asking nicely, but he'd been on his way to collect a falcon. Bad timing, he'd said.

She'd put her request to have access to the aviaries in writing and received no reply.

Third time lucky, right?

In her hand she carried yet another request for her to have access to the aviaries and this time the request came from Cas. Tomas—if he had a subversive bent, which he absolutely *did*—could deny he'd ever received such a request if she didn't deliver it to him personally, so here she was, about to do exactly that.

She'd warned him she was persistent.

Claudia found him in a white-walled office crammed with filing cabinets along one wall and several computers set up haphazardly on any available surface. He sat behind a corner desk with a phone to his ear and a frown on his face that deepened when he saw her. He didn't motion for her to sit, but she placed the letter dead centre on his desk and swivelled it so that his name on the envelope was facing him, fully aware that he was watching her every move.

She'd spent a ridiculous amount of time on her hair and make-up this morning. She'd tried on three different sets of outdoor 'work' clothes. She'd armoured up in preparation to see him again because apparently she was perfectly capable of having a crush on him with all the avid obsession of a hormonal thirteen-year-old.

What joy.

Smiling tightly, she then turned her back on him and proceeded to poke around his office.

Okay, not poke, she wasn't quite that rude, maybe prowl was the description she needed. There was a wall of bird photographs, with names neatly printed beneath each image. Once she'd inhaled all that, she memorised the weekly roster and the names and duties of his apprentices. And of course she listened to his side of the phone conversation.

'I don't have any room,' he said more than once. 'We're full. I know. Leave it with me. I'll call you back.' Two more rapid phone calls, one to France, the other to Latvia, and he was indeed calling that first person back and giving them the contact details of the raptor sanctuary he'd organised to take their breeding pair of endangered goshawks. Finally, he put the phone down and stared at her.

She'd been waiting over twenty minutes.

'Hello,' she murmured now that she had his full attention. She was certainly prepared to offer him all of hers in return. 'Good job on rehoming the goshawks.'

She loved the way he exuded healthy masculinity in his

rough labourer's clothes that included wide leather bands wrapped casually around both forearms. Muscles bulged. Angels sighed. Falconers had an unfair advantage when it came to looking effortlessly sexy. Not that she was inclined to mention it. She was all about keeping this meeting professional. Mostly professional. She'd see how she went.

'Are you the president of some kind of raptor relocation outfit?'

'No.' He gestured towards the envelope. 'What's this?'

'Another request for access to the royal aviaries. I've also included my falconry experience, starting from age seven. It's extensive.'

His eyes narrowed as he stared at her—a suspicious-hearted person might have even called it a glare. And then he turned his attention to the envelope, discarding Cas's covering letter after a swift glance in favour of scanning her C.V.

Quite voraciously. It was very gratifying.

'It says here you're a Master Falconer.'

Claudia beamed.

'Where are your birds?'

'Still in the mountains. And while I'd happily bring them here, I'm currently busy taming Cas's courtiers, and it sounds like you don't have room to keep them. I'd like to discuss it though, just in case you can find some way to accommodate them.'

'There's an onboarding process for anyone wanting access to the royal aviaries,' he said.

'Of course.' She expected no less. 'And I am here for it. Are you free now?'

She'd ambushed him, used her position to corner him, and he didn't know whether to be resentful or impressed. Just another set of opposing emotions to add to the collection he carried deep within whenever he thought of her. And with the newspapers and magazines and fortress gossip fair bursting with talk of the political demands she was making and the family gowns and tiaras she was wearing, not to mention her ever growing influence over her brother and his family, he thought about the returned princess of Byzenmaach *plenty*.

She didn't even have to be *present*.

'I'm here for the next two days and I'd really like to get my onboarding on track,' she was saying, and he seriously considered making it happen.

Maybe if he onboarded her himself, he could form his own opinion on the type of person she'd grown up to be and stop buying into all the gossip she created just by breathing in a particular direction. He could stop watching the many television interviews she'd taken to giving, because they downright did his head in. It was impossible not to admire her grit, even as he wondered what the hell she thought she was *doing*, dabbling in political minefields that were minefields for a reason.

'Let's do it now,' he said of the onboarding, choosing for once to step up and wear the emotional turmoil of connection.

Go him. Such outreach. His former girlfriends would hardly recognise him.

'Really?'

*Don't beam at me. Don't shine like you've just won the lottery.*

'Yes.'

She beamed at him, and he scowled right back because the world needed balance.

But he gave her the respect her qualifications deserved

and took her on a comprehensive tour, the VIP colleague version, and she was knowledgeable, enthusiastic and full of praise. She cooed over his rare mating pairs. Told a featherless but talkative parrot he was her new favourite, and when they entered the aviary full of peregrine falcons and he handed her gloves and a bucket of feed she proved herself more than capable of feeding them by hand in orderly fashion.

She kept enough physical distance from him to render him comfortable, right up until they rounded a bend outside aviary three and she lost her footing on a slippery rock step and he shot out his hand to steady her. These paths could be dangerous, especially when covered in late afternoon shade.

'Sorry,' she murmured, righting herself. 'Slippery.'

He probably should have anticipated the sudden pounding of his heart—either from touching her or at the thought of her falling. Nothing to do with sexual attraction at all. Probably.

'Give me your shoe size and I'll order some boots in with rubber tread like mine.'

'You'd do that for me?'

'I do that for everyone who works for me. Not that you do work for me or that I expect you to. But if you want unlimited, unsupervised access to the aviaries, you may as well have all the gear.'

'And will you allow me that access?'

'Yes.'

Her eyes lit up, the same way they always had done when they'd been kids and she'd done well and been praised for it. Made him want to preen. Made him a little too slow to drop his hand and withdraw that physical support. More fool him.

He'd embarked on project *Make Claudia Welcome* in an effort to get over her, not to become ever more in thrall to the woman.

By the time they got back to his office, the sun had slid behind the distant mountain range and shadows painted the ground. He scanned the clipboard on his desk, and the long list of tasks and ticks and the comments column for anything in need of his attention. She was still there. Still eager to know everything.

'You've expanded so much. It's brilliant! Imagine what you could do with more resources,' Claudia was saying.

If only.

And why was she still here? They'd said their farewells five minutes ago, hadn't they?

'Do you want more resources?' she asked perceptively.

'Your brother and I have discussed it.' Tomas hoped that with their recent speed trial wins that they might take another look at avian resources, but it hadn't happened yet. Cas was busy, not least with reining in his long lost and in no way dead sibling. 'It'll happen eventually.' He wanted to believe it. 'Your brother means well.'

'Damned by faint praise,' she murmured.

'But it is praise. Your father's rule was…difficult. People are understandably wary, and your brother has yet to prove himself. I know what you're doing, by the way. Making *your* views the target of political outrage when anyone with a brain knows they're your brother's views as well. Nice little sidestep he's got going there. Letting you take all the heat.'

'Careful, Tomas. I'll start to think you're a political being.'

'Never. Spare me the company of craven courtiers. I hate them all.' He meant it.

'And yet my brother speaks very highly of your ability to deal with them.'

'I serve as I ever have.'

Claudia snorted, and even that managed to sound fetching. 'I certainly hope not. From memory, you and your father and the rest of the staff here were extremely adept at limiting my father's impact on the world around him.'

He grunted in reply. No point incriminating himself or others.

'So what do you think of the water rights treaty?' she asked. 'It's exciting, right? With conservation at the forefront and guaranteed access for those who need it.'

Always with the questions, luring him into unwanted conversation.

'As you say, things are changing, and people are hopeful.'

He watched her cross to the picture board with the names of all the falcons on it. She'd been captivated by that earlier too. He usually asked new apprentices to memorise it within a week. Instinct told him it wouldn't take her that long.

'Do you still think we can't be friends?' she asked quietly.

'You're a princess, I'm a servant.'

'Oh, c'mon,' she scoffed. 'We did away with that distinction twenty years ago.'

'We certainly did *not*.'

'In private we did.' When had she become all angles and impossible beauty? So utterly compelling? He didn't want to be her friend, that still hadn't changed. But since when had he wanted lovers' rights? A fully adult and possibly X-rated relationship? Had he come to that con-

clusion five minutes ago? Ten? Was the featherless parrot to blame?

Because he really wanted to blame *something* for his
appalling lack of judgement.

'If you want access to the royal aviaries, you have it.'
Time to get this briefing back on track. 'If you let me
know how many birds you want to bring in I'll make
space for them, even if we have to house them in the
fortress proper—we've done that before and we can certainly do it for you. They'll need vet checks and a clean
bill of health before they arrive and I'll send you an information questionnaire that needs to be filled out for
each bird. If you can't take them to the palace when you
go there to be your brother's political scapegoat—which
I don't agree with, by the way, he's doing you no favours
by letting you take point—I'll put them in my personal
flight rotation. I'll even give you updates. Just don't ask
me to send pictures of them with little voice bubbles or
videos with them dancing to music or wearing cowboy
hats and neck ties, because I won't do it. Is that a good
enough extension of the hand of friendship?'

'Well, when you put it like that,' she said, golden eyes
shining, holding out her hand for him to shake, and damn
her for making his pulse spike again. 'I'll take it.'

Claudia spent the rest of the evening riding a wave of
happiness. She had dinner with Silas and Lor in the big
kitchen, with her wolfhounds at her feet and Sophia's as
well. Casimir had kept the wolfhound name traditions
going. The heavily pregnant wolfhound stretched out in
front of the huge stone hearth was Jelly Belly the elev-
enth. Or was she the twelfth?

Coming home had been harder than expected. She'd ridden in with a heart full of hope that she would be accepted and a deeply buried fear that she would prove useful to no one. Not the northerners, who expected so much from her bulldozer-style advocacy. Not her brother, whose rule had invariably become more complicated upon her return.

She needed to succeed in all her roles. She needed to be strong and powerful, politically invaluable, and above all confident. Make Cas look good. Take the extreme position if she had to so that he could swoop in with a more moderate stance and yet still make ample progress. That was the plan. Her only plan.

But Tomas had clocked it and criticised her actions and she too had underestimated just how much courage it would take to face suspicion and outright hostility from the select few politicians who, first and foremost, were still her father's men. Cruel, powerful men with years of alliances and information to trade upon. Ugly business, the ruling of worlds. Corruption never far from the centre.

She hadn't factored in how much energy it would take to keep her emotional armour permanently in place, and her reserves were wearing thin.

Tomas's friendship, or whatever he wanted to call it, was a godsend.

Her mobile rang and she glanced at the screen for the name of the caller.

Cas.

'Brother! You rang?'

'I did. How did it go with Tomas?'

'I like to think I wowed him with my poise, maturity and falcon-feeding skills and maybe even reclaimed the threads of an old and valuable friendship. The reality is probably a lot less rosy, but progress has been made, which makes me happy.'

She could almost see her brother picking over her words, analysing her good humour, and coming to conclusions.

'I never realised how close you and Tomas were as children.'

'He was safety,' she offered simply.

'How did I not know this?'

'*Secret* safety.'

'And now what is he?'

'Who knows?' A reluctant champion? Her latest late-night fantasy? Definitely the latter. 'He's incredibly hard to read. All that iron control, and I know he needs it for his birds, but it's annoying. Cas, stop laughing. It's not helpful.'

Her brother did stop laughing. Eventually. 'He's not an easy man to know, our master falconer. By all accounts, he's a demanding but fair teacher. He's not a fan of small talk. He could barely stand to be in the same room as Sophia when she first arrived. I believe it was because she reminded him so strongly of you. Now she tracks him down whenever she visits and his patience with her is a sight to behold.'

'I refuse to feel jealous of my niece,' she told him loftily. 'Even if I am.'

'Tomas knew you had returned the moment you rode into this valley. The facts were all against it. He could barely bring himself to voice the words lest everyone think him a madman, but he knew it was you. Ana will tell you that he never truly released you from his heart, even though everybody said you were dead, but that's just…wild.'

Yes, it was.

'I'd love to see him with the capacity to expand his

role beyond being merely your falconer. He's worth investing in.'

'*Merely* the King's Falconer? Is that not exalted enough?'

'He needs more resources. Would you like to hear my plan?'

'Perhaps. But first I have a question. What is it you want from him? Not *for* him. *From* him.'

She thought long and hard before answering. 'I want him to feel more comfortable around me than he currently does. I want him to like me.' There it was. 'And I can't get it out of my head that he's hurting because of me. Because I left. Because I'm back. Because I didn't write to say *hi, I'm still alive*. I don't know *why* my presence pains him, but it does. All I can do is guess.'

'And guess badly,' Cas admonished.

'Maybe if he thought of me growing up at all, he imagined someone different from who I turned out to be. Maybe I'm a disappointment. Not worth spending time on.'

There it was, her primal fear revealed—nurtured by years upon years of having to justify her existence.

'What if it's that?'

'It's not. *You* are a survivor. You're smart and strong and incisive and caring and open. And you could have turned out differently after all you've been through. You could have been hard-hearted and resentful, suspicious and untrusting, and no one would blame you, but you're not. You're an inspiration. Don't let the falconer get you down.'

'Aw.' She had a champion. 'Thank you. Music to my ears.'

'Besides, maybe you're looking at this the wrong way around. Maybe Tomas thinks he let *you* down by not preventing you from being taken in the first place. Guilt might be part of his response to you.'

'That's just stupid.'

'I speak from experience. Guilt plagues me that I did nothing to prevent your abduction. We lost *years*.'

The pain in his voice was only too real and she stopped to consider his words more carefully and form a more appropriate reply.

'If you need my forgiveness, you have it. But Cas, you were just a kid. You and Tomas were both kids. What could you possibly have done to prevent my kidnapping?'

'Something,' he muttered darkly. 'All I'm saying is that if Tomas was your unofficial secret protector, he would have guilt. I guarantee it. And our falconer doesn't particularly like being reminded that he has feelings. That's all I'm saying.'

'I'm not giving up on him.'

'What a surprise,' he replied dryly. 'I'm on your side, Claudia. I'm glad it went well today.'

'Thank you for the new perspective. I'm going to keep it in mind when I corner him next. And, brother, just so you know, I'm going to knock any harbouring of guilt for the life I've led right out of your head too.'

'Please,' he offered drolly. 'Do.'

# CHAPTER THREE

CLAUDIA DECIDED TO start small when it came to desensitising Tomas to her ongoing presence in his life. She owned a falconer's training journal written in 1770 that she'd often found useful, so she had it forwarded to her and left it on his desk with a note to look at page sixty-three and see if he agreed with the method presented for treating bumblefoot. That had led to a chance encounter out by aviary three and a lively argument about the merits or otherwise of using harsh chemicals to clean perches. Tomas had argued against it, which left Claudia to take the for position.

Neither had realised how loud they'd been getting until one of the apprentices had interrupted, with every indication of having been trying to get their attention for a while.

'What about using a good old antiseptic soap, sunshine, and using a variety of perches and rotating them in and out?' he'd suggested.

There'd really been no way to argue with that. Tomas had apologised for his temper, headed for open space and refused to re-engage with her for *weeks*.

'He's not one for raising his voice,' his most senior apprentice explained when Tomas rescheduled her appointment with him yet again because of some new crisis that took him away from the fortress. 'He'll be kicking himself about the argument he got into with you last time you and he butted heads and trying to make sure it never happens again.'

Claudia stared at the older man, bewildered. 'But he didn't lose his cool. We were having a spirited intellectual debate. No falcon feet got damaged in the process.'

'He raised his voice. To him that's a failing.'

Tomas Sokolov was a big baby. A big, beautiful, unforgettable infant.

'Is there anything *I* can help you with?' the man continued.

'I want to set a date for bringing two of my falcons here permanently.'

'With due respect, ma'am, you're the Crown Princess. Pretty sure you can do that whenever you feel like it.'

'I know. But I know it'll be a stretch on resources, and he said there was an information sheet I had to fill out...' And she'd wanted to see him again... 'He wasn't really upset about that loud conversation, was he?' She refused to call it an argument.

'It's like this. Staying calm and in control is like the first commandment around here. We need it when handling the birds. We need it when conveying information respectfully and effectively to titled idiots who think they know everything about falcons when really they know nothing.'

'You mean me.'

'No, ma'am. No one here has any complaints about the way you handle and care for the birds. But you don't know Tomas, if I may say. And he doesn't do strong emotions. He locks that sh— stuff down. Maybe he got trained to bank it down hard, you know? Maybe it's just his way. But riling him's not the way to make a connection. He won't stick around for it.'

'So you're saying it'd be a bad idea if I confessed to him that I quite liked seeing him all heated, and that I was enjoying myself. Immensely. He's very, ah—' she waved a gloved hand around in the air to explain what she meant while she searched for the right word '—compelling.'

The man couldn't quite hide his amusement. 'Right.'

'But I certainly don't want to rouse his, ah—'

'Passions,' supplied the apprentice, suspiciously deadpan.

'Right. I wouldn't want to rouse those to the point of no return. That would be bad.'

'Nah, do it. Do him good,' said another apprentice, sticking his head out of an enclosure to join the conversation. 'Junior apprentice Bran at your service, Your Highness.'

'Hello.' So many apprentices with advice and no Tomas. 'Call me Claudia.'

'No can do, ma'am. But I'm the one in charge of the paperwork this week and if you don't mind walking with me to the office I can print out those information sheets you're after.'

'Great. And when will Tomas be returning?'

'The problem is that when he sees you flying in, he heads out,' said the ever-helpful Bran.

'Tell him he's a coward.'

Bran laughed long and loud and the older apprentice simply shook his head. 'Yeah, I don't think anyone's going to be telling the Master Falconer that.'

# CHAPTER FOUR

WHEN IT CAME to hatreds, Tomas strove to be even-handed. Take capital cities swarming with people, and royal palaces swarming with courtiers, for example. Tomas happily loathed both. Not for him the niceties needed to traverse such terrain. He didn't suffer fools. He wasn't one for idle conversation. Even his conversations with Casimir bordered on brutally brief.

He was heading into the mountains tomorrow to check on the greater spotted eagle pairs, because at some point he wanted to introduce a new pair. All he had to do before he left was dress up in his royal finest and travel to the palace for an afternoon audience with his king and some kind of banquet in the evening. Didn't matter that he couldn't remember what the banquet was for, they were all the same. Get showered, get dressed, go to the capital and the palace he loathed because it was too full of random guards he didn't recognise and Claudia hadn't been safe there, and see duty done. That was the shape of his day, and he was all for getting through it efficiently.

Shower first, to wash off the stench of owl droppings and get clean again.

And then the rest.

Five minutes later he made his exit from the shower as Lor entered his quarters without knocking. She didn't usually intrude on his private space unless she felt it necessary. Like that time when a golden eagle had scored his shoulder and all down his back in a botched landing. Or when that fighting hawk had almost taken his finger off. Or like now, as she carried a pile of spruce green fabric and gold braid over one arm.

'I freshened your coat. It was dusty.'

'Thanks.' He tightened his grip on the towel that covered him from low on his hips to the start of his knees. While the trousers and shirt of his dress uniform fitted him well enough, the coat was a masterpiece fit for a coronation. It was tight fitting through the shoulders and chest and split back and front for ease of riding, but that was where practicality ended and the dust-collecting gold braid began. Embellished cuffs ran from wrist to elbow, tightened by leather buckles. He supposed a raptor could land on his forearm easily enough without damaging his skin, but the heavy gold braid embellishment didn't stop there. It formed a stiff collar around his neck, became a tight belt around his waist and dripped from the coat shoulders. It was terrible, and beautiful, and ridiculous. It was the King's Falconer's ceremonial dress. 'Do you have any idea what all this is about?'

Lor too wore her finest royal livery and her eyes, kind as they were, suggested she knew something he didn't.

'I'm afraid Lor is bound to secrecy,' said another voice from the doorway, and he sighed, because of course it was Claudia and doubtless his emotions would start acting up again.

His heels came together and he bowed his head as befitting his status and hers. Enforced formality was his last line of defence against Claudia, bane of his existence. That and speechlessness. Not that he ever seemed to stay speechless for long in her presence. His grip on his towel tightened.

'Hey.' She smiled and he didn't trust that *very* appreciative smile one little bit. 'You're running late.'

'Someone brought in an owl with a broken wing.'

'And not one of your apprentices could see to it without your supervision, hmm?'

'Exactly.'

'Nothing at all to do with you not wanting to go to the palace in the first place.'

'Nothing at all.'

That was the other problem with Claudia. She knew him too well and he didn't know *how*. He was a closed book. An impenetrable fortress. A cypher of his own making.

Who'd been blabbing about him?

'The helicopter leaves in twenty minutes,' she murmured in dulcet tones. 'The King is expecting you, me, Silas and Lor to be on it.'

'I'll be there.' She wore a royal purple travelling cloak and her long, thick hair had been wound in an elaborate crown. Her make-up was perfect. He tightened his grip on his towel, wondering if her composure would falter if he dropped it. Maybe she'd flee and give him some small reprieve from those all-seeing eyes. There was no earthly reason for her to even be in his quarters. Was there? 'Was there anything else?'

'I'll take it from here, Lor. We'll meet you at the helicopter,' Claudia said, and Lor nodded, hung the coat from a hook on his wardrobe door, and left.

Claudia stayed.

'I need to get dressed.' Chivalry demanded he give fair warning.

'What a good idea.' Claudia glanced at her delicate wristwatch that doubtless cost more than his annual wage. 'Eighteen minutes.'

Frustration bubbled. 'Leave.'

But all she did was lift an eyebrow. 'Your bathroom's right there if it's privacy you need. Your King, my brother, tasked me with getting you to the palace on time and I take my duties extremely seriously.'

He didn't need the twitch of her lips to know she was teasing. Her capacity to break rules, tradition and anything else that stood in her way was fast becoming legend.

His capacity to ignore her was rapidly becoming non-existent.

There was absolutely no ignoring this woman.

He didn't even know if he *wanted* to ignore what had been brewing between them.

With a shrug and what he hoped she took as unconcealed irritation rather than challenge accepted, he dropped his towel to the floor and strode to his chest of drawers in search of underwear. He took his time, allowed himself a flex of muscle here and a slight stretch there. His lifestyle hardly encouraged softness and his body was the result. Strongly muscled arms and shoulders gave way to a sculpted midsection that carried no fat. Long legs, strong thighs, and heavy manhood that he had every right to be proud of. He could almost feel her gaze travelling from that spot between his shoulder blades, all the way down his spine and over the globes of his buttocks. Modesty failed him in the same way propriety constantly failed her.

He half turned, noting with satisfaction the hot colour that rode her cheeks. 'What's wrong? You look a little glazed.'

'Hmm?' She dragged her gaze away from his nether

regions with no small amount of effort and finally let him see the expression in her eyes. It was hot, fierce and appreciative, and his body stiffened in all the right places. 'Glazed, no. This is my so impressed I'm practically speechless face. Sixteen minutes.'

A lot could happen in sixteen minutes.

He could reach for her. Muss up those perfect lips with biting needy kisses. Bury his fingers in her hair and tilt her head just so, the better to see every tiny expression to cross her face.

Instead, he stepped into his underwear and reached for his trousers, smiling wolfishly at the regretful little sigh that reached his ears.

He reached for his shirt next and let the buttery soft ivory linen encase his arms and shoulders as if it had been made for him and not his great-grandfather. He didn't fumble the buttons at his chest, but the tiny buttons on the cuffs of the sleeves were another matter.

'Here.' She crossed the room to stand in front of him. 'Let me help.'

So he held his arm out, wrists turned up like a supplicant, as she fastened the half dozen buttons on first one cuff and then the other. He'd never been this up close and personal with her before—not as an adult. Those times when they were kids and had stretched out on the rug in front of his father's hearth as they pored over picture books of falcons didn't count. He hadn't been aware of her back then as anything but a forbidden friend who needed protection.

Her fingers were warm against his skin and her delicate touch set up a chain reaction that fizzed along his veins. She brushed her thumb over his wrist when she was done and he wondered whether it was normal for a man's pulse rate to triple beneath the act of a woman helping him put his clothes *on*.

'Coat next or boots?' she asked, and the words were plain as could be but the husky intimacy of her voice did nothing to slow his heart rate.

'Boots.' He sat on the hard wooden seat of the blanket box at the end of his bed and reached for them. Never had his room felt so small. 'Why are you here?'

'To help you prepare for your meeting with my brother. For some strange reason, he suspected an emergency might lead you elsewhere.'

She went to kneel before him and he stood abruptly and stopped her with a hand beneath her elbow. He shouldn't be touching her uninvited, but he couldn't be thinking about that now. 'Don't ever kneel before me.' He might never let her up.

'It's not weakness to honour a man so.' She held his gaze with a steady one of her own and he was the first to look away.

'Within the borders of intimacy, maybe. Not for the likes of you and me.'

'Why not you and me? You might like it.'

He definitely would like it just a little too much.

'You're sister to a king. I am my father's son. We shouldn't be doing any of this. Not the fighting. Not the flirting. Not this.' He let her go and stepped into his boots and lifted his foot up on the chest and started on the laces. 'I am but your humble servant.'

'Humble servant?' He glanced up just in time to see the ghost of a wry smile on her lips. 'Hardly. A week ago, the falcon you bred and trained for speed won the most prestigious race in four kingdoms and fifty million dollars in prize money.'

So it had.

'Your brother's bird, your brother's money.'

'And *your* win. Your face as it happened was as proud and fierce as any king's.'

'You should have been watching the falcon.'

'And miss seeing you in action? I'm not that stupid. As for my royal blood being a barrier to any future association between us, my blood may not be as blue as you think. My so-called father believed my mother slept with his brother and had decided I was no child of his long before I was born. A cuckoo in his nest, so to speak.'

Tomas couldn't hide his shock. He'd never heard such rumours—and he would have if they'd ever been circulated. 'Who told you that?'

'Cas.'

He didn't want to believe any of it. And yet…

'Explains a lot, doesn't it,' Claudia continued. 'My mother took her own life—can't ask her. Cas believes his father murdered my father. Fratricide, they call it. All of them taking their secrets to the grave. Cas doesn't care who sired me so long as I stand by his side as his sister, serve as a bridge between Byzenmaach and the north, and keep our family secrets secret.'

'Then why tell me? Why not do as your king commands and *hold your tongue*?'

'Because before we reach the palace, I want you to believe beyond doubt that I'm in no way bound by titles and blood status. You could have befriended me at any time these past months. You must know I crave your company.'

'I know you *think* you do. I still haven't figured out why.'

'Look to your character. I like it. Hell, look in a mirror. Think about what happens whenever we touch.'

'Nothing happens.'

'Speak for yourself. I get shivers.'

'Nothing happens.'

'Imagine what would happen if we ever had sex. If you say nothing happens I'm going to revert to toddler-hood and pull your hair.'

He smirked. He couldn't help it.

'Are you ever going to put more clothes on, or am I just going to stand here and pant?' She slipped his coat from its hanger and held it out. The coat obscured her face but the impatient shake she gave it spoke volumes. 'I'm about to be presented with a new title and home. I don't know if I'm excited about it or not. Lor and Silas are getting stuff too. You're being honoured for winning that falcon race. I can't believe you haven't guessed that last bit already. Thirteen minutes. Hurry up.'

Moved to action, he thrust his arms into the sleeves and shrugged into the ceremonial coat. He stayed abso-lutely still as she fussed with the positioning of the shoul-ders and brushed her hand across his broad back.

'Hmm,' she murmured.

'What now?'

'Tight fit.'

He knew that. 'It'll be worse when the buttons are done up, so I'll leave them loose until we get to the capital.' He'd done this before, he knew how to stay as comfort-able as possible for as long as possible.

'What about the buckles on the sleeves?'

'They can be done now.' He turned and caught a waft of faint fragrance, something velvety and rich. 'Is that why Leonidas refused your return after the kidnapping? Because you weren't his?' It took a while, what with all her talk of craving him, but his brain did eventually kick in around their earlier conversation thread.

'Probably.' She reached for the first buckle, her fingers quick and nimble. 'They'd have had better luck taking Cas. Instead, they snatched a second-born girl child and likely not even his. Little wonder the King reacted as he did.'

'And yet your captors let you live.'

'I know plenty of my political opponents think I've got Stockholm Syndrome, but my captors were not bad people. Misguided, yes. Naïve to think they'd just be able to hand me back and take a seat at the negotiating table—Leonidas would have been perfectly capable of sitting them down and slaughtering them, don't you think?'

'Well, I do *now*.'

'But my captors weren't child killers. They didn't cut off any of my body parts and send them back in the post. In many ways they were very kind to me. They reminded me of you and your father.'

He was aghast. 'Is that supposed to be a *compliment*?'

'Clearly you don't think so.'

He could do nothing but stare.

'I had my very own pony, wolfhound and falcon, and substitute parents who treated me far better than my own ever had. I had other children all around me and a nomadic lifestyle that made every day an adventure. I begged them to keep me. Promised I'd be useful to them one day.'

He didn't like her captors and never would. He would sooner gut Lord Ildris, her advisor, than look at him, and the other man knew it. They claimed ground around each other very, very carefully.

'They took you as an act of ill intent. Ripped you from

your home because they wanted more for themselves.' Tomas *didn't* forgive them their sins.

She'd finished with the buckles on one vambrace. He lowered his arm and raised the other. 'Did you ever think of the people you left behind? The ones who grieved for you and thought of you and blamed themselves for years because they couldn't keep you safe?'

As soon as the words left his mouth, he knew he'd revealed too much. He might as well have screamed *What about me?* Her fingers faltered, clumsy, and then she found the strap again and pulled the buckle way too tight. 'Easy,' he muttered.

'Sorry.' She loosened it and found the right buckle hole.

'The apology is mine,' he offered gruffly. 'What you did to survive, how you coped after being taken, is none of my business. I'm glad your captors realised your worth and treated you kindly. I reserve the right to question their humanity.'

She dropped her gaze to his vambrace, long lashes shielding her expression. 'I missed Cas terribly at first. Then I decided he'd take far fewer beatings if I wasn't around because he wouldn't have to protect me. I decided I was protecting him for once. I was a hero in my own imagination.' She finished doing up the buckles and he let his hand drop as she looked up at him through her lashes, her eyes glittering with tears. 'I missed you and your father and the falcons most of all. I knew you'd be worried and that you'd...grieve...if you thought me dead.'

'I prayed for you,' he confessed gruffly. He'd hidden himself away in places no one could find him and prayed as hard as he could for her safe return. 'I grieved.'

She'd held a special place in his heart for so many years. Beloved. Untouchable.

Dead.

And yet here she was, spinning him round, twisting him inside out, because he didn't know what to *feel* when he was in her presence.

'I'm sorry.' She was going to ruin her make-up if she let those tears fall. 'All I wanted was to feel safe. And loved. Both. That's still my guiding star and something I seek again as an adult. In a lover.'

There was too much honesty in this conversation for him to reply.

He shrugged away from her instead. Heaven, give him space.

'I called my first pony Tomas. My first wolfhound Tom-Tom. My first falcon Toot Lolo,' she told him and then took a step back. 'Call me obsessed. I won't deny it. I wanted to remember you any way I could.' Delicate colour stained her cheeks as she tugged the sleeve of her travelling cloak aside to glance at her wristwatch again. 'Three minutes,' she said, as if she could force briskness upon them. 'You might want to do something with your hair. It's sticking up all over the place.'

He retreated to the bathroom, feeling flayed around the edges. Heartsore over the naming of a bird. He normally took a towel to his hair then ran his fingers through it for good measure, but he was six weeks past due for a haircut and maybe this time he could use a comb.

Maybe doing something so menial would bury the urge to take his fingers to her hair and mess it up beyond redemption as he pressed slow kisses to her cheeks and her eyes and inevitably her mouth.

He met his own gaze in the mirror and narrowed his

eyes and flattened his mouth until he looked fierce and forbidding, all other emotions forcefully contained.

Better.

She smiled when he exited the bathroom and he scowled his reply, but did that deter her?

'You look amazing,' she murmured approvingly. 'I'm grateful you're not yet married or otherwise attached. Why is that? Lack of opportunity? Hidden vice? A solitary nature?'

'I am what I am.' It wasn't his fault he'd never yet found a woman who could handle him in the long term. 'Don't analyse me.'

'You're asking the impossible.'

'You've risen from the dead once already.' As far as he was concerned, she was mistress of the impossible. 'Just do it.'

Claudia waited impatiently as her brother's equerry stood by the closed double doors to the throne room and ticked her, Tomas, Silas and Lor off the guest list. It was an honours day with Cas in residence, intent on bestowing riches on the worthy. Silas and Lor—being well past retirement age—were being gifted a grace-and-favour cottage within the walls of the winter fortress and a generous stipend to replace their wages. If they weren't yet ready to retire, there was now a plan in place for them to step back gradually from their vast responsibilities. Silas's bones had been brittle of late. It was time to slow down.

Claudia was being gifted a previously mothballed duchy on Byzenmaach's northernmost border, and it encompassed the winter fortress in its entirety. Henceforth, she would be known as Princess Claudia, the Princess

Royal, King's Counsel and Duchess of Ayerlon. So many daunting titles and she vowed to do them all justice.

As for Tomas, he too would receive his due.

She'd had a hand in it, of course. All he had to do was keep an open mind.

The King was waiting for them just inside the doors and Tomas entered and bowed as he was introduced by name and lineage. His family had been falcon masters for centuries and in service to the King for the last three generations, and he was proud of that legacy. He knew he would have to take a wife soon to secure the family name, but he was still in his early thirties. There was still time to find someone suitable.

*Don't go there*, he told himself fiercely. Do *not* picture Claudia of Byzenmaach in your bed.

He who'd spent years honing his senses so he would always be in control of his reactions and his raptors had a dominant streak a mile wide in the bedroom. He *liked* being in control. It was a point of pride that he could just as easily satisfy his partners with soft, slow kisses and attentiveness as he could when he got his edge on. The point was, he *never* lost his head. He never stopped noticing and analysing everything about the person he was with.

He did not want to think about what might happen if he added Claudia and a mountain of unresolved feelings to *that* mix.

He stood in line, waiting his turn to stand before his King, and tried not to look too shocked when Claudia—regal and resplendent in a rose-coloured ballgown and diamond choker and earrings—received a duchy that encompassed the finest mountain wilderness in all the land. It included the winter fortress. That fortress so casually traded was his *home*, and indignation prickled at his skin, already held tight by the fine fabric of a coat that had been made for ceremony rather than for him.

He watched, silently seething but outwardly a picture of calm, as her brother held out his hand and she took it and rose and kissed him on each cheek before moving on.

Silas and Lor then took her place in front of Casimir and Tomas wondered, not for the first time, how old they were. Were they in their eighties already? Late seventies? They'd been old when he was a kid. Kind and patient with him, the grandparents of his heart in lieu of blood kin.

Tomas listened as Silas and Lor were given a pathway towards living out their days in a manner both generous and respectful of the many years they'd called the winter fortress home. It was fitting, and Tomas grudgingly approved.

And then it was his turn and he wondered exactly what Casimir had in mind for him.

He was too young to retire, so why was he here?

'Tomas Sokolov, son of Andreas, grandson of Yos,' King Casimir began. 'Your skill and dedication to the sport of falconry has brought Byzenmaach great standing. Your breeding programmes for endangered species are acknowledged worldwide. My sister vouches for your kindness and protective nature when we were children. My wife and daughter cherish your patience and gentleness with them. Beyond that, I know you, Master Falconer. I see your dedication to the welfare of all in your care and your passion for your causes. It's time to spread your wings.'

'Are you firing me?' Because he couldn't. *Surely* he wouldn't? Tomas had been nothing but loyal, and although he had apprentices to pass his knowledge on to, it would take years before any of the current crop could replace him. 'Fair warning, many of the birds in my care will go where I go.' It wasn't an idle threat. 'There's no other way.' Casimir *knew* this, surely. 'They're imprinted on me.'

'Good thing I'm rewarding you rather than letting you go, then, isn't it.' Casimir sounded exasperated. 'Happy surprise, my arse. I knew I should have warned you in advance.'

Tomas held his tongue as Equerry Dorn approached with a weathered scroll sitting atop a velvet pillow. Claudia held a similar scroll in her now gloved hand.

'Kneel.'

Tomas held his tongue some more, bowed his head and knelt before his King.

'Tomas Sokolov, I bequeath to you the Barony of Aergoveny, henceforth to be held by you and your descendants, male or female, for as long as your bloodline exists. The land is mountainous, with summer grazing in the high passes. There's a village with several families in residence within your borders and they pay pennies in local government taxes in return for being left largely to themselves. I'm reliably informed that several people there have expressed interest in becoming apprenticed to you, should you want to encourage it.'

'I already have apprentices,' he murmured beneath his breath.

'Have some more. A modest manor house surrounded by solid outer walls lies east of the village—I have stonemasons working to bring it back in good repair. There are aviaries, stables and animal enclosures that should please you. As for funds, which you're going to need, I bestow upon you the prize money recently won by the falcon Sweetybird McTender Heart, otherwise known as Cloud—we seriously need to work on those bird names, Master Falconer, if we're going to keep winning major competitions.'

'Blame your daughter.' Tomas sneaked a glance at the other man, unsure if this was some kind of elaborate joke, or maybe just a dream. But he'd never dreamed of being an aristocrat—and it wasn't because he lacked ambition. He ran one of the most ambitious endangered raptor breed-and-release programmes in Europe. But he emphatically didn't want the responsibility to *people* that came with an aristocrat's title, and he'd make a terrible Lord. Could he refuse the honour? Maybe not publicly, maybe not now, but later?

Did he *want* to refuse fifty million dollars?

Casimir's eyes narrowed and Tomas swiftly bowed his head.

'In addition to the prize money, as per the competition rules of 1649, I grant you permission to keep *two* wives, now that you have the monetary means to do so.'

*What?*

'Rules are rules.'

Tomas felt the tap of a ceremonial sword on each shoulder. This wasn't real. It couldn't be. He was no nobleman. He barely had table manners. But Casimir was smiling and taking a scroll from a purple velvet pillow and handing it to him and people were applauding, so maybe it wasn't a dream after all.

'Arise Lord Sokolov, King's Falconer, Baron of Aergoveny. Welcome to the circus.'

# CHAPTER FIVE

HE WASN'T TAKING it well. Claudia scoured the banquet
hall that heaved with all the people and the families of
the people who had received honours that day. Tomas
stood alone, silent and forbidding. There'd been no Sokolov family to invite—his parents and grandparents were
dead and, according to Silas and Lor, who'd acted as his
surrogate family for years, he had no extended family.

The way he stood with his feet slightly apart and his
arms behind his back suggested a man perfectly at ease.
The tension in that perfectly chiselled jaw and the ice in
his eyes for anyone he didn't know suggested otherwise.
The look he'd given her a few minutes earlier had been
glacial enough to compete with the highest mountain
peaks. She'd raised her chin and offered her most challenging smile in return.

*Your move, my lord.*

Sadly, he'd yet to move an inch.

'You're glaring,' said a voice from beside her and she
turned to survey her brother, resplendent in ceremonial
garb. 'Little wrinkles around your eyes, here and here.'
Cas touched his own face in ever helpful fashion. 'Why
are you glaring?'

As if he didn't know. 'Two. Wives.'

Cas smirked. 'Don't look at me. The right to two wives

came with the prize money. Of course, the rules go on to say that should a man's first wife object to the taking of a second one, the first wife gets the inflationary indexed equivalent of all the prize money. She can do whatever she wants with it.'

Claudia contemplated this latest bit of information. 'How perfectly brutal.'

'I knew you'd like it.' He touched the space between his eyebrows. 'Still with the little wrinkles.'

'I don't like these events.'

'Who does? And yet they serve a valuable purpose. Who should praise and encourage good deeds and excellence if not a country's leader?' Her brother's smile cooled. 'You were the one who came back, Claudia. To advocate for change, you said. To be of use. Well, the price to pay is your presence in my inner circle and that means a million more banquets like this one. You know this.'

She did know.

She'd made that devil's bargain. She had her brother's ear. He *listened* when she spoke of the concerns and needs of those who straddled the borders to the north. More than that, he'd offered consultation and collaboration and respect for a nomadic way of life he couldn't possibly understand because he'd never lived it.

But she had lived that life of freedom, throughout her childhood, teens and early adulthood, and sometimes she missed it so much she wanted to weep and rage at the loss of it.

Now was one of those times.

She'd lobbied hard for Tomas to be given the barony and the prize money. He needed more room for more birds and the ability to expand his activities in that arena as he saw fit. He could be so much more than just a king's falconer, and Casimir needed strong, steadfast noblemen who could help preserve the mountain regions.

She hadn't realised until this moment, watching Tomas glower at her from across the room, that he might not have wanted to trade freedom for riches.

'It's going to work,' she murmured, suddenly desperate for reassurance. 'It has to.'

Cas stared and she lifted her chin high, even as fierce heat flooded her cheeks. She didn't usually display her vulnerability, at least not in public. She was the stolen princess who'd returned to her country, fierce and unbroken, some twenty years later. She had a myth to uphold. Desperately wanting approval for her actions didn't fit her image at all.

'Don't stare,' she told her brother. 'It's impolite.'

'I'm so sorry.' The tenderness in his voice slid through all the cracks in her armour and she silently cursed him for it. 'I didn't realise your feelings for our falconer ran so deep.'

'Well, now you know, and I'll thank you to keep your newfound insight to yourself. Tomas is going to love Aergoveny when he sees it. He'll be his own man, free to live and love as he pleases, and maybe he'll live well and choose to love me. That's my big master plan. Lame, isn't it.'

'It has a few holes in it, Cas conceded. 'You do realise that being pushy might not get you what you want?'

'Well, that's going to be annoying.'

Cas snorted. 'Poor Tomas.'

'Not any more.' She fixed Cas with her sternest gaze. 'You *are* getting ready to leave so we can all get out of here, right?' No one could leave before Cas made his exit.

'Rudolpho's been eyeing his watch and giving you stern glances for at least fifteen minutes.'

Rudolpho was Cas's valet or equerry or private secretary—it depended on requirements. Rudolpho kept her brother's days doable.

Cas nodded but made no move to leave. 'If I may be so bold as to make a suggestion concerning our newest baron?'

'You may. Provided it's *only* a suggestion.' One she could ignore.

Cas rolled his eyes and then leaned over to whisper words for her ears only.

'*Patience, sister.*'

Claudia had five minutes, if that, once Casimir took his leave before others started leaving too. So while Cas headed towards Rudolpho, Claudia made a beeline for Tomas.

'I have the keys to the map room,' she said as soon as she reached his side. 'Would you like to see drawings of the lands now under your care?'

'This is your doing.' The repressed fury in his voice gave her pause. She'd never seen Tomas properly angry. He was a man of infinite patience when it came to his birds, and horses and wolfhounds. Any beast, really. Even their occasional, ahem, arguments, hadn't involved full fury. Until now. '*You* put this *reward* in your brother's ear.'

The way he said the word *reward* made it perfectly clear he thought of it as something else entirely.

'Cas didn't need any convincing—if that's your problem.'

'I don't want a barony and great piles of money. I don't need them. I have enough responsibility.'

'To your birds.'

'Exactly. I don't need any responsibility to people. I don't generally *like* people.'

'Is that really true, though?' She nodded and smiled at her brother across the room as he finally took his leave. Tomas noticed, he always had been observant, and sketched a brief bow of his own towards the retreating monarch. 'Because you get on well enough with Silas and Lor. And Ana and Sophia and the stable master and his family and your apprentices.' There were others she could name. 'And they like you. You're firm and fair and I hear tell you have a kind heart.'

For those who could find it.

'Maybe what you don't like is thinking that you're going to somehow let people down, but I don't think you will.'

His scowl had intensified and she redoubled her efforts to convince him that she'd done the right thing for everyone concerned.

'The people of Aergoveny have been ignored for a very long time and they've heard of you, Tomas. They want their high country preserved, and who better to do that than a baron in need of vast tracts of wilderness, into which he can release all manner of wild creatures? They're willing to show a lot of respect to a man who can honour them and their children and preserve the old ways of falconry. They're already tuned to protecting habitat, as are you. As am I. You're going to be an excellent fit, and I, as mistress of the winter fortress, am going to support you in every way I can.'

Did he really not understand what she was trying to do?

'Aergoveny is yours now. And it's a big change from what you're used to, but think of what you can achieve. You can appoint a steward to help with the day-to-day management of your household and the surrounding lands. You can employ people to help you accomplish goals. You know how important remote settlements can be for those who inhabit them. You know how they run.'

His silence unsettled her.

'You can expand your breeding programmes, take on seasonal apprentices, invite experts from all over the world to stay under your roof. Hatch plans that reflect your values and no one can stop you now. It's freedom.'

'It's a cage.'

'You've been bound since birth by your family's service to the Crown. That's a cage too. This cage is bigger,' she snapped.

*Patience, sister.*

So much for sound advice.

She focused on her breathing, slowed it down, and tried not to push too hard and too fast.

All he had to do was give his new life a chance. Give *her* a chance. She was a woman of great confidence and clarity—everyone said so, and most of the time it was true.

She wouldn't disappoint.

'And, in addition, presenting you with the means to excel even more in your chosen field, as a nobleman, you and I are now on a far more level playing field.' And if he still didn't get it, 'Meaning that if you want to, you're now well placed to pursue me. Romantically. *Openly.*' Because that was important too.

Had she really imagined the fire in his eyes all those times he'd looked at her before turning resolutely away? Had she misjudged the way he watched her when he thought no one was looking? Had he been unable to keep his eyes off her because she dazzled him or had he simply been keeping watch to make sure she wasn't spirited away again by forces unknown?

'I'm not written into your future. I wouldn't do that,' she assured him. 'But I am a possibility. I always have been. I've just made things a bit easier for us, should you ever actually want me.'

He was like a big, silent wall. The resplendent King's Falconer, with his iron will and magnificent body and eyes of deepest brown.

'It goes against my nature having someone else call the shots *the way you so very clearly do*,' he said finally.

Was that meant to be a warning?

'You like being in control, yes, yes, I know. Probably in the bedroom too, am I right? I've heard rumours of your, um, prowess. I am here for you in that regard. I know what I like and I definitely like that. You be you. I'll be me. I'm very fond of saying please.'

More silence greeted her earnest words. Startled, bemused silence, dripping incredulity all over the marble floor.

'So would you like to see the map room now or would you rather take another decade or two to think about it?'

She'd had such good plans for them this evening. Was it too much to ask for a thimbleful of cooperation?

'I'm going home.'

She could work with that. Privacy was all they needed.

'I'm getting out of these stupid clothes.'

*Yes, yes, exactly!*

'And then I'm going to do what I planned to do all along, and take a trip into the mountains for a couple of weeks and do my job, and fulfil the commitments I made before you so helpfully rearranged my *world*.'

He had no idea how badly she wanted to pull on her travelling furs and ride out there with him. The problem with that plan being that she had political commitments all next week, along with two royal luncheons and a trip to a neighbouring kingdom as her brother's envoy.

'If you can postpone your trip for a week, I could come with you.'

'No.'

'You are *so* infuriating.'

'Me? You think I'm the infuriating one in this—' he made a sharp gesture with his arm as if he couldn't find the right word '—this...'

'Relationship?' she supplied hopefully.

'Conversation! That's all this is. A conversation.'

'I'm disappointed in you. At least call it a battle of wits.'

'No.'

'Robust courting?'

'Wrong again. You made me a lord. On a *whim*.'

'It wasn't a whim. It was a carefully considered reward for your service to falconry, a savvy political move on Cas's part, and an act of utmost faith in your character.'

He stared at her for what seemed like an eternity.

'And I'm not giving up on you.' Might as well get that out in the open too.

'Oh, for the—

'For the what?'

At least he was talking again.

'Show me the blasted map room!'

* * *

He wasn't capitulating. Just because he was walking down a long, empty corridor in a section of the palace he'd never been in before, with the terror that was Claudia leading the way, didn't mean that he thought any of this was right and good, or that he deserved to be called anyone's lord.

He was doing this because public showdowns had never been his style and he and Claudia had been heading straight for one.

He was following her lead because he'd needed to get away from prying eyes and fawning courtiers and she'd offered him a way to do so that afforded him minimal contact with others.

That was what he told himself and he mostly believed it.

Right up until they entered the map room with its vaulted ceilings and wooden tables and feature lamps illuminating priceless parchment. A fire crackled merrily in the enormous stone hearth, and supper had been laid out on a sideboard.

Claudia smiled her approval and let out a little sigh as if she too had found the ceremonial events taxing. 'Make yourself at home,' she said, and proceeded to remove one earring and then its pair. 'You have no idea how heavy old jewellery is. It was my mother's and I'm supposed to have some sort of mystical emotional connection to it, but I don't. It feels like a noose.' Her hands went to the clasp of her necklace and she moved closer and turned her back on him. 'Would you mind? There's a clasp disguised as a flower with a little pearl in the middle and you have to push on the pearl and then—oh, okay, you've done this before.' The clasp came apart and she caught the necklace before it could fall. 'Thanks.'

The fact that she looked so put-out by his apparent expertise put him in a better mood than he'd been in all day. He didn't bother to say 'No problem', figuring his smirk spoke for him.

Non-verbal cues were his strength, after all.

She slid him a sideways glance as she placed the jewels on a nearby table and started tugging on her gloves, one fabric finger at a time until she'd taken those off too.

'Feel free to take off your coat,' she murmured, knowing full well that he couldn't do so without her help.

'I won't be here long enough to settle in.'

She made that small hmm she was so fond of. The one that never failed to make his manhood stand up and take notice. 'There are ledgers here too. Stocking rates and harvest figures courtesy of the last Baron of Aergoveny back in 1672. Are you sure you don't want to at least undo all those buttons on your coat?'

'Positive.' He was one hundred percent sure she was downright evil, knowing as she did that he'd left doing those buttons up until the last possible minute. But he needed to be in control of something, even something as insignificant as when he undressed. 'You're bossy.'

'I prefer to call it having leadership skills.' Now she was the one with the smirk, and it was infuriating.

'Not quite the same thing.'

'Hmm.' She headed for one of the far tables and turned on a lamp to illuminate the map placed upon it. It had the ripples that came of being rolled up for a long time, and someone had placed strips of lead around the edges to keep it flat. He wanted to remain unmoved, but the weight of history and continuity wore him down. Even so...

'How can this be owned by anyone?'

'It can't,' she said simply. 'We just pretend. But you can be a steward, with protection your goal.'

'I never asked for this.'

She traced the outline of the estate with her forefinger. 'The land suits your needs perfectly. It may not seem like home to you at first, but as the years pass, surely that will change. Your Barony could become one of the greatest reserves in northern Byzenmaach and beyond. Cas is already pressuring neighbouring kings to dedicate land in that mountain range to preservation. You can lead conversation and influence policy and all you have to do is believe.' She turned to face him, her eyes beseeching. 'Protection for this land. Financial independence and opportunity for you and yours. Why can't you see this as an opportunity? Is it because I'm the one who fought for it?'

The things he wanted to *do* to her.

'My hands are rough. *I* can be rough. My sexual appetite is strong. Coarse. Greedy.' So he'd been told. 'I'm not a nobleman.'

Her eyes glowed.

'Claudia, it's a *warning*.' He couldn't be more plain. 'I would ruin you if I let desire rule me. Rule *us*.'

'Please try. You have my full permission. Because I certainly want to ruin you. I'd even put you back together afterwards. You have my word.'

'You are so—'

She stopped his words with her lips against his and as far as tactics went it was ridiculously effective.

His coat was too tight and her lips were too warm. The skin of her cheek was softer than feathers against his calloused fingers. She was finer than any woman he'd ever kissed and his mad, hidden desire for her made itself well and truly evident. She was a gossamer butterfly beneath his hands and he still had control—a slender silken thread of it. He hadn't ruined anything yet.

Only after her eyelashes fluttered closed did he slip his leash enough to savour her, tilting his head for better access and taking his fill. He fitted her body to his so easily, or maybe he gathered her in—was he holding her too tightly?—hard to know his own strength, and he felt honoured, and hounded and completely adrift from reality in this room of maps and traps and other people's history. He didn't know who he was any more or where he fitted in the grand schemes of kings, but he knew without doubt that if he could kiss like this every day he would be a wealthy man.

And for every bit of common sense that said no, Tomas, back up a bit and *think*, desire made him stupid.

He didn't stop her when she unbuttoned his coat and the shirt beneath it too, because he wanted her hands on his skin so badly, and she seemed intent on delivering. When her nails scraped lightly across his skin and edged across his nipple with a quick and sudden change in pressure, digging in like a claw, he shuddered his approval. When her lips left his to trail across to his jaw, pillow-soft right up until that moment when she nipped the sensitive skin just behind his ear, he groaned. New kink. Formerly unknown hotspot.

'Do that again.'

And she laughed against his skin and soothed with her tongue, catching his earlobe and, hello. He wouldn't object to her spending more time there too, but right now her kisses were more important. He could lose himself if he wasn't careful.

And right now, he definitely wasn't being careful.

When he lowered the zip at the side of her gown, a hidden item he'd spent some time looking for in the ballroom when fantasising about undressing her, his only thought was *yes*. He could be gentle, and the smooth slide of haute-couture undoings proved it.

See?

She was beautiful in the lamplight, all golden skin and rosy flushes, and he bent his head to her breast and drew a cry of pleasure that would stay with him for ever.

She was generous in her praise of his every move. So willing to go where he led. That he wanted to savour every moment, and she wanted to rush, made her huff and him laugh. Slowly, he unwound for her and let the fire between them burn hot and needy.

When his fingers dipped beneath her panties, she swiftly got rid of them and stood before him, naked but for her glittering pearl-coloured stilettos, as she placed the palm of her hand over his manhood and claimed his mouth with kisses that grew wilder with every breath.

There was a tabletop *right there*, and she scored his back with her polished nails as he shoved his trousers out of the way, lifted her up and dragged her against him so she was barely resting on the table edge and the rest of her rested on *him*. She closed her thighs and legs around him, cradled him, and it only took a moment to lift her up and on, and his forehead connected with hers as she whimpered and they both looked as, inch by inch, she took him in.

He'd never felt anything like it—this haunting, perfect homecoming.

She gasped, or was it a whimper, as he clenched his teeth and clutched the hard edge of the table rather than leave bruises on *her*, as he fought to stay in control so that he didn't drive too deep, but her whispered words weren't exactly helping, broken curses smattered with '*yes*' and '*don't stop*' and '*more*'.

'Lie back,' he muttered harshly, hoping to make their joining more comfortable for her. 'Let me.'

Let him put his calloused thumb to her centre and press it against his thick ridge as he tried so hard to be gentle with her and limit the power of his thrusts. Let him raise her arms above her head and clasp her wrists together as he teased and suckled her areolas to pointed nubbins.

*Let me lose my way in the slap of flesh against flesh and hope you like rough edges.*

*Watch you twist and brace as I steal whimpers straight from your mouth, and I warned you it would be like this.*

Heaven was opening up before him, warm and slick, and, no matter how hard he tried to be otherwise, Tomas was not a gentleman.

Claudia had relatively modest expectations for the concept of heaven on earth, right up until the moment Tomas entered her and unleashed his emotions. His earthy, uninhibited desire flat-out worked for her—so much for his muttered words of warning—and he was beautiful in the lamplight. A golden-skinned warrior, finally hers to hold. A hard man, barely able to contain his fascination for her softest places because he had none of his own. He was like an aphrodisiac made especially for her, and she was rushing towards a finish line that was far too close, because once she crossed it the pleasure might stop.

'No,' she whispered when he repositioned them both so he could put a thumb to her centre. She clutched at his wrist and felt him freeze. 'I'm not going to last.' She guided his hand north and pressed a kiss to his knuckles.

He smiled then, and all but melted her with its sweetness. 'You can go again.' But this time when he began to move, his hips were slow and sure, with a sensuous roll and drag guaranteed to send her into orbit anyway. 'Better?'

She closed her eyes on a particularly close brush with the end. 'Not exactly going to fix my problem.'

'How sad,' he murmured into the skin of her neck, and did it again, and again, as she arched up into him, chasing whatever wild magic he was delivering. There was no going back now—only up, up.

And over.

'*Bastard.*' It had to be said.

Tomas found his completion moments after Claudia left earth, and she laughed, because it was all so glittering bright and perfect.

His hair clung to his forehead in damp curls. Her princess bun likely resembled a bird's nest. She pressed a kiss to his temple as his ragged breathing slowed and so did hers. Their bodies were so in sync. She laughed again, inviting him to share her joy. 'Whatever will we do for an encore?'

Tomas said nothing, and she re-entered the earth's orbit with a searing sense of disappointment. Their bodies hadn't lied but minds lied all the time. Memories lied. Self-evaluation was notoriously unreliable.

'Don't say anything awful,' she begged.

'You'll bruise.' She could barely hear the words within his gravelly rumble.

She could work with that. 'My lover's desire mapped out on my skin. A compliment.'

'Don't humour me.'

'There's no shame in honest desire. My marks will be on you too. I want you to regret their fading.'

He drew a ragged breath.

'I want this.' Could she be any more direct? 'I want to be with you like this again. Don't pack all that fierce, gorgeous emotion away. There's nothing wrong with it. I don't bring out the worst in you, do I? Because, from where I stand, this is the very best of you and I am here for it. Why can't we see where this attraction ends?'

'You're a myth.' He loosened his hold and stepped away and moments later she was sitting naked on the table while he tugged his trousers into place.

'And you're not?' She began to laugh, harder this time, and wondered whether he'd still be here when laughter turned to tears. She'd known that rushed intimacy might deliver a rough landing, and that she would feel fragile in the face of his withdrawal. She'd taken that risk anyway. 'You've been my rescuer since I was seven years old. For real to begin with, and then in my dreams. But I'm prepared to consider you a real person—complex and flawed—if you'll do the same for me.'

'I'm no rescuer,' he said, and the tight fury in his voice made her stop and listen, even though she'd scooped up her dress and the best thing to do would be to put it on rather than strangle it with her bare hands. 'I wanted to find you and keep you safe but, no matter where I looked, you weren't there. I failed you.'

'No! You saved me from so many beatings. You spoke up for me and persuaded your father to take me under his wing and gave me a getaway place and moments to look forward to. Once they took me, I didn't really expect you to—' *Save me.* But she had expected that, and maybe deep down she *still* expected him to make life here in

Byzenmaach more bearable. 'I knew you wouldn't come for me. How could you?'

And yet how many nights had she stayed awake *hoping* he'd crawl into her tent, hold out his hand and whisk her to safety? Especially in those early days. Maybe Tomas wasn't the only one who needed to deal with the past and admit *all* the emotions. Even the ugly ones.

'I mean, I could dream, but you were just a boy and I *knew* there was nothing you could do. You were powerless, like me.'

'Is this conversation meant to make me feel *better*?' He'd half turned to stare at her from beneath a lowered brow and he was every bit as forbidding as the apex predators he served.

'I'm rather hoping it's not going to send you straight to therapy,' she muttered, slipping the gown over her head. 'Who cares if I'm a fantasy princess to you and you're a Galahad figure to me? We can work with that. Neither of us is powerless *now*. We *have* control of our lives going forward. We're outstanding together in bed, even if our communication elsewhere still needs work. And I for one have worked my arse off to get to this moment and I'm exhilarated.'

By the time she'd wrestled the gown in place, he had the buttons on his shirt done up and was helping himself to a glass of water over by the sideboard. He poured one for her too, but didn't bring it over.

'So, can I pencil you in for a private dinner and dessert some time soon?' she asked. 'After you return from your trip into the mountains?'

'You're relentless.'

'Is that a yes?'

He shrugged and drew attention to those stunningly

broad shoulders, and she tried not to let her eyes glaze over with renewed sexual appreciation. Probably too soon. But he noticed her reaction, and was that a slight shoulder muscle flex just for her? Maybe there was hope for them yet.

'I'll be away for at least three weeks.'

She'd waited longer for less. 'Okay.'

'I might swing by Aergoveny on my way back.'

'You should.'

He nodded, still with his back to her, and then gestured awkwardly towards the array of bottles on the sideboard. 'May I pour you something stronger?'

'I'll have the Highland single malt Scotch, please. No ice.'

'There's ice?'

'In the silver ice bucket with the lid.'

'How *anyone* thought I'd make a decent aristocrat…'

'You will.' He had a generous and deft hand when pouring, a certain grace about him as he crossed the room and handed it to her. 'You could join me in a drink.'

A tentative knock on the library door diverted his attention. Alarm flashed in his eyes as he looked at her. 'What is it?' he barked, every word forbidding.

The door stayed closed. 'A messenger from King Casimir, Lord Aergoveny. He says to tell you the helicopter is leaving for the winter fortress at ten p.m.'

'I'll be on it.'

Claudia glanced at her watch. Twenty minutes from now. So much for persuading him to stay the night with her.

'Your brother's protecting your reputation,' said Tomas with a frown, once the sound of footsteps had retreated.

'Or yours,' she pointed out. 'Possibly his. Likely all

three. You don't need the added complication of being known as my lover while establishing your new position. Cas doesn't need people thinking him a soft king who would bestow a barony on you at my request—not that he *did*.' Basic statecraft. She *knew* this. *Patience, Claudia*. 'He's looking out for us.'

'You mean he's controlling the situation because we've failed to do so.'

'Nonsense. We've got this.'

'Princess…'

They were back to honorifics and her heart broke a little because she'd thought they were done with that.

'Don't Princess me.'

'Today has been…a lot,' he continued, without uttering her name. 'And while I'm ambitious in my own way, I've never sought a barony. I've never thought about what that could mean. I've never imagined this, us, being something that could happen openly, and I need time to think about that too.'

'Unbridled passion not about to sway you?'

He huffed a reluctant laugh. 'Clearly it *did*.'

'I want…' Did it even matter what she wanted in the face of his retreat? 'My brother warned me about being pushy. I should have listened to him.' *Patience, Claudia*. Let the man catch up. 'To your freedom, Tomas. To happiness and fulfilment, no matter where your road leads. My hearth is ever open to you and yours.' She set her drink down and pressed her hands to her chest and then extended them towards him, one cupped hand sitting atop the other to form a heart shape. It was a formal farewell offered by the people of the high north. A pledge of unconditional support, no matter what the future might bring. 'Safe travels, Master Falconer, Lord Sokolov of Aergoveny.'

He brought his heels together and bowed his head. 'Thank you. I'll…be in touch.'

She hated slippery words and empty promises. Especially from a man who'd already pleaded his need for space. 'Break my heart now and quickly if you must. I hate false hope.'

'Isn't that all I've ever given you?' He was back to being harsh and distant.

'Why would you even think that?' If he didn't leave soon, hot tears would fall. 'No,' she said earnestly. 'You gave me reason to hope. Nothing false about it. Just like there's nothing false about what I'm offering. But if you don't want it, go. Leave me some dignity.' As much as could be gathered with her lopsided hair and sated body and heart he had no desire to claim.

'I'll be away for three weeks, maybe more. Will you be at the fortress when I return?'

Her fortress now. Also the only home he'd ever known. Awkward. But then, she'd left so many places in her lifetime, even special ones. If Aergoveny didn't work out for him and he wanted to return to the winter fortress, she would move on. She could occupy the rooms set aside for her here at the palace. She could build something. 'I return there on the eighteenth. And you have another helicopter to catch in…eleven minutes. Time to go, Lord Sokolov.' See? She could do stilted formality too.

He ran his fingers through his hair and straightened his vambraces. Checked that his belt was positioned just so.

'You have a bit of lipstick…' She demonstrated the spot by pointing to the area on her own face, but he got the wrong cheek. 'Other side.'

'Thanks. You have…'

He made a flapping motion with his hand that seemed to encompass her entire body.

'I'm in need of a mirror, yes. I'll see to it.'

'You look…'

'I *know*.'

'I was going to say beautiful. Better than any dream I've ever had.'

Oh.

'The phones never work up in the mountains where I'm going,' he said steadily as opened the door a crack. 'Look to the skies for my homing pigeons bearing news.'

# CHAPTER SIX

IT WAS ALL very well to promise news and load up with homing pigeons to release at various stages on the journey—should other birds on the mountain be willing to leave them alone, but it was another issue altogether to try and write cramped little messages that were in any way meaningful.

Tomas was a man of very few words. He'd had more as a boy, but his trust in others had waned with Claudia's disappearance and been shattered when her father, the King, had refused to barter for her return. This new world with Casimir in charge was kinder, and the politics progressive, but Tomas still struggled to trust others—even his apprentices, who had proven themselves capable many times over. Giving him a barony and even *more* people to oversee just meant more work for him until he learned how to delegate.

Maybe he should write about that.

Today I thought about how to find staff for a manor house. And whether I seriously need to know what tableware to use for any given situation. Is this why I need two wives?

He couldn't finish a message there. Could he?

Mt. Saer: three golden eagle pairs, all plus eggs. On to Mt. Raeschi.

That would do. No need to overthink it, or to mention just how often he thought of Claudia's softness, her fierce strength, or the warm cradle of her body. Of course, there was always the slim chance the pigeon might not find its way home, but if it did his team had instructions to make sure the Princess Royal received the message.

A week later, something appeared in the sky that looked like no bird he'd ever seen. Something that startled his horses and made his falcons flap their wings in alarm. A drone. A drone, flying royal ribbons—it hovered in front of his face. This was a travesty. Gross misuse of airspace. Falcon fakery of the highest order. Maybe he'd club it to bits.

'Good morning, Master Falconer. Nice bushy beard you've got growing there.' Claudia's words rang out loud and clear.

'Why is this mechanical thing tracking me?'

'Well, I could hardly send a homing pigeon to you, now, could I? That's a one-way trip. Whereas this communication method…once the satellite picked up your coordinates, all I had to do was feed them into the program and hope for a sunny day. Marvellous, isn't it? Solar-powered. It's a military prototype.'

'I loathe it.'

'Hence the scowl, yes, I see. I was rather hoping you'd be impressed by my ingenuity.'

'The fact that he couldn't *see her* irritated him mightily.

'So, to answer your questions about the troubles inherent in having too many wives—I predict many, *many* troubles, too many to count. I don't recommend it.'

'You're not sitting in a room full of generals, are you? Because now would be a good time to tell me that.' He put his finger up against what he thought was the camera lens.

'Stop messing with my tech,' she ordered. 'Don't make me zap you. And there's no one else in the room with me. I'm the only one who can see and hear you.'

'That you know of,' he muttered darkly and kept his finger right where it was. There was nothing wrong with a little paranoia.

'You're going to need Lillis & Co pattern number PT12CBQ, white ribbed bone china, times twelve, plus banquet dishware. RWBee stainless steel cutlery plus full banquet mix additions for a table of eighteen. Veni glassware—crystalline with silver, design number CS32, and no one wants to skimp on glassware so you'll need the full set, meaning twenty-four of everything they can think of.'

'When you say "going to need…" Am I? Am I really? What if I've decided to be a no-frills baron with simple tastes?'

'I've sent you a list to look at when you return. You do intend to return to civilisation at some point?'

'Yes.' The drone rose into the air, dislodging his finger as it began to slowly circle him. 'That's cheating.'

'So, this is your camp.'

The drone stopped to hover over his tent and small campfire where three falcons perched unhooded—two of them with their bellies full of rabbit entrails, the third hungry and ready for flight. A pair of pigeons sat caged, awaiting release, and his three horses had been pegged out on a sweet grazing patch.

But had he sensed disapproval in her words rather than curiosity?

'What's wrong with it?'

'Needs more people. No one has your back.'

'I can protect myself.' He had enough hardware hidden on his person to stop single predators cold and a pump shotgun in the tent to defend against pack wolves. His birds and horses were more than capable of letting him know if he should be concerned by anything nearby. 'I'm not without survival skills.'

'That's so sexy.'

'I *really* hope no one's listening to you right now.'

'That I find you sexy isn't news. Find me someone of our acquaintance who *doesn't* know I'm hunting you and I'll show you a unicorn. Do you believe in unicorns, Tomas?' She sounded slightly wistful.

'I stay up here long enough, I start believing all sorts of things are possible,' he admitted gruffly. 'Although being tracked by a stolen military drone wasn't one of them.'

'Have you been thinking about us?'

'A lot.'

'I like honesty in a man. Also decisiveness. Are you ready to have dinner with me yet?'

'I thought we'd already established this as a possibility.'

'Hmm.' In no world would he ever mistake that little hum of hers as full agreement. 'Care to make it a certainty? When will you be back?'

'End of the month, maybe.' But he wasn't making promises. 'Depends what kind of reception I get in Aergoveny, and whether I think it's a good idea to interview for household staff and apprentices.'

'I like the way you're thinking.'

All this time on the mountain had at least clarified his dislike of having decisions made about his future from on high.

'I don't like being led, coaxed, cajoled, steamrolled, overruled—it's just the way I'm built. Your willingness to think you know what's good for me is a problem. It's not what I want in a lover, a partner or even a casual companion.' He wished he could see her face. Anything was better than the noise of the drone and Claudia's complete silence. 'I respect you and admire you. You're a powerful, influential individual who lobbies hard and gets results. But the very strengths that make you so effective in your brother's court are the same qualities that give me pause when I think about forming an *us*. We both like to be in charge.'

'I can...see how that might be a problem,' she said finally. 'I think, though—within the parameters of a sexual or romantic relationship, or both—that I wouldn't always need or want to be the one in control. It would be a relief not to be.'

Her answer floored him more thoroughly than the sudden appearance of a flying elephant would have.

'You might find the real me not to your liking,' she continued. 'But don't assume you know how I'll be if we enter a relationship. The Princess Royal you're basing your assessment on is a carefully crafted political weapon. There's more to me. And less. And I'm sorry I misunderstood your pigeon message. I took it as an invitation to engage. I didn't realise your next step would be to say sorry, not interested, but I'm not without ears. Message received.'

The drone rose.

'Wait!'

The drone hovered.

'I may have spent too much time with my own thoughts

of late,' he admitted carefully. 'I still don't quite grasp what you want from me.'

'Same thing I've always wanted. A chance to know you properly, without artifice, titles or any other expectations getting in the way.' The little machine whirred and hummed. 'You said you needed a chance to think about it. If you've thought about it and don't want to take that chance, say so and I'll leave you to get on with your life. I *can* be told things I don't want to hear. I won't make your life difficult upon your return, if that's what you're worried about.'

He hadn't been worried about that at all.

'I don't even have to be there.'

'Claudia, stop. Can we start this conversation again? This time without your push and my defensive indecision. I'll start.' He felt such a fool, talking to a machine, but he'd dug his own hole when it came to communicating with this forthright, challenging woman and it was up to him to find a way out of it. 'Would you like to have dinner with me when I get to Aergoveny? Either somewhere in the village if there's a tavern or restaurant or at my manor house if it's privacy you prefer.'

'There's a tavern,' she said. 'We could meet there and keep plans fluid. The only thing I will ask from you now is a date and time. My calendar fills up fast.'

'August the fourth at six p.m.'

'A full moon,' she said after a moment. 'A blue moon, in fact.'

He knew it. But then, it was his business to know the wax and wane of those things that affected the creatures in his care. 'Is that a problem?'

'Of course not. Makes for an interesting night. Your apprentices are getting used to me dropping in on them.'

'How's the little peregrine with the twisted toes?'

'She's with me now. The others were picking on her.'

'You imprinted her?'

'I took her with me when I visited a school group the other day and have yet to return her into general care. She's so sweet. There was a young girl there with twisted feet. Serendipity, but it started a discussion on limitations and potential and set me to thinking. What are your thoughts on putting together a travelling show for schools featuring little peregrine hatchling Suly and various other injured birds that the apprentices tell me can't be released and are permanently in your care?'

'I'll consider it, but only if you stop stealing my birds.' He probably shouldn't be smiling so hard. 'I start my new apprentices on those birds.'

'You take one new apprentice a year, Tomas.'

'And the years add up!' He currently had four. 'And I'm considering adding more.'

'I do hope you include girls in those interviews.'

'If they come, I consider them.'

'If you invite them, they will come.'

'Why does my brain hurt every time we talk?'

'It's expanding with possibilities.'

'No, I think it's you messing with me.' He knew it was. The drone flew higher. 'You're smiling again.'

'I wish I could see your smile.' The words flew out before he could call them back. 'You sound insufferably smug.'

'I'll see you next blue moon. Don't be late because I will be there.'

'Can I shoot the drone now?' Because he was really, really itching to.

'You realise you could use one of these to get around

all your golden eagle mating sites in an afternoon? You should get one.'

He withdrew his Ruger and took aim. Why on this glorious earth would he want to do that? 'I hate progress.'

It only took one shot.

Claudia had a stomach bug. A three-day wouldn't-go-away stomach bug that saw her lose the previous night's meal before breakfast each morning and made her feel like a marionette going through the motions the rest of the day. She'd tried keeping her distance from others lest they catch the bug too, but this morning Ana and Sophia had brought a breakfast tray to her room and sat with her while she sipped at the thin chicken broth in a porcelain cup and pushed dry toast soldiers around a pretty fluted plate.

'Why are you here? You'll catch it too,' Claudia protested for at least the tenth time.

Ana's smile was just that little bit too knowing, and Claudia knew just what she was thinking. 'I'm *not* what you think I am. I took a test.'

'A blood test?'

Well, no. She'd peed on a stick and heaved a giant sigh of relief when the result had come up negative. As it should have, because she'd had an injection against becoming pregnant some three…possibly four…months ago. She'd been well and truly *covered* when she and Tomas had temporarily lost their minds and joined bodies in the map room.

'It's impossible.'

'Been there, done that.' Ana smiled gently and reached for her cup of tea. 'Meet my daughter.'

'Hi,' said Sophia with a grin.

'I can't be that right now.' She couldn't even say the word—just thinking it was enough to make panic bloom. Tomas was still getting used to the idea of doing couple things in public, let alone aligning future goals. A future together—that she took great pleasure embellishing, in the privacy of her own mind—was in no way a sure thing. They hadn't even had their first date yet!

The thought of pressuring him into a relationship because she was pregnant only made her more nauseous.

She set the teacup down with a clatter and pushed the tray to the bottom of her bed, where Sophia sat watching with the innocent curiosity of childhood. Put a photo of Claudia at seven and Sophia at seven side by side and they could be mistaken for the same child. It was how Cas had known instantly that Sophia was his. He'd stopped at nothing—even kidnap—to bring Sophia under his roof so he could protect her and her mother, Ana. He'd been driven by fear and the need to protect them, and guilt too, for leaving Ana with no way to contact him. Claudia couldn't imagine her brother's emotions when he'd first set eyes on his daughter. He'd once said, over too many drinks, that he'd never felt more blessed and afraid in equal measure.

Watching her brother hold so tightly to Ana and Sophia in that revelatory press conference had sealed the deal when it came to Claudia returning to Byzenmaach after their father's demise. Not only would her return cement Casimir's claim on Sophia, he needed someone to help him make the most of the olive branch he'd publicly held out to the people of the north.

Claudia had real power now and changes were coming, and she could be proud of her role in bringing peace to her country. But with that role came certain expectations.

Being unmarried, pregnant and unwilling to name the father would give her political opposition way too many clubs to beat her with.

'I can't be,' she repeated thinly. 'I have bigger responsibilities.' She deliberately avoided her niece's golden gaze in case longing for a child of her own flooded through her. 'Cas would—'

'Understand,' said Ana firmly.

Would he? He'd warned her to take it slow where Tomas was concerned, but had she listened to his most excellent advice? No.

She couldn't even begin to wrap her mind around what Tomas might think. Or say. Or do, at this lack of anything even resembling a controlled courtship and emotionally steady way forward.

No.

Just no.

Ana removed the breakfast tray from the bed and set it on the table by the window. She pulled the curtains aside, her actions befitting a maid rather than the Queen Consort. 'I'm here to support you.'

It was a strong position to take for someone who—a year ago—had been a single working mother living an ordinary life. Or maybe that experience was *why* Ana was here. She knew Claudia would need allies if she was…

Should she be…

Carrying.

'And what of Byzenmaach's broader population? Would they support an unmarried pregnant princess? I think not.' Claudia knew she sounded snappy. Maybe it came of being half scared out of her mind.

'You're their Iron Princess. You're indestructible,' Ana

countered, turning back towards the bed. 'They'll get used to it.'

'And then there's T—the father.' Last but emphatically not least. They'd never discussed children. They'd barely discussed dinner.

'Yes.' Ana's sympathetic gaze was almost too much to bear.

'He's not one to be trapped.' Understatement. 'He'll think I did it deliberately.'

'Maybe. Or he might trust that you wouldn't deliberately do such a thing.'

In her experience, trust was something that had to be earned.

'I let him think I was dead.'

'Due to circumstances beyond your control.'

Claudia liked this compassionate, clever woman who kept Cas grounded and worked so hard to be the figurehead her brother and this country needed. Even if her confidence in Claudia's ability to cultivate trust was misplaced.

'I pushed him out of his comfort zone.'

'He *is* rather rigidly self-contained. Probably do him good.'

'You don't even know who I'm talking about.'

Ana smirked and arched an elegant brow. Okay, she absolutely did.

'Of course, if you're not expecting, it won't matter what I know,' Ana said. 'Might be just a stomach bug. Shall I send the doctor up once she's finished with us?'

It wasn't the worst idea ever put forward, now, was it?

'Yes,' Claudia managed belatedly. 'Please. Let's put that fantasy to rest.'

# CHAPTER SEVEN

TOMAS RODE INTO Aergoveny trailing two horses, three hawks and an empty pigeon cage. His arrival in the small mountain village did not go unnoticed. He'd been expecting a glance or two—the falcons always created interest and any newcomer to a place as isolated as this one was always greeted with some measure of suspicion. The silence as he dismounted in front of the only tavern didn't worry him as much as the smell of himself after spending so much time living rough. Hasty washes in almost frozen streams had barely taken the edge off the odour and he knew it. He had two days to get clean-shaven before Claudia arrived and he didn't know whether to take a room at the tavern or take his chances and keep going until he reached the property he now owned. Instinct suggested that, either way, it would be good manners to introduce himself, seeing as these villagers were soon going to be his neighbours.

The groom that rushed out to take his horses—shedding a serving apron along the way—was small, wiry and female. 'You're him,' she declared without preamble. 'The King's Falconer. We've been wondering when you'd turn up. The Princess Royal's people called two days ago and reserved a room for you, and the bathhouse and a barber. They said you'd scowl like that too. Da's inside and I can see to your horses. We've stables out back, with lowland hay and grain.' She looked longingly towards the falcons. 'I can take care of your birds too.'

'They don't leave my care.' Preferably his sight. 'They room with me.'

'Probably for the best. I saved a falcon once. The cats had it trapped and were going in for the kill and the stable doors were closed and it couldn't get out. It was exhausted, poor thing. I could pick it up and everything.'

Being showered with falcon stories was part and parcel of being the King's Falconer. It was his duty to listen and offer words of encouragement and advice. 'What happened to it?'

'I brought it inside and checked for wounds. It didn't have any I could see, but it wouldn't eat. Da said it was probably full of mice.'

Tomas and his animal entourage followed her to the stables, relieved when they were clean and warm, with wide stalls and several ponies already in residence. The girl slanted him a glance, took one of his packhorses, clipped it to a lead rope attached to a post and began to relieve the horse of its load. 'Use these three stalls here. They're ready for you.'

She knew her way around horses, and he joined her in the offloading.

'What happened to the bird?'

'We kept her overnight so she could recover her strength and then let her go.'

'Did you ever think about keeping her?'

'Dreamed of, more like,' the girl said with a snort.

'Why didn't you?'

'She was wild and grown and used to being free. Wouldn't have been fair. I'm Caitlin, by the way. Daughter of Bain, and hopefully wife of Balo one day—but don't tell him. He doesn't know yet.'

Tomas snorted. So did his horse. Poor Balo. 'Tomas.'

Such enthusiasm in her nod. 'I knew it! Who else would you be? The woman on the phone described you perfectly.'

'Did she now?' Surely Claudia wouldn't have been the one to make the call? She had aides for that. Didn't she?

'Big. Scowling. Shaggy dark hair and eyes you wouldn't dare disobey. And when he asks you to do something, you're moving before your brain even catches up.'

'Did she give you *her* name?'

'No.'

Could have been Lor having a laugh at his expense. 'You did the right thing with the wild falcon. You might have been able to train it to get used to you but you'd have never been able to trust it to return if you flew it.'

'I know.' She sounded wistful. 'That's what Da said.'

'I'll be interviewing for apprentices tomorrow.' Just like that, his mind was made up. 'I'll need at least half a dozen, maybe more.'

'Oh, man! The guys are going to go ape. Balo, okay? Remember the name!'

'Why not you?'

Her eyes widened with shock and excitement before she slowly, ruthlessly snuffed that light out. 'I work for Da. He needs me more than you do.' She set his packsaddle on a nearby table and returned her attention to the horse. 'Don't worry. You'll get plenty of interest. Is there an age range?'

'Not children—although I'll take falconry classes for children once the manor is up and running.' Go him. Being his own man and winging it and feeling good about it. And all because Claudia had challenged him to let go a little and loosen up on his emotions. He was doing it. 'Apart from that, anyone of any age can apply.'

'Do you need household workers too?'

'I'm thinking about it.' He'd make better decisions about that after he saw the place. He had ideas about open days to bring in income for running costs. Even the prize money he'd been given would run out eventually if he didn't figure out how not to bleed money when it came to running all the programmes he'd dreamed into existence while up in the mountains.

'I'll get the word out,' she offered.

'I'll do it myself.'

She wrinkled her nose and probably bit her tongue in an effort to keep her many opinions to herself.

'What now?' he grumbled.

'I mean, first impressions and all. You need a bath.'

The next day Tomas took interviews, got to know the people of Aergoveny. He'd sent word of his arrival to Claudia by text once his phone had recharged, and received a thumbs-up in reply.

He'd sent another short message about interviewing for apprentices and got a laughing smiley face in reply and nothing else. For a woman who had a lot to say in person and via drone, she was surprisingly circumspect by phone.

At six thirty-five on the morning of Claudia's arrival, he got a text from her.

Tomas, I have to cancel. I have a dreadful stomach bug and travel just isn't going to happen. You've got this!

He told her to get well soon in reply.

Maybe she really was sick with a rapid onset stomach complaint. Bad seafood at the royal banquet luncheon. A bad chicken wing during her afternoon snack.

He had to give her the benefit of the doubt.

He bundled up his disappointment into a tight ball and swallowed it whole, along with the breakfast on his plate. Claudia, the Princess Royal, had responsibilities to more than just him. She didn't owe him a longer explanation or for him to hear her voice while she explained away her absence. They were still at the start of a very long journey that could lead anywhere.

She didn't owe him anything.

The Aergoveny manor did nothing to curb Tomas's burgeoning dream of setting up a specialty raptor sanctuary. Situated in the middle of a hidden valley, surrounded by mountains, it stood harsh and plain, a grey fortress surrounded by high stone walls. A barren nest long since abandoned, but there was so much promise here, and the stonemasons and carpenters had made a good start on repairs. The stables were to the east, along with entrance gates and bunkhouses. The aviaries were to the west. The kitchen garden and orchard lay to the south and consisted mainly of weedy garden beds and ragged fruit trees that had once been espaliered against protective stone walls. What a place to train birds to the glove!

He could see it already. This tiny jewel in the Byzenmaach crown could one day become a raptor breeding and rehabilitation centre that could easily earn its way by putting on open days and re-enactment fairs and providing education opportunities for children in the summer months. If he wanted company in the main house, it could potentially accommodate a handful of environmental researchers and ornithologists all year round.

He claimed a room on the ground floor near the kitchens for his meagre belongings, and maybe one day he'd graduate to feeling comfortable inhabiting the master bedroom but that day had yet to come. He spent another week organising aviary repairs and ordering materials and trying not to read anything into the fact that Claudia hadn't contacted him.

He invited Silas and Lor and stablemaster Ivan from the winter fortress to visit and give their opinions on staffing and maintenance, ever grateful for their cheerful support and practical experience. He moved back and forth between the fortress and his new home for another two weeks, running himself ragged trying to do his job and oversee the work happening in Aergoveny.

For a man who'd objected so strongly to becoming a baron, he wasn't lost to the fact that he was wholeheartedly *embracing* the reality of it.

Claudia was right. Having the freedom to build something for *himself* was addictive.

He wasn't actively trying to avoiding Claudia but she was never in residence when he returned home, and on the one occasion he'd asked Lor where she was, Lor had got the strangest look on her face and muttered something about her being tied up at the palace while multinational water negotiations took place.

It sounded perfectly reasonable. There was no earthly reason for him to suspect something was off.

Claudia was an important woman.

Lor had never steered him wrong.

And yet, if a falcon in his care had prompted this kind

of uneasy feeling he'd be keeping it under close observation.

When the royal helicopter landed at the fortress that afternoon, he thought he might get his chance to catch up with Claudia that evening, but the helicopter spat out Ana and young Sophia and no one else.

To say he hid his resulting foul mood from his apprentices would be a lie. He tried to limit the damage done by giving them all an impromptu half day respite from general chores. Instead, he asked them to go home and write a two-page response to the idea of rotating them in and out of the Aergoveny manor one or two at a time for one or two months at a time while he continued to travel between the two sites. He needed people he could trust at both places, needed them to provide continuity of care for the birds and alert him to any problems. Two of his apprentices had young families to consider, two didn't. No one would be penalised for speaking out against such a move. No one would lose their apprenticeship. They should consider their two-page spiels to be expressions of interest, or disinterest. He simply wanted to know what their circumstances would allow.

The silence that followed his announcement wasn't encouraging.

Finally, his fourth-year apprentice spoke up. 'What are *your* long-term intentions? As the King's Falconer and now lord of your own lands?'

'I intend to expand the King's falcon breeding programmes and open up the Aergoveny manor to the public. I'm looking into housing other endangered birds and eventually reintroducing them into areas where researchers think they will survive. There will be monitoring programmes. Research opportunities. Learning and exchange of ideas because I sure as the sky don't know everything. I know you're all encouraged to leave at the end of your four years here. I know you can count on finding key positions worldwide. And if your goals and dreams have always lain elsewhere, I say go for them. I'm setting you up for success *anywhere*.' He meant every word. 'But I'm opening up two permanent positions immediately as part of my goals for the future. One here, one in Aergoveny. Maybe even four permanent Master Falconer positions in the years to come, and four apprenticeships offered each year. I've been given a sackful of money and the most beautiful raptor sanctuary location in the world and I'm going for it.'

Silence greeted his words. Silence, sideways glances and finally grins.

'Whatever you want done, I'll do it,' his fourth-year apprentice replied firmly. 'I want in on the ground floor.'

'Mad not to,' said his third-year apprentice. 'Count me in too.'

'And me,' said Bran, the youngest, hurriedly. 'I have family in Aergoveny. My father grew up there. I'll go there any time and be happy about it.'

'And I'll go with him.' His remaining apprentice smiled broadly. 'Have you *seen* his cousin? She's the prettiest woman in the world and sweet along with it.'

'She lives in the capital, Romeo,' countered Bran.

'And when she returns to visit her family, I will be standing there flying falcons and looking majestic by association. King's Falconer's apprentice. Never fails to impress.'

Bran puffed up like a little barnyard rooster. 'That's an unfair advantage!'

Bran had been using that unfair advantage to devastating effect ever since he'd got here. Tomas didn't bother to disguise his smirk.

'Are you sure you're all with me?' He hadn't expected such instant support. Was leadership always this easy with a vision in mind and the resources to make it happen? 'Thank you, I'm humbled.' He was also hungry to see what could be achieved and how fast they could begin to make it happen when working as a team and taking on extra responsibilities. 'I'll have new employment contracts for you to look over by the end of the week. I still want your thoughts on rotation planning. Add a paragraph on what you're most looking forward to being part of. I'll take looking *majestic by association* as a given.'

He was still smiling at that one later that afternoon when his apprentices were long gone and he was finishing the last of the weigh-ins and deciding that the time had come to properly embrace computer records in addition to the trusty notebooks that had served his father and grandfather so well. Especially now that birds and people would be travelling back and forth between sites.

He saw Sophia pause in the doorway to the weighing room, her trusty wolfhounds Jelly and Belly at her side. He saw her raise her tiny fist to knock on the doorframe and then pause, her gaze shifting from him to the eyas on the tray in front of him. Best not to knock right now and startle them. He liked the way she'd paused to think about that. Another falconer in the making, he decided with no little satisfaction.

'You can come closer if you're quiet,' he murmured. 'Make the hounds sit by the door.'

The King's daughter did exactly that as he recorded the weight. 'Do you want to feed her?' he asked of the bird in his hand.

'Yes, please.'

He pointed towards the bucket of meat and nodded. He liked this little girl with her affinity for animals and Claudia's eyes, even if it had taken some getting used to her. It had been like seeing a ghost at first, and he hadn't been the only one to think so. Cas had been blindsided by his daughter's resemblance to Claudia too.

Claudia's presence had gone a long way to making Tomas regard young Sophia as a person in her own right. It wasn't Sophia's fault that her looks and mannerisms sometimes left him spinning with memories of his childhood and Claudia's.

He would do better by this child. They all would.

For starters, young Sophia knew her parents loved her and cared for her as they should.

'Does she weigh enough?' the little girl asked.

'Yes. See how the numbers on the chart keep going up slowly but surely? That's what we want to see.'

'How old is she?'

'Four weeks.'

He answered more questions while she helped him weigh the next set of hatchlings. He watched her eyes grow round when he told her he was thinking about placing one with a young woman in Aergoveny whose main job was to help her father run a tavern. He thought the young woman had a way with animals and people too, and he wanted to teach her and many others the art of falconry and experience the practical partnerships between people and birds.

'I want to experience the practical partnerships too,' Sophia assured him earnestly.

'It takes a lot of time. And right now you're learning

other big skills. Don't you have a new pony to ride and a wolfhound puppy coming soon?'

Sophia nodded.

'Show me how well you care for them, over and over for years, and we can talk again about getting you your own hatchling.'

'Aunt Claudia had a falcon of her own when she was seven.'

'Did she now?'

'And so did you. Aunt Claudia told me.'

'*Did* she now?'

'She says you were her best teacher ever.'

Ha. 'I was eleven at the time and my father was teaching us both. It's good to learn things alongside a friend.' He hoped his new apprentices proved his words true.

'So you and Aunt Claudia are friends. Is that why she doesn't want to trap you?'

'What do you mean?'

'With a baby.'

She wasn't making sense. 'A—*what*?'

'Aunt Claudia's baby. In her belly.'

Still not computing. He lifted the last of the eyas off the scales and back into the bucket, and wrote the weight down in the record book. Miracle of miracles, his hands stayed steady throughout.

'Aunt Claudia has a baby in her belly?'

The little girl nodded.

'Did she say that?' He should be ashamed, pumping a child for information, but here they were.

Another nod. 'And then my father said, "He needs to know" and Aunt Claudia said, "Why would I trap him when he's just been set free?" and my father said, "It's your duty to tell him" and that's when they really started yelling.'

'So you overheard this conversation but you weren't part of it.' Sophia was beginning to look scared. He hadn't raised his voice but if he could track the tight tension in his words, doubtless so could she.

'Am I in trouble?'

'Not with me.' He tried to make his voice sound less harsh as he crouched in front of her. 'No, but princesses have rules they need to live by. And one of the first rules of princessing is that you don't repeat conversations you're not part of in the first place. You might be giving secrets away to the wrong people.'

'Indeed,' said a voice from the doorway, and there stood Ana, her pretty face grave as she stared down at them. He straightened, crossed his arms for good measure and held his Queen's gaze with a flinty one of his own.

'Thank you, Tomas. I can take it from here. Come on, Soph.' Ana held out her hand for her daughter to take. 'Let's get you cleaned up for dinner. Your father will be joining us.'

He hadn't started this conversation but, one way or another, he would hear the end of it. 'Will the Princess Royal be joining you too?'

'Do you have business with her?'

'You tell me.'

Ana was the first to look away. 'With the water rights negotiations completed, she was heading north with Lord Ildris for a time. To celebrate.'

'Ildris's horses are here.'

'I believe they flew. Lord Ildris will be returning at the beginning of next week. He's accepted a permanent consultancy position within the palace.'

More fool Cas.

'Did you just...*growl*?' asked Sophia with no little fascination.

'I'm sure the Lord Falcon Master was just clearing his throat,' Ana murmured. 'As for the Princess Royal, I believe she's staying up north for a week or two longer, maybe more. The mountains were calling.'

He had mountains. He had mountains on his *doorstep*. This very fortress had been carved into the side of one, should anyone want to get pedantic about their proximity to shouty big blocks of stone.

'Come on, Soph. Time to go.' Ana ushered her daughter to the door but spared him a glance at the very last moment. 'You speak mountain man, don't you?'

# CHAPTER EIGHT

IT WAS COLD in the north. Claudia had forgotten the icy bite of the wind on any part of her not covered by wind and waterproof clothing. Not for this place the ballgowns and jewels of her brother's palace. Not for these people the unbearable judgement because she was too confident, too immune to bribery and way too satisfied with her own good self to be of use to those who thought blackmail a legitimate political tool, just as long as it served their greater good.

Or maybe these people of the north had been there and done that with her already and figured she could use a break.

She was second-guessing everything about her world and the people in it. Why not second-guess them too?

Only the doctor, Ana, Cas, Sophia and probably Lor knew she was pregnant, but it wouldn't be long before solid rumours started swirling. A small but powerful group of politicians and courtiers from her father's era had already called for her removal from Cas's court. They said she'd been seduced by the northerners and pressured into being their voice, as if she'd never had a conscience of her own. They called her a survivor of abuse, as if the abuse had originated with her captors rather than her parents. They underestimated her strength and her influence, those little men and women with their fat bank accounts and political portfolios and no interest whatsoever in fairness. They would pull her down at the earliest opportunity if she couldn't find the strength to withstand them.

Unfortunately, she spent most of her strength these days on getting up in the morning and staying up rather than crawling straight back into bed after a bathroom stop, her mind a fog and her body not her own to command. What did she know about motherhood and babies? Her own mother had been a shadow of a woman—pitiful and broken. Her so-called father—King Leonidas—had been a monster. Her real father had thought nothing of bedding his brother's wife. What kind of a family tree was that?

As for the people who'd kidnapped and then kept a small child out of pity and a vague idea that one day they could use her to advance themselves, she'd paid them back, hadn't she? She'd secured their rights and way of life and owed them nothing more. She was square with them now. Surely they could ask for nothing more?

And maybe they wouldn't want her around now she'd served her purpose, but she had nowhere else to turn to for comfort and support and possible solutions to a problem of her own making.

Why did she no longer know which way was home?

She'd been welcomed with fanfare. Her tent had been set up for her, bursting with warmth and furs and food after her journey. She'd been hugged and lauded—she and Ildris heroes. A feast was happening right outside her door.

And all she could think was that she didn't belong here either. She wouldn't wish this duality on her enemy, let alone her daughter, and since when had this baby become a daughter? She didn't know that for sure. No one did.

'Claudia, are you in there?'

She knew that voice. It belonged to her not-sister who'd been at Claudia's side since they were seven years old. 'Enter.'

Alya entered with a flurry of movement and a dusting of snow on her hair and the shoulders of her cloak. 'Why are you missing the party? You're the guest of honour.'

'Just tired, I guess.'

'You guess or you know? Because unless you haven't slept in days, I'm going to drag you back out there. People want to see you. You're our champion.'

'I'm pregnant.' There. She'd said it, but didn't feel any lighter for sharing her load. If anything, she was waiting for the weight of Alya's disappointment to rain down upon her.

Alya pushed back her hood, bringing her ebony curls, heart-shaped face and shocked brown eyes into the light. 'Oh.'

Yes, oh.

'Change of plan on the drinking front,' Alya said next.

'Indeed.'

'And I guess it explains why you're looking so pale and worn.'

'More than likely.' And she'd tried so hard to add a bit of colour using make-up.

'Do I, ah, know the father?'

'You mean is Ildris the father? No, of course he's not.'

'Is that because he's too old for you?'

'Twelve years isn't that big an age gap if plenty of other things align. It's because I don't care for him in that way and never have, no matter how handy he is to have in my corner. No, Ildris knows nothing about it.' Or maybe he knew more than she thought. He was a secretive soul, more suited to politicking than she would ever be. 'I slept with the King's Falconer.'

'You mean…you slept with Tomas? The boy hero?'

She could blame childhood confidences on Alya knowing all about him.

'What can I say? He grew up well.'

Alya shed her cloak and took a seat at Claudia's table, reached for the untouched wine and poured herself a glass. She reached for a sweet pastry too, giving every indication that she wasn't going anywhere. 'Does he know?'

'No. It was a one-off. I was being my usual pushy self. I don't even know if he wanted to be naked with me in the first place.' Not that he *had* been naked.

'He can't have been too much against bedding you if he got the deed done.'

'I can be very persuasive.'

'Given that we're out there celebrating that very fact… I know.' Alya waved her hand with the pastry in it towards the tent flap, before popping the honey-soaked confection in her mouth.

'I don't think this is the result he would want if given a choice,' Claudia confessed baldly.

The other woman chewed thoughtfully and then reached for her wine, taking her time. 'Choice is a luxury some people don't get to have. You of all people know that.'

'I can choose not to implicate him.' She'd been thinking about that avenue a lot.

'No man worth a hero badge is going to let you get away with that if he thinks that baby's his. He's going to want to be there for that child. Maybe he'll want to be there for you too. Let's call that *his* choice.'

'You're saying I should tell him?'

The other woman nodded. 'If you're keeping it, yeah.'

'I'm keeping her.'

'Oh, it's a *her*, is it?'

'Only in my stupid head.' Claudia felt hot tears start to well. 'I don't even *like* my role at the palace. The public are fed this notion that I'm this indestructible princess, back from the dead. Some kind of icon, preferably in a tiara, only the more people get to know me, the more they realise I'm just human and I make mistakes. Fitting in is tough. Cas wants me there but has warned me to back off on some of my advocacy until I'm more settled. Even my parentage is in question—my real father was likely the man I thought was my uncle, which is why Leonidas never wanted my return. And now I'm pregnant. How is that helpful? My position is so precarious. I don't know how I'm going to be of use to *anyone* going forward.'

'Hush, Claudia. You can always stay here. We'll have you, and gladly.'

'Will you? Or have I delivered on the water rights and now you're done with me too?'

'See, that's just crazy mixed-up baby hormones talking,' Alya said firmly. 'Come back outside and I'll *show* you that's not true. People are in awe of what you have achieved. We love you and we've missed you.'

'I don't know what I'm doing or where I'm going.' She was a compass dial, endlessly circling. 'I don't know which way's home.'

Alya rose and embraced her. 'I'll help you find the way. I'll come with you on that journey, but be warned, I'm going to be the naughty auntie.'

Claudia clutched her honorary sister's hand and clung with all her might. 'Thank you.'

'Don't thank me yet. I'm going to be a very bad influence. The stories I can tell about what we got up to as kids. There's the stolen pony story.'

'Rescued pony.' Claudia smiled through her tears.

'The duck egg substitution story. That was one very confused owl.'

'I now have a great deal of sympathy for that owl. I'd be confused too if this baby turned out to be a duckling.'

Alya squeezed tight and then gently stepped away. 'Rug up and come back to the feast, at least for a little while. Let's celebrate new beginnings and the peace and prosperity on the horizon. I won't even mention your part in the negotiations if you don't want me to. You can watch me try and fail to catch Ildris's attention. It'll be like old times.'

'He's taken a position in Cas's court.'

'I know.' For all that Alya tossed those two words around lightly, there was heartbreak behind them. 'Don't remind me. I too am not all that happy with reality today. Shall we face it anyway?'

*This* was the attitude that had guided her way. *Try*, and know that failure was part of that process. Be *honest*, with yourself if no one else.

'I want Tomas to be with me because he wants to be, not just because there's a baby. I'm afraid he's going to offer marriage and I'm going to say yes, and I'm never going to know how he really feels about me.'

'I get it. You're screwed. He's screwed too. But, whatever happens, I say this baby is going to be incredibly lucky to have you for a mother, because you have so much love and passion to give, and you're strong and fierce and capable of making life *better* for everyone around you. Forged in fire and all that. Be proud of your remarkable journey through life in search of your happy place. One day you're going to find it. You've got this.'

'You make me feel better than I've felt in weeks.'

'That's because I know what you need.' Alya stood and linked her arm around Claudia's. 'Come outside for a while and let us love you.'

'One hour, and then I'm coming back in.'

'One hour,' the other woman agreed. 'And I'll bring you breakfast in the morning.'

'I don't do breakfast any more.'

Alya's glance was full of concern. 'When do you breakfast, and what will tempt you to eat?'

'Around eleven and soup is good. Thin and brothy.'

'Have you seen a midwife? Let's do that tomorrow.'

'Tomorrow,' agreed Claudia, relaxing just a little bit.

Maybe things would be better tomorrow.

Claudia lasted an hour, and then another, with Alya at her side, bubbling over with festive good humour and cloaking Claudia's forced enthusiasm. She *was* glad to be back, even if she knew in her heart that her status here had changed and there was no going back to her old life. Not easily. She had become a creature of politics, with the same pressure here as the one she felt in her brother's court, namely that she couldn't please everyone all the time. And what then? Who would even want her?

Bleakness had bled into her bones and she didn't know how to reverse the condition.

She'd settled before the open fire, Ildris to one side and Alya on her other as the celebrations continued and the fire began to show a hint of embers. There were a million stars above her head, a cloudless sky and a waxing crescent moon. She had shelter nearby and warmth on her face and there was simple comfort in that.

*Take the simple, fleeting moments of comfort and security and be grateful, Claudia.*

Make every breath, every moment, count. Just like old times.

She didn't know at first why Ildris rose to his feet so suddenly. It was late, she was weary, and she'd begun to let her mind drift.

But a woman was heading towards them and behind her strode Tomas, big and solid and contained as only he could be. He wore ordinary outdoor work boots and trousers and a warm winter jacket with wide cuffs made of leather. The firelight did little to soften the sharply drawn planes of his face and jaw, and his eyes were narrowed and not just against the smoke from the fire. He was set against Ildris, regular observation had told her that much, but he was usually somewhat better at hiding it. Hostility had a hold on him now, though. And then he saw her, and his hostility increased tenfold.

Maybe Ildris wasn't the problem after all.

'Well met, Master Falconer, Lord Sokolov,' Ildris began. 'What brings you amongst us?'

'I'm here for what's mine, mountain lord, and you can object to my claim, but know that I'm already disposed to think of you as my enemy. My grievance spans *decades*.'

Alya squeaked, Ildris crossed his arms in front of him and held his ground as Claudia scrambled to her feet and stepped between the two foes. 'Have you lost your mind?' she demanded.

'Not yet. Have you?' The next minute, she was viewing the world upside down on account of being slung over Tomas's shoulder, bottom up and head down, as he strode away from the fire, the crowd parting for him like butter, with him the hot knife.

'Are you kidnapping me?'

'Yes. You should be used to it by now. Or I could be rescuing you, or saving your life, who would know?'

'You! You should know what you're doing! And you can't just take me. You're outnumbered. People will stop you.'

'They can try.' Tomas gave a piercing whistle, the one he used to call birds down from flight, and a short time later she heard the flapping of wings as a majestic golden eagle landed on his outstretched forearm.

She looked up. The bird looked down. 'Oh, aren't you a beauty,' she cooed. 'Tomas, where have you been hiding *her*?'

'Stop trying to win over my attack bird.' He had his hands full so there was nothing to stop her rooting around in the pocket of his trousers for a strip of dried meat that would surely be stuffed somewhere on his person.

Front pocket, deep, deep down.

Hello.

'Feed my bird that particular bit of meat and I may not be able to forgive you,' he warned.

A man of humour, how lovely. Claudia withdrew, but not before trailing admiring fingers along his delectable length. She found the food in his inside coat pocket and held it out for the eagle, praying that her odd position and all the jostling about as she held the food up for the bird wouldn't encourage it to take a finger as well.

'What's her name?'

'Never you mind.'

'Claudia!' Alya had come up beside them, almost running to keep apace as she bent to look Claudia in the eyes. 'What's happening?'

'I'm being kidnapped.' Claudia felt oddly cheerful. 'But thanks for asking.' Tomas still hadn't broken his stride. 'Alya, meet Tomas. Tomas, Alya.'

But the other woman was having nothing to do with formal introductions and Tomas didn't seem that interested either.

'Do you *want* to be kidnapped?' Alya sounded anxious.

'I'm thinking about it.' The eagle took the meat. Her fingers stayed attached to her hand.

'Because if you need saving, I'll save you. His nethers are currently unprotected. He'll likely drop you and the eagle will pluck out my eyes, but I'll do it.'

'And I will never forget such a beautiful offer,' Claudia assured her just as earnestly. 'But I'm very comfortable, really.'

Tomas made a noise that sounded a lot like pure frustration, and Alya squeaked again. 'Did he just *growl*?'

'He does that. And yet I've still decided I'm willing to be kidnapped. Again. Or rescued. Or taken to dinner. Whatever.'

'If you're sure…'

'I can paddle your backside if you don't take this more seriously,' Tomas warned.

Ha! Stretch goal. 'What with? Your third arm?' They were slowing down. They'd reached the edge of the camp, where a group of horses were staked out. 'Are you planning on stealing horses for us too? Because I'm not sure you'll get away with *that*.'

'He shouldn't push his luck,' agreed Alya.

'I brought the Range Rover.' He deposited her on her

feet and opened the back doors and set about containing his golden eagle.

Claudia took a moment to embrace the sister of her heart. 'I'll be fine,' she whispered.

'He's glorious,' Alya whispered back.

'I know. Good luck with Ildris. He was not tempted by anyone in the capital and you've more than enough soft power and courage to make him a very good match.'

'If you've quite finished planning the next generation of leaders,' said Tomas from behind them. 'Well met, Lady Alya. Princess, we're leaving now.' He opened the front passenger door and handed her in and buckled the seatbelt for her, and was it her imagination or did his hand linger over her stomach? Did he know? Was that the reason for all the theatrics? The very definitive swooping in to take what was his?

'Tomas…' She couldn't hide the hesitation in her voice.

'Not now.'

*Call me*, mimed Alya as the door closed. Claudia heard more voices outside and then he was getting in the driver's side and starting the engine. Her bravado—what was left of it—fizzled away, leaving only the occasional bubble of confidence in a sea of flat bewilderment.

Five minutes went by in silence. Ten. Another ten. Apparently, he'd used up all his words when claiming her. He didn't seem at all eager to reveal why he'd done so.

'Why did you come for me?'

He didn't glance her way. Never even took his eyes off the road ahead, but his hands tightened on the wheel and the tension in his body was contagious. 'Because you have something to tell me.'

He knew. Somehow, he'd discovered her condition.

'Who told you?'

'Sophia.'

Hard to take revenge on a little girl.

'And you think it's yours?'

He spared her a scathing glance. 'Don't even try that line. It won't hold.'

Possibly not. Everyone knew where her interest lay.

'My head was covered last time I was kidnapped. My hands were tied and travel was by horseback. This is a luxury abduction by comparison.'

'There are blankets and pillows on the back seat.'

Now he was making her feel ungrateful.

'I would have told you.' Maybe. 'Eventually.'

'Big of you.'

'I'm not trying to make the problem go away, if that's what you're worried about.'

'It's not a *problem*, it's a baby.' Oh, he could sound vicious when he wanted to.

'Right. I'm not trying to make this baby go away. I'm adjusting to its unexpected presence. I *was* protected. I thought I was. It wasn't a trap.' She wanted to make that clear. 'I'm...' Would honesty suffice? Could she say she was scared this baby would ruin her life and his? 'I'm trying to get my head around what it means, going forward. I took some time to shore up my defences.'

Nothing.

'Where are we going?' she asked, mainly to fill that awful silence with something other than tension.

'Home.'

She laughed, short and sharp. 'You might need to factor in the Claudia effect. Too bold for my brother's court. A weapon spent as far as the north is concerned. I have no home. I seem to have run out of options.'

'I'm taking you to the manor. And if it's not home to

either of us yet, I trust that in the years to come it will be. A bolthole like the room we had in the fortress wall. *Our* place. A safe place. We can make it happen this time.'

Oh, those words and the memories that followed. The promise of safety was her Achilles heel.

'We'll be married as soon as it can be arranged,' he added gruffly.

It wasn't a question, but still…

'You want to marry me?'

'Who knows?' He hadn't looked at her once. 'But there's a baby coming so we're doing it. It's the only way.'

Dogged chivalry. Not that there was anything wrong with it, but it wasn't love, and it was love she craved, almost as much as safety.

'Actually, there are many other ways to approach impending parenthood.' Probably best not to say *impending doom*. 'You've had a shock, I understand that, but what if I don't *want* to marry you?'

'I think you'll choose to do so anyway.' Was that the voice of reason? She hated it. 'Our child will be legitimate and loved and I will protect you both with all that I am. Any political opponents that seek to undermine you will suffer for their sins because I'm a vengeful man and my aristocratic veneer is thin.'

Well, when he put it that way…

'You're quite a forceful guy when you decide you want something.'

He smiled tightly. 'I have no idea why you sound so surprised.'

'I like it.'

'How fortunate for us all.'

She fiddled with the delicate ring on her finger, a diamond and pearl Art Deco concoction from the royal collection. She had a few vague memories of her mother wearing it, and it served to keep her tethered to her duties as the Princess Royal of a nation. The thought of wearing Tomas's wedding ring alongside it gave her pause, because she knew she would treasure his ring more.

'Do you even like me?' She hadn't meant to voice the question. She'd meant to keep those doubts locked in her subconscious, hidden from scrutiny. Clearly, her heart had other ideas. 'I mean, it's a starting point, right? Liking each other.'

'Correct.'

'I'd take my wedding vows seriously,' she said next. 'I'd give it my all.'

'As would I.'

'I'd take no other lovers.'

'Fewer bodies for me to bury.'

'I can't quite tell if you're being serious or not.'

He smiled at that, wide and wicked. What a weapon. It made her feel all jelly, not that he needed to *know* that.

'Still can't tell,' she informed him loftily.

'I'd probably just feed them to the birds. No gravedigging at all.'

'The fact that you've even thought about feeding people to the birds is giving me pause.'

'So it should.' He'd relaxed his grip on the steering wheel and his upper body looked less stiff. 'I'm joking. But I'm also a proud, possessive man and I don't share. If I'm going to surrender to my emotions, I aim to do it properly. I'm calling it the Claudia effect.'

And, oh, how she adored this accessible new side of him.

'So, it's a proper marriage you're suggesting. None of this in-name-only business.'

'Definitely not.'

'What happens when I have to do my brother's bidding and be a princess for the people?'

'Do you *want* to do your brother's bidding and be a princess for the people? Because, to my way of thinking, you give them too much unfettered access. With a child on the way, I'd expect you to pick your battles carefully and create more time for personal home-building.'

'At your manor.'

'*Our* manor. Correct.'

She was beginning to feel very hopeful about this unexpected kidnapping with marriage attached.

'I hear make-up sex is really intense. We should try it.'

'I'm sure we will.'

'Although not too often,' she hastened to add. 'Upon reflection, sex with you is already intense enough. I loved it.' Maybe if she used the word love around him enough his subconscious would get the hint and associate the word with her. She closed her eyes and conjured the memory of him striding towards her in the light of the campfire. His certainty. His utter willingness to stride into camp and claim her, as if he had every right to do so and an army at his back. 'The golden eagle was an exceptionally nice touch,' she murmured sleepily. She hadn't slept well for days, possibly weeks, and for the first time in weeks she wanted to surrender to the dark, knowing that Tomas would be there when she woke. 'What's her name?'

'Alhena.'

'You named her after a star.'

'I did.'

'You'll wake me when we get there? It's just… I'm so tired.'

'Then sleep.'

She loved his voice, his presence, everything about him. 'Don't make me wake alone.' She remembered that from her long-ago abduction, and the terror that had invaded her soul. 'I don't like waking up alone in a strange place.'

'I won't let you wake up alone.'

'Promise me.' She barely knew what she was saying. Fatigue had a hold on her now, slurring her words and robbing her of caution. 'I'm scared I've done you wrong and that you'll come to your senses and leave.'

'On my word, you won't wake up alone.'


Tomas drove through the night and kept his eyes on the road, never mind that they felt full of ash and grit. He'd never carried a more precious cargo. He'd never felt more sure that this was the road they should be on. No matter the fallout—and he expected plenty—he could not sit back and do nothing, not this time. He had another chance to do right by Claudia of Byzenmaach and he would not let her down. Not this time.

Claudia roused only briefly when he pulled over and took the pillows and blanket from the back and tried to make her sleeping position more comfortable. Was this normal? Was he going to spend the next many months worrying about her health and that of the baby she carried, and doing everything in his power to make her feel at home?

Yes…yes, he was.

He called Caitlin and arranged a room at the tavern, and a hearty breakfast for two, and said he'd be there in the early hours of the morning, and that he wouldn't usually ask for someone to be waiting up for him but it couldn't be helped. He'd pay double the rate. Triple.

'Da sleeps light, Lord Falconer. Will you have birds and horses with you again?'

'Just a golden eagle.'

'Holy sh—moley!'

'Are you sure you don't want to be one of my apprentices?'

'If wishes were horses, Da would be able to afford to employ enough people to replace me. Then I could.'

'If the opening of the manor brings in enough people, Aergoveny will grow and he'll be able to.'

'Keep dreaming, my lord, and so will I. Come in the side door closest to the stables. There's parking there. Gotta go. Tables won't clear themselves and it's Friday night.'

She rang off before he could murmur his thanks. Claudia stirred as he reached out to turn the phone off—he didn't like those things tracking him, and no one could tell him they weren't. He caught the gleam of her eyes in the dashboard lights.

'Who was that?' she murmured.

'I called the tavern in Aergoveny. They're keeping a room for us.'

'But who were you speaking to? It sounded like you knew them.'

'The innkeeper has a daughter, Caitlin. She's about, I don't know, fifteen or so. Does the work of three people, alongside her father. She has the best instinct for my birds that I've ever seen since, well, since you.'

'Did you offer her an apprenticeship?'

He nodded. 'She considered it for a wistful heartbeat and then informed me she couldn't be spared. She probably can't. But circumstances can change.' He tried to gauge how Claudia was feeling after her two-hour nap, but the low light made it difficult. 'How are you feeling? There's water here and some of Lor's sweet pastries.'

'Maybe later. You said we were going to the manor. Why are we now staying at an inn?'

'Changed my mind when I remembered I only had tinned beans and bitter coffee in the cupboard. This way, you'll get breakfast.'

'It really wouldn't have mattered,' she offered dryly, sitting up straighter, tucking her hair away from her face and looking out of the window at the darkness thrown by a quarter moon and a cloudless night. 'How far away are we?'

'We'll be there in an hour.'

'I need to call Cas. Ildris vouched for my safety when we went north and I don't know where my guards are. I don't want to start another war.'

'Call him by all means, but your guards are a couple of miles behind us and have been all the time. Cas knows where you are, even if he doesn't know the why of it yet.' Silently, he gestured towards his phone. 'You'll have to turn it on again and hope for a signal. And it'll come up as me when you dial anywhere so don't expect to have a direct line to the King.'

'Okay.'

Casimir picked up on the first ring.

'Huh,' she murmured. 'I guess you have a direct line to the King now too. Fancy that.' She put the phone on loudspeaker—a courtesy Tomas hadn't expected. 'Cas, I'm with Tomas.'

'So I heard. Ildris says your abduction was quite the spectacle.'

'I enjoyed it,' she answered dulcetly. 'We're almost in Aergoveny. My fiancé—that would be Tomas—has arranged a night at the inn for us before we travel on to the manor.'

'So you've told him about the baby.'

'Well, *someone* told him and I confirmed it, so yes. Let's not sweat the details. He knows. We're eloping. Think of the money you'll save.'

'I see.' Cas didn't sound impressed.

'As if you've never got ahead of yourself,' she reminded him.

'Put him on.'

'I can't, he's driving. Very safely, I might add, if I wanted to ram home the point that I'm in good, safe hands. We're working out our future and it's a delicate negotiation, as you might imagine. Can you tell the guards to keep their distance?'

'You wouldn't be sitting there if I hadn't already done so.'

'You're a wonderful brother. The best.'

'I'm glad you think so. I'm also Byzenmaach's King, so put your fiancé on the phone and turn the speaker off. I want a private word.'

She hesitated. Tomas didn't, reaching out to pick up a set of earphones from the console and handing them to her. She gave it all back, set up for privacy, and he sighed and put the earbuds in his ears. He'd known he was pushing his luck. It was a measure of the King's trust in him that no one had yet interfered. He wanted to keep it that way.

'Your Majesty.'

'Ballsy move, Lord Sokolov.'

'Unavoidable. Your sister was being uncommonly indecisive.'

'That or she's playing the long game and has you exactly where she wants you.'

'Maybe.' He hadn't ruled that out. 'Makes no difference to me. I need special dispensation to wed. The innkeeper's a celebrant.' He'd discovered that on his last visit. 'It can happen tonight if required.'

'Hey!' said Claudia indignantly. 'That is *not* required.'

Tomas liked to think he quelled her with a glance, but it seemed unlikely. 'Tomorrow, then.' Look at him, changing his plans at a moment's notice. And they called him intractable.

'Sunday,' she countered.

*Two* days away.

'Your sister says we're marrying on Sunday. I say tomorrow *evening*.' There he went, being tractable *again*. He shot Claudia a swift narrow-eyed glance. 'That's it. I'm done negotiating.'

'I'll clear my weekend,' the other man offered dryly.

This was his *king*. 'My apologies, Your Majesty. I was speaking to your sister.'

'I think we shall just turn up at this inn of yours tomorrow afternoon and take it from there. It'll add to the mystique. Ana says she'll bring Sophia, Silas and Lor, and clothes for us all, and will inform your apprentices and the horse master.'

'I appreciate it.' What else could he say? He was being given far more leeway than he deserved.

'Make her happy, Tomas. My sister deserves to be loved for exactly who she is. She's a remarkable woman. A unique treasure. I don't surrender her lightly.'

'Noted.'

'Several of my father's old guard politicians are trying to tear her down because of the progress she represents, and they'll come for you as well. No more flying under the radar. You're going to be too close to the throne. They'll shred your reputation and try to ruin whatever you attempt to build. You need to learn to play the power game.'

'Not a problem.'

'One last question. Do you love her?'

What was love? He was attracted to Claudia beyond measure. He wanted to spend time with her, laugh with her, fight with her, and *be* that person she turned to in the darkness. He wanted to see her cradling his children, teaching them the names of the stars and mountains nearby. He would die before he let any harm befall her. No matter how unruly his feelings, they were fixed on her.

'I'm getting there,' he muttered. 'And, as you can imagine, it's quite the trip.'

# CHAPTER NINE

THE TAVERN WAS clean and rustic and Tomas had liked it well enough when he'd stayed there before. Innkeeper Bain met them at the door several hours after midnight, sparing a swift glance for the sleepy, silent Claudia and a longer one for the eagle as he led them up the stairs and along a dimly lit corridor to the room Tomas had stayed in before.

'Fire's lit and we made up a couple of perches for your birds after last time. Don't know if they're the sort you usually use—Caitlin and Balo put their heads together and came up with them. You'd have thought they were making a throne, the time and care they put into it.' Pride laced his voice.

Tomas transferred Alhena to the tall, sturdy perch and removed the hood to let her survey her new surroundings. He'd put it back on soon enough, once he tethered her for the night. The bath pan below the perch was empty, but it was a nice touch.

'You know, if it's capital you need in order to bring in paid help in order to free Caitlin up so she can follow her dreams, I have it to spare. You're never going to lose her completely. She loves you and she's part of the fabric of this place. She could apprentice to me through the day, a four-day week even, I'd make that concession for her and for you, and she would return to you at night.'

'Has she asked this of you?'

'I asked her a general question about interviewing for an apprenticeship with me. She wouldn't even consider it. Said you needed her more.'

'Everyone has childhood dreams of becoming something fancy.'

'That they do, Innkeeper.' Claudia entered the conversation gently. 'You must be so proud of your daughter for the answer she gave my fiancé. I know I would be. And a little bit sad about that answer too.'

The man didn't seem to want to look at her. She had that effect on people sometimes, when she chose to cut straight to the heart of things.

'There's bread and cheese on the table, wine and water as well, and stew downstairs if you want it reheated. I wasn't sure,' he muttered.

Claudia shook her head, so Tomas answered for them both. He was hungry but not that hungry. 'Thank you, no. This is good.'

'You'll be wanting breakfast too, I suppose. Downstairs like before?'

'Up here,' said Claudia before Tomas could answer. 'Please.'

The innkeeper nodded and headed for the door. 'Think that's all.'

There was one other thing. 'We want to get married tomorrow,' Tomas told him. 'Are you available to perform the service?'

The grizzled older man turned back towards them but barely raised a brow. 'I need two weeks' notice to get the paperwork in order. It's the law.'

'The paperwork will be waived.'

'Never heard of that happening.'

'Trust me,' Tomas murmured. He had a king in his pocket. 'It can be done.'

'In that case, m'lord, I'm available.'

Claudia chose that moment to lower the hood of her dusky blue travelling cloak. The material was a coarse woollen weave, nothing special. Her face, however, could stop a man's breath. Unless Bain had been living under a rock lately, he would know who she was. 'Thank you, Innkeeper,' she murmured. 'I didn't catch your name.'

'Bain, m'la— Your Gr— Royal… Princess… *God*.'

Claudia smiled. 'That's quite an escalation, but don't worry about it. I'll write my name out in full for you for tomorrow.' She nodded towards Tomas. 'His too.'

Bain bowed and nodded at the same time. 'Thank you, Princess. I'm just going to…get you better wine.'

'Don't bother,' Tomas told him. 'You can expect a team of guards to roll in soon. They'll station themselves around the tavern tonight. You might want to warn people.'

Bain pulled out a set of old-fashioned door keys. 'Let me just make sure the *second bedroom* is open for your use.'

'Plausible deniability, how *thoughtful*,' murmured Claudia. 'Thank you so much. Your service is impeccable.'

'It would have been even *more* impeccable had we known you were coming. Will any *other* guests be joining your wedding party tomorrow?'

'They will,' said Claudia smoothly. 'Discretion is required.'

He closed his eyes and ran his hand across his face.

Squinted at them from between his fingers before dropping his hands to his sides. 'You're still here.'

Tomas sighed. 'Yes.'

'Discretion it is.' Innkeeper Bain made it through the door and shut it firmly behind him.

'We should marry here. At the inn,' declared Claudia.

'It's more of a tavern.' She hadn't seen the downstairs bar yet.

'It'll be a wedding venue before he knows it.'

Tomas couldn't help but smile. 'That's just cruel.'

She headed for the table and unwrapped a block of hard cheese from within a waxy cloth and took a knife to it. 'It's soft cheese I shouldn't be eating while pregnant.' She nibbled an edge. 'I think this is Cheddar.' She slipped a slice between a bread roll and bit in, before loosening her cloak and draping it over a chair by the fire. 'This is a nice room. Lived in. Not quite as nice as my tent, but acceptable.' She took another bite and studied a faded painting on the wall.

She hadn't always lived as a princess. She didn't mind taking her meals in Lor's kitchen. He needed to keep reminding himself of those facts or he'd go mad thinking that she'd never be satisfied with his version of normal. 'I'm a plain man,' he warned.

'You're definitely not that plain. Possibly a little deluded, though.'

He tried again. 'I like plain things.'

Her mouth was full but her eyebrows spoke volumes.

'You, of course, are not plain at all,' he added quickly. 'What I mean is that I don't want to live a fancy life. A simple one will do, and I'm not sure that's going to suit you.'

She took her time swallowing her food. 'Because I'm a princess, and princesses can't live simply?'

'Yes.' Why did he feel as if he was eleven years old all over again, telling her she couldn't be a falconer? He'd been wrong about that. Maybe he could be wrong about this too.

'Have I been living lavishly at the fortress?' she asked. 'Redecorating? Insisting on formal dining? No. I eat in Lor's kitchen as often as you do.'

'And then there's your princess clothes,' he offered heavily. There was absolutely no arguing about those. 'Can I afford to keep you in clothes? I'm thinking no.'

'My official clothing requirements are covered by the Crown. All part of the job description for the Princess Royal. But when I come looking for you at the aviaries, how am I dressed?'

'Simply.' He had to admit that.

'And you haven't seen me of a morning lately. Be warned—my morning sickness is brutal. Why do you think I'm cramming this food down now? Because I'm practical and I like good plain food, a warm fire and a clean bed. I think it's time that you put your thoughts about us not sharing similar values behind you. Deal?'

'Done.' He took a deep breath and recommitted to the path he'd chosen for them both and dug for the inner strength and confidence required to walk it. 'So.' He shed his coat, emboldened by the way her gaze lowered to the snug fit of his trousers and his plain cotton shirt that did have a few buttons at the neck but otherwise pulled on and off like a T-shirt. Very plain. Possibly flattering, according to the sudden appreciation in her eyes. 'We have no nightwear.'

She arched one single elegant brow. 'Surely you have a spare shirt somewhere.'

Such a long way to go to the car and get his duffel and bring it in. 'No.'

'Well, then.' She removed her cloak and placed it over a nearby chair, and then set her socks and boots beside it. Tidy. Her embroidered shift followed and then her trousers. He didn't look away as she sauntered towards the bathroom. 'I think Alhena should sleep in the other room, don't you? Wouldn't want to disturb her.'

'I can sort that.'

'Will you be showering before bed too?'

'And then joining you in bed, naked. Yes.'

She slid him a brilliant smile. 'Perfect.'

Only when she'd disappeared from view did he put his hands to his face much as the innkeeper had done. She'd been outfoxing him from the moment she'd seen him again and he showed no signs whatsoever of gaining the upper hand. But he had a true heart, his course was set, and his bed skills had pleased her last time around. If he could keep his head in that regard, reduce her to a quivering wreck *first*, maybe there was hope for him.

He crossed to the eagle. 'I'm going to pick up your stand with you still on it and put you in the other room. No protest, now, you'll like it. And tomorrow I'll take you downstairs and introduce you to Caitlin and Balo. You'll like that too.'

The eagle stayed quiet for him as he set her up in the adjoining room and tied her off. To call her an attack bird was doing her a disservice, given her placid nature. She'd been with him for over seven years and he'd been putting potential mates before her for the past three. She liked being around people too much to pay attention to any of that, though. Alhena the star had quite forgotten how to be a bird.

That or she was excessively picky. Emotionally un-
available, much like he had once been, but look at him
now. Getting married tomorrow and all that. Rushing
in to stake his claim and protect, protect, *protect* what
was his.

He was shirtless by the time he returned to the main
bedroom. He was completely naked by the time he
reached the shower cubicle.

Claudia smiled and moved aside to let him enter.

He took his place, every nerve alive and reaching.

And let the future in.


Claudia loved it when Tomas took charge. She needed
him to take control in order to surrender. No more thinking or planning or trying to stay one step ahead and be
safe. She was *already safe* with this beautiful man, and
with that came the freedom to follow wherever he led.
She closed her eyes as the kiss they shared deepened,
relearning the taste of him and the warm expertise of
hungry lips. He lifted a hand to the back of her neck, his
thumb below her jaw, the better to tilt her head, and there
was a sensuality about him, a willingness to let pleasure
rule, that left her flushed and breathless.

He took the soap from her and placed her hands on
his chest. He soaped up his hands and started at her fingertips, and then the vee between her fingers. He circled
her wrists and kissed her as he worked soap up her arms
and over her shoulders. She shuddered into him when his
hands cupped her breasts, gentled by slick suds as warm
water rained down her back.

Her nipples pebbled for him, and it wasn't just because
his skilled fingers were attentive. It was him. Her Tomas.

He turned her so she could lean back against him as he

took the shower hose and directed it to remove the soap on her arms and breasts and then he moved the pressure lower, and between the water and his fingers coaxed her to swift orgasm.

'Cheat,' she murmured when she'd recovered breath to speak.

'I'll make it up to you.'

She took her leave a short time later while he got clean, but not before she let her gaze linger over his erection. 'That's for me, right?'

He gave himself a leisurely stroke, his eyes never leaving her face. 'Yes.'

'And you won't be long? Because all I'm going to do is be in bed trying to arrange my body to best advantage. That's going to drive me mad with indecision in *very* short order.'

She'd made him smile. Impossible not to feel smug about that.

'On your back, hands beneath the pillow.'

She could do that. 'And my legs?'

'Apart.'

But of course.

He put his face to the spray and she put her mind to drying off and pushing back the bedclothes. Wouldn't want to obstruct his view.

He took her to pieces all over again once he finally joined her. Generous with his tongue and touches in all the right places and when he finally entered her she could no longer keep her hands to herself, weaving them in his hair and putting all her joy and hopes for them into a kiss that brought tears to her eyes.

'I dreamed of you,' she murmured when he broke the kiss and rolled his hips and made her gasp. 'Soon as I saw you after all those years away, I started dreaming of being spread open beneath you and feeling so cherished.'

'Are you feeling cherished yet?' He set his lips to the tender skin of her neck and she was so close to orgasm she could almost reach the stars.

'I am.' And then he rolled her atop him and put the pad of his thumb to her centre and surged up into her with those strong, muscular thighs and she closed her eyes and surrendered. 'I'm feeling everything.'

When she clenched around him and stilled his hand and brought it to her stomach, he tumbled after her.

Mornings were hell. This was Claudia's reality. Not even a night of bliss and a soundly sleeping Tomas at her side could alter that reckoning. She slid from the bed and made it to the bathroom without retching but she was glad to shut the door behind her. She clung to the basin, head down and begging for her nausea to recede before glancing at her reflection in the mirror. Bird's nest dark hair, pale face, and redness on her neck where Tomas's facial hair had rasped her skin. He had no beard but he must have to shave every day. Soon she would know many such personal details.

Husband. She touched the extra colour around her nipples. He'd used her incredibly sensitive breasts to ruthless advantage last night and she'd loved every bit of it.

Father. Her father had not been a kind man. Tomas's father, for all his sternness and adherence to rules, had been patient, protective and kind, and Tomas would be too. He would be the kind of parent every child deserved. Her hand went to her still flat stomach. All she needed to concentrate on right now was bringing this baby safely into the world and being a decent wife to an honourable man who would never have chosen to marry her if not for the way she'd pushed.

'Work with it,' she whispered to her reflection. Hadn't that been her motto for all the long years she'd spent in exile? *Make it work for everyone involved.* She took a deep breath and stood up straighter and summoned a smile.

*C'mon, Claudia, where are you? You don't have to be loved to be happy. You don't even have to be especially wanted as long as you're useful to have around. You can be useful, can't you? Just do it and don't think too much about what could have been. Just make the most of whatever you're given.*

*There you are, girl. Don't fail me now.*

Claudia the unwanted child, the resourceful survivor, the woman who, for all her faults, had never hardened her heart against hope. Bravado too would see her through, because she had plenty of that. Bravado and hope.

'It's the best way forward for all of us,' she murmured and sealed the deal with a nod.

And promptly doubled over and lost the contents of her stomach.

By the time she poked her head around the bathroom door, Tomas was up and dressed and the fire was crackling in the hearth. His dark eyes searched her face, a frown between his eyes.

'I used the bathroom in the other room,' he said. 'How are you feeling?'

'I'm pretty good by mid-afternoon, but most mornings are a bit rough. Would you mind passing me my clothes?'

He moved gracefully for such a big man.

'They're bringing breakfast,' he said as he gathered

up last night's clothes and gave them to her. 'I ordered everything.'

'I hope you're hungry enough for two then, because I'm making no promises when it comes to keeping anything down.'

'Is that normal?'

'Apparently.'

'Is there anything else you need?'

Where did she begin? This was her wedding day, after all.

'I can ask people to bring your belongings here. I can go and get them.'

'No!' She took a deep breath and promptly swallowed hard on a fresh wave of nausea. 'No leaving me.' And boy, was it going to take a world of therapy to unpack that little outburst. 'I can make do. We discussed this last night. I'll be out in a minute.'

She dressed quickly and braided her hair and made good on her promise to emerge from the bathroom. She'd only taken a few steps before there was a knock on the door and a cheerful girlish voice called out, 'Breakfast!'

What was the young woman's name again? Kaity? Catherine?

The girl breezed in when Tomas opened the door, carrying a laden tray piled high with food. 'Da said to make it an extra special tray. He even wanted me to pick flowers, but you try finding roses in the mountains at this time of year, and besi—' The young woman stopped abruptly, her lips forming a perfect O to match her startled eyes. She tried to curtsey, tray and all. The tray tilted and rattled alarmingly until Tomas rescued it and set it on the sideboard.

'Morning, Caitlin. Meet my fiancée.'

'Your—? That's the Princess Royal!' whispered Caitlin.

'And also my fiancée.'

Caitlin slid him a beseeching glance and nervously smoothed her apron skirt. 'What are the words? What do I call her?'

'*Your Royal Highness* the first time you see her, and if you see her again the same day you call her *ma'am*.' He was quiet with his directions, no fuss, and it seemed to steady the young girl.

If Claudia hadn't already been besotted with him, his behaviour these past twenty-four hours would have made her so.

'Your Royal Highness, ma'am!'

'And now stand up,' murmured Tomas, and Claudia wanted to put the girl at ease too, the way Tomas had, but the rich smell of cooked sausage and bacon was her undoing. She barely managed a nod before bolting to the bathroom and starting with the stupid morning sickness all over again. It didn't matter to her brain or her stomach that there was nothing left to bring up. She would go through the motions anyway until her throat burned with the sour taste of stomach acid and she felt like a wrung-out rag.

An eon later, when she slid to her knees and leaned her head against her forearm on the toilet bowl, she saw a damp wash cloth dangling in front of her.

The hand holding the cloth didn't belong to the girl.

Tomas settled on the floor beside her and lifted her into his arms as if she weighed barely anything at all. She tucked her head beneath his chin, too embarrassed and grateful for words.

'I sent the breakfast away.'

'Thank you. The smell…'

'I figured.'

'She'll guess I'm pregnant.'

He made a humming noise that might have been agreement. 'Is that something you want to hide?'

'I'm undecided.' Part of her wanted everyone to know now that Tomas knew, so she could go about changing her life to fit the circumstances. Part of her knew her reputation would take a hammering and it would reflect badly on the royal family—best to get it over with. And then there was Tomas's reputation and new position to think of. 'Do you want me to pretend I'm not pregnant until we've been married a while?'

'I think we're past that.'

Who knew pragmatism could be so attractive?

'Let's just shape our lives and the life of our child to best advantage. No lies, we're just doing things our own way. Why *wouldn't* we marry with a baby on the way?' he continued.

'Do you really want to do this?' She was having second thoughts. That or her earlier thoughts were back to haunt her. 'You'll be trapped and resentful.'

'I'll be *grateful* and do everything in my power to prove my worth as a husband and father. You keep telling me I'm good enough to stand with you, so get out of my way and let me fight for us. I'm ready. Besides, I'm not the only one here whose life has been turned upside down.' His voice had grown gruff. 'Yours has been upended too. You get to bear this child, ready or not. You get me for a husband, whether you want me or not.'

'I'm ready.' Her love for the child growing in her belly was already a fierce and twisty force. 'I want it all. Anyone who says you're not good enough to stand at my side is going to get schooled on the many reasons why they're *wrong.* I'll slay all those demons and I'll *make* you a believer, see if I don't.'

'Funny. You don't *look* all that fierce, curled up here in my arms.'

The steady beat of his heart beneath her ear seemed like a good start. She closed her eyes and let herself relax. People thought she didn't have nerves or insecurities. Even her brother saw her as some kind of indestructible force and, right or wrong, she tried to live up to the hype.

'You know how we're talking about our insecurities...'

'I heard you talking about *mine.*'

Dry as dust, this man who'd soon be hers for life.

'I have some too. People think I'm strong and fierce because I want to make a difference in this world and I'm prepared to make enemies along the way,' she mumbled into the well-worn weave of his shirt. 'I know how to fight and wait and play the long game and win. And sometimes being that person is easy and sometimes I run on pure bravado. I need—' *you,* her helpful voice supplied, but she could be more specific, and less '—I would love to have someone who can lend me their strength when mine runs out. I'd weep with relief to know that you too will have our baby's best interests at heart. I can let go and know you'll do everything in your power to keep us safe. That's a gift I've *never* had before and I'll give it the respect it deserves.'

'I won't fail you.'

'I can be strong again. I *will* be. I won't always feel so low.' She closed her eyes and soaked up his warmth.

'And I'll never think less of you for saying you need me,' he murmured. 'Say it as often as you like. My insecurities will thank you.'

Good to know their insecurities were compatible.

A soft knock sounded at the door of the outer room. 'Ma'am and Lord Tomas? It's Caitlin. I have two mugs of weak tea with some slices of lemon and ginger on the side. I'll leave them outside the door and if you want them, good, and if you don't, I'll collect them later.'

Tomas rubbed his thumb over her shoulder in a gesture she found comforting. 'Shall I tell her to bring it in?'

Claudia nodded.

'Come through, Caitlin.'

Moments later, the girl was kneeling beside them in the bathroom. 'My ma used to swear by lemon and ginger tea for soothing the stomach. The tea is Mrs Lee's mountain blend. She's Balo's *nonna*. Balo's the man I'm going to marry, but he doesn't know that yet, so if you could keep it to yourself for another year or two while I grow up, I'd appreciate it. Is there anything you'd like *me* to keep to myself? Because I can. This old place sees its fair share of secrets. Da says not spilling any is as much a part of being an innkeeper as not spilling the drinks.'

Such earnest eyes.

'I can see why you want Caitlin for your falcons, Tomas.' Claudia leaned forward and added lemon and ginger to both mugs and picked one up before settling back against him and bringing the mug to her lips to take the tiniest sip.

'Speaking of…' Tomas had a gleam in his eyes. 'Caitlin, there's a golden eagle in the spare bedroom and a gauntlet on the bed. If you could take her downstairs and find a chair or another perch for her by the fire, I'd be grateful. She's well behaved and enjoys watching people moving about.'

'*Me?*'

'You.'

'And we need another suite of rooms for our guests this afternoon,' he continued.

'Da said we have incoming and to give them the best room we have, but you're in it.'

'Make this room up fresh and we'll move to another,' said Claudia. 'Let's aim to keep my brother in a good mood, hmm?'

Caitlin's eyes grew impossibly round. 'I—the King? And Queen *Ana*? Here? As in *today*?'

'For our wedding,' Tomas supplied gravely, and never again would she suspect him of not having the most sublime sense of humour. Caitlin was already on the move. 'I guess your Da *can* keep a secret. Don't forget the eagle. Her name's Alhena.'

Ten minutes later, Claudia was almost halfway through her tea and they'd moved from the bathroom floor to the armchairs by the fire. For a woman on the morning of her wedding day she felt delightfully unbothered by details. The only detail that mattered was to marry the right man, and he was on the phone to Ildris, inviting him to their wedding through gritted teeth because she'd asked him to. She smiled into her cup when she heard him take it upon himself to ask Ildris to bring Alya too.

His future wife obviously valued them, and they owed her, he said next.

Maybe he'd learn to be a little less heavy-handed when it came to wielding power or maybe he'd never get the hang of it. Claudia was looking forward to a lifetime of brutal honesty, absolute trust and fireworks, no matter what. A pox on emotional containment. It was overrated.

'What?' he asked as he ended the call and pocketed his phone. 'They'll be here mid-afternoon. I told them they might have to share a room if they were staying on.'

'So I heard. But, by my reckoning, Caitlin said there are six rooms in total, and if the King and Queen are in one, with Sophia in an adjoining room, Silas and Lor in another, and you and me in one, the count is only four rooms taken. Why would Ildris and Alya have to share a room?'

He smiled wickedly. 'Never said I could count.'

This man. This life stretching out ahead of them.

*Savour the moment, Claudia. Those funny, fleeting, happiest of moments.*

*They'll sustain you.*

# CHAPTER TEN

TOMAS MADE HIS way downstairs the moment Cas and his entourage arrived, and he might have been driven to drink as a way of settling the nerves that had crept up on him but for the steadying presence of Rudolpho and horse master Gabriel, who'd also hitched a ride in one of the two royal helicopters now sitting in a field behind the inn. He knew these men and they knew him. He was happy to see them and took great pleasure in watching Balo's *nonna*—who'd been put in charge of the wedding flower arrangements—pin sprigs of flowering thyme and wild mountain heather to their shirts.

News of the wedding spread through the village with the arrival of those royal helicopters carrying the royal family. Far from this wedding being an impromptu and modest affair, the people of Aergoveny seemed hellbent on embracing their King, country and especially their new Lord, and making Tomas's wedding to the Crown Princess an evening to remember.

Tomas and his companions were herded to the outdoor fires where the men of the village had gathered, and music and dancing was already in full swing. Women walked past on their way to the inn, bearing armfuls of wild mountain flowers and baskets of food, and everyone shared wide smiles and teasing glances and embraced the festivities with a skip in their step.

Rudolpho and the village mayor had taken it upon themselves to form an alliance and see to it that Tomas met as many people as possible in the hours before the ceremony began. Gabriel harnessed the younger men and encouraged their most prized steeds to be brought to him immediately for examination. The King's wedding gift to the village included a year's access to royal racehorse bloodlines, he told them, and promptly turned the wedding gathering into a horse traders' paradise.

'Just making it a wedding to remember,' he said.

'My father grew up in a mountain village,' Rudolpho told Tomas a short time later as the men co-opted by the women to help with preparations began bringing out ornate soup tureens and tables. Tomas gratefully accepted a cup of strong hot coffee brought to him by the mayor's grandson.

People started turning up with their hawks and, well, what was a falconer to do in the face of that kind of temptation but set a prize of first pick from his next hatching and help set out a flight path for time trials?

Rudolpho, being a courtier well used to keeping wayward kings on task, warned Tomas not to get too involved, this being his wedding day and all, and then the women signalled they were ready for him, so he jostled his way to the head of the crowd, straightened his trousers and shirt and the stunning fur cloak Ildris had slung over his shoulders at some point, and made his way towards the village square, where his bride waited with her family.

At some point the small, intimate gathering Tomas had imagined had become a celebration for all, because how else would this place beneath the sky and in the

shadow of a great mountain range have become ringed
with mountain wildflowers and pine boughs, and made
raucous with rhythmic clapping and spirited vocals? With
his blood quickening and his gaze searching ahead for
that moment when Claudia would be revealed to him,
he gave himself over to the moment, cupped his hands
over his mouth and let out a piercing war cry of his own.

He didn't even have a gift to lay at her feet—he really
hadn't thought this marriage moment through. And then
he saw her and the air around him stilled and the music
faded to nothing.

She wore a royal tiara and a simple white gown and a
fur-trimmed cloak similar to his, and she smiled at him
as if there were no other place she'd rather be than here
with him.

He led an army of Aergovenich warriors, young and
old, who would follow his lead, and he didn't know when
he'd become their figurehead but they put the weight of
their wedding songs and customs and posturing behind
him and it was glorious.

Bain the innkeeper stopped him from reaching Claudia's side by the simple act of getting in his way and holding his ground until they stood chest to chest.

At the raising of Bain's hand, all sound stopped.

'Crown Princess Claudia of Byzenmaach, is this him?'
'It is.'

'King Casimir of Byzenmaach, do you consent to placing your treasured sister, the country's beloved Crown
Princess Royal, into this man's hands?'

'If she insists, yes.'

'Lord Ildris of the mountain clans, do you object to
the placing of your beloved jewel of the north into this
working man's hands?'

'I dare not object.'

'Lord Falcon Master Sokolov, are you worthy of this beloved woman?' roared Bain at his most formidable volume yet.

Tomas realised why Bain had so suddenly developed a taste for theatre when the army of men behind him bellowed, 'Yes!' until Tomas raised his hand for silence.

The resulting hush nearly stole his breath.

And then Lor stepped up. He hadn't expected her to play a prominent role in the ceremony, but nothing so far had proceeded as expected and her kindly face was reassuring.

'Tomas Sokolov, you were born in my presence and, as you stand here before me, I claim my role as representative of the spirit of your parents. Do you object?'

'No.' He probably should have gone over the details of this wedding in advance…

'Your future wife stands before you and us all,' continued Lor. 'And, as is customary, I demand you open your heart for examination.'

Did she want him to cut it out? This might shorten his life span considerably, which might even please Cas and Ildris. Cas was smiling broadly and Ildris looked annoyingly pleased with himself. Neither seemed to want to clue him in on his options regarding this particular part of the ceremony. Then again, he'd winged it so far.

'I have nothing to hide,' he offered grandly.

Although a little bit of mystique when it came to lording it over the people of Aergoveny might have come in handy.

'Will you honour her?' Bain asked.

'Yes.' The answer was his alone, but no less compelling than the hundreds of voices that had gone before.

'Will you cherish her?'

'Beyond measure.'

'Will you protect her from harm?'

'With my life.'

Lor smiled proudly. How much more was there to go? 'Do you love her?'

There was such hope in her eyes and a faint plea not to embarrass her by saying something ridiculous like 'No' or 'I might' or 'We'll see'. That time had passed.

'I love her with every breath I take, yes.' And probably beyond, but no one had asked for that.

Yet.

Lor turned to Claudia, who stood tall and still, eyes shining. 'Princess Claudia of Byzenmaach, Lady Falconer of the North, he is worthy and he is yours. Will you have him?'

Claudia stepped up close and trailed a finger around his jaw, tilting his face first to one side and then the other. She was enjoying this horse-trading segment just a little too much. She strolled a leisurely circle around him, measuring the breadth of his shoulders with her fingers and the strength of his patience while he awaited her answer and his army looked on.

'Yes.'

And the celebrations began in earnest.

'I can't believe you didn't have to say any of the vows,' he muttered hours later in the privacy of the tavern's second-best bedroom. The room had been lit with so many candles, he figured the Vatican must surely be missing some. And Claudia sat in a chair with her hair down, her feet up and her tiara on the table while the celebrations continued elsewhere.

She looked tired but gratifyingly content. He, on the other hand, rubbed at the place where his heart used to be, firmly convinced that she'd picked it up and put it somewhere with casual abandon. It was probably underneath that priceless diamond and sapphire tiara on the table.

'I still don't believe that there I was, lying prostrate at your feet…'

'Figuratively speaking,' she said airily, with a languid wave of her hand.

'Pledging my all for eternity…'

'Or face a public hanging, I did like that bit.'

He'd always suspected she was the bloodthirsty sort.

'And all you had to do was say, *He'll do, thanks. Yes.*'

'You're the one who thought an Aergoveny village wedding would be a cinch. I mean, who knew they'd make you their essence of masculinity for the day? That looked fun. Was that fun?'

Maybe if he'd known what he was doing…

'I thought you represented them *very* pleasingly. I counted at least three new unions to come of it.'

'Please tell me Caitlin didn't corner Balo.'

'Not yet. Her father knows her heart and so does Balo. It will happen in time, but not yet.'

'Alya and Ildris?'

'I saw them leaving together arm in arm,' she murmured.

'Ha.' His gaze flew to Claudia's stomach. 'How are you feeling?'

'Married.'

'Good, because I'm only ever going to do that once. How is our baby feeling?'

She'd closed her eyes but cracked one open, just a slit. 'Too small to tell, but I think it's all good. Tomorrow morning will be a repeat of this morning, but with more cake involved. I did eat a lot of cake. The vanilla frosting was on point.'

Where had the people come up with enough food to feed and water six hundred at such short notice? And they were still going, those wedding celebrations, and somehow, he was going to have to make good on those vows he'd made before everyone and God.

'I'm sorry you had to lie about loving me. I know you don't. Not really.' She had her eyes closed again, so missed his double-take. He opened his mouth to tell her that although he'd been put ruthlessly on the spot in full public view, he hadn't been lying when he'd made those vows. He'd meant every word.

How could she not have recognised his sincerity? Even if he had just been grumbling about the unevenness of their vows.

'I—'

But she was already speaking again, her voice coming in over his. 'I want you to know that I'm going to do everything I possibly can to make this union work. I don't want to disappoint you. I'm determined to be of use.'

*Of use.*

She was *of use* to her brother.

She'd been *of use* to Ildris and his ilk.

Why was being of use so important to her sense of self? Was she really so motivated by service to others or had it merely been a survival tactic for far too many years?

He hesitated before speaking his mind, not quite knowing how his next words would be received. 'You have a thing about being useful to others. You turn yourself inside out for people and put their needs above yours, but that's not how I want this marriage to work. You don't exist to be used by others. Let's figure out together what moving forward means, and go easy on the one-way self-sacrifice.'

She put the heels of her hands to her eyes as if his words hurt her. His heart ached for her.

'For example,' he continued doggedly. 'You've talked about not feeling at home in the places you live. Should creating a home base where we feel completely and utterly ourselves be our number one priority?'

'Yes.' It sounded like a sob, but it was a yes.

'Could a modest manor house in the middle of nowhere, with no old memories attached, ever become such a place for you?'

'Yes.'

'Clean slate. New beginnings. A baby on the way. We can make new memories. Beautiful ones. No matter what has brought us to this moment, will you do that with me, and *for* me, and, most importantly, for yourself?'

'Yes.'

'Good.' He pulled her into his arms and she curled into him and clung as if she'd never let him go. 'It's not so bad, this being married business,' he declared gruffly. 'We're going to nail this.'

# CHAPTER ELEVEN

BEING MARRIED HADN'T actually changed his way of life all that much, decided Tomas several months later. He'd known from the beginning not to expect Claudia to be a stay-at-home wife, eagerly awaiting his return after a day of blissful homemaking, but the time she spent in service to the Crown and the various charities she'd adopted, and her continued service to Ildris and his northerners, meant she didn't actually spend a lot of time in Aergoveny.

Likewise, he was busier than ever as he travelled between the manor and the winter fortress and carved out the time to join his princess wife at the various state banquets and luncheons Casimir insisted they attended.

Far from his reputation being sullied, it had been thoroughly gilded once his high-country wedding to the Crown Princess had become common knowledge. The people of Byzenmaach approved of Claudia's choice of partner. Photos of him and his eagles had helped. He was of Byzenmaach and his pedigree went back generations. He brooded photogenically.

He was the new Lord of Aergoveny, and Aergoveny had claimed him.

As Casimir had warned, he now had his own political capital to spend.

It had only taken one excruciatingly boring state dinner and a round of idle conversation between him and some of the courtiers who'd been stirring up rumours about Claudia's legitimacy and planting stories about her unfortunate Stockholm Syndrome. They'd even begun wondering aloud, and in his presence, when Claudia might give birth. Apparently, they'd thought themselves beyond reproach or justified in their smear campaigns. Perhaps they'd thought him toothless.

How deluded was that?

He'd begun by reminiscing about a particular hunting party some of them had attended at the winter fortress many years ago under the rule of the late Leonidas. Pity about those heinous rumours of sexual assault on the son of the Duke of Laire, wasn't it? Such a tragedy, the boy's subsequent suicide. Such a shame no one in attendance had ever seemed to have the stomach to get to the bottom of it.

Wasn't it?

So many stories of those dark times towards the end of King Leonidas's life.

Weren't there?

Claudia had called it extortion, or was it intimidation? One of those big words suggesting borderline criminal behaviour.

Tomas called it small talk.

They shared a bed once or twice a week—enthusiastically, he had no complaints—but as their baby grew, his touches became more tentative. There was a baby in there! What was a man to do but be very, very careful in his approach?

He spent hours of every day setting up the new falconry the way he wanted it, and Claudia spent almost every waking moment deep within the political bowels of her brother's court, buying into the crisis of the day. And there was always one of those.

He was everywhere and nowhere, always playing a part these days. Only in the sanctuary of Lor's kitchen did he allow himself to drop the mask and be himself again. Claudia's wolfhounds were at his feet more often than not, and he always had at least one falcon with him. Sometimes Ana and Sophia would likewise find refuge from the demands of the Crown while Claudia and Cas debated policy and execution late into the night.

He might have even been content with his marriage of—what had they called it?—two spirited individuals, if he didn't already carry with him the memory of what a loving marriage could be.

His parents had shown him the sweetness of silences that did not clamour to be filled.

The intimacy of private glances and perfect understanding. The cups of tea in the morning, made with care by a loving hand and served in a favourite mug. Foundation memories. He wanted them.

His morning coffee whenever he stayed in Claudia's suite at the palace came on a silver tray at exactly seven a.m., lukewarm, too weak and utterly impersonal. Just this morning he'd barked at a maid who'd entered their bedroom just as he'd exited the shower. He hadn't expected her to be there.

He hadn't liked the way her sly sideways gaze had flicked at him.

'Did you really need to send her away so curtly?' Claudia had chided.

'Did she really need to freshen the linen at five minutes past six in the morning?' he'd snapped back.

He hated losing control of his responses and being found lacking.

And for all their fine talk about making a home for themselves and loving memories to go with it, neither he nor Claudia were making that happen.

Lor took that moment to place a hot mug of beef broth on the table in front of him and although he said his thanks, he promptly got lost in the thought that Claudia wouldn't even know it was *his* mug, let alone that he'd made it at school one year and given it to his mother as a birthday gift. The last time Claudia had set a cup of anything down beside him… Nope, she never had.

Lor, Ana and young Sophia all knew more about him than his wife did.

And off he went, being morose again.

This right here was why letting emotions rule your life was a *bad* thing.

And then Sophia clambered up on the stool next to him, bringing her special soup in her special cup with her, and regarded him solemnly. 'Did one of your falcons die?'

'No.' He certainly hoped not. Sophia's fixation with death was well known, mainly because she'd been told from a young age that both her father and aunt were dead when they weren't.

'Did you make a mistake and get into trouble?'

'Maybe.' He huffed a laugh. 'Why?'

'You're sad.'

'Nah.' He held up his forefinger and thumb, set approximately an inch apart. 'Maybe this sad. I was thinking about my mother, who died a long time ago. I made this mug for her when I was about as old as you are now. Have you done mug making yet?'

She shook her head with vigour. That would be a no, then. 'But I want to.'

'And you will,' said Ana. 'Say goodnight, Sophia. It's bedtime for you and me.'

Everyone in the kitchen began the goodnight chorus and by the time the heavy kitchen door swung shut, Tomas was halfway through his soup and determined not to look sad again, even if he was.

'Are you happy about becoming a father soon?' asked Lor with far more of a read on him than he was comfortable with.

'Sophia's a nice kid. I like kids.' Which didn't exactly answer the question. 'Raising a kid who's a member of the royal family to have similar values to the ones I grew up with won't be easy, though.' First time he'd voiced that thought. 'How do you teach someone to value a misshapen mug when they have access to the best of everything? Does Claudia possess anything belonging to her mother, other than royal jewels? I don't think so.'

'Maybe not, but in my experience it pays to think of Claudia more as an orphan raised by a foster family. She's not going to let on that a particular possession of hers is important, even if it is. She may say some of the falcons are hers but there's no loyalty from them in return—she knows that just as well as you do. She has a horse she treasures, but it's cared for and ridden by Gabriel and his grooms these days because of her pregnancy. She does have two very loyal wolfhounds.'

They both looked down. Those wolfhounds were currently sitting at Tomas's feet.

He hadn't meant to take them on, but Claudia's palace meetings ran for days sometimes, whereas with him at least the dogs got a run.

Lor wiped her hands on her apron. 'Has she talked about their defection to you?'

'I didn't realise it was a competition.' But what if Claudia thought of it as such? 'I thought I was helping.'

'You are very caring, very competent and very helpful, yes. You bring rules and safety with you—I predict that your children will idolise you. But with that happy head start into parenting comes a warning. Don't cut your wife out of the child-raising if she doesn't take to it as naturally as you do. That woman has been surplus to requirements all her life. *Include* her. Make her feel essential to your wellbeing and happiness. *Talk* to her about what you want from this new world the two of you are creating. There is her northern world, to which she is beholden for keeping her alive. There is her brother's world, into which she brings challenge and reform—a world where she's more often cast as a villain so that Casimir can be seen as the good King. And then there's *your* world, and to my old eyes she's doing her damnedest to make you happy. It doesn't help that you disappear for days on end, leaving her to get on with paying her dues.'

'She wants me to go,' he protested. 'She encourages me to get on with paying mine.'

'And in a secure relationship, individually working hard and coming together when the work is done would be enough. Is your relationship secure, my stalwart heart? Or is there still so much to learn about each other and discuss? Can't do that when you spend most of your time apart.'

Who knew that having Lor point out the obvious could make him feel so miserably unfit for the role of husband?

'She comes in here some nights when you're away and without fail she reaches for your mug, and she treats it with the same care you do, even though she doesn't know its history. She just knows it's yours.' Lor eyed him shrewdly. 'It's the little things that reveal so much, isn't it. Who you really are. What you value most. Even if you don't know how to keep hold of it.'

'Keep talking.' Might as well admit he needed some tough love. 'I don't know what I'm doing wrong, but my marriage is withering.'

'You need my wise words.'

Yes, he did. 'I need to fix it.'

'Claudia doesn't want to let anyone down and they use her and you know this. She'll work herself to the bone in service to others, it's happening in front of your eyes. She finds it very difficult to even state her wants and needs, let alone follow through. So get in there and put your foot down, Tomas, and make it easier for her to follow through.'

He was listening.

Two days later, Tomas braved the underground swimming pools of the winter fortress in search of his princess wife. He didn't like the watery caverns carved into the side of the mountain, no matter how many sconces lit his way. He didn't see luxury in the fluffy towels and scented oils placed strategically. He found the place eerie, truth be told. Give him sky above his head, not solid rock all around him. Maybe he just wasn't a cave person.

But Silas said Claudia had taken to bathing here of an afternoon, so he swallowed his dislike and journeyed forth, into the gloom.

Claudia sat by herself beneath the waterfall, a wrap tied around her rapidly changing body, her head slightly forward to let the water from the underground riverway pound down on her shoulders and neck.

By the time he'd removed his clothes she'd seen him and had made her way to the shallow end of the pool where the steps were, her amber eyes alight with curiosity and…dare he imagine pleasure?

'I thought you were away for two more days,' she said by way of greeting.

'I heard from Lor that your meeting was cancelled, so I asked Balo's grandfather to step in and supervise the apprentices through to the beginning of next week. Might work, might not. Delegation is not my strong point, but I'm trying to build teams that won't fall apart in my absence.'

'He must be good for you to even consider bringing him on.'

'He reminds me of my grandfather.' Tomas settled on the step beside her, half in the water, half out. 'He handles the goldens in ways I've never seen before, but it works. I can learn from him. That region is a treasure trove. Have I thanked you for choosing it for me lately?'

'Not lately.'

He leaned in and captured her lips in a kiss that started gently and then he very deliberately set about adding layer after layer of gossamer passion and promise.

'Thank you,' he whispered when his body had stirred sufficiently to make it abundantly obvious that he was pleased to see her. 'I can't wait to get you there more often. Did I tell you that Caitlin's father has taken on a new manager? I interviewed her for an apprenticeship yesterday.'

'Really?' Delight looked good on her.

'I offered her the position on the spot. It's people, isn't

it. Key people in key positions who can change the world. She's one of them. You're one of them too.'

She smiled and leaned against him and it was enough to make him happy.

'I like it when you touch me or lean against me or trail your hand across my shoulders when you walk by,' he rumbled, mindful of Lor's advice that he should be more forthcoming. He was getting used to having to use his words more in all sorts of situations, rather than expect others to pick up on his non-verbal cues.

'You like it when I scratch the feathers at the back of your neck too.'

He huffed a laugh. So he did. 'Blame it on my early childhood conditioning. My father was a man of gestures rather than words. When I was younger, he'd carry me on his shoulders. When I got older I'd work my skinny little kid guts out to earn a pat on the back. My mother was big on putting my favourite food in front of me in my favourite bowl. Then she'd run her hand through my hair and mutter about there being more twigs in it than a bird's nest.'

'So touch is an expression of love for you. Good to know.'

'And you work yourself to the bone for the people you love. It's what you do. Baked into your psyche. It's what I want to talk to you about.'

She eyed him warily.

'You're doing too much for others and too little for us.' He came right out and said it.

She was silent a long time. Long enough for him to immerse himself in the water completely and rise, shaking the droplets from his hair and pushing the hair from his face. Hardly Aquaman, but she always seemed pleased enough with his body and that in turn pleased him.

'They need me.'

'They can't always have you. I and our baby are going to need you more.'

She dropped her gaze and skimmed her hands through the water in lazy figure eights, making ripples but not splashes. A turbulence that lapped at his skin rather than attacked it.

'One of my ways of showing love as a kid was to try and be as invisible and unobtrusive as possible,' she offered finally. 'If I could just be still enough and silent enough, they could pretend I wasn't there, and Cas wouldn't have to try and protect me and end up taking a beating. Not breathing too loud was my version of love.'

And that was just heartbreaking, but he should have guessed. He'd seen first-hand what her childhood had been like, never mind that she'd never been like that with him as a kid.

'Was it like that for you in the north as well?' He moved closer, putting his hands to her belly, and measuring growth in finger spans.

'To start with, yes. I breathed very quietly and I was always wondering where I would go or what I would do if they simply packed up and left me behind. Then I overheard one of the elders saying I'd be of more use once my father was dead and Cas became King and I clung to the thought that somehow I could be of use. I tried to learn as much as I could. I was forever putting myself forward, being the first to volunteer for anything and everything so I could *be of use*.'

'They manipulated you. I'll never think differently.

But more to the point, don't you think you've repaid that debt in full?'

'I—don't know.'

'Ask them what more they want from you. Tell them your focus is shifting to your baby and allocate what you do for them to other people for the next six months. When they prove competent—and they will—leave them in those positions.'

He sneaked a glance and could see she was thinking it over as she chewed delicately on her bottom lip. Her matter-of-fact recounting of that time in her life horrified him. It sat at odds with how she usually spoke well of her time in the north. Maybe both versions could be true. Maybe all that mattered was that he understood her duality and listened to her concerns.

'It makes sense that you would swing from being barely visible to being all up in the thick of things, determined to be useful.' He pressed his lips to her belly. 'It makes sense that you're struggling to find a middle ground to reside in, but I'm here to help you find that balance if you'll let me. You are half a fingernail wider across the belly,' he declared.

'You think I'm failing you and our baby.'

'No,' he countered firmly. '*No.* But I want us to remember what we talked about on the night of our wedding and that we chose to make our relationship, our baby and our home, our first priority. And we haven't been, so let's do a reset. Both of us. Okay? I've been just as guilty as you of letting other things get in the way.'

He gathered her close and she clung to him. He hugged her tight and bobbed them up and down, dunking them at one point to wash away her tears. He cast about for something to show how deeply he wanted to make her feel wanted and secure.

'Balo's *nonna*'s a potter, so I made you a mug when I went to see them about his grandfather stepping into that supervisory role.'

'You went to offer a man a job and ended up making a teacup?' Her smile was watery, but she wasn't crying that he could tell.

'Yes. It's wobbly but I think I've improved since I made that one for my mother—you'd recognise that one. It's the one in Lor's kitchen that I always use. I couldn't decide on a colour for your glaze—it's a toss-up between the blue of the sky or amber like your eyes. I have to go back to paint it once it's dry.'

'Blue. Blue for the sky.'

'You could come too and see what you think of the blue tableware for our day-to-day use at the manor. I liked it.'

She pulled away as far as he would let her—which wasn't far. 'Tomas Sokolov, are you *nesting*?'

'Is that what you call it?'

'What do you call it?' she demanded.

'I'd rather not think about my newfound fascination for pottery at all, but I do want you to come to Aergoveny with me tomorrow and stay the night if you have the time. The wolfhounds have missed you.'

'That's a lie. They miss their nomadic way of life. At least with you they get to ride out every now and then.'

'It's not a lie—I stand by what I said. They miss your company. So do I.' Words, words, using all the words until he broke through to her. She wasn't the only one who could learn new tricks. 'Please, I need you to take some time for yourself. We could ride out and explore. What did the doctor say about you riding?'

'Not to,' she replied dryly. 'I'm allowed to swim, so here I am, lolling about in the shallows because Cas has forbidden me to jump in the river opening, even though he still does.'

Tomas had been in that fast-flowing coil of darkness only once. Between the swiftly moving undertow and the grate at the end that could pin a person like a fly on a swat, he'd been fearful for his life. 'To be fair, it's a death trap.'

'Exactly. So Cas is now banned from swimming there too. He can't die until he and Ana have offspring that are old enough to sit on the throne without me having to be Regent. And you're not to take any notice of the rumour going around that I tried to poison my brother yesterday. That is not in my wheelhouse.'

'So…ah…what *did* happen to the King yesterday?' He dreaded the thought that Claudia would ever have to take her brother's place, but it could happen. She was next in line. Sophia hadn't been born in wedlock, so would never rule Byzenmaach. Royal succession rules were archaic and absolute.

'He got a stomach bug from Sophia, who got it from school. But don't let that get in the way of a good royal poisoning plot. Some courtiers work tirelessly to plant a wedge between me and Cas.'

'Who? I want names.'

'You can't have names if all you're going to do is threaten to reveal all their dark secrets if they oppose me.'

'Says who?'

'Says me.'

'Spoilsport. Claudia, listen to me. No one is ever going to come between you and your brother. The bond you forged in childhood grows stronger by the day. He needs

and wants you in his life because he loves you. That you
choose to support him so thoroughly is a blessing in his
life, but you could step back tomorrow and he would still
love you just the same. Talk to him about taking more
time for yourself. Blame the baby, or me, but talk to him
about placing your political focus where he needs it most
and delegate the rest. You don't have a royal secretary—
why not? Ask Rudolpho to train one and then *delegate*.
You'll get more done in less time. I'm sharing my newfound wisdom with you freely so that you too may learn
what I'm learning.'

'You're a saint.'

'Hardly. I just want more of you to myself.'

'Why didn't you just say you were feeling neglected?'

'Wouldn't have learned nearly as much about you if
I'd come straight out and said it, now, would I?'

'You're *sneaky*.' She sounded delighted with that dis-
covery.

'No, I'm not. I'm honest to a fault. And stalwart.'

'And naked.'

He hadn't forgotten. 'Have I mentioned how very
pleased I am to see you?'

'Well, you have now.' She locked her legs firmly
around his waist and began to rub herself against him.
'But I know how much you prefer nonverbal communication. Maybe you could show me.'

Challenge accepted.

# CHAPTER TWELVE

KING CASIMIR AND Lord Ildris were negotiating. They'd
been at it for hours and Claudia's interest had long since
dwindled to nothing. The chairs around the negotiating
table were outrageously comfortable but her lower back
ached regardless. They kept calling for coffee refills
for their tiny ceremonial coffee cups, but she'd stuck to
water throughout the day, so not only was she not buzz-
ing with caffeine, she'd had four toilet breaks in the past
two hours.

Each time she excused herself the two men would
stand and break the meeting until she returned, before
once more getting down to business without her needing to say a word.

She'd spent two glorious days beforehand with Tomas
at the manor that was fast becoming her favourite place
in the world. They'd discovered a storeroom stacked with
floor rugs, at which point Claudia had also discovered
that an afternoon spent lounging on a sunny window seat
stuffed with cushions while her husband and several of
his apprentices revealed carpet after carpet for her to
choose from was an excellent way to pass the time. Especially when said apprentices brought their falcons with
them for socialising.

Returning to the palace so soon after watching Tomas

effortlessly train and entertain and retain his authority throughout… Surely, she could be forgiven for thinking this high-level politicking a comedown from glorious heights?

As far as she could tell, her brother and Ildris were in agreement for the most part of this extended water use negotiation and were now haggling over minor details. Of course, those minor details weren't minor at all to the people who were affected by them, but she'd long since lost interest in the earnings projections of the Sorl River salmon farmers versus the hopes of the orchardists further downriver. She'd lost track of the many pros and cons of each five hours ago, which was around about the last time she'd made any meaningful contribution to the discussion.

Ildris was a good leader. So was her brother. Byzenmaach did not stand on the precipice of civil unrest and nor was it warmongering against its neighbours.

Could it be that these two men simply enjoyed talking decisions to death? More power to them, if that was their jam, but, well…

Did she really have to be here?

She stood and stretched, her hand on her lower back, which pushed her stomach out—and while she wasn't huge, there was no mistaking her these days for anything but well along in her pregnancy. Cas's eyes flashed from irritation to concern as he too rose from his chair. The ever-present Rudolpho pulled her chair back as Ildris rose too.

'Again?' asked her brother.

'Again,' she murmured just a little too cheerfully. 'Your Majesty, Lord Ildris, I must beg your leave. My mind wanders, my back aches, and we're down to discussing minutiae. You don't need me here. That's a compliment, not a complaint.'

Ildris remained impassive, her brother frowned.

She wasn't above wondering if she should put her hand on her belly to further emphasise her need to be elsewhere, but that was guaranteed to make her brother frown more.

Cas's eyes narrowed as if reading her mind. 'Do you need to see your physician?'

'Only if I want her to tell me—again—that it's perfectly normal for pregnant women to have aching backs and get tired and go to the bathroom a lot.'

Rudolpho, bless him, was already opening the outer door for her.

'You'll be here tomorrow?' It was Cas her brother and not Cas her King asking. She was almost sure of it.

'No, I'm heading back to the mountains for the weekend. I want to be there when Tomas's black-necked and red-necked grebe pairs arrive.'

'His what?'

'Ducks.' She winked at Rudolpho. 'Yes, the sexiest falconer in the world collects endangered waterfowl and I am there for it.'

'Are these my ducks or his ducks?' Cas called after her. 'When did I agree to become king of the ducks?'

'You didn't. They're not yours. They're ducks of the world.' A playful Cas was an absolute delight. He didn't let himself go there nearly often enough. 'You're welcome!'

With her priorities rebalanced and Tomas more often by her side, Claudia began to spread her time more evenly between the royal palace, the fortress and the manor. She'd loved the Aergoveny manor house from afar and the reality did not disappoint. It had the potential to reflect the best of all her worlds and it suited Tomas to perfection. He had vision, natural authority, rock-solid steadiness and fairness at his command, and people responded by working hard for him. Falcons and learning and research and renewal of resources long forgotten. Why wouldn't people gladly follow him to the top of the world and back?

She was just over seven months pregnant now and last week the palace had released a statement saying she and Tomas were eagerly expecting their firstborn in November. Yes, people could count and would know that she'd been pregnant before marriage. Who cared?

Her life balance was better than good; it was amazing. Happiness had never been so easy to find.

Until the night Claudia stood alone in her dressing room in her brother's palace as she readied herself for yet another long afternoon of political jockeying disguised as small talk and noticed blood on her panties. Not a lot of blood. A few spots. Four. Maybe six spots overall, none of them big. But the blood was a bright, vibrant red and it rocked her confidence and put a fear in her that nothing else ever had.

She couldn't lose this baby.

Tomas would have no reason to stay with her if she lost the baby, no reason at all, and *no*. This wasn't happening. She wouldn't run, she'd just sit down, but not on a chair where the blood would soak in, and not on any carpet either. Just for a moment, she'd sit down on the floor in the bathroom, or lie down, that was better, and put her feet up on the edge of the bath and everything would right itself and there would be no problem at all.

She cradled her belly with tender hands. She didn't want to think about what might happen if there was no

November baby for her and Tomas, Lord and Lady Sokolov of Aergoveny.

Would his vows stay true in the face of all that gaping nothing?

Who in her life had ever stuck around if she didn't deliver what they wanted?

'It's just your insecurities talking,' she told herself between jagged, too-loud breathing. 'Tomas's regard for you is real. You know this. He shows it every day.' He wasn't a man of love poems and verbal declarations of undying devotion. Actions counted more. He was committed to her and this life they were building. That wouldn't change. He was not a shallow man, this man she'd chosen. Loss might even bring them closer.

But later that night, after she'd begged off her meeting due to feeling unwell and had seen the doctor, who'd ordered more rest and fewer engagements…much later, after she'd returned to the winter fortress and taken herself to bed early, she didn't tell Tomas about those seven, eight, bright little spots on her panties. She pretended to be drowsy, already half asleep, and let him hold her, just hold her, as he drifted off to sleep.

While bits of her bled and she remained stubbornly, fearfully silent.

If she didn't say it, it wasn't happening.

Claudia took it easy the next day and the day after that.

She slept late and cancelled so many appointments that Rudolpho turned up, demanding to know what was happening.

The bleeding had stopped but fear kept her cautious, and she should have mentioned her spotting to Tomas before he left for Aergoveny for three days without her.

She'd told him to go alone when he'd floated the idea of her going with him. She could tell he'd noticed her uncharacteristic need to sleep late and read quietly in her rooms of an afternoon. She wasn't walking her wolfhounds or taking care of her falcons. Even in the most vicious throes of morning sickness, she'd always managed to do those things if she was within doing distance of them.

But pregnant women were not questioned when their habits changed abruptly, she'd come to notice.

At least, not by men.

Rudolpho being the exception, and that was only because he answered to the King.

'I have to tell him something,' Rudolpho emphasised for perhaps the hundredth time since he'd requested an audience with her. 'When is your current incapacity likely to end?'

'I don't know,' she told him tersely, not to mention truthfully. 'I don't feel up to sitting through a state luncheon today.'

'Have you seen your doctor? What did they say?'

'They told me to rest, so here I am. Resting.' The edge to her voice didn't go unnoticed. She stood abruptly, unable to stay still. 'I realise Cas is relying on me to help win over his senior courtiers to this new change to the water distribution plan, but the deal is done. They can whine all they want but the kings of four interlocked kingdoms are making this happen. Cas's old guard are just going to have to get over their vapours or be *replaced.*'

'Princess—'

'Don't you agree? It's time he stopped indulging them.'

'Quite, but—'

'It really is that simple. He. Is. Their. King. His word is *final*!'

Rudolpho was standing in front of her now, his dark eyes flashing concern. 'Your Highness, *please* sit down.'

'Stand up, sit down, come to lunch—what is it you all want from me?' Couldn't she even have a proper meltdown without someone trying to guide her through it?

'Princess, sit *down*.' The crack of a whip in his voice broke through her indignation. 'Let's not be alarmed, but ma'am, you're bleeding, and this concerns me *greatly*.'

She did as he said, sitting on the bed at first, and then lying down as a cramp in her stomach struck hard. 'Don't tell Tomas.'

'Why in the world not?' He was already at the door to her suite, gesturing to someone outside. 'Find former housemistress Lor and bring her here. You, call the royal doctor and ask her to come urgently. *As in now, man, don't just stand there.*' He closed the door and turned back to Claudia. 'Feet up. Don't move.'

She closed her eyes on his forbidding frown. 'Please don't tell Tomas. He'll leave me if there's no baby to stay for.'

'Now I know you're out of your bleeding mind. No. No, brain bleeding at all,' he amended quickly. 'Out of your clearly addled mind. What have you been eating or drinking of late? Is there any chance you might have been poisoned?' She felt a smooth palm on her forehead. 'You're burning up. What about any unguents or skin potions? Have you used anything new?'

'Bath oil. I've been soaking in it. Bergamot and rose and…other smells. Lady Ester gave it to me.'

'Your late uncle's bitter mistress, who hated both your parents with a viciousness even I found impressive, gives you a gift and you didn't think to have it checked?'

Well, when he put it like that…

'Wait? Was Lady Ester my father's mistress? You tell me this now?'

'Your uncle's mistress.'

'Who was in all likelihood my—wait, do you know?' Was it her stomach or lower down? Hard to tell with the stabbing headache that had so recently arrived. 'No, you don't know *that* secret. No one does. Doesn't matter. Let it go. Shh. Keep trying to make me feel better instead.'

'How do you suggest I do that? You're burning up, I'm quizzing you about poisons, and your nose is bleeding.'

'My nose?' Her hand came up to examine it. 'Yes?' There was blood on her hands now too. 'Yes! So I'm not bleeding from anywhere else? Forgive me while I— Oh, there's nothing. That's brilliant.'

Rudolpho by now had his face in his hands and his back turned towards her. 'I'll tell your brother not to expect you for the rest of the *month*,' he pleaded. 'If you'll just lie back and wait for a *female* attendant to turn up before you go examining any other body parts. I beg you.'

She lay back and swiped at her nose. How had she not felt that? Had she been too mired in righteous indignation to notice a popped blood vessel? 'You said blood. I thought I was miscarrying.'

'If you could wait there in *silence*,' he pleaded even harder.

'What's going on?' said a gruff voice from the doorway, a voice Claudia would know anywhere.

'Oh, hi. You're back.'

'I never left. My departure was delayed by a wounded falcon and I was worried about my wife. I repeat, why is the King's valet in your—*our*—bedroom?'

'Thank God you're back,' muttered Rudolpho. 'She's

all yours. She has nosebleed, fever and she's not herself. I've sent for help.'

'I thought I was having a miscarriage, Rudolpho thinks I've been poisoned by the bath oil, and Cas wants to know when to expect me for lunch.'

'Barking, the lot of you,' Tomas muttered, and turned to the other man. 'Why are you still here?'

'Possessive.' Claudia approved.

Rudolpho strode to the bathroom, reappeared with the Venetian glass bottle of oil in hand. 'I'll be in touch,' he said, and vanished.

'Care to tell me what's been troubling you for *days*?' Tomas asked with an excess of bite. 'Or would you rather I hear it from somebody else?'

Possessive and out of sorts. 'I had a little spotting the other day.' He looked none the wiser. 'Of blood. From down here.' She motioned with her hand and watched all colour drain from his face. 'The doctor said that can be very normal but to take it easy, so I have been. Except now I have a fever and I'm bleeding from my nose and here we are.'

'And where exactly does the poison theory fit into all of this?'

'I cannot be responsible for Rudolpho's wild imaginings. Only mine.'

'You're telling me you thought you were miscarrying and chose not to tell me, and waved me off to work this morning as if this was just another day in the life of the world's most independent woman. Did I not have a right to know?' His voice was getting louder. 'Did you think I wouldn't cope?'

'I didn't know! And I didn't want to worry you in case there was nothing to worry *about*.'

'Because you've got this miscarriage event covered all by yourself, is that right? Was all your wedding night talk about needing to lean on me sometimes a lie?'

'No!'

'Because I don't see you leaning, Claudia. And I need you to.'

'Not for every little thing! I said that too, on our wedding night.' She swiped at her nose with the side of her hand—it was bleeding again, or maybe it had never stopped. 'Damn.'

'Don't move.' He pointed his finger at her for good measure and went into the bathroom, returning with tissues and a damp facecloth. 'Thinking you might be losing your baby is no small concern. Thinking you might have been poisoned by the bath oil—why haven't you ever raised that as a possibility?'

'Because I doubt it is one.' The wet cloth felt cool against her burning skin as she lay back against the pillow and savoured the temporary relief. 'I'm not that disliked, am I?' Maybe she was. 'I have a nosebleed and a temperature. Or a fever that might have caused the nosebleed. The doctor will shed some light.'

'And the other bleeding?' He turned the rapidly warming cloth on her head over to the cool side. 'What happened there?'

'A little bit of blood on my panties, not much, but I panicked. The doctor wasn't too worried but did say to take it easy for a while. I didn't want to worry you until I had to,' she murmured again. 'I didn't want to lose you.'

'Lose me how?'

She deliberately kept her eyes closed so she wouldn't have to look at him. 'You only married me because of the baby. I know that. The world knows that.'

'I married you because I'm worthy, and if you think I'd leave you if you lost this baby, you're out of your feverish mind. You *have* to stop working so hard for others! I've asked for this and now I'm begging. Stop! It won't make us love you any less. How can you not know this? Get it through your head!'

Her Tomas was yelling now. It was a sight to behold and somehow it *did* make her feel loved.

She was so screwed up.

'You love me?' she asked quietly. 'Really?'

'*Yes!* Baby or no baby. Whether you love me or not. Regular as sunrise. *Yes!* How can you not *know* this?'

'You never said.'

'I told you on our wedding day. Do you think I'm in the habit of making false vows? Don't answer that. You thought that. And you thought wrong. I've been trying to show you how much I love you ever since. You want to hope you haven't been poisoned,' he added next.

'I *do* hope that,' she told him earnestly.

'Because my vengeance will not be kind,' he added. 'I'm a lovelorn man on the edge.'

Her smile broke through his emotional frenzy, but only because it was blinding. 'I love you, you know that, right? I've only ever wanted to make your life better, never worse. I want…' The temptation to tell him she wanted whatever *he* wanted was *so strong*. She was fighting to stay awake—surely that wasn't normal after a full night's sleep and a morning spent lazing around. 'Tomas?' She reached for his hand and it was warm and big, with pleasing callouses. Not as overheated as she was and surely that couldn't be good for the baby. 'If something really is wrong and you have to choose betw—'

'I choose you,' he interrupted. 'No debate and no apology. I will always choose you. Please don't make me prove it.'

His answer was… 'Acceptable.' Enlightening. 'For now. We may have to have this conversation again once our baby is on the ground and the light of our lives.'

'We are *never* having this conversation again. You're not miscarrying, you've not been poisoned and you're not dying on my watch. Never again, without me going with you. There's nothing else to discuss.'

She sighed and couldn't tell where sorrow ended and delight began. 'I suppose we could consider that settled.' Feverish she might be, but there would be no forgetting that promise. Tomas was perfect in every way and she was a bad wife for not trusting him to be rock-solid there for her, no matter what.

'No more protecting you from pregnancy worries.'

'No more.'

'We can share the panic.'

'We can.'

'I'm really glad you hung around this morning.'

'I'm not a mind-reader. Next time say, *Tomas, would you mind staying with me this morning? I'm not feeling great.* That is all it's ever going to take!'

'Yes, but *not feeling great* is fairly common for me these days. How do I tell the difference between morning sickness, a bad scallop and a right royal assassination attempt?'

'I'll ask around. Maybe Ildris will know.'

'You're bonding with Ildris now?'

'No way, nohow and never. But I'm not above instilling overwhelming concern for you in his heart. He deserves it.'

'I didn't realise I'd married a comic genius masquerading as a madman,' she murmured.

'Didn't you?' he grumbled, right on cue. 'Well, now you know. Claudia?'

'Mmm?' So weary.

'You can't die again. I won't let you. You're going to beat this. Whatever it is.'

'I'll do my very best.'

'And I will ever be with you.'

There was no poison in her blood. The bath oil had been declared safe and Lady Ester had been indignant. The spotting had stopped but a piece of Claudia's placenta was flapping. It was all very manageable for a man of reason capable of exerting great control when needed.

And if that no longer described him in full, Tomas was altogether on board with fudging it.

He'd called on Casimir and told him to stop using Claudia as his personal scapegoat.

He'd cornered Ildris and requested, on Claudia's behalf, more support from the northerners during her complicated pregnancy. Alya lived with them at Aergoveny now, alongside two other young women from the north, and three young men from Aergoveny, the younger ones duly added to the apprenticeship roster, and staying in the west wing of the manor house.

Outreach, Tomas called it. Surrounding Claudia with people who knew and accepted her as her own good self was what Tomas *meant*.

He'd made it happen. Simple.

He'd braced his big body as he'd stood in front of all comers, crossed his arms and reminded every last one of them of all she'd ever done for them and the love she deserved. He'd warned them ever so politely that should they ever feel the urge to use his wife's overarching need to make herself useful for their own benefit they should do so extremely carefully. If anyone broke her, he would break them. No exceptions. He was being very reasonable!

How fortunate everyone agreed.

'I need your help these next few weeks to supervise Alhena,' he said to Claudia one morning as he pulled up a chair to her bedside. There were dozens of chairs in the room and yet not one of them seemed like a useful place to sit. 'She's not immune to one of the male goldens we introduced her to and I want to bring them both in here for you to keep an eye on.'

'You mean in this room?'

'Yes.'

'And you chide me for bringing my work home with me,' she murmured with a roll of her eyes. 'Okay, yes. I'll do it. But only because I like Alhena.'

'Perfect.' He sighed. 'But if she has taken to him, they'll need close observation. That'll take weeks. In here. Under your watchful gaze.'

'Now you're just making stuff up.'

'You noticed. You can always sit and watch the grass grow. I'm trying to be supportive about the fact that you'll be spending these next few months on bedrest until this baby is born. You'll crack unless you have something to do, and I need you whole when the baby comes. You're going to be the most amazing mother, have I mentioned that? Adventurous and unconventional, tender and encouraging. There will be hugs. So many hugs, and falcon jesses. It takes a village to raise a child and I'm all for building one right here around you. We're going to add a table and a couple of comfy chairs by the window, and in the mornings I can push the screens aside and let the mountains in. And we'll put the baby's bed over in the corner, and once she arrives she'll sleep long and well, until we're ready to greet her every morning.'

'Oh, you poor deluded soul, but please continue. Are there tapestries on the walls?'

'Er...yes?'

'Excellent.'

'What else do you want me to set right in our world?' he wanted to know. Big or small, petty, silly or serious— he'd make a deal with the devil if it meant keeping his wife hopeful.

The doctor arrived for her weekly check-up, and asked questions and took Claudia's temperature and blood pressure, then collected a blood sample and a urine sample and finally pulled out her stethoscope and listened to the heartbeat.

Then she sat back on the edge of the bed, arms crossed, and levelled them both with a no-nonsense gaze. 'Here's the deal. You're too far away from proper medical care here and we need to do some investigating.'

'I can relocate to the palace,' offered Claudia, but the doctor was already shaking her head and Tomas's heart was dropping to his toes.

Just when he'd thought he had everything under control.

But it came with the territory and he was there for it.

'Pack your bags,' the doctor said. 'You're going straight to the hospital.'

From bad to worse and worse again, Tomas paced the hall of the hospital and King Casimir, Ana and Ildris paced with him. He wasn't built for narrow halls and tiny waiting rooms, he wasn't used to this kind of terror. None of them were.

Part of him wished Claudia could see them all falling to pieces at the thought of her absence. She'd know she was loved then, without doubt, rhyme or reason. Her usefulness had nothing to do with it.

He couldn't stop pacing.

He wanted nothing more than to return with her to the mountains.

'You love her,' Ildris murmured. 'I wasn't sure of that.'

'You need to stop talking.'

'Mr Sokolov?' A woman had appeared by way of the door at the end of the corridor.

'Yes.' There was no need for titles here.

'You can see your wife now.'

He looked to Cas. Tomas had no intention of giving up his place for the other man but, y'know... King. 'I'll tell her you're here. I'll tell her you're all here.'

'Go,' said Cas. 'Get in there.'

Everything was so white when it came to hospital rooms and beds. It wasn't soothing, thought Claudia. It wasn't soothing at all, but she was in good hands, the doctor kept telling her. The best hands in the country were here and if she could stay put for even one more week, with her baby in her belly, the baby would benefit. Partial placental abruption was manageable. In her case, continuous external foetal monitoring of the foetal heartbeat was recommended.

No problem.

Whatever she had to do, she'd do it.

The door opened and Tomas stepped in and she willed her heart to stop beating faster at the sight of him. He looked at the machines she was hooked up to, paying particular attention to the heartbeat monitor.

'That's our baby's heartbeat,' she told him. 'She's okay for now.'

'She?'

'Oh. I actually don't know. The technician who did the ultrasound absolutely knows but I didn't ask. She, he, either way, I'll be happy and grateful.'

'I love you,' he said. 'I'll be saying that more often.'

Brilliant.

'I'll be staying here until this baby is born,' she said. 'Doctor's orders.'

Her favourite falconer in the whole wide world digested that news with the shrug of his very capable shoulders. 'Makes two of us. I'll be here when you go to sleep of a night and I'll be here when you wake up each morning. You don't like waking up alone in strange places.'

She looked to the doctor. 'Can that…?'

'Be arranged? Of course. We can move you to a double room with a window view. Of course, there should be no intercourse between now and the birth.' Tomas looked scandalised. The doctor looked apologetic but resolute. 'It is my duty to state that.'

Rock-solid Tomas said, 'Thank you, Doctor,' and looked to Claudia. 'I love you and you need me. Which is the only reason I haven't completely lost my mind yet.'

'I will always need you,' she said.

'Thank you,' he said again. 'That's very useful.'

He was so delicious. 'I'm confident this is going to end well for us.'

'I love you,' he said again. 'It bears repeating. Repetition is very effective in a learning environment.'

'You're the falconer,' she murmured. 'By all means,

prime me to fly into your arms. You probably don't even need to use food.'

The doctor snorted and the attendant who'd done the ultrasound covered her smile by way of rubbing her hand across the lower half of her face.

'Moving *on*,' said the doctor. 'I'll go and brief the King and Queen and the northern lord who's out there in the waiting room with them and then see about a room change, and someone will arrive in due course to take down your dietary requirements.'

'No hospital food will be necessary,' said Tomas. 'The palace considers poisoning a high risk. There will be guards. There will be food coming in from outside. You'll meet Rudolpho. He'll organise everything and you will endure.'

'Because they love me to bits.' Saved Tomas having to say it, but he was nodding most seriously.

'Yes. Yes, we do. Isn't it obvious?'

'Very,' said the doctor with a wink in Claudia's direction. 'Claudia, I'll leave it to you to keep your loved ones in check. May I suggest no falcons, no parades, no dinner parties in your room and no press? If you think of anything else I need to ban, let me know.'

'Thank you, Doctor.'

And then it was just her and Tomas, with his mighty heart packed full of love to give. 'You don't really have to stay here with me until I have this baby, you realise. At some point I fully expect you to come to your senses.'

'I don't think so.' Gently implacable was his stance.

'Because you love me?' She could get used to such devotion.

He smiled and it was just for her. 'Now that you mention it, yes.'

# EPILOGUE

BABY SOKOLOV MADE her way into the world at thirty-four weeks and six and a half days, by way of Caesarean section. She greeted the world with wide eyes followed by a lusty bellow, and her father was there to hold her and fall in love, and later place her gently to her mother's breast.

It had been a mammoth effort to keep mother and child healthy and thriving these past few weeks, but Tomas had put in more effort for less during his time as a falconer, and every moment had been worth it. There was a potter's wheel in the corner of their hospital room and a view of the city skyline out of the window. They'd made all the plates, bowls and vases they would ever need and every one of them was misshapen.

Their daughter, though, she was perfect, with a shock of silky black hair and eyes just like her mother's. They stared steadily at him as she nuzzled at the breast and finally latched on and wasn't that a sight to fill a heart to overflowing.

'What do we call her?' They'd made a list. They'd made a lot of lists during their time indoors.

'Oreah.'

From the Greek: my mountain home.

'Oreah Alya Ana Sophia Lor—'

'Stop.' They couldn't do that to a child. 'Oreah Alya will do.'

'Oreah Alya Sokolov. She's so beautiful,' Claudia whispered. 'Look at her.'

'I think we should keep her,' he suggested.

'Your father thinks he's such a wit. You'll get used to it. I actually think he'll return to normal once we return him to the mountains.' She leaned closer. 'Too much time in a small room.'

He would show his daughter the mountains soon enough, and the stars in the sky and the falcons. She would meet Silas and Lor, her honorary grandparents. She would be passed around to her aunt and uncle and only years later would she discover that they ruled a small country. She would meet wolfhounds and ponies and sleep in a tent in the far northern mountain passes and think she was on a camping trip. She would groan at his dad jokes and he'd hug her to pieces.

He climbed onto the bed as he'd done so many times these past few weeks, and tucked in behind Claudia so she could lean on him and because loving arms meant safety and safety was important. 'Welcome to our world, little one.' And what a brilliant world it was. 'You're going to love it.'

\* \* \* \* \*

# COMING SOON!

We really hope you enjoyed reading this book.
If you're looking for more romance
be sure to head to the shops when
new books are available on

## Thursday 26th September

To see which titles are coming soon, please visit
**millsandboon.co.uk/nextmonth**

MILLS & BOON

# MILLS & BOON®

## Coming next month

### ITALIAN BABY SHOCK
Jackie Ashenden

'I'm so sorry,' Lark said quickly as the phone vibrated again. 'But I really need to get this. It's my daughter's nanny.' She bent to pick the phone up off the table, turning as she looked down at it.

He could see the screen over her shoulder. On it was a photo of a baby, a little girl dressed in pink. She had a cloud of soft, rose-gold curls and blue, blue eyes.

It was a singular colour that rose-gold, as was the intense blue of her eyes. He'd never met anyone else who'd had hair that hue apart from his mother. And as for that blue…

That was Donati blue. Two hundred years ago the Donatis had been patrons of a painter who'd created a paint colour in their honor. And that's what he'd called it.

Cesare went very still as everything in him slowed down. Everything except his brain, which was now working overtime. Going back over that night. Going over everything.

Because if there was one thing he knew, it was that the baby in that photo was his daughter.

*Continue reading*
**ITALIAN BABY SHOCK**
Jackie Ashenden

*Available next month*
millsandboon.co.uk

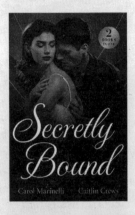
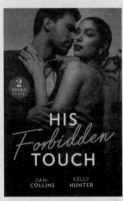
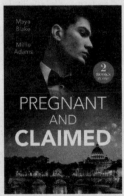

LET'S TALK

# Romance

For exclusive extracts, competitions and special offers, find us online:

f MillsandBoon

X @MillsandBoon

📷 @MillsandBoonUK

♪ @MillsandBoonUK

Get in touch on 01413 063 232

For all the latest titles coming soon, visit
millsandboon.co.uk/nextmonth

# afterglow BOOKS

Afterglow Books is a trend-led, trope-filled list of books with diverse, authentic and relatable characters, a wide array of voices and representations, plus real world trials and tribulations. Featuring all the tropes you could possibly want (think small-town settings, fake relationships, grumpy vs sunshine, enemies to lovers) and all with a generous dose of spice in every story.

♪ @millsandboonuk
◎ @millsandboonuk
afterglowbooks.co.uk

#AfterglowBooks

**For all the latest book news, exclusive content and giveaways scan the QR code below to sign up to the Afterglow newsletter:**

SCAN ME

# afterglow BOOKS

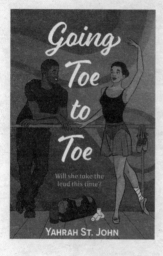

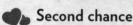 Second chance

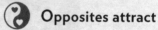 Opposites attract

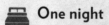 One night

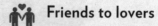 Friends to lovers

 Spicy

 Spicy

# OUT NOW

Two stories published every month. Discover more at:
**Afterglowbooks.co.uk**

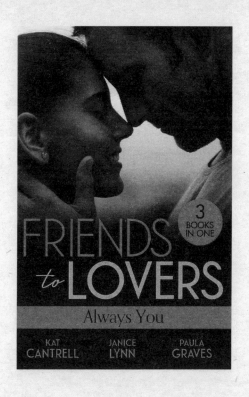

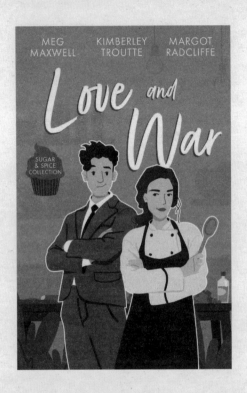